The Road to Gambela

Roger Quam

xulon PRESS

The Road to Gambela
by Roger Quam

Printed in the United States of America

ISBN 1-591609-93-3

Xulon Press
www.XulonPress.com

Xulon Press books are available in bookstores everywhere, and on the Web at www.XulonPress.com.

CHAPTER 1

Friday—Day 1

The airport was within three minutes and I had yet another delay.

As I was traveling down the freeway, my eyes were fixed on the light blue Honda two hundred feet directly in front of me. The person driving the car was about to change lanes, probably to get to the exit lane. All of a sudden, another car moving at excessive speed first passed me, then the Honda, in the exit lane on our right.

The sudden appearance of the second car caused the Honda driver to cut back. The startled Honda driver lost control and started to weave side-to-side. The Honda was heading for a rollover. I quickly glanced in my rear-view mirror and stepped on the brake. The Honda slammed into the curb, bounced and rolled, just as I passed by.

God suddenly spoke to me: "Stop and help those people!"

I pulled off to the side of the freeway, quickly backed up, jumped out of the car, and ran to the tipped-on-its-side Honda. Adults were screaming and little children crying! The smell of gasoline was strong and smoke was rolling out of the engine. Through the smolder, I could see a small red flame. This car had all the appearances of a vehicle ready to explode!

As I ran to the topside of the Honda, I could see gas gushing out of the ruptured tank. I needed to get the people out fast—within a few seconds. The screams from inside the car were getting louder and more hysterical.

I frantically yelled out, "Please help me, God!"

The people inside of the car may be injured, but most likely not too bad—they were making noise. If the car exploded and burned, no one would escape. All my moves needed to be precise and swift.

I placed my shoulder against the car and started rocking it with all of the power I could muster. Within a few seconds the car was teetering on its driver's side tires. Another burst of my energy caused it to gradually roll back into the upright position.

The resulting "thud" may have worsened any injuries of the occupants, but that was not the immediate concern. In a matter of seconds, there may be several human beings burning alive with no escape.

I ran around to the opposite side, grabbed the front door handle and pulled. The door was jammed. The Honda's occupants needed to be removed from this side of the car, as the ground on the other side was gas-soaked. Any spark would immediately ignite the ground.

I tried the back door—it opened. Within seconds I had carried three small children—a load of a hundred pounds—to a spot of ground some fifty feet from the car. Their injuries seemed minor.

I raced back and jumped into the Honda's front seat from the rear. There wasn't much room with two adults and an infant. They had stopped screaming, and were just sitting there dazed. None of the occupants had been strapped in.

I hurriedly stretched out on top of the two adults—two women. With my back and shoulders solidly against the driver's door, I rammed the passenger door with the heels of my shoes and all the power in the lower part of my body. The door flung open. I quickly pulled the still stunned two adults out onto the ground, and by their ankles, pulled them to where the three children were lying. My task was almost complete.

As I turned and started back to the car to retrieve the remaining infant, who was now crying, I saw people coming to help. Two men, having stopped on the service road, had climbed the fence and were racing down the incline. I yelled to them, "Get these people further away from the car—it's about to explode."

The men ran toward the three children and two adults to quickly carry them to a spot well away from the Honda.

I gently seized into my arms the baby who was lying on the floor of the front seat and quickly turned around to begin the race back to the other injured people. As I swung my arm around, the back of my wrist hit a jagged piece of metal on the door.

I was on my way back to the other occupants and only 10 feet from the car when I heard a "Woomph...Woomph!" The smoking and burning engine and the gas vapors caused two almost simultaneous explosions around the engine and then on the gas soaked ground. There was a sudden burst of heat on my back.

I ran and gently placed the infant beside her brother and sister and mom or whoever they were. More people were now helping out, giving first aid, and calling for help from the police and paramedics. The fire had quickly spread and the entire car was now burning out of control.

I made a quick decision. I needed to leave and drive quickly to the airport or I would miss my flight. My work here was done—someone else could do the rest. I raced back to my car and took off. As I was driving away, I looked up at an over-the-highway footbridge and saw another group of people. One of them was on a cell phone, as they had just witnessed the accident and were probably calling for the police. The situation was well covered and under control.

My hand was hurting from hitting it on the car. I looked down, saw my wrist bleeding, with blood on my pants and shirt. I never realized that the cut was this serious, but, unfortunately, it would have to wait.

While I was stopped for a red light, I took my large handkerchief and wrapped it around my wrist, tying the ends with my right hand and teeth. I had medical supplies in the bags in the trunk, but they were inaccessible and I wouldn't have time to give myself first aid at the airport.

At another stoplight I closed my eyes, took a deep breath, and tried to contemplate the previous 10 minutes. I was glad that I had stopped. "Thank You, God, for helping me."

****

I was going to be late arriving at the Indianapolis International Airport. There had been so many details that needed to be taken care of, and I should have started them days sooner. On top of everything, I left my airline ticket at the apartment and had to drive back five miles to get it. My traveling companions were probably waiting impatiently at the ticket and luggage check in counter, wondering where I was.

The trip was a culmination of four months of planning by a recently assembled medical mission team from three different cities, but only six weeks of planning for me. Three of us would fly from Indianapolis to Chicago, where we would meet up with the rest of the team. Then it was on to Frankfurt, Germany, where we would have a short layover and the team's first planning session.

The times on my wristwatches indicated that I would just make it to get my bags checked in, and then to the departure gate.

I was wearing two watches—current time on my left wrist and Chicago time on my right wrist. I would change the time on my left wristwatch as we entered the various time zones. The right wristwatch would not be changed during the entire trip. It may be of some value to know what the current time was back home.

We were traveling to Gambela, Ethiopia, where a team of eight people would set up and operate a medical facility for about two weeks. Gambela is a city in western Ethiopia not far from the border of Sudan. The city is seriously short of medical care. This is especially true for the Sudanese population, as they are refugees of the continuous ongoing brutal civil war in Southern Sudan.

James and Samuel, two of my many new Sudanese friends, were going to meet me at the ticket counter. I had known them for only six weeks. We met at my church, Sunshine Covenant, where the Sudanese refugees meet for their Sunday afternoon Nuer language worship service and fellowship.

The one remaining major item on my checklist was to call my ex-wife, Abby. During the past weeks, I hadn't been able to get her off of my mind. Maybe I could call her from Chicago, Frankfort, or Gambela. I had a very important message to give her.

Since I was a latecomer in joining the mission team, I didn't know all of the names of the other people making the trip. I did know that there were two medical doctors, two registered nurses, a retired missionary who is also serving as the team's leader, my two tall Sudanese friends, and me. The team leader's name is Cameron Johnson from Denver. He has been instrumental in arranging the trip schedule, logistics and itinerary; and he was to serve as the keeper of the trip's money purse.

Each of the team members provided his or her portion of funds to allow Cameron to pay for the land cruiser's cost from Addis Ababa to Gambela and back to Addis, hotel accommodations, food, and any other miscellaneous expenses. We each paid for our own airfare, purchased at a group rate.

I was invited by Samuel and James to make this trip. Since I am a new believer, I was eager to make a trip somewhere and to do something that would help what many called a "hurting world." Maybe I just wanted to make up for all of the years I had wasted trying to please only myself. I had another reason, also.

Each of the three large bags that I would check in at the airport contain about 70 pounds each of medical supplies: rolls of tape, Band-Aids, antibiotic ointment, gauze pads, Batadine, soap, bottles of Tylenol, Q-tips, rubber gloves, alcohol, etc. The church ladies had rolled a large amount of white cloth bandages. All of the medical supplies were donated or paid for with funds provided by the people of the Sudanese Church in Indianapolis.

I received a separate list from Samuel and James, who had obtained it from the team's two doctors in Minneapolis. The list consisted of: saline, IV tubing, IV needles, syringes, antibiotics, quinine, x-ray film, stethoscopes, otoscopes, blood pressure cuffs, and other items, all of which I obtained and carefully packed.

One of my bags contained a collection of 300 Hot Wheels cars—30 pounds packed tightly in a box 10" x 10" x 10." If there were little boys and girls in Gambela, they surely would enjoy some fun with Hot Wheels racing.

The mission team leader had received special permission from United Airlines and Lufthansa for each of us to carry an extra bag up to 70 pounds if the contents were used for humanitarian purposes. Since eight people were making the trip, this provided us with an extra eight bags.

Contained in another bag were other items—ballpoint pens, baseball caps, women's scarves, bubblegum and chewing gum—all to be used as giveaways to the Sudanese pastors and people. A woman in my church gave me sixteen Swiss Army knives. I wasn't sure how I was going to use them; maybe I would just give them away. The woman who gave them to me received them from the redemption of cigarette UPC labels she had collected from her friends at work.

My discretionary funds to spend on this trip were limited. Some people at my church provided me with most of the money needed, since I had no money saved up. One man gave me a twenty-dollar bill to help buy gum for the Gambela children. In one of the bags is a box of 800 colorful three-quarter-inch diameter bubblegum balls purchased at Sam's Club. They are destined for the children of Africa.

I had volunteered to do the work of purchasing, collecting and assembling the three bags of medical supplies. Most of the items are from surplus stores and from medical supply houses. It took two weeks to locate and obtain the contents of the three bags. James, Samuel and I will each check in one of these bags.

The doctors and nurses are carrying with them other medical supplies and some of the prescription drugs needed for treating cases of malaria, leprosy, and other infectious diseases that are found in that part of Africa. They also have a bag containing a small, portable refrigerator unit.

****

By the time I arrived at the airport, James and Samuel had already checked in. They grabbed my three heavy bags and placed them on the baggage scale. The weight of each bag was just less than the maximum allowable limit of 70 pounds. We hurried down to the departure gate, not any too soon, as the plane was already boarding.

I buckled myself in. I was exhausted. My back was starting to hurt, probably from pushing the Honda back to its upright position or kicking the door open. There was also pain in my wrist. I unwrapped the bloody hanky and looked at my injury. The bleeding had stopped, but the wound was wide open and very deep.

Maybe I should have stayed longer at the scene of the accident, since I was a witness. But this delay would have only caused me to miss my flight. I had no money to spend on another ticket, and I would have missed the trip completely. No, I had made the correct decision.

It was 12:30 p.m. James and Samuel were sitting together about ten rows up the aisle, and I was next to the window. It wasn't long before I was beginning to doze off. There were so many things that flashed before me as I gazed up at the floating white clouds.

I thought about the freeway accident and I began to shake. What did I do back there? I looked out the window as we were taking off and saw the scene of the accident. Now I remembered. Flashing red lights told me that all was taken care of. I stopped shaking and closed my eyes. "Thank You, God."

****

I was born Jack Teegardin Franklin in a small rural community forty miles south of Kansas City, Missouri. My dad was a fan of the big band leader, Jack Teegardin—thus my middle name.

My parents were not professing Christians but did occasionally attend a Baptist church in our small town. They would send me to Sunday school, and I enjoyed it until I got into Junior High and became a worldly teenager. I graduated from high school in 1988.

My youth had been wild and I gave my parents fits. They were finally relieved when I took off for college. They even told me that. Soon after I was in college my parents moved to Indianapolis, where they finally divorced. I was their only child.

In the summer of 1988, I made the decision to attend the University of Minnesota in Minneapolis. The university had a good engineering program, and I was interested in pursuing a degree in mechanical engineering. My interest in anything mechanical gave me the desire to go into this field.

I had a passion for disassembling cars and motors, reassembling them, and fixing anything broken. As a boy, I became the neighborhood expert in Hot Wheels technology. I discovered exactly what made the cars go down the track fast, what caused them to become slow and how to make them fast again. I built a 50-foot portable Hot Wheels racetrack that could be easily assembled in any garage and driveway.

Show me anything that is broken or doesn't run right and I'll soon have it running smoothly.

My first two quarters at the university were not academically exceptional—just squeaking by with a 2.0 grade point average. The spring quarter was even worse. My study habits were bad and I lacked enthusiasm.

In February I met Abby Olson in a speech class. She was a beautiful young woman, and I was immediately attracted to her. We sat next to each other on the first day of class and became very involved from the start. I lived near the Dinkytown section just north of the campus, and she lived in an apartment near the hospital complex.

My studies fell behind and by the summer I was on academic probation. Abby was in the nursing program at the University and was able to keep up with her studies. She was a brilliant student.

On June 25, 1989, my world suddenly became complicated. Abby announced to me that she was "great with your child," as she so aptly put it. When she informed me, she cried. I didn't know how to react, which was an indication of my immaturity. I was a typical teenaged boy interested only in having his fun and not considering the consequences of any actions.

Abby was three months "along," and we made the decision to travel immediately to her home in Tulsa, Oklahoma, to tell her parents.

On our way down to Tulsa, Abby and I had a long talk about religion. We each came to the same conclusion that we were not Christians—as her parents were, as she had been taught, and as I had learned during my Sunday school days. Like Abby said on that rainy day traveling down Interstate 35, "Going to church doesn't make a person a Christian any more than going into a barn makes him or her a member of a livestock family."

Abby's parents, although showing a significant amount of disappointment with their daughter, were seemingly realistic about the situation and encouraged us to get married right away. We did just that the following day in the Pastor's study and drove back to Minneapolis on Sunday.

Was marriage the right thing to do? Only God knows. We never had a honeymoon, and we never fell in love with each other.

During the next five years we had three children—all boys: Charles, born in December 1989, Jack Jr. in 1992, and Steve in 1994. They are all good boys mainly because of their mother. Abby is a good mom. I would like to think I was a good father, but I now realize that during those five years I was neither a good father nor a good husband.

The marriage did not work out. Abby and I would argue about everything from money to religion. Also, I had a big career conflict.

Immediately after our marriage, because of my bad grades and a baby coming, I had to quit school and go to work at a service garage as a mechanic. Abby, because she had been doing well in her studies, continued her nursing education. It took her two extra years to complete, after taking off time to have babies, but she graduated and did very well scholastically.

She had her parent's financial support, a college fund, and had obtained some scholarship money even before she graduated from high school. Abby's parents had even set aside funds for childcare. I often wondered how they knew she would someday need this extra support. I had no such support—financial or otherwise.

When Abby did graduate from the University Nursing School and went to work at a hospital, her salary was almost twice the money I was earning at my job. This became an increasingly bitter pill for me to swallow, and it soon became a huge obstacle in our marriage. I was the typical man who thought that I should make more money than my wife. Because that was not possible, I bitterly resented the fact that Abby was making the big bucks. To add insult to injury, her salary increased greatly and mine only slightly.

I began to rely on the bottle more than normal to hide my troubles, staying out late and becoming more and more a burden to Abby.

Finally, one day, I decided to take off for my home in Indiana. Looking back, it was a big mistake. I was throwing away the part of my life that was more precious than any amount of jewels or gold—Abby. She was a beautiful and wonderful woman. Our children were well-behaved and intelligent, in spite of their dad. I wanted Abby to have a second chance at marriage—and maybe a happy one—so I divorced her in October of 1995. That was six years ago.

It wasn't long after the divorce that I began a new job at a car repair shop in Indianapolis. I continued to financially support our three boys by working at a second job delivering pizza. This only added to my humiliating and unfulfilled life.

The owner of the auto repair shop where I was working decided to retire and put the business up for sale. I wanted to buy and expand it. I called Abby one night and talked to her about my idea. She said it would be a bad move for me. "You don't have the smarts to run a business, and it's more important for you to provide steady child support for our three sons."

These were very cutting words to me. Maybe the truth, but still cutting and I finally hung up on her.

About a week later, the shop burned down. At first, the fire investigators tried to put the cause of the fire on me for using a cutting torch, but that was soon proved false. About a week later, investigators found the cause: arson. It seems that the owner had just taken out a new fire insurance policy and started the fire himself. He was charged with arson. I was left without a job and with no chance of owning my own repair shop.

I then drifted from job to job, lacking any purpose in life. I missed Abby and the boys, but couldn't get myself to go back to her and try to reconcile. I kept thinking that she would not take me back, which was probably right. To her, I was a loser.

Abby's life, on the other hand, all of a sudden became exciting! She never remarried, kept my last name, and started attending a neighborhood Bible study in Minneapolis. I'm sure she did this for support, as there were some women in the group who were in the same situation that she was in—being a single mom.

It wasn't long before she found the Lord as the master of her life.

I remember the night she told me—or rather tried to tell me. She had called me because I had failed to sign a check that I had sent her for the support of our boys.

"Guess what, Jack! I am a new person. God has changed my life. I have given my life to Him."

I was stunned and very quiet for at least fifteen seconds. I think she thought I had hung up on her. I changed the subject to our sons, but before she said goodbye, she told me that she would pray for me. That was even more astonishing. *Maybe she is just trying to get back at me*, I thought at the time. Deep down, I knew that what she had found, I also needed.

Over the next few months, I became despondent, lazy, and without much ambition. I worked at various jobs, gained 20 pounds, and was once again drinking. In two years, I think I established the record for the most job changes ever. I had no goal in life, and it was hard to get up in the morning and face the world.

Then one momentous Saturday night, I happened to meet a man at a high school basketball game. He asked me a very simple but penetrating question: "Do you have any kind of spiritual belief?" I answered "yes," not realizing that he would then ask what my belief was, followed by a series of probing questions. This fellow had to be a super salesman, because he was soon at the core of my problem—sin. In all of this, not once did it cause an argument. I never even got the man's name.

That night, at the basketball game in the bleachers, I accepted the Creator of the Universe into my life. That was only 6 weeks ago.

The next morning I decided to drive until I found a good church to attend. I found it at the Sunshine Evangelical Covenant church. They had a good worship service and a very effective missionary ministry.

The church was involved in helping to resettle a group of Sudanese refugees from the camps in western Ethiopia. The first Sunday I was in church I became involved with this group.

After the morning worship service as I was walking to my car, James, one of the Sudanese refugees, asked me if I could help him get his car running. He couldn't have asked a more qualified person. Was that a chance meeting? I don't think so. Ten minutes later I was working on James's car motor. The problem was a broken wire to the spark plug. I had the needed tools in my car trunk and a spare wire.

The church's senior pastor happened to stop by and we talked. I made the suggestion that the church help these refugees with their car needs. That Sunday noon, in the church parking lot, I was put in charge of coordinating the Sudanese Automobile Education Ministry. Since that Sunday noon, my entire Saturdays and some weeknights, have been spent teaching the new refugees how to drive cars, purchase cars and car insurance, and maintain cars.

James and Samuel were planning this trip to Gambela, Ethiopia, to help with a medical ministry. They were working at a local hospital as nurse's aides, with the goal of eventually becoming nurses. They invited me to make the trip with them. They then called Cameron, the trip coordinator, and asked if I could tag along if I paid my own way.

Cameron was somewhat reluctant, without knowing my background or how I might fit in on the medical mission trip, but he agreed. I think my Sudanese Christian brothers persuaded Cameron to let me go along. None of the doctors and nurses knew that I was making the trip or that I lacked any medical training or experience.

I had received all of my shots in the past six weeks, which normally takes several months to complete. Somehow God made it possible to have everything completed just two days ago with the arrival of my visa in the mail.

I had found another job and everything seemed to be improving, until last week when I lost that job. This trip happened so fast and I had failed to tell my new employer. When I requested three weeks off, he refused. "Chose between your job or the trip," he told me. I had already obtained funds for the medical supplies, committed my share of the trip's expenses to the team, and my $1,800 no-refund ticket had been purchased.

So, I am now on my way to Ethiopia. It is like a dream. I close my eyes and wonder how in the world I got into this situation. I can come up with only one answer: God is in control.

For the past five weeks I have wanted to tell Abby about my conversion, and the resulting change in lifestyle. I tried three times—twice her line was busy and the other time there was no answer. On that occasion, the answering machine went on, but I hesitated. I thought to myself that if I left a message, she would think

I had been drinking. Her trust in me was very low—in fact there was no trust at all. She told me that on more than one occasion.

My heart ached for Abby and the opportunity to make things right between us. What I wouldn't give to go back, have a second chance, and start over. But this was only a dream and I knew it.

I sent Abby a check last week and was planning to tell her in the letter. But I was afraid that without seeing some evidence of a change, her belief in me would go even lower, if that was possible. Abby is too nice of a woman for me—she deserves someone better.

This is the other reason for my taking this trip.

I need to prove to her as well as myself, that I can do something for someone other than myself. Then maybe I will have the courage to tell her about my conversion, backed up by some solid evidence to prove it. This is the reason I've decided to keep a diary of this trip—to record my activities. I'll then send her the completed diary and surprise her. Maybe.

****

We arrived in Chicago on time. Cameron and the two doctors met us and we had a session of introduction. We were immediately told that the two nurses, an Elizabeth and an Abigail from Minneapolis, would be delayed for another three hours. Their plane had mechanical problems at the Minneapolis airport. The doctors were also from Minneapolis but had taken an earlier flight.

The decision had already been made to continue on to Frankfort as scheduled. The nurses would take a later flight and, barring any other unforeseen circumstances, catch up with us before our scheduled flight left for Addis Ababa, Ethiopia.

I went to the bathroom, cleaned off my wound, and rewrapped my wrist. The scissor from my Swiss Army knife provided me the means of cutting one of the tee shirts from my overnight bag. The wound was two inches long and very deep. It had quit bleeding, but looked awful. I had nothing with which to treat it. Maybe the doctors could look at it.

The departing gate was not far away and we were soon ready to go. The bags the Sudanese were carrying had to be examined. They apparently contained items that looked a little suspicious. They were bringing gifts to relatives in Gambela from people attending the Sudanese church in Indianapolis.

****

Occurring at the same time as the clinic is to be conducted at the church in Gambela, pastors of the 300 South Sudanese Covenant churches located in Western Ethiopia and Southern Sudan are to have a seven-day prayer conference. One of the items that will be discussed is the need for community health education in certain areas of South Sudan. Cameron told me in our phone conversations that the two doctors and nurses were preparing sessions on this subject.

I kept wondering what exactly I would or could be doing on this trip. The value of my services on a medical team was in question by me and would surely be even more in question by the two doctors and two nurses. I was starting to get worried.

****

We left Chicago for Frankfurt on the Lufthansa airline at 5:30 p.m. It would be eight hours of flying time, plus seven hours of time changes. Our team was located in separate sections of the airline, and it was difficult to communicate with each other. Cameron did visit with the two doctors on a couple of occasions. I tried to sleep during the flight, but my mind was too preoccupied with so many things.

I wonder how I can make a phone call from Frankfurt to Abby in Minneapolis? What should I say to her and what will her reaction be? I wonder if we'll have any trouble getting the medical supplies through Ethiopian customs, if the people in that Honda are OK and what was the extent of their injuries?

I thought about what Abby looked like. I had her photo in my wallet, but it was an old photo. I've had it out of my wallet at least a dozen times in the past weeks. When I get back to America, maybe I'll get up enough guts to ask her for an updated photo. She may not give me one.

I reached for my wallet, turned on the night-light and looked at Abby's photo.

Abby is five foot seven inches tall, is very well proportioned, has long blond hair and big blue eyes and is always quick to smile. She has a distinct stride in her walk.

Her photo was soon carefully placed back in my wallet and I turned out the light.

I need to forget about her in the next three weeks, otherwise I will become useless to the team. My present need is to focus on the mission trip and our purpose for visiting Africa.

Oh, what might have been!

CHAPTER 2

Saturday—Day 2

It is now completely dark as I look down outside the window of the Lufthansa airline. We are flying over the clouds. As I look upward, the sky is clear and I can see the star-studded heaven. I keep dozing off and then waking up. My left wristwatch tells me I haven't slept much and the TV monitors hanging from the ceiling indicate where we are over the Atlantic headed for Europe.

I removed the hanky bandage from my wrist and looked at my cut. It didn't look good, it hurt and I needed to get some ointment and clean covering for it. When the flight attendant made her next pass down the aisle, I asked her for a couple of package of ointment and several Band-Aids. Four minutes later she returned with what I needed. As I applied the ointment to the wound, I could feel the healing begin. The wound probably needs stitches, but where would I go? Maybe the mission team doctors have a stitch kit in their carry-on case.

****

My Sudanese friends have filled me in on the details of the plight of the Nuer people in South Sudan.

Second only to the holocaust, the death of two million human beings in Southern Sudan is considered to be the greatest genocide of the 20th century. Sadly, it is continuing into the 21st century with even greater violence. This story has been pitifully under-reported by the mainstream news media, with some media outlets leaving it totally unreported. I had not been aware of this ethnic cleansing until James and Samuel informed me.

What was the reason for the genocide? The answer: Because the Sudanese Nuer are Christians. They are being slaughtered like animals in their own villages and churches, yet these people seem to be so vibrant and passionate about their faith that it caused me the desire to have even a fraction of this dedication and commitment.

I remember the day when my Sudanese brothers told me some of the personal stories of persecution they and their families had suffered. It was the first Sunday that I heard these brothers and sisters pray—the day after I became a Christian.

I had just finished fixing James's car in the church parking lot and needed to return his car keys to him. I walked into the church and into a room where about fifty of the Sudanese refugees were meeting. They were about to pray. I handed James his keys and he invited me to sit down.

One of the Sudanese brethren began to pray. The atmosphere in the room became quiet and peaceful, as if God Himself and some of His angels had decided to visit the prayer meeting. The group was praying in the Nuer language and I didn't understand a word of it. Yet I felt their spiritual passion. I was very new to the faith, and this passionate season of prayer made me feel spiritually insignificant. I longed to pray like they could.

What had happened to make these people so spiritually strong? Maybe this trip would provide the answer to my question.

The Southern Sudanese people, especially the Nuer tribe, have been targeted by the Khartoum government sponsored National Militia since 1984. To counter this aggression, some of the Southern Sudanese tribes have formed a fighting force in an alliance called the SPLA, Sudan People's Liberation Army. This group has met with some success in stopping the armies of the Khartoum National Militia (KNM), but much of the time they are hampered by squabbling among themselves.

****

Our flight arrived early into Frankfort at about 7:00 a.m. on Saturday. Cameron went to the Lufthansa information counter to find out if the nurses were coming and on which flight. They were on one of two flights, both scheduled to arrive at 9:00 a.m. Since one of the flights would be arriving at the same gate ours had, we decided to stay where we were.

I had never been in a foreign country before, and it was all new to me. We had three hours to kill. There was nowhere to sleep, so we found some coffee, sat down and visited. Up to this time, the six members of our team had barely talked to each other. If we were going to work with each other for the next three weeks, we needed to start becoming good friends.

****

James and Samuel, young men in 1989, were living in the same village in Southern Sudan, when one day a small militia came driving in. The unexpected and uninvited mercenaries all had their guns out and ready to use. The militia leader demanded that all of the people in the peaceful village group together in the center of the town.

One of the teenaged girls started to run away, when two of the heavily armed militia shredded her to pieces with a barrage of bullets as she was running. Some of the bullets that missed her also killed her puppy. Immediately, everyone began to gather as demanded.

The militia picked out all of the Nuer men and women who had markings on their foreheads and faces. Some women had raised points from the top of their noses, going around to the top of each eyebrow. Some had the same raised points from the nose and going to the backs of their cheeks.

Many of the men had raised lines circling horizontally around their foreheads in half-inch intervals. These markings had been made as children and signified their identity with the Nuer tribe of Southern Sudan. It had been a rite of passage for them as young people.

The government militia led all of these marked Nuer people out to the edge of town and summarily shot them. James said there were about fifty people in that group. The militia then picked out all of the remaining young men and women, loaded them into two trucks, and drove off.

James and Samuel somehow managed to escape off of the trucks, cross over the border to Gambela at night, and walk to one of the refugee camps where they asked for political asylum. They came as refugees to Indiana in 1994.

The medical doctors on our team are using some of their vacation time to make this trip. Dr. Terrance Howard was born in Iowa and schooled there. Dr. Michael Peterson was born in New York and educated in Minnesota, where his parents moved when he was just in grade school. I decided to call them Dr. Mike and Dr. Terry out of respect for their profession. They seemed to be very fine men.

Cameron Johnson and his wife had been Covenant missionaries in the Congo before that civil war force them out. Since then, he has been semi-retired. His wife has had some medical issues, according to what Cameron told me in our conversation over the phone the first time I talked to him. He never elaborated.

I decided to approach the two doctors about my cut wrist.

"Can you good doctors help me? I cut my wrist on the way to the airport and would like to have you look at it."

"Let's have a look," Dr. Terry replied.

I un-wrapped the hanky-bandage from my wrist and showed the wound to the two doctors. Dr. Terry gently took my hand and spoke. "Whoa! You really need sutures, Jack. I've got some butterfly bandages in my bag. In fact, I have some Steri-Strips; they're better than butterflies. We'll put four of them on and it should heal properly. You may be deformed for life, just so you don't sue us."

"Don't worry, I'm already deformed."

Our team was displaying a sense of humor. This would be needed to counter the expected atmosphere of heartache, pain and poverty of the clinic patients in Gambela.

"How long has it been since you've had a tetanus shot," Dr. Mike asked?

"About two months."

"How did you cut it?"

"I banged it on a car."

"You're lucky you got the back of the wrist and not the front. Then you'd really be in trouble."

The doctors finished fixing me up in just a few minutes, with the wrapping of gauze cloth around my entire wrist. The bandage was quite noticeable, but I felt much better since the ointment they applied was giving me the needed relief from pain.

Both Dr. Terry and Dr. Mike seem to be really good men. I had become the first patient on our trip.

****

The time came for us to meet the flight from Chicago. We were not sure if the nurses would be on this flight, but we took the chance. We all walked over to the gate where they would maybe arrive and found a section where we could all stand and watch. Most of our team was looking a little groggy from the jet lag. The plane was scheduled to arrive about twenty minutes early.

This part of the airport was very busy with people waiting for passengers. The incoming plane may or may not be full, since it is a delayed flight. I stood in a place where I could see directly down the boarding ramp and view the passengers, as they would come out of the plane door.

They began walking slowly up the ramp. Since I didn't know the two women arriving, I figured that they would stay together and this would be a good way to identify them. I didn't even know their ages, imagining them to be older nurses—maybe middle-aged.

All of a sudden, I panicked and my heart started racing!

Coming up the ramp after just turning the corner from the door of the plane and carrying two bags, a purse, and a camera case, was someone who looked just like Abby. I caught only a momentary glimpse of her and her load, and then my view was immediately blocked. It appeared she was walking with another young woman. Both of them looked like they were in their mid-twenties.

What was Abby doing here? Could she be one of our team nurses? My eyes must be playing tricks on me. It couldn't be her. I quickly turned away.

I closed my eyes, slowly turned back, and looked again. She was now almost to the arrival gate door. It *was* Abby. She was the nurse Abigail from Minneapolis. When I heard her name in

Chicago it hadn't registered with me. Cameron had used only their first names when mentioning the nurses.

In the past six weeks my mind had been constantly preoccupied with the thought of Abby—what she was doing, her talk, her walk, and her smile. Maybe God was preparing me for what was about to happen. She had cut her hair and had filled out a little, but she was still the same beautiful Abby that I remembered.

Oh, what a fool I had been to leave her! In just a matter of the past few weeks, my mind had transformed her from an ex-wife into someone whom I wanted to worship. Only God could cause my mind to go through such a transformation.

What was I going to do now? Should I welcome her immediately or wait and acknowledge her introduction? which was surely going to happen. I even hoped it wasn't Abby but someone who looked exactly like her.

I quickly prayed, "God, help me to know what to do." This is going to be more difficult than getting the people out of a tipped-over Honda.

The six of us stood in a single line and met the nurses as they came to us. I was the last in the lineup and Abby was behind the other nurse. When Abby was almost next to me, I reached out. "Here, let me help you with your bags."

My familiar voice got her quick attention. Abby's mouth suddenly dropped and her eyes became as large as soupspoons. She looked at me and stood motionless for a few seconds. Then she whispered to me, "Jack, what are you doing here?"

My right hand accidentally touched her soft warm hand as I took the heavy carry-on bag from her. There was a bewildered look on her face. I whispered back, "I didn't know you were coming."

"Where are you going, Jack? Are you passing thru to…somewhere?"

"I'm with the medical mission team; the same one that you're with."

"You're kidding me. You can't be. How is that possible? Jack Franklin on a medical mission team? I don't think so."

Abby's reaction and comment were expected. She had no confidence in me. It didn't bother me that she said it; I was just glad that no one else heard it.

We were interrupted when our leader Cameron spoke to us. "Let's all move over here."

He talked as we shuffled over to the wall separating two terminal boarding areas.

"I just received the disappointing news that our flight to Addis is being delayed for twelve hours due to runway construction at that airport. Let's eat breakfast and then we can have a session of introduction and figure out how to spend twelve hours in a foreign airport. There's a McDonald's upstairs. Let's grab a couple of carts for our stuff, and two of us will take the carts up using the elevator. The rest of you can go up using the escalator. We'll meet up there."

We piled all of our carry-on bags, camera cases, and jackets onto two carts. Cameron and I took them up the elevator to the McDonald's restaurant. The line of people waiting with carts to use the elevator was long. It took us 15 minutes to finally make it to the second floor.

The area looked exactly like any McDonald's in the United States, and it wasn't as busy as we thought it might be. We walked right up to the counter. We all ordered breakfast using the English language on the menu board. Abby and Elizabeth were still together. I was afraid of embarrassing Abby, so I stayed in the background and was the last of the team to obtain food. Once, Abby looked back at me with an even more bewildered look on her face. This was a shock to both of us!

I peeked back as they walked to a table. I needed to see where they were going to sit. It was then that I noticed Abby was now holding onto Dr. Terry's arm, and he was carrying both of their trays of food. I wondered what that was all about. The answer was easy. It seemed that they knew each other—and evidently quite well.

None of the team knew that Abby and I had been previously married. I had given my last name, Franklin, when the introductions were made back at the arrival gate. Abby gave only her first name. Maybe she was ashamed to give her full name, since I was present.

There wasn't any more room for me at the table with the rest of the team, so I found an empty place around the corner. A five-foot wall separated us. Only Abby and I could see each other. I glanced at her a couple of times, and she glanced back with the same some-what-worried and perplexed look on her face.

Even before I had finished eating, Cameron started talking. The restaurant was quiet, allowing me to hear every word.

"This will be the first of what will be daily staff meetings where we will discuss individual medical cases, specific problems, inventory of medical supplies, schedules, transportation, and other pertinent subjects. We'll meet every morning at the clinic or maybe at the hotel where we will be staying in Gambela."

"By the way, do any of you know the greeting in the Nuer language? How do we say 'hello' in Nuer?" There was no response from any of the team.

Cameron seemed to be talking to the doctors and nurses. James and Samuel, my two Sudanese friends, had gone to phone their families back in Indianapolis. Cameron could not see me. Abby looked over at me once with a look that seem to indicate that she also thought I was not part of the staff meeting. At this point I had nothing to contribute to the discussion. I began to feel like a square peg in a round hole. I didn't belong here.

Abby was not yet aware that my life had done a "180 degree turnaround" and I wondered if the thought even entered her mind. And if ever I did find the courage to tell her, she may not even believe me. She knew me too well in my former life.

I focused my eyes out of the airport terminal window where mammoth planes were taking off and landing every minute. Abby would occasionally glance at me with the same puzzled look on her face. She and the rest of the team needed an explanation, the sooner the better.

I began to recall all of the grief and disappointment I had caused her during our marriage. It was painful to think about it. Many things that happen to us in life are uncomfortable to bring to mind. There had been so much heartache for her that I decided to stop thinking about it.

Then there was the subject of child support or, in my case, the lack of it. I was behind—and not by just a little bit. I had been sent several notices from the county officials in Minneapolis warning me of dire consequences if I didn't comply with the agreed upon child support.

Abby was a beautiful woman even ten years after I had first met her in the University speech class. But there was something even more beautiful about her now. I guess it was my new attitude toward what once was. Now she was once again in my presence. The world calls it "serendipity" or "fate." I viewed it as God's will, as divine intervention.

I suddenly felt within me a burst of passion for Abby that I had not felt in all of the years I was married to her! There was also a burst of confusion within me, not knowing if this feeling was a new love for Abby or love for a Christian sister who happened to be my former wife, the mother of my three boys, and now a team member on a missions trip to Africa.

I quickly prayed for discernment and that God would direct me in what to do or say. More importantly, I prayed for guidance in the timing of any such action on my part.

The staff session continued for another 30 minutes. I just sat there and pretended to be reading the copy of *USA Today* that I had found abandoned in the plane we had arrived on from Chicago. Cameron obviously didn't know that I was sitting just around the corner listening to his every word. He probably thought I had gone with James and Samuel. He then made a comment that made me feel like I was two inches tall.

"I'm not sure what role…ah…what's-his-name, Jack, will be playing in our mission trip. In fact, I'm not certain why he is here or making this trip. He probably thinks that this is a vacation. I'll need to discuss that with him before we leave Frankfort."

He stopped talking momentarily as everyone became quiet, and I fixed my eyes on the clear German sky outside of the window. I should have gone with Samuel and James. I wanted to find a hole and crawl into it. Abby looked at me. Her head turned—I could feel it. Her voice finally broke the silence, as I looked back at her. "Jack is sitting around the corner, maybe we should ask him."

The situation and Abby's words had suddenly become very awkward for me, but it also forced me into doing something fast.

I stood up, walked around the table, and sat down across from Cameron, who was by this time crimson red with embarrassment.

Cameron's expression told me that he was totally unaware that I had been listening. I was now sitting next to Abby, the closest I had been to her since just before our divorce was signed five years ago.

I didn't know quite what to say to the team, but I figured God would put some words in my mind and then guide them as they came out my mouth.

"I owe you people an explanation. What I am about to say will be a surprise to all of you; Abby and I were once married! We have three fine boys in Minneapolis. We still share the same last name, Franklin. Abby has chosen to keep her married last name and not change it back to her maiden last name as many divorced women do. I was totally unaware that she was making this trip, and I am sure that she was unaware of my being here."

The two doctors, the other nurse, Elizabeth, and Cameron were in a state of complete surprise—almost to the state of shock. There was a long pause as I waited for the news to sink in.

"I became a Christian only six weeks ago in the bleachers section at a high school basketball game, believe it or not. A group of Sudanese refugees have a fellowship at the Covenant church I am attending, and I became involved with these fine people less than one day after that basketball game. Two of them are James and Samuel, and they invited me to go with them on this trip to Ethiopia. I accepted, never realizing that I may have nothing to contribute and might even be a burden on this mission.

"Maybe God has a reason for me to go. He must have or He wouldn't have let me get this far. He made it possible for the visa process, medical shots, and needed financial support to sail right through without any delays or problems. I think you all know what I am talking about."

Abby sat still with her mouth open and with a look of absolute amazement. She was probably wondering why I didn't tell her about my conversion after it happened and in a more private setting. She may have even thought that I was not telling the truth. I continued to keep my eyes fixed on her.

"Abby and I have talked only occasionally in the past year, and until just now she has been totally unaware of my conversion."

I paused long enough to catch my thoughts and to see the reaction on the faces of each of my teammates. They couldn't believe the story that was unfolding before them. Once again, I turned my head and looked straight at Abby.

"At this point, maybe I should take the plane back home. I have twelve hours to decide that."

I turned to the other team members.

"Before I leave to get some more coffee, walk around the airport, and make my decision, I want to pray for this mission if you will permit me. And if I decide to return home, I will continue to pray for you every day from back in the States."

There was again a quiet awkward moment. None of the team could think of anything to say. Everyone was quite embarrassed, including me.

Dr. Mike finally spoke up. "Please, do pray."

I didn't wait for the rest of the team to bow their heads.

"Lord, I pray that You will bless this group as they travel to Gambela to help a people who love You and who are being persecuted merely because they want to follow You. Guide the doctors' and nurses hands and minds. Give them extra energy in the hot African sun and in the midst of extreme poverty. Give us all wisdom to decide what to do with me. Last, but most importantly, send down a group of angels to protect this medical team as they drive to Gambela and set up a medical clinic. I understand that the road to Gambela is a tough one, Lord. Keep our brothers and sisters in Your strong and protective hands. Amen."

When I had finished, I looked up at Abby. She still had the same bewildered look on her face.

No one said anything. Tears had suddenly started to roll down my cheeks and everyone saw them, including Abby. This was the first time I had cried since I was a child. I remember that I didn't even cry at the divorce settlement. I was a macho man—it wasn't proper for a man to cry. It was also the first time Abby had heard me pray.

I picked up my empty coffee cup and travel bags and began to leave. Turning back to the team, I spoke. "By the way, the Nuer greeting is, 'male magua,' which sounds like 'molly ma gua.'" My spelling of the greeting and how it was pronounced was written down by all of the team—all except Abby. I then strolled away without looking back at any of the gathered group. I bought another coffee at McDonald's and started walking around the airport. I needed time to think.

I stopped at the Lufthansa information counter and asked what a ticket would cost back to Indianapolis. The changing of the ticket would be very costly, since the original ticket was purchased at a group rate and provided no refund. It would require a substantial fee to change.

I worked my way back to the busy international restaurant close to the escalator on the second floor. The airport had suddenly become very busy. I found a small unoccupied table, sat down, nested my arms, and laid my head down. My head was spinning from a combination of things—the noise of the dishes clanging in the restaurant kitchen, the many languages being spoken at the tables next to me and from people walking by, my jet lag—produced tiredness, and the feeling of being left out of the world. Then God came down, seemed to put His hand on my head and said to me, "Not to worry. Everything is going to work out."

I relaxed and fell asleep for a few minutes. My sleep was so sound that the tap on my head had to be repeated. I looked up and saw Abby.

"Have a seat, Abby. Do you want something to drink?"

Abby just stood there. Her expression told me that she had plenty to say but didn't know where to start.

"No, I just want to tell you that Cameron is looking for you."

"I didn't embarrass you back at McDonald's, did I?"

"No, you didn't. Well, yes you did. But...I should be happy for you. I hope it turns your life around."

"Have you got a minute? I need to ask you something, Abby. Please have a seat."

"No, I'd prefer to stand."

I looked directly at her.

"Abby, will you forgive me for the past ten years of living like a fool and leaving you without a husband and a dad for our boys? I realize that it's a mountain for you to forgive. You really had four boys, you know. I would love to go back, start over, and make up for past sins. But that's unrealistic."

I stopped and waited for her to say something. Abby wasn't responding to my request for forgiveness, at least not verbally.

"Abby, I want you to know something. In the past few weeks, I've acquired a whole new outlook on life, love, marriage, family, God, and Christian friendship that I never thought was possible. I feel so bad about the kind of person I've been. My mind is now fixed on becoming what God wants me to be. That's first.

"I need to prove that I can be a decent human being—just a fraction of the person that you are. You're kind, considerate, and most of all, true. I can't believe you didn't get remarried to some rich doctor or lawyer or some other good person. If we could just become good friends—you and I—it would make this trip worth while."

Abby continued to just stand there. I had spoken my mind, and now it was her turn to say what was on her mind. Whatever she would say, no matter how bad, I had it coming and was prepared for the worst.

"This has been a real shocker, Jack! I can't believe that you're here. What could you possibly contribute to our team? There will be no cars to repair. I think you should turn around and go back to the United States. It would be the best for all of us.

"I need to be honest with you and tell you that Dr. Terry and I have been seeing each other for the past year. He's the one who recruited Elizabeth and me for this trip. Your sudden appearance is going to make this trip somewhat difficult and uneasy for Terry and me. We've started to make plans. You are no longer any part of my life."

Abby's voice was trembling—like she was frightened, or maybe angry. This was not like her.

"I saw that you were hanging on to Dr. Terry back at McDonald's."

"Jack, I also have to be honest with you and tell you that I have little feeling for you. Let me rephrase that, I have a lot of negative feelings toward Jack Franklin. You just asked me to forgive you. I'm having a difficult time with that request. The thought of you and me as a team, even with the compassionate and benevolent work we are about to do in Gambela, gives me the shivers. I don't think it's possible; and, furthermore, I don't want it to happen. I have other interests now. My sons need the dad that you never were to them.

"You say you want to prove that you can be a decent human being. Well, you can start by showing some respect for other people. It's a trait that you never displayed at any time during our marriage—especially to me. You were always thinking about yourself, never about other people. Put other people first, Jack.

"Another thing. I don't think you have one ounce of compassion in your body! Unless God has really done a number on you, Jack, you would be of no value on this trip. The doctors have the same opinion—we've discussed it. What did you do to your wrist?"

"Nothing, its just a little scratch."

I don't know if she was just trying to change the subject or if she was genuinely concerned about my injury. Her question was interrupting her tirade and that was good. Abby continued to stand. I looked at her with disbelief in the manner she was speaking. She was speaking the truth but in an irrational and emotional manner. This was not the Abby I once knew. Her spirit of unforgiveness toward me hurt me the most.

"We also need to talk about child support or, more appropriately, your lack of providing some."

I decided to not say a word. I just turned my head and looked at the escalators and at the continuous sampling of the world's population moving on it. After about ten seconds, Abby abruptly turned around and walked away. I was hoping that she had emptied her reservoir of negative bits and pieces about me. But it may continue later.

I felt like a whipped puppy. This was the second time this morning I had felt beaten. Maybe I had been so bad that forgiveness was beyond reach for her. Something else was at work inside of Abby—a struggle that only I could detect.

Cameron suddenly appeared at my table. He sat down but said nothing for a few seconds. He was embarrassed about what he had said about me, and I didn't know what to say to him. "Jack, I want to apologize to you for what I said at McDonald's. Please forgive me!"

"That's OK," I said giving him a smile to let him know I truly forgave him. "I can understand your doubt about my role on this trip. It was my Sudanese friends who really wanted me to go. However, I believe the Lord had something to do with it. I'm sure I can be of some help to the team. Maybe you should meet with the rest of them and let them vote. I'll abide by the outcome."

Cameron seemed relieved. Six weeks ago I might have punched him in the nose for his comments. "You're going to need a mechanic and a handyman to help set up things or to run errands, aren't you, Cameron? And what if our driver gets sick?"

Cameron was quiet for a few seconds as his eyes roamed the various people sitting at tables around us. It appeared as if he hadn't heard my question, maybe from the noise. He ordered a cup of coffee from the waiter coming through and then answered my question.

"Come to think of it, yes. Your presence would free me up to do more visiting with the Sudanese pastors. It would also give more time for the doctors and nurses to treat people. You can also serve as a driver, should we have need for one. And some special task may come up that you can do for the team. Tell me about your vocational background, Jack."

"Well, for most of the past ten years I've been working at fixing cars. You name the car, I've worked on it. I delivered pizza for a while, and that's about it. It's not exactly the required background for a medical mission team member, is it?"

"I want you with us and you'll be of good use. God will see to it. Let me get the input of the doctors and nurses, and then I'll convince them of your value with the team and that you should continue the trip to Gambela."

We continued our conversation. The waiter brought Cameron's coffee and gave me a refill in the paper cup I had carried from McDonald's. We talked about what tasks I could be involved with on our trip to Gambela. After some thirty minutes, we shook hands and walked back to McDonald's where we sat down and chatted some more. It was the start of a great friendship between us.

After about ten minutes, Cameron walked over to where the doctors and nurses were sitting. I could see them and they could see me, but I was out of ear range. They talked for a good thirty minutes while I continued to drink coffee, watch people, write in my trip notebook, and catch minute naps. I could tell they were talking about me, and I could imagine what they were all thinking about me. Maybe I should have moved so I was out of their view.

James and Samuel were tired and decided to get some rest on one of the benches along the wall. They used their coats for pillows. I thought this might seem unusual until I looked around and saw other people doing the same thing. Since it was the middle of the day in Frankfort, I guessed these people might be from half a world away and probably didn't have the extra money to sleep the few layover hours at a nearby motel.

Soon Cameron walked back to where I was sitting. He had a concerned look on his face, which worried me. He started to talk in a lowered voice as he sat down next to me.

"There's one other item I need to talk to you about. This is going to be a mission trip, and I hope any romance competition won't inhibit any of our work. We need to keep focused on our mission's objective, okay, Jack? I can see a race for Abby's hand going on between you and Dr. Terry. I've discussed this particular subject with a couple members of the team."

His face quickly lost its concerned look and he said to me, "Good news, however, Jack. They have all agreed that you should continue this trip with us."

I wondered if Cameron had brought up the subject of romance during their meeting, or if maybe Abby or Dr. Terry did.

"I fully understand the situation and I'll be a good boy," I assured him.

"Just be aware, Jack, that I have an opinion—or shall I say "favorite,"—on any such romantic competition. But the fact remains that we all need to keep our focus."

"Can I enlist your prayer support in this possible competition?" I asked.

"How do you want me to pray, Jack?"

"Pray that God's will be done and that a broken family and marriage be restored."

****

Two hours later, the two doctors were sitting at another table talking and I decided to join them and chat. I needed to become their friend.

"May I interrupt this discussion?"

"Sit down, Jack."

I sat down and decided to begin the conversation. There was a moment of awkwardness, reflecting the differences in our socio-economic situations.

"Tell me about yourselves—where are you from, where'd you go to school, where do you work, about your family—you know, all of the important stuff."

"I'm Terrance Howard. I was born in Iowa City, Iowa, went to school at the University of Iowa, work at Midway Hospital in St. Paul, and I'm single."

"Can I call you Doctor Terry?"

"Yes, you may, but just call me Terry."

I turned to the other doctor. I had been introduced to both of these physicians in Chicago, but this was the first time I had been able to talk with them at any length.

"I'm Michael Peterson. I come from New York, moved to Minnesota, schooled in medicine in Arizona, and have a wife in Minneapolis. I too work at Midway hospital."

"What field of medicine do you doctors work in?"

Dr. Mike spoke first: "I'm an obstetrician—I deliver babies."

Dr. Terry broke in, "I'm a orthopedist—I work at fixing broken limbs and other bones."

"I hope I can help you guys in some way in Africa."

"Well, I'll tell you what. Terry and I are going to need someone who is mechanically inclined to fix our equipment and tools if they break down. We've got a small portable refrigerator that operates on batteries, and I'm not very mechanical. Maybe we'll need to have you Gerry-rig some artificial limbs for patients out of bamboo and baling wire or masking tape."

We all had a good laugh.

Dr. Terry and Dr. Mike told me about their church backgrounds and how Cameron had recruited them for this trip. They both attend the same Covenant church in one of the Minneapolis suburbs and play golf together. Even though our career levels were different, we had one single objective in mind on this trip: to glorify God by reaching out to the people of Gambela and give them some needed medical help.

"Again, if I can be of any assistance to you guys at any time, just let me know. If I can't fix it, then it probably isn't broke!"

"How is your wrist?" Dr. Mike asked.

"A little sore, but I'll be okay."

"Just keep me informed. You're our first patient on this trip, and we don't want to lose you."

****

The doctors and nurses decided to take a taxi into Frankfurt and shop. I felt I needed to save my money, so I remained at the airport. I also felt like I would be a fish out of water and needed to maintain a social distance from Abby. She would have to make the next move toward any reconciliation as merely a friend or a fellow Christian. If she didn't make that move, I was prepared. After what Abby told me this morning, I questioned if she ever wanted to be in the same room with me. I needed to keep away from her, at least for now.

****

At 9 p.m. Cameron came up to me with a surprise.

"Jack, where were you at 8:00 p.m.? We had a team meeting at the tables by McDonald's."

"I didn't know that. Did I miss an announcement of the meeting?"

"Didn't Abby tell you?"

"No. I saw her and Dr. Terry at about 7:30; she never said a word to me."

"She was supposed to tell you about a change in our departure gate and about the meeting."

I looked at Cameron with a blank stare, that slowly turned to an understanding expression for both of us. We each seemed to know what had happened. Abby purposely didn't tell me about the meeting. This was not good. There was a wall of ice being built between us. Something had to happen very soon to cause this ice to break—or at least begin to melt.

I sat down and quietly asked God to order events to happen in the next two weeks that would cause this wall to be removed. The entire mission trip could be in jeopardy.

****

We all gathered at departure gate fifteen at 10:00 p.m. with everyone both excited and tired. We were all suffering from jet lag and no sleep. I glanced over at Abby. She was purposely looking away from me, not wanting to chance any eye contact.

Dr. Mike approached me sitting by myself. "Do you want something for your pain?"

"Do you have something?" I asked. "Both my wrist and back ache."

"I'll see if the girls have any pain killers. Let's go ask them."

Dr. Mike took my arm and walked me over to where the nurses were sitting. He sat down on an empty seat between the girls. He may have done this purposely.

"First, let's have another look at your cut."

He carefully unwrapped my wrist. Abby was sitting and drinking some hot herbal tea. She was blowing on it in an attempt to cool it off. She tried to appear disinterested in whatever Dr. Mike was about to do.

"What in the world happened to you?" Dr. Mike asked, as the last wrap came off. "You've got a bad cut on your wrist and you have a back ache. Are they connected, Jack?"

I didn't answer his question. I was having a little trouble myself remembering exactly what had happened on the freeway. My tiredness was not giving me a clear mind, and it all seemed like a dream.

"Do either of you girls have anything for pain? Jack could use something."

The treated wound had begun to heal. Elizabeth looked at it and expressed her concern with a sigh and a groan. Abby was not interested. Elizabeth then expressed herself verbally. "You really gashed yourself, didn't you Jack? Dr. Mike, will his wrist be okay?"

"He should have had stitches. We're really supposed to leave the Steri-Strips on. But I needed to check for any infection."

Dr. Mike then put on new strips and rewrapped the wound. Abby reached for her purse, retrieved a bottle of Ibuprofen, and placed four in Dr. Mike's hand. He then gave them to me. All of the team was watching, and Abby's not giving me the Ibuprofen directly gave all of us a clear signal that something was amiss between us.

"What happened to your wrist? How did you injure it?" Abby inquired.

"I bumped my hand on a car when I was helping some people along the freeway."

"Well, that was nice of you, helping someone," Abby retorted. She said it as if she were inferring that I wouldn't help the people—another putdown. Again, I decided not to respond to her comment. Elizabeth looked at me with a disapproving facial expression to Abby's comment.

I looked at Dr. Mike and said "Thank you, Abby."

****

Our departure was smooth. If the quality of the remainder of the flight was like this, we were in for a night of rest. We were soon in the air and heading from Europe to Africa.

With Abby informing me that she had been dating Dr. Terry, and with her not talking to me in an agreeable manner, the whole mission's trip had suddenly become difficult. The team was small and it was going to be difficult to accomplish our goal without Abby and me talking and working with each other in a reasonable manner, let alone doing it as Christians. I decided to be the best team member possible, be available to do anything that would help Abby, and let God sort it all out.

But I also began to pray for a miracle and a second chance with Abby. I had just fallen in love with her. Her falling in love with me would never be possible without a miracle from God Himself. The decision would be up to Abby.

CHAPTER 3

Sunday—Day 3

About two hours into our flight, the plane encountered some turbulence. It woke everyone up after they had fallen asleep while sitting on the Frankfurt runway for at least 45 minutes. I tried to get back to sleep, but that proved fruitless. There was too much on my mind.

Only three seats in front of me sat Abby and Dr. Terry. I had never been a very jealous person, but that changed in Frankfurt. I suddenly had become a jealous ex-husband of a former wife and her relationship with a medical doctor. It sounded much like a soap opera. It was difficult to relax and not think about the past, the present, and the possible future, as far as Abby was concerned.

As we began to fly over the continent of Africa, I looked out the plane window. The sky was clear, the moon full and bright, and the ground fairly visible. The land looked rocky and uneven—almost like some of the badlands in the States. There seemed to be very few towns with only occasional single lights. Maybe they are small villages where only one light is present. Some of the lights might also be small outside cooking fires still ablaze.

I asked the flight attendant what country we were flying over. She leaned over and whispered the answer. "Egypt."

As we got closer to Addis Ababa, with the dawn just beginning, I saw what appeared to be agriculture fields. The different plots made the ground appear like a giant quilt. Some squares of the quilt looked like they had small haystacks on them. From the air they looked like someone had arranged neat little piles of uniform colored doggy do-do into rows. The color of the do-do was the color of straw, which may have been what the stacks were.

Cameron moved to the empty aisle seat beside me. He sat there quietly for a moment like he wanted to talk with someone. He was waiting for me to start the conversation—which I did. "Tell me about your family, Cameron."

"Well, we have two sons and a daughter. They're all married and live in three different locations in the United States. My wife and I have three grandchildren. Ruth, my wife, is the one I am worried about."

"What seems to be the problem?"

"Her mind."

"What is it?" Cameron hesitated for a bit and then turned to me with his voice slightly breaking as he spoke.

"Something has snapped. All of a sudden, she's stopped communicating with our children, the people in the church, the neighbors, me—everyone. She stays at home and just watches television."

"What do the doctors say?"

"They think it's some kind of depression. At least that's what they're treating her for. I really should have stayed home with her. I'm having one of ladies from the church stay with her for these three weeks."

"I'll remember to pray for her." I hesitated, then asked, "what do *you* think the problem is?"

"I think she misses the life we lived, loved and left in the Congo. We had to leave because of the civil war. She loved the work, the people, and the land—even the animals. Maybe we stayed there too long. On top of that, because of her age I think that she's going through some physical changes"

We continued to talk until the pilot announced that we were coming into Addis Ababa. I would have liked to continue our discussion as he seemed to want to share the burden he was bearing. Before he moved back to his seat, I prayed for Cameron and his family, especially his wife.

"Thank you, Jack. Keep praying and I'll keep praying for your situation. I think you're the one that really needs the most prayer."

"Well, God's in control and He orders the stars to move. I think He can order human hearts to move also, even if one of them seems frozen at the present time. Just keep praying."

****

We arrived at the Addis Ababa airport at 7:00 a.m. and were told we would have a long taxi ride to the airport terminal aboard buses. There seemed to be runway construction everywhere. We were soon heading toward the customs building and wondering what trouble we would have with our carry-on bags. Added to that were the 24 checked-in bags of personal items and medical supplies. Would the customs inspectors open them? What delay would they possibly cause? Some of the bags were packed so tight that it was difficult to close them. This was on the minds of the entire team, and I think everyone was praying during our ride.

It was worry for nothing, at least for the carry-on bags—an answer to prayer. Our team looked harmless and all of our bags went through without any difficulty. We walked over to the conveyor area and waited for the carts of baggage to arrive from Ethiopian customs.

Abby, Elizabeth, Dr. Mike and Dr. Terry were talking together. I glanced over at Abby several times. She finally saw me looking at her. I stopped when I saw her wrinkle up her face. I think that's what she was doing. Maybe she was just getting ready to sneeze.

As we were waiting for our luggage, Abby all of a sudden became distressed. It seems she had left her camera case in Frankfurt.

"I thought I had it stuffed in my carry-on bag. I think I left it at McDonald's. How could I forget it?"

Dr. Terry, trying to calm Abby down, asked her a question. "Was it just your camera in the case? Because, we can get you another one someplace in downtown Addis."

"I also had my family photo album to show to the Sudanese

people and all of my film. My parents gave me the camera especially for this trip. I feel just terrible."

"They're cheap here in Ethiopia. We'll go look for one later this morning, as soon as we get checked in and have a chance to shop."

It was quite obvious that Dr. Terry wasn't as concerned about the loss of the camera and case as Abby was, and she didn't seem relieved with Dr. Terry's offer. The case and its contents had great personal value to her. I felt bad for Abby, but what could anyone do? Someone probably found it and it's now on the way to a faraway country.

We finally retrieved everyone's luggage, piled it onto several carts, and pushed the carts together side-by-side.

Some of us went over to the airport bank to trade a few dollars for the Ethiopian birr. This would get us by until tomorrow when we would find a large bank and exchange larger amounts of American money.

While standing in line at the exchange bank, I met the foreign desk chief from one of the major newspapers in the United States. I asked him about the war in Sudan. He was very frank. "This war is much underreported and even unreported."

I agreed and asked, "Why is that?"

"Friends can be upset easily. The Southern Sudanese are Christians, and if we report what is truly going on in South Sudan, our Moslem friends will become upset. We buy oil from many of those countries. To make matters worse, the Khartoum Government is receiving assistance in their attempt to wipe out the South Sudan people. This will make it easier to drill for the oil that has been discovered, since it's where these people are living. Several western oil companies are financing the oil exploration. Meanwhile, the killing goes on."

"Have you been to the war area?"

"Yes, I have. It's horrible. People are starving; some are walking and crawling around maimed. There's even reports of men and women being captured and sold as slaves. At least two million people have died in the past 20 years. I just wish CNN could be in Sudan 24 hours of the day. But maybe they and the world still wouldn't care." He paused for a moment, shook his head, and asked, "Why are you in Ethiopia?"

"I'm with a mission team that's going to set up a medical clinic for two weeks in Gambela. Most of the people that we'll be treating are the Sudanese Christians from the Nuer tribe."

"Are you a doctor?"

"No, in fact, I'm an auto mechanic."

"I've been in Gambela. Boy, do they need medical help there, especially the Nuer people! I wish you well on your trip. In fact, I wish I could go with you. I need to get away from my rat race for about two weeks. Hey, my wife's a nurse! She could apply Band-Aids and I could dig out slivers—or maybe it would be the other way around."

"Where are you going now?" I asked.

"Back to the United States and then on to New Zealand to see my wife's family."

"Are you going through Frankfurt?"

"Yes, I am. I have the normal 8-hour layover."

I suddenly had an idea. An opportunity had just presented itself. "Would you do me a big favor?" I asked, somewhat tentatively.

"What can I do for you?"

"One of our team members left a camera and its case in Frankfurt. It was a gift from her parents, and she feels just terrible about losing it."

"Write down her name, the description of the lost items and where she left it. I'll see what I can do. Where are you staying?"

"The Blue Nile hotel."

"I've stayed there before and I have the phone number."

I wrote down all of the pertinent information, including the color of the camera case. It was light blue with a dark blue shoulder strap. I remembered the color when I first saw Abby at the arrival gate in Frankfort.

"Here's my card. Give me a call when you return to the USA. I'd like to hear how your team did. Maybe we can do a story on it. Be sure you take good photos and notes."

I would have liked to talk with this man further, but it was his turn to exchange money and then he was gone. As he left, I gave him my name and address on a piece of paper I had in my pocket.

He placed it in his small notebook.

I walked back to the busy baggage area, rejoined the team and turned toward the nurses. Abby turned toward Dr. Terry when she saw that I was about to say something to them. "Here is some Ethiopian money for you girls to divide. You may need it until we get to the bank tomorrow." I handed a stack of bills totaling 500 Ethiopian birr to Elizabeth. Abby may have refused anything I gave her.

"Thank you, Jack. I'll share it with Abby. We'll pay you back when we exchange money tomorrow. I imagine you don't have much money, do you?"

I didn't answer. If I did, the next subject may be child support, but maybe not. Abby had covered that subject already. She apparently had also shared portions of my life—financial and otherwise—with Elizabeth. But that was okay. At least Elizabeth seemed to show some civility toward me.

We rolled the carts carrying our luggage down two ramps to the taxi parking lot and there was at once a flurry of confusion! Every taxi driver wanted to take us to the hotel. Cameron would negotiate the number of taxies needed and which ones. I spotted a driver not selected starting to grab one of our bags. I quickly stopped him— and none too soon. A host of other drivers had the same idea. If they could get one of the bags in their car, it would mean that their chances of being picked by Cameron would be greatly enhanced.

I continued walking around our baggage carts watching them like a hawk. I called the two nurses over to assist me. We were carrying some valuable medical supplies, without which there would be no medical clinic in Gambela.

****

Our ride into the city of Addis Ababa was interesting and gave us a preview of what we might see in Ethiopia. The city seemed to be old, dirty, and dusty. The evidence of poverty is the first thing that we noticed. People were pushing carts filled with all kinds of saleable items. Donkeys and mules were pulling carts—if the people were lucky enough to own these beasts of burden.

People were sitting along the road selling their wares. Small old women were carrying huge hard-to-balance loads of sticks on their frail and sickly bodies. They were bent over so far that their faces were positioned directly downward toward the ground. Many children were playing everywhere, sometimes on the road. As we got closer to the hotel, the crowds seemed to become increasingly dense.

We arrived at the Blue Nile hotel where Cameron did the registering of everyone on the team. A secured room was provided where we could keep some of our bags. It took a lot of work to make sure they were all accounted for, placed in the room, and locked behind the door.

After I had been to my room and freshened up, I decided that some breakfast with good strong coffee was in order. I walked into the restaurant and sat down at a table. The waitress came over with some water and handed me a menu. I choose not to drink any of the water as I had read of tourists getting sick from the local water. What I was going to do in Gambela for water was a big question on my mind. I may have to use my water filtering bottle.

I ordered some Ethiopian coffee, scrambled eggs, toast and a bottle of Ambo. I had never tasted Ambo, I'd only heard about it from James. He said that it tasted like soda water. He was right. The restaurant coffee was very strong.

The restaurant was like any restaurant in the United States. The tables were heavy, the chairs padded, the floor carpeted, the ceiling dripped with chandelier light fixtures, and table settings and tableware were made in Korea—just like home.

As I looked around the restaurant, I saw many different ethnicities. There were many who looked like they were tourists, some from the United States, some who were definitely Sudanese, and some who were Ethiopian. One table of people looked like they may be from some country in Europe. I think the people sitting at the table next to me were Chinese as their language sounded Chinese. Across the room I could see a table of people who looked like they may be from Spain or maybe Mexico. I could hear the Spanish language.

It was just like being in the Frankfort airport.

****

Cameron had a friend in Addis Ababa who was working for a business in the United States and wanted to give us a tour of the city. His name was Eyob and he was Ethiopian. Cameron told us that he spoke English, Amharic, Tigrigna, Arabic, and some Italian. He had a car that seated only eight people—and not very comfortably. He picked us up at 11:00 a.m.

As we drove around the central part of the city of Addis Ababa, beggars came up to the car and begged for money. Little boys came leading by the hand their crippled mother or relative and began to beg. They would say, "Please—mother—sick—blind—no food," in English, of course.

The little boys knew exactly how to position their one hand and configure their face in a manner that was supposed to "melt our hearts." Maybe this is being a little too cynical, but it didn't take long to see a pattern to what was going on.

The doctors started giving the people coins out of the car windows. Abby and Elizabeth were reaching for their purses when I spoke up. "Hey folks! You're going to run out of money, be careful. These people are professional beggars and there's probably a million people within a radius of two miles from where we are driving."

"How do you know that?" was the question from Abby.

Hey! She spoke to me, although she was still in a combative mode. The ice wall was still very solid. I didn't answer. I had read about the beggars in a travel guide at Barnes & Noble only one week ago.

The car was moving slowly enough so that it may have been possible, or even quite likely, for the beggars to alert their buddies up the street of the handout prospect coming their way. The crowd seemed to be impenetrable with our car barely moving. I needed to say something.

"I'm sorry team, but I cannot in good conscience participate in the act of giving at this time and this location. My limited funds were given to me by my church people to fulfill a specific mission these three weeks, and I need to be a good steward. Besides, we could have a C5A loaded with Ethiopian one birr bills and still run out."

The giving suddenly stopped. Cameron turned around and winked at me. The doctors just sat there quietly. Abby broke the silence as we turned a corner and drove down an even more crowded street. "Jack's right. The poverty here is overwhelming."

Abby had finally agreed with me about something. I was amazed.

Eyob's car was not in the best running condition. Several times it stopped and he had difficulty starting it again. The starter sounded like a bearing was going out. Also, the idle was set too low and the car needed a major tune-up. That would be 1.6 hours of work by an auto mechanic, plus parts. I would probably be the one to look at and fix the engine if it stalled. I wasn't too keen on working on a car in the midst of an army of beggars in the central part of Addis Ababa, Ethiopia. Besides, how long would my set of tools remain untouched? In this crowd, they would be stolen in about two and a half seconds.

We saw the burial site of Haile Selasie from the car only. Some of the Ethiopians stopped us from parking and walking around. Again, these people were trying to get money from us. They could tell we were American tourists. We had it written all over our faces and in the manner in which we were dressed.

We toured other historical sites, churches, memorial gardens, a gift store, and a wealthier area of central Addis.

In between visiting the sites, we would drive through what I would label as "squalor towns" or "Unpleasantvilles." They were complexes of thrown-together shelters made of old wood, roofing tin, and any type of material that could be utilized to build a structure. "Existing" in these living quarters were countless numbers of people. It appeared that animals also lived there.

We went down a street where an old man was lying on the ground. One of our doctors judged that he was dead. I wonder who would pick him up or if anyone even cared. It was quite obvious that I was already becoming used to the poverty—even cynical toward it. The most important question was, of course, had he ever heard about Jesus?

We visited a small convenience store on a street of businesses. The store reminded me of "The House of Hanson" in Dinkytown by the University of Minnesota. They sold the same basic items. I decided to buy a case of 2-liter bottled water. Our entire group wondered why. "They'll come in handy sometime in our trip," was my answer. I also bought a few other items, which I believed I would be able to put to good use in Gambela.

Abby seemed to be having a good time, although she wasn't smiling as she once did. There was obviously something on her mind. I think she was worried about her lost camera, about my presence complicating her relationship with Dr. Terry, and maybe the fear of the unknown adventure that lay ahead of us. This was Abby. When we were married, she would worry about many things. Of course, I didn't help the situation by trying to calm her fears or being a support for her. I was just another of her worries.

I wonder what her reaction will be if and when I tell her that I have fallen in love with her. She may think that I'm crazy or that she would be crazy for even responding to such a notion. Maybe that opportunity would present itself during our trip. God would need to tell me what to say to her and when to say it.

Our tour lasted two hours. It was depressing but very revealing. I concluded that unless a person sees first hand the poverty in a third-world country, one could only imagine what it is like. A person has to smell the putrid odors coming from rotting organic material, see the pathetic and dejected look on people's faces, and hear some of the wailing of humanity, sick and waiting to die.

We stopped at a small restaurant in a home and let Eyob order for us. We sat on the large porch around a coffee table. I ordered a bottle of Ambo. It was quite warm and I wondered if any ice existed in Addis Ababa. I doubted it. Also, how could we possibly eat anything after ingesting the foul Addis air for the past two hours?

I was becoming negative and needed to dwell more on the positive things in Ethiopia. If I didn't, I'd be of no use to the people I'd come to help. I needed to change my attitude. *God, please help me.*

Eyob ordered injera along with two large trays of various items that were to be eaten with it. I asked Eyob what the items were. "Beef, vegetables, goat cheese, mutton, and a few other things that I'm unable to identify," was Eyob's reply.

Injera is a flat, thin sheet of baked pancake-like food, similar to a sheet of pizza dough or Norwegian lefse. Tearing off a small piece, it is used to grab a portion of the meat, veggies, etc., and then stuff the whole thing into your mouth.

After we had eaten, Eyob gave us the shortened history of Ethiopia.

"Ethiopia is the oldest country in Africa, having its beginning at least two thousand years ago. We celebrate May 28 as our National holiday, when the Mengistu regime was overthrown. Sudan and Ethiopia, as well as much of Africa, were sacked by drought and famine in the early 1980s. The government of Mengistu and his brutal policies only intensified the famine here in Ethiopia. Millions of people starved to death.

"Once his regime had been overthrown by the Ethiopian People's Revolutionary Democratic Front, the EPRDF, the country's food situation improved. In Sudan it was another story as an authoritarian leader ruled that government.

"Ethiopia has been engaged in a civil war since the early 1970s with it's largest former state, Eritrea. In the middle 1990's Eritrea voted to become a separate country. Even the Eritrean refugees in America were able to vote."

When Eyob had completed his discussion, I asked him a question. "Eyob, if you were elected mayor of Addis Ababa, were given a reasonable budget plus extra funds from the Ethiopian government, and had a mandate to improve the city, what are five things you would do?"

Eyob sat back and was quiet for about thirty seconds. We could tell that his mind was racing and that he was eagerly accepting the challenge. Finally, he looked at us and spoke.

"That's quite a question. I don't know where to start. There is one more precondition you would need to add to this assignment— no corrupt political involvement by anyone in my term of office.

"I think I would improve on the education system as much as I could and as fast as I could—for adults and children. Then I would fix the roads and streets—I would widen them. Then it would be the water and sewage system—it's awful! I would improve the housing. I would get the people away from the center of the city. If the city keeps moving in on itself, people will be on top of people. Number

five would be to improve health care. Number six: I would introduce computers. We cannot operate successful businesses in a
world economy without computers."

Our team approved his plan for the city. We then voted unanimously for Eyob as the next mayor of Addis Ababa. He smiled and
took a bow.

****

We were to meet at 5:00 p.m. in the hotel restaurant for dinner
and to have an informal chat. I spent two hours finally getting some
quality sleep. For about the first five seconds after I woke up, I wasn't
quite sure where I was. Then it suddenly dawned on me that I was in
a hotel in Addis Ababa, Ethiopia. Once I was fully awake, I felt good.

It also quickly came to me that I would see Abby again in just a
few minutes. I was beginning to miss her and desired to be able to
see her more often. Even getting a glance from her, friendly or not,
would be welcomed.

How could I miss someone who seemed so bitter toward me?
Maybe that was a good sign. I couldn't reveal my feelings since she
very possibly despised the ground I walked on. As a Christian, I felt
no ill toward her; it was quite the opposite. I just hoped that this
passionate feeling would become mutual as the next few days and
weeks progressed. But before that happened, forgiveness needed to
flow between us.

I opened the window and looked out. The noise of Addis was
much different than that of Indianapolis, Indiana. There were no
sirens piercing the air and I was able to hear people talking and
producing all sorts of strange sounds. The carts people were pushing
or pulling could be heard on the street below. Donkeys and goats
made their non-familiar sounds. An occasional jet could be heard
passing overhead on its flight path to and from the Addis airport.

A short distance from the hotel was an Ethiopian Orthodox
church with the loudspeaker on full volume. The sound from the
music and speaking in the Amharic language was very loud and
even distorted. I decided to keep the windows closed in order to
keep myself from getting bitten by any mosquito still lingering

from the previous night.

After freshening up, I walked down the stairs from the third floor. On my way down I noticed a large picture on the wall. The man in the painting looked like John the Baptist—an Ethiopian version. He was dressed only in a pair of shorts, had long black hair, and was standing beside a boat in the water. I decided that the artist was attempting to paint good ol' John waiting for some repentant sinners to baptize.

When I arrived at the restaurant, the waitress was waiting to seat me. Someone in our group must have told her I was arriving. She led me to the back corner where I saw some familiar faces. The two doctors and the two nurses occupied one of the two tables. My Sudanese brothers, James and Samuel, and Cameron occupied the other table, where I was seated.

My teammates ordered drinks—coffee, tea or water. I ordered hot tea and a bottle of Ambo. For dinner, I ordered a bowl of vegetable soup and the Nile River trout. At the airport I was told that this restaurant had the best tasting Nile trout in Addis, maybe in all of Ethiopia and Sudan.

Our table spent time discussing a variety of topics, including our tour by Eyob. We all concluded that the tour was going to be one of the highlights of our trip.

I looked over at the other table wondering how Abby was. As soon as she saw me looking at her, she immediately jerked her head and looked in the other direction. She was really not appreciative of my presence; that was for certain.

Something would have to happen to get Abby and me involved with each other. If we did not make peace with each other soon, the rift would spread and it would place the mission team's work in jeopardy. In our present state of mind, we were of little value. A sense of compassion and love was needed for the work that was going to be done in Gambela. But first it was needed within our own team.

The soup and trout were delicious. I noticed that some of the food ordered on the doctors' and nurses' table was not being eaten very fast or enthusiastically. They had ordered injera. My Sudanese friends had ordered it and ate it like it was their first meal after fasting for ten days. Samuel gave me a taste. It had a sour taste.

James had told me how they made injera—mixing with water the flour from a grain called teff. The Ethiopians and the Sudanese would let the injera lie in the open air for many hours, allowing it to spoil slightly prior to baking. Some of it tasted like vinegar had been added.

I decided to do a neighborly thing and offer some of my trout to the medical table. The chef had given me a very large portion, covering the entire large plate, and I had eaten only half of it. I cut what was left into five pieces, placed them on an empty bread plate, and slid one piece back on to my plate. I stood up, walked around to the medical table, and handed the plate to Elizabeth. They each began to take a piece.

Doctor Terry sitting next to Abby must have been hungry, or maybe he didn't follow the count, or perhaps he wasn't paying attention. He took the two pieces remaining and placed them on his plate. By the time the plate got to Abby, there was none left.

Abby handed the plate to Elizabeth, and she handed it back to me. The girls gave each other a puzzled look. I started to wonder if the doctor was totally awake. Maybe he was yet going to slide a piece onto Abby's plate. I didn't wait to find out. I pushed my chair back, stood up, grabbed the plate containing my piece of trout, and again walked around the tables. My action of emptying the remaining good-sized piece of trout onto Abby's plate apparently got the good doctor's attention. He suddenly realized what he had done, became embarrassed, and immediately apologized to Abby.

As we were finishing our meal and getting ready to leave, one of the hotel clerks came in and interrupted us. "I have a message for Abby Franklin."

"I'm Abby."

"This fax just came in."

Abby took the sheet of paper from the hotel clerk and he left. She read the message to herself. Her facial expression suddenly turned to joy. "My camera case was found! I can't believe it! The Ethiopian Airlines is going to deliver it to the hotel tonight. Wonderful!"

My media friend from the airport currency exchange bank line had not forgotten my favor. We all shared and expressed Abby's joy.

I decided to leave and go to my room. As I was almost to the doorway of the restaurant, Abby read the final sentence of the fax out loud.

"P.S.—Say hi to Jack."

****

After dinner James and Samuel visited with many of their Sudanese friends in the hotel. They had all attended the Addis Nuer Covenant church service in the afternoon and were sitting in the lobby engaged in a spirited discussion on the war, according to what James told me.

These people also were asking James and Samuel for money. Cameron had warned me about this happening. "The Sudanese think that everyone in America is a millionaire. They keep asking for money. Be careful," he told me. I had conveyed this message to James and Samuel in advance by telling them, "I will have no money to give you."

I sat down with three of the Sudanese and asked them if any would share their story of what happened to make them leave South Sudan. Daniel volunteered, with James translating.

"Let me take notes, if you don't mind," I told him.

"My name is Daniel, and I was in South Sudan in 1989 when the government militia from the north put me in jail. I remember it was Christmas Eve, and normally our church would be meeting in our regular church building for a Christmas service and fellowship. However, because there were children involved, we met under a large tree with overhanging branches. We sang Christmas songs accompanied by a single drum.

"The government forces heard the drum and decided to surround the tree instead of bombing it with a plane. They shot ten people while we were singing. Four of them died and the rest were carried to their homes without medical treatment. The militia followed me to my compound hut and arrested me. The guards beat me in front of my family and then took me to jail.

"The next thing they did was horrible. The guards led me out into the courtyard and proceeded to shoot people right in front of me. Before they would kill the victim, they asked me to renounce

Christianity and Jesus. They told me if I did, they would stop the killing. When I refused, they would either shoot the person or cut his or her throat. I pleaded with them and cried during the entire time."

Daniel stopped for a minute as he was overcome with emotion and cried openly. We all sat quietly until he finally regained his composure.

"Daniel, how did you escape or get out of jail?" I asked.

"A man came to visit me in the jail. He was my size, and he was dying of cancer and did not have family in the village. He wore layers of clothes. Apparently, he had a nerve condition and complained constantly of being cold. He convinced me that God told him to take my place in jail. I put on all of his clothes and heavy cap, and I was able to escape. Shortly after I left, the guards shot him and he went to heaven to be with Jesus. That man gave his life for me.

"I had my entire family of sixty people leave my village within the hour and begin the walk to Gambela. We took various trails and roads, which allowed us to elude the government's militia soldiers as they came after us. We all prayed as we walked. We split up into groups of not more than five. God was with us and must have confused our pursuers."

"Why did all of your family have to go with you?"

"The government soldiers would surely have killed my entire family."

"Are there more stories like yours?"

"There are thousands of stories that could be told—and will be one day in heaven."

"Thank you for sharing your story with me."

At that point, the hotel manager asked the Sudanese to leave, as it was getting late.

****

It was 8:00 p.m. when some of us met in the hotel lobby. The girls wanted to go out for a walk and both went up to their room to get their jackets. The doctors decided to turn in early, and Cameron had already gone to his room. He wasn't feeling well, probably from a combination of fatigue, the heat, and being worried about his wife.

The nurses' going out for a walk was not a good thing to do. Addis Ababa was a big city with all types of people roaming the streets at night, just like in any large city of the world. Anything could happen.

It was my intention to not ask the girls if I could go with them, but rather to just follow them in case they ran into trouble. They took off and I began to follow at a reasonable distance. The girls had their purses in clear view for anyone to see.

It wasn't long before they realized that I was following them. They stopped and I caught up to them. Abby spoke before I reached them and could provide an explanation for my following. "Jack, I thought you were going to crash for the night. I think Elizabeth and I can walk on our own. Is that too much to ask?"

There was so much anger in Abby's voice. It probably was an expression of her independence from me that she wished to communicate more than anything else. Maybe she was expressing her frustration at my posing a threat to her new relationship with Dr. Terry. Not every girl meets an up-and-coming star in the medical field.

"You may not wish to have me follow you, but I don't think you girls should be out on the street this time of night. You may not care, but it is important to me that nothing happen to you!" I was looking directly at Abby as I spoke.

"Why?" Abby asked, noticeably irritated.

"Because my sons need their mother alive and healthy, that's why!"

Abby quickly turned and stomped off. Elizabeth stood there looking first at Abby and then at me. She followed Abby, walking fast to catch up. I continued to follow them and watch them closely. Abby knew I was right.

Everything went fine until they walked down a street that began to narrow into an alley. The street was on a downhill slope, and only a dim light from one of buildings was available.

All of a sudden, four young men came out of the shadows and approached the girls. They may have been waiting for the girls in particular, or they may have been waiting for just any other unsuspecting tourist. The four looked like they were Ethiopian teenagers—maybe from an Addis street gang. They were unaware that I was following the girls and never saw me.

Soon the four had surrounded Abby and Elizabeth, forcing them to stop. I could hear the anxiety and fear in their voices as they continued to talk to each other in a sudden terrified manner. They assumed that the four young men couldn't understand English.

I needed to make my presence known as quickly as possible. I also needed to be willing to take on four street youths in an alley in central Addis Ababa. They may even be armed with knives or guns.

I walked up to the girls and the young men and made my presence known in a loud authoritative voice. "Girls! Police officer! You girls are under arrest!"

Within seconds the four young men were racing down the alley. Surprise—my street friends understood English. They also must have been guilty of some type of violation. Their rapid departure certainly showed their guilt, if not their unlawful intentions with the nurses.

I grabbed the girl's arms and began walking them back up out of the alley and back to the hotel. They gladly walked along with me. Neither of them said anything.

When we returned to a main street, I said to them, "Okay, girls, go on ahead, I'll get out of your hair."

I was angry. Not with the girls personally, but because of their stupid decision to go out alone after dark in a strange city.

"No. Please stay with us," was Elizabeth's trembling response.

"Thank you, Jack. You were right," Abby responded in a noticeably shaken voice.

When we returned to the hotel, I escorted them directly to their room. As I left, neither of them said a word. I may have been a little too stern, but all three of us had just had the living daylights scared out of us.

I went to my room and was sleeping within minutes.

CHAPTER 4

Monday—Day 4

At the breakfast table in the hotel restaurant, the nurses never mentioned the ordeal of the previous evening. They were both still scared and probably embarrassed at what had happened. I had saved them from getting robbed, if not worse. Addis Ababa is no different than any other city in the world—there are good people and there are bad people.

Abby and Elizabeth were at a table by themselves. When I arrived a 7:00 a.m., I could have joined them, but the doctors who would sit with them had not yet arrived. Since my presence seemed to make Abby uncomfortable, if not angry, I decided to remain at a social and literal distance. I walked to their table and whispered.

"Not a word about last night, okay?"

"Not a word, Jack. You are our hero," was Elizabeth's reply.

"One other thing, please forgive me for being angry with you two last night. I'm sorry if I made you more upset than you already may have been."

I strolled to my table.

Abby just sat there with a blank look on her face, not saying a word. Maybe she couldn't as yet get herself to admit that I could do something right. I couldn't blame her, but maybe it was time that she gave me a chance.

Our team had a good breakfast and meeting, with Cameron leading. Everyone seemed to be refreshed and ready to depart on the next leg of our journey to Gambela.

Abby handed me a note on her way out of the restaurant. It surprised me. What could this be all about? I was almost afraid to read it, but I slowly opened it.

> *Jack—Thanks for getting my camera and case back. I appreciate your thoughtfulness and timely action. Thanks, also, for protecting Elizabeth and me last night. —Abby.*
>
> *—P.S.—Don't read too much into this note. Okay?*

Good—she ended the note with a question. That meant that I could answer her with a note. I would need to have one ready to give her; maybe breakfast time would be a good time to pass her a note.

Her words meant that warm weather may be on its way and the ice could be soon melting. I can only hope and pray.

Elizabeth and I were the last of our team to remain seated in the restaurant. Abby needed to make a phone call back to the United States from the hotel lobby. Since we were seated at separate tables, I turned my chair around and joined her, bringing my coffee cup with me.

Elizabeth was a very nice woman of about 30 years. She and Abby worked at different hospitals in the Twin Cities, but they attended the same Covenant church. I had no idea if she had a boyfriend, had been married before, or was even looking for some relationship. I only knew that she was not married at the present time. I also knew that Elizabeth was nice to me, and at this point at least, my only way to communicate with Abby. I decided to use her to try and build on this connection.

"How's Abby doing?"

"She's fine, but I wish she would get over being so negative toward you. It's spreading to Dr. Terry now. I've never seen her act like this. It's almost like she's a completely different person when she's around you."

"Will you ask her a question for me?"

"Sure. What?"

"Ask her if it's okay for us to communicate with notes? It'll be non-threatening, and I'll only include subjects that pertain to her, our sons and me. Tell her that I'll give the notes to her when Dr. Terry is not present—probably at breakfast."

"She'll probably agree to that. I'll ask her when I go upstairs now."

"Just give me a thumbs-up or down signal when she's not looking."

****

Our vehicle arrived at the hotel parking lot at 8:00 a.m. It was a black Land Cruiser. As soon as we saw it, we immediately knew that it would be impossible for this vehicle to carry a total of nine people, their carry-on bags inside, and the 24 bags on the top carrier. The entire weight was probably more than could be safely transported over the rough roads. No one knew what type of vehicle we were getting from the Addis Rental Company. Maybe we would need a second vehicle, but what we really needed was a bus.

The team had a quick parking lot conference and decided that the best thing was to send all of the medical supplies in a separate vehicle to Gambela. Cameron went back into the hotel to call and find out the cost of this option. The other option mentioned was to airlift the bags to Gambela on Ethiopian Airlines. That could be price prohibitive.

The doctors came over to me and asked how my wrist was.

"Let's take another look," Dr. Mike said. He unwrapped the bandage, and they and the nurses observed the wound.

"It's a little red, but I think it's healing nicely. I was afraid of infection, after first seeing it in Frankfort. You'd better keep it wrapped for a few more days. The wound is in a place where your wrist movement may keep it from healing normally. How's your back?"

"It's still sore and aching but I'll live."

"What on earth happened to you to cause so much pain and misery?" Elizabeth asked. I didn't answer her. I should not have mentioned my injury to the doctors back in Frankfurt.

Elizabeth suddenly forgot about her unanswered question and became more concerned about communicating a message to me. She caught my eye when Abby was looking the other way and gave me two thumbs up. That meant I could now talk to Abby using a pen and a piece of paper. Maybe this would soften the ice, if Abby so desired.

Cameron soon came outside with the news that Ethiopian Airlines was willing to cut us a deal, mainly for humanitarian purposes. The transport costs would be no charge. We would only need to pay for insurance and storage costs at the Gambela Ethiopian Airlines office until we arrived to picked them up in two days. This was welcomed news! We needed to get the bags out to the airport as soon as possible.

Our driver's name was Gabriel. I immediately asked him if I could call him Gabe. He agreed with a nod of his head.

Gabe was Ethiopian and spoke Amharic, English, and some Tigrigna, the language spoken in Eritrea. He also knew a little of the Sudanese Nuer and Arabic languages. He was a likeable fellow, and I somehow knew it was the start of a great friendship.

We were all waiting in the parking lot for Cameron and a hotel clerk to unlock the storage room, when I decided to break the silence with a stupid question.

"What should we call our vehicle?"

Everyone looked at me for a few seconds. Doctor Mike asked the obvious question.

"Why do we need a name for it, her, him, or whatever?"

"Well we're going to be on intimate terms with it, especially for the next two days and then for most of the next two weeks. Let's give it a name. It's going to be our legs, and we'll be relying on its ability to get us to and around Gambela safely and then back here to Addis."

"You come up with a name," Doctor Terry replied. "Let us know."

I think he may have questioned my sanity at that point. He turned and shook his head. Maybe it was a silly idea.

Gabe, Cameron, and the two doctors loaded the 24 bags and headed out of the driveway and to the airport. Dr. mike thought it best for me to not risk further injury and pain to my back by lifting the 70-pound bags. I decided to go inside for another cup of coffee.

"Hey nurses, do you want to join me in the restaurant for some after breakfast refreshments?" I invited.

"I think we'll just go to our room and get a few more winks of sleep," Elizabeth answered. "You go ahead, alone."

It was twenty minutes later and the two girls joined me in the restaurant. Something had changed their minds. They ordered some hot herbal tea. It surprised me that Abby wanted to sit at the same table with me.

"What should we call our vehicle? Hmm…I've thought of a name."

"What?" Elizabeth asked. The girls didn't seem very interested.

"Well, the vehicle is going to have to be rugged, not gentle. Therefore it is a 'he.' And, he has to have a name that is enduring. Also, the name needs to be Ethiopian, maybe even historical. So let's name it Selasie! Selasie is an Ethiopian male name, and it's a name that is endearing to the Ethiopian people."

The question from the girls came in unison and was expected. "Who in the world is Salasie?"

"He was Ethiopia's most popular leader—Haile Salasie. Remember, we saw his tomb yesterday. He was called *The Lion of Judah* and lived during the mid-twentieth century. He was one of the most admired leaders in the world during that time period."

"Where did you read that?" Abby asked.

"From a book I bought at Barnes & Noble in Indianapolis."

"That sounds like a good name, Jack. When did you start going to Barnes & Noble?" she retorted.

Again, I decided that no answer was the best answer. It was another put-down and it was beginning to get a little old. But I now had much more patience than I did a few weeks ago. At some point, Abby would run out of negative comments and, I hope, talk to me in a more civilized, if not Christian, manner. At least, that was my hope.

My silence spoke volumes. It was quite noticeable to both girls that Abby had once again humiliated me. I just looked at the table-ware.

I decided to leave and let Abby and Elizabeth visit by themselves. As I was walking away I heard Elizabeth speak to Abby. "Why don't you try to be nice to him? He seems like a decent person."

Abby responded, but by this time I was out of ear range and didn't really care to hear what she had to say.

****

Around 10:00 a.m. the airport baggage detail returned. As we were walking up the steps to check out and get our carry-on bags, I once again brought up the vehicle's name.

"I have come up with a name for our Land Cruiser. We'll call it Selasie."

Gabe, our driver immediately became excited. "That's a good name."

This was the first anyone had heard Gabe speak since our first introduction. There was no comment from any of the other team members. They just ignored me. It confirmed my suspicion that they thought I was crazy.

We loaded up our gear, tied everything down, and took off. Before we left for Gambela, we needed to obtain written permission from the UN Refugee Agency in Addis to spend at least one day each at two different refugee camps. We drove over to where the agency office was located. Cameron and Dr. Mike went inside to talk to the head official.

Their reception by the agency director was very cold. He told them that we needed either an official from our church in the United States, or an official at the American Embassy to fax him a request to visit the camps.

We drove over to the American Embassy and guess what. It was closed due to it being President's day in the USA. It was Monday, February 19, 2001. None of us had thought about it. Cameron went inside to see if any official might be there on this holiday.

The guards at our embassy were all Ethiopian, dressed in American army uniforms. It made sense to have non-American Marines guarding the embassy at the center of Addis Ababa. My few words with the guards yielded no response. I asked one guard if I could take their photo. With the movement of his head, he indicated a definite "no." They were all well-trained.

For some reason the door to the embassy was only about five

feet high. Cameron had to duck as he passed under. I wondered what that was all about? Maybe it was designed for Ethiopians, many of whom are not much more than five feet tall. The door wasn't designed for the tall Sudanese people, for sure. Some of them are well over six feet tall.

Cameron was inside for only a few minutes. There was no official around.

We stopped at the Bank of Abyssinia, and each team member exchanged American dollars for the Ethiopian birr. The exchange rate on that day was 8.363 birr for each dollar. Elizabeth walked over to me and handed me 500 birr, the amount I had given her and Abby at the airport. "Thank you for thinking about us."

Abby was with Dr. Terry when they both exchanged currency. It was difficult to keep my eyes off of her, and it was going to become increasingly frustrating for me. Abby seemingly knew this and was staying along side Dr. Terry whenever possible and whenever I was present. It was apparent to me that she was sending me a message.

****

As we were about to take off for Gambela, Cameron suggested that we stop and pray for a safe trip. Gabe pulled Selasie over to the side of the road, and Cameron began to pray:

"Lord, keep us safe on the road to Gambela. Bless our driver and give him good judgment and vision. Bless Salasie as he goes down the road. May he remain in one piece and in good working condition! Prepare the way for the team and the church where we will be setting up our clinic in Gambela. Keep us all healthy, and be with our families at home. Amen."

At least Cameron caught on to the name of our vehicle.

At 1:00 p.m. we were finally on our way to Gambela. The road out of Addis was sometimes paved, sometimes tarred, and at all other times covered with dirt, dust, rocks, and potholes. Everyone inside our vehicle was busy viewing the activity along the road.

It seemed like on each side of the roadway there was a sea of vendors. Everyone was trying to sell merchandise—stones, brush, lumber, fruits, vegetables, etc.—anything that people would buy.

Capitalism is alive, well, and living in Ethiopia!

The road went southwest out of Addis, and by the looks of the map it would be a short drive to Jima, where we were to stay the first night. But maps can be misleading. They do not tell the story of the ever-present dust that comes from moving vehicles, the random potholes, animals, human and motor traffic, narrow roads and curves, and other obstacles that may make the ride both exciting and miserable.

Up ahead we could see what looked like small hay or straw stacks coming down the road toward us. As we moved closer and then finally passed them, we realized that they were stacks of hay heaped on goats, with only the goat's head sticking out in front. On this particular occasion there were fifteen of these haystacks all in a single file.

We stopped in the traffic next to a public garbage dumpster. I noticed these dumpsters in Addis also. People were constantly going through them, looking for anything that may be edible, burnable, or usable for any purpose. Next to the dumpster was usually a pile of one item—plastic. It is one substance that cannot be recycled, at least without expensive equipment. Nobody wants scrap plastic—not even in Ethiopia.

****

We stopped at a small town to get some gas for Selasie. Gabe hadn't filled up in Addis and apparently knew of a place where he could get gas at a reasonable price. Everyone was thirsty, so I opened up a bottle of water. It was warm, but it was also wet. I had some paper cups and gave one each to the team members. From the sounds of their gulps, everyone seemed to agree that the warm water was refreshing.

I ordered some tea at a small café. The tea was very hot, which meant that any bad water was pure and free of any living microscopic bugs. Dead bugs won't hurt you, I don't think.

As I walked into the café, bar, or whatever it was called, I looked around to observe the clientele. I was carrying a lot of American money and an even greater amount of Ethiopian currency. The bulge on my hip showed any observant potential pickpocket where the loot was.

The café was a small building made of straw, branches, and mud. It had a dirt floor and a single low-wattage bulb hanging in each of the two small rooms. There were tipped-over barrels for tables and crude handmade benches and chairs for seating. The patrons of this establishment looked like something out of an American western, but with the Amharic language being spoken. A small radio was blasting Ethiopian pop music.

When we resumed our journey, Abby and Dr. Terry were in the front seat, he with his arm around her. It was quite obvious that the good doctor was making a play for Abby and that she seemed to be a willing participant of this attention. I'm sure that the other members of the team were also aware of what was going on.

Somehow, I needed to let Abby know that I had fallen in love with her and that I would keep trying to gain her interest in me. Maybe that was a foolish thing to do, but I really didn't care. Timing of any interaction with her was going to be crucial.

****

It was becoming increasingly more difficult to take notes.

Our driver is crazy. At least Gabe drives like he is. I believe that he aims the car instead of steering it. I also believe his shoe is glued to the accelerator. When we go through a town, he doesn't slow down. Everyone in the car cannot believe it, and I can feel everyone tensed up. Maybe the Ethiopians drive like this on these roads and maybe it's normal, but it's scaring the wits out of us.

I prayed for God to send down some angels to protect us, although there wasn't much extra room for them inside of Salasie. The angels would have to ride on top of our vehicle, or I may have to give them my seat.

When Gabe comes to a town, he will survey the

roadway with his eagle eyes. He will see a bustling town of local people, children playing—some clothed, some not—beggars doing their thing, and ambitious vendors selling their wares, all on the road just ahead of us. He will observe an occasional crippled or blind man, and hundreds of animals. Gabe's goal is to move through the town without slowing down. I wonder if there is a speed limit in these towns or any other part of Ethiopia.

Gabe looks ahead for potholes. If he sees them he travels on any part of the road just to miss them. An observer would suspect that he is driving drunk. It seems like the people on the road are the least of his concern.

All of a sudden, the people ahead of us just move out of our way. It's almost like there's an invisible snowplow traveling fifty feet in front of the Land Cruiser. As the vehicle makes its speedy journey through the town, the people, the animals, and the mobile haystacks suddenly fan away to the sides like two long rows of dominos collapsing horizontally. To make it more exciting, our movement is not in a straight line, since Gabe is continually dodging potholes.

Gabe has apparently driven this road many times, and maybe the people sense when he's coming. Maybe the news of his coming through town is placed in the local paper. I wonder if he has ever hit anyone or anything.

May God protect us!

****

I was wearing a baseball cap and had another one inside of my carry-on case. Abby and Elizabeth's hair was going to get filthy and dusty if they didn't get something on their heads. Since I only had the one extra cap, I had to make a choice.

I found the second brand new baseball cap in my bag and placed it on Abby's head. The extra attention I gave to make certain the hat fit properly took longer than normal. I lingered—on purpose. I even patted her on both sides of the cap.

It was apparent to the other team members that I was playing favorites with Abby. I sat back, watched the girls, and could read their minds. They were saying, "Why doesn't he give up *his* hat, the rat." After a few seconds, I took mine off and placed it on Elizabeth's head. "That's better," they seemed to say by the looks on their faces.

Dr. Terry just shook his head. Cameron smiled.

As we drove we were constantly passing trucks. Our driver was driving so fast that nothing passed us. The trucks were medium-sized and were usually empty. I asked James what they were hauling, or on their way back from hauling. He said that they were probably coming back empty from hauling grain and other commodities.

The trucks usually had at least three people riding in the cab and many riding in the box. They were probably paying riders who added to the driver's pay package. The dust from these large vehicles at times created a rolling cloud that caused us to start coughing and choking. Everyone was hot and miserable.

****

At about 2:00 p.m. Gabe suddenly slowed Selasie down. There was a big problem up ahead. A bridge over the roadway was missing due to construction. A new bridge was being readied, with a huge crane nearby. Big rocks had been placed on the bottom of the creek to allow the heavy road equipment to move on it. A detour route sign was crudely printed in English and Amharic, indicating that the drive would be an extra twenty miles. The traffic had to be rerouted; nobody even attempted to drive their vehicles across the rocks.

We stopped, got out, and surveyed the situation. It looked like the entire team had suddenly become civil engineers. Gabe shook his head. "I'm not driving on that. It'll break something on this Land Cruiser." Apparently, something like this had happened to

Gabe in the past and he was very hesitant to attempt it.

One of the doctors spoke. "Now what do we do?"

Cameron answered him. "Maybe there's a bypass or alternate detour back on this road."

At that point I needed to display one of the few talents I had—driving. I walked slowly the length of the temporary rock roadbed, surveying the driving path possibilities. At one point I stopped, lifted some rocks, and carried them to fill in an apparent gap between small boulders. From the other side I returned and jumped into Selasie. Dr. Terry was the first to respond, thinking that I was out of ear range. "Now what is Jack going to do? He'll wreck our vehicle. He's not very smart, is he?"

Everyone seemed to doubt that I would make it—or should even attempt it. I was taking a risk with a very expensive piece of equipment, but I had done this before in Indiana. A crowd had gathered to watch.

I started the engine, observed the roadbed ahead of me and proceeded to drive the four-wheel-drive Land Cruiser to the other side. The lowest gear of Salasie provided the stability and power to inch the length of the rock road. When I reached the other side, I got out of Selasie. Elizabeth, Cameron, and Dr. Mike applauded.

An Ethiopian man came up to me and offered me a job with his bridge construction company. I kindly thanked him, but declined. We all jumped in and were on our way once again.

****

At 4:00 p.m. we stopped at the top of a hill so Gabe could check Salasie's vital signs. He knew what he was doing, and the team needed a break. We all decided to go exploring.

We hadn't notice at first, but we were stopped next to a small Ethiopian village. It was well hidden behind large trees along the road. Over the wooden pole fence was a compound where the inviting smell of the evening meal was drifting through the cracks. We slowly strolled to the entry of the compound.

An older, stately looking gentleman, who looked like he could be the mayor of the town, walked up to us and greeted us. "Hello, I am Racso Nirtse. Welcome to the village of Notlef. What can we help you with?"

His English was very good. Cameron spoke to him as they shook hands. "We just stopped to check our vehicle. We're on our way to Gambela, from America."

"Ah! Americans! Would you be our guests for the evening meal? We have plenty of food."

We all looked at each other, smiled, and gave him our enthusiastic approval. We could smell and imagine a mixture of foreign cooking. The aroma of spices was almost overpowering. The man led us to an open hut and seated us in a circle on a large round homespun carpet spread out on the ground. I removed my shoes and placed them in back of me.

"Why did you remove your shoes, Jack?" Elizabeth whispered.

"It's the custom when eating in someone's home," I whispered back.

"I suppose you learned that at Barnes & Noble, too," Abby replied.

"As a matter of fact, I did, Abby. It was under a section called 'Customs to Follow when Visiting an Ethiopian Home.' I don't remember the page number, but I could find it if you wish."

Elizabeth reached in back of me and patted me on my back.

Soon the center of the carpet was teeming with hot, steamy Ethiopian food. There were several wooden bowls of assorted meats, steaming vegetables, rice, and, of course, the traditional injera. Several of the townspeople joined us in our meal. Our cameras were busy recording the event.

We ate a little bit of each item. Most of it was very tasty. Hot—but tasty. I asked our host to tell us what the items were, how they prepared them, and what spices were used. He seemed to be very interested in us and displayed a great deal of hospitality.

After we had eaten our fill, the nurses decided to stroll out of the hut to take some more photos. Everyone wanted his or her photo taken, especially the children. It was then that Abby and Elizabeth noticed some of the children having leg, hand and other body infections. Both nurses came into the hut as we were about to leave. "Do we have any medical supplies with us? We need to treat some of the children."

"I don't think we have the time right now," Cameron said. "We need to get to Jima by nightfall. Besides, our medical supplies are in storage waiting for us in Gambela."

Both Abby and Elizabeth turned and looked with compassion and disappointment at the children outside of the hut.

I stood up, walked out to Selasie and found one of my carry-on bags. Inside was a medical kit stuffed with all of the items needed to fix minor wounds and infections. It was made up for just such a need as this. I walked up to Abby and handed her the medical kit. "Here, Abby, go give the children some of your loving medical attention."

Abby looked directly at me and smiled.

It was the first time that had happened in the past ten years. I held on to the kit as I handed it to her, smiling back and lengthening the moment.

I think I even heard the sound of ice cracking.

For the next hour, the medical team worked at treating all types of wounds and infections. The doctors became involved in an advisory manner, sharing some of their medical knowledge and know-how with the girls. They worked as a team. It was a good warm-up session for what we would be doing in Gambela. I hoped this cooperation and teamwork would continue.

A woman walked into the temporary clinic area carrying a small girl. Elizabeth felt the little girl's forehead. "This girl has a high fever, and I see what the problem is. She has a badly infected arm."

The doctors looked closely and determined that there was some foreign object deeply embedded in the girl's arm. Dr. Terry's response was next. "We don't have any tools with us to operate, but we need to do something."

I spoke up. "How about a Swiss Army knife?"

The doctors looked at me and then looked at each other. "Why not, as long as we sterilize it first."

I gave the knife to Dr. Mike. He opened the smallest knife blade and sterilized it using the fire that had been used to heat our meal. He cleaned the blade thoroughly with alcohol and gave the knife to Abby.

With Dr. Mike guiding her, Abby carefully extracted a piece of stone embedded in the little girl's arm. What came out of the wound next was not very pleasant to look at. Elizabeth cleaned out the wound, placed a generous amount of ointment on it and covered it with Band-Aids. The little girl was noticeably relieved from her pain.

As we walked back to where Gabe and Selasie were at on the road, I caught up to Abby. "You do good work, Abby. You were my hero today."

She again managed half smile. The ice was definitely starting to crack. I wondered if anyone else heard it and realized what was happening.

After we were all seated back in Selasie, I handed everyone on the team a Swiss Army knife.

"I have a knife for each of you. I was planning to give them to each of you just before we left Gambela to come home. However, I can see now that you can use them while we are here in Ethiopia. A woman from our church gave me these knives. I felt that God told her to do that, and now I know why. Please use them as needed for major or minor surgery—or to saw a tree in two. I had even thought of giving them to you after we arrived in Frankfort and before we left for Addis Ababa. However, my mind was occupied with something else at the time."

Everyone was quiet for a moment and then one by one said, "Thank you." The team seemed to be happy to have the knives, especially the girls. Gabe was overjoyed to have his.

I recorded this event in my notebook, so I wouldn't forget to write a thank you note to the woman who gave them to me.

****

We took off once again and made good time. Many of the team dozed in and out of sleep for much of the way until it began to get dark.

Gabe was just as crazy in his driving at night as he was during the day. Maybe he was a skilled driver, but he took too many chances. A light-skinned person would be hard enough to see at night, let alone a black person. Most of the men had very little attire on, so the black skin served as little contrast to the sometimes pitch-black night background.

As we drove on to Jima, we saw the campfires of the people living along the road. Once in a while we would open the windows of Selasie and catch a whiff of the meals being cooked and the other odors that permeated the Ethiopian countryside.

****

We arrived in Jima at about 8:00 p.m.. Jima is known for its coffee; it is the capital of the Kafa region. It was dark and we were all tired and thirsty. All of us had lost our appetite. The road to Gambela had thus far been bumpy, dusty, rocky, pot-holed, sometimes missing, and covered with people, animals, and garbage. We all longed for the American freeways.

Cameron was taking his turn at riding in the front seat. He turned to us and spoke.

"Supposedly, there is a spot in the river somewhere near here where a community of hippos make their home. Shall we go find them and give them a greeting from America?"

"No thanks," was the general response.

Fortunately, we didn't encounter any hippos.

We found the Jima Hotel, registered, and got cleaned up. The rooms were nice and the water cold. The cost of the single room was 54 birr or about $7.00.

We ate at the hotel restaurant, since it was the only one close by. The doctors and the nurses again sat together. When Cameron came in, he had us push two tables together.

"Tonight we eat as a team."

Abby and Dr. Terry noticed his comment and action—and its significance.

I sat quietly during the dinner. Most of the discussion was about the trip so far, but I chose to not participate—just listened. I figured that if I said anything, Abby might say something negative back to me.

I ordered spaghetti. It wasn't too bad, but it had no meat. That was good news, as any meat might be hippo. The toast was not like the garlic toast that goes so well with spaghetti back in the States. I asked the waitress if she had anything for desert. She brought what looked like pound cake with some tan syrup on it. It tasted terrible. It was one bite for me—only a half a bite for the rest of the team. Everyone agreed with my evaluation of this dessert.

Samuel was concerned about his wife back in Indianapolis. Her car had broken down after we took off on Friday, and it needed to be fixed. I could have helped out, but I was here. I was familiar with her car and had worked on it several times. Their apartment was two miles from the nearest grocery store. The other Sudanese would need to help her out in Samuel's absence.

As we ate, Samuel told us about his decision to marry his wife, Mary. He had agreed to pay 24 cows for her. This was the going price for the ordinary bride in Sudan and, as it turns out, in America also. The customs and traditions were continuing in the new world for the Sudanese refugees. The cows, or the value thereof, would go to the family of the bride. I needed to find out more about this custom.

After dinner I hit the sack. It was almost 10:00 p.m. and I was exhausted.

****

I woke up at 11:00 p.m.—I couldn't sleep. There was too much excitement and too much on my mind. My body was tired, but I was in love. The thought of Abby kept me from falling asleep.

I walked out to a two-seat swing hanging from a tree next to the hotel, sat down on it, and gave it a push with my foot. The soft, warm Ethiopian breeze was keeping the mosquitos away. I swung for at least fifteen minutes, during which I prayed for the team's safety and for Abby. I also prayed for my three sons back in Minnesota.

The calmness of the evening and the moment was interrupted when Abby and Elizabeth suddenly appeared. They were surprised to see me. Elizabeth did the talking, as Abby continued her stubborn look-away attitude toward me. "Hi! You having trouble getting to sleep, also?"

"Too many things happening and too much excitement—especially with Gabe driving." I replied.

"You noticed that, too?"

"I think I'd rather face a bunch of crocodiles."

"We couldn't sleep. Must be the jet lag," Elizabeth stated.

Abby didn't say anything and looked off in the distance. She obviously didn't wish to be there.

"Here! You girls sit here. I'll find another spot to enjoy the warm breeze." I offered.

Elizabeth quickly answered. "We'll sit here with you, if you don't mind."

"If you wish, please do."

I stopped the swing while the nurses stepped on and sat down on the opposite seat. A gentle push of my foot got the swing going once again. I decided to engage Abby in some conversation with Elizabeth present. She could cushion any negative comments from Abby.

"Abby, tell me about the boys. What's happening with them?"

At that point Elizabeth realized that I might want to talk to Abby alone. She excused herself and walked back to her room. Abby, sitting quiet for about a half a minute, finally spoke. "I thought you weren't interested. We have three boys you know, and they need a dad around the house," she retorted.

The ice may have begun to thaw, but it was still pretty thick.

"I know, and I've had little to do with raising them. I'd like to say that I am going to spend a lot of time with them when I get back, but you probably doubt a promise coming from me."

"They're very interested in their dad and keep wondering where he is. I don't know what they tell their friends. You do have so much catching up to do, and I wonder if you can do it." She paused for a moment. Her face softened a little and she said, "I guess I really shouldn't say that. Jack, I want to apologize for being so negative to you. I haven't acted very much like a Christian, have I?"

"Well, I can understand your feelings toward me. I would just like to be your friend, for now anyway."

"I'll just have to weigh my words before I express them, when I speak to you."

"I plan to spend some time in Minneapolis and look for a job. I'm between jobs you know."

"Where will you stay in Minnesota?" she asked.

"I may have to stay in my car, temporarily."

"But it's cold this time of the year in Minnesota."

"I'll figure something out. How are your parents?"

"They're fine; Dad's planning on retiring early at age 55."

"You may want to refrain from mentioning my name to them the next time you write or talk to them. I think your dad and mom hate my guts. I don't blame them. Back then, I even had trouble liking myself."

Abby began to get a little impatient and edgy. "We'd better get to bed. The morning will come early and we'll be on the road to Gambela for another nine hours."

"Don't remind me. Today was bad enough."

Abby got off the swing and walked back to her room. I sat and swung for a while longer. It was good to be able to talk with her in a welcomed civil manner.

I decided to spend some more time swinging and attempting to become tired. The warm African breeze was very relaxing and had a nice calming effect.

I thought about Abby and what might happen to us in Gambela. We would become involved with each other with our ministry, and would see each other several times a day. I couldn't decide which had a more calming effect on me—the breeze I was now experiencing or the thought of seeing Abby for the next two weeks.

I continued to pray for a miracle—a miracle that would give me a second chance with Abby. It was going to be a challenge to convince her that I was serious about her and that my life had changed drastically. At the same time, I needed to work with her and the other team members, including Dr. Terry. God would need to give me great wisdom and direction.

I made a promise to myself that I would do anything to get Abby back.

CHAPTER 5

Tuesday—Day 5

M y alarm went off at 6:30 a.m. Once I had finally fallen asleep, nothing could have disturbed me. It rained sometime during the early morning, and the room was comfortable—once yesterday's dead air had circulated out into the Ethiopian atmosphere.

As I lay in bed, I looked up at the wall where the day's first light reflected off of the dresser mirror. There were two other guests in the room—some lizard-like creatures apparently talking to each other. They were different colors. One was probably a male and the other a female. I just hoped that their family wasn't asleep under my mosquito tent, under my blankets, or in the pillow my head was lying on.

I decided to get up and attack the day by taking another shower. The water was cold and the floor colder. I hoped the pair of rubber slippers that I wore as I walked around on the wet floor of the bathroom would keep my feet from picking up any little bugs. They may wish to live between my toes for a few days or weeks. Maybe they would want to raise a family—possibly even several generations. I wasn't going to let it happen.

After my refreshing shower, I packed my gear together and walked outside. The sun was shinning, the African birds were singing and talking to each other, and the street below the hotel was busy with the commerce of Jima. School children were talking amongst themselves in the Amharic language with their books and lunches on their backs.

Only a few people were eating in the hotel restaurant when I walked in. The team and other guests were sleeping late. It's no wonder, since they all had traveled the same road yesterday, either to or from Gambela. The trip had been hard on all of our team. I sat alone at a table, writing notes in my trip notebook.

Abby and Elizabeth walked in together.

"Good morning," I said.

"Good morning," they answered in unison.

The discussion about our boys last night with Abby had been good. She and I needed to communicate, if only about that subject. It may eventually lead to us discussing other topics.

The nurses sat down at a separate table. I could have invited them to join me, but I felt more comfortable being at a distance from Abby. The doctors would soon walk in, and Dr. Terry would expect to sit with her.

I ordered scrambled eggs, toast, a bottle of Ambo, and some hot coffee. In addition, I ordered a small pitcher of hot water. The coffee served in Ethiopia is at the top of the "strongest coffee in the world" list. When the waiter brought my liquids, I made three cups of normal strength American coffee by pouring the cup of Ethiopian coffee into the pitcher of hot water.

I requested to the waiter to make certain that the eggs were well done. The kitchen complied and they were very good.

I had a note ready for Abby. After I had eaten, I walked over and handed it to her. She opened it as I returned to my table to sit down. The note read:

> *Abby—It's my turn to write a note to you. I'll try to pass my notes so your "new friend" doesn't see them.*
>
> *Thank you for talking with me last night. As you might not know or expect, I have a greatly renewed interest in our sons. However, my interest in you is even greater, as I have fallen in love with our sons mother. It happened in Frankfurt.*
>
> *Many good things are going to happen on this*

trip and you are one of them. I promise to behave myself, but you should know that it is my intention to steal your heart. I am praying for a miracle and another chance with you. —Jack.

The remainder of the team walked in over the next 20 minutes—the two doctors together. Cameron requested that we once again push tables together and eat as a team, at least this morning. The entire team looked tired, but they were all conscious.

Everyone ordered from the menu, I ordered more coffee, and we were soon busy discussing the remaining ride to Gambela. None of us was looking forward to it. Maybe some excitement would occur that would take our minds off the dreadful road. The hot weather was continuing to curb my appetite.

Cameron spent some time providing us with information and advice on working with the peoples of Africa. He had spent fifteen years in the Congo and had valuable general knowledge of the various cultures and religions, the family unit, the government, local laws, etc. We spent thirty minutes listening to him, followed by a question and answer time.

We had a session of prayer and left the restaurant.

We packed up all of our overnight gear and loaded up Selasie. We were on the road at 8:00 a.m. Gabe had stayed with some friends in Jima and looked tired. He probably didn't get much sleep and I might need to drive for a while later in the day. I was ready.

Everyone was taking a turn sitting in the front seat next to the window, as it was the least crowded and, thus, the most desirable. There were three people in the front seat; four in the back seat and two in the way-back uncomfortable seat. Abby and Elizabeth sometimes sat together. It was Dr. Terry's wish to sit next to Abby whenever possible. Abby probably didn't want to sit by me, and I understood this and accepted it. James and Samuel sat together and spent much of their time talking to each other in the Nuer language.

It all made for an interesting shuffling of people into seats whenever we stopped and then loaded up again. I decided to let everyone else find the seat they preferred and take the remaining seat, wherever it was. I just waited until everyone had entered

Selasie, was comfortable, and then moved to where the remaining spot was waiting for me. It wasn't long before the team realized that I was purposely staying in the background during our entry into the vehicle.

****

Our first excitement of the day began when one of the doctors started to feel nauseous. Something he had eaten or drunk, the bumpy road, or a combination of all three, was making him sick. We stopped and let Dr. Terry empty his stomach. Maybe it was the water. The doctors were using a water bottle with a filter. Up to this point on our trip, I was strictly on Ambo. The soda water drink seemed to quench my thirst.

Our second bit of excitement occurred as Selasie started to sputter right next to an Ethiopian village. Then the motor killed. Everyone became quiet. The two doctors were the first ones out of Selasie.

"Open the hood Gabe. Let's have a look at it," Dr. Mike said as he walked to the front and opened up the hood. The two doctors fixed their eyes on the motor and said nothing for the next two minutes. They wiggled a few wires, took off the air cleaner cover and finally shut the hood.

"Something's wrong," Dr. Terry announced.

Up to this time, none of our team except Abby knew the full extent of my auto mechanic expertise. While some people may think this is a talent, my view was that it was undignified. I always thought I was capable of—and should have—a more secure and reputable job. Abby knew my expertise. "Jack, fix it!" she shouted.

Abby spoke to me with confidence in her voice. It was probably the only thing about me that she had confidence in. The doctors said nothing and stepped back. I walked to the hood and opened it once again.

From the sounds Selasie's motor made when it sputtered and died, I could tell that the problem was the gas. Something was constricting the flow of gas somewhere.

It was just a few seconds and I found the problem. Dirt had

caked into the air cleaner, and the filter needed to be cleaned out. In order to do the proper job, I would need to remove the dirt using some gas. We could get gas from the gas tank if we had a hose. I looked around and saw the people inside a compound eating lunch. Maybe they would have a hose.

I walked in and with James translating into the Amharic language, I asked if anyone had a hose. Someone did and quickly retrieved it for us. I used it to siphon gas out of Selasie's tank into a small plastic pail, and I placed the air filter into the pail to soak for a while.

The people in the compound then asked us to have dinner with them. We quickly and enthusiastically accepted the invitation. This was the second time in as many days that we had been invited to dinner in Africa.

The food was Ethiopian and was exceptional. The woman who prepared our meal was from Asmara, Eritrea. She had married a local. By all outward appearances and their hospitality, I could feel that these people were Christian.

As we were finishing up our tasty meal, I suggested to the doctors they take the medical kit and see if anyone needed medical attention. It wasn't long before we had a line of people wanting relief for their infected toes, sores, aches, colds, etc. One older man wanted something for his malaria. The doctors reluctantly told the man that they had nothing to help his condition. Cameron stood around visiting with our host, but soon he became a little eager to get back on the road.

A crisis occurred all of a sudden in the village. As we were completing the mini clinic and preparing to leave, a man and his wife rushed into the compound and into the hut where we were working. Their little girl had climbed a tree in an attempt to retrieve her pet monkey. She was too terrified to come down.

The family led us to a huge tree where the little girl was stranded. Her sisters and brothers had been attempting to coax her to climb down. I could hear her sobbing frantically. When she looked down to the ground, she would become almost hysterical. I looked up and saw the monkey sitting on a close-by branch and looking puzzled at the little girl.

The tree was very old, according to the father. "It's one I used to climb when I was a child." The little girl was over half way to the top of the tree.

I looked at the situation for about two minutes wondering what I could do to help get the little Ethiopian girl down safely to her parents. Maybe I could climb up and rescue her and I was willing to try. But I knew someone who could do it better than anyone.

I turned around and looked to where the doctors and nurses were standing and shouted, "Abby!"

At first she didn't respond to my call. She was in the noisy crowd that had gathered a few feet from the base of the huge tree. I decided that she might have not heard me the first time. "Abby? Where are you?"

"Here I am. What?"

She slowly emerged out from the crowd of children and parents and walked to where I was looking up at the tree.

"We need you. Abby, climb up the tree and rescue the little girl. You are an expert at climbing trees."

"How do you know that?"

"Your dad once told me."

Soon Abby was climbing up the tree. Her physical agility impressed everyone. She hugged the little girl and told her to hug her. Once the little girl had secured herself to Abby, Abby reached over and gently grabbed onto the monkey, who put up no struggle. She not only rescued the little girl, but the monkey as well.

By this time, the entire village of 75 people had gathered to observe the rescue. Everyone applauded as Abby, the little girl, and the monkey were about to jump back on to the ground from a horizontal tree branch. As the trio hit the ground, I steadied the three of them.

"Hold it. Let's get a picture of the little girl, her monkey, and Abby," I suggested.

I made sure that we took photos, using Abby's camera, of the little girl's family along with Abby. She wrote down the family's name and address and promised to send a copy of the photos.

The little girl gave Abby a big hug and thanked her. Her parents gave their daughter a serious look, conveying their concern for her safety. The father said something to her in Amharic, which I assumed was, "Don't follow the monkey up any tree again, unless you are certain that you can return to the ground safely."

As we were all walking toward our vehicle, I caught up to Abby. "Abby, you were great. You're a hero! Thank You!"

"Thank you for thinking of me, but I didn't think you knew that much about my childhood."

"Your dad and I spent five hours fishing one summer, and I got to know many things about you. I also know that you used to be a doctor to any wounded or sick animals in the neighborhood."

"That's right."

"No wonder you're a nurse."

The air cleaner had been soaking in the pail of gas throughout the entire commotion, and it cleaned easily. I reinstalled it and Selasie was running smoothly. As we started to take off, the people of the village invited us to stop again on our return to Addis Ababa.

****

As we approached Gambela, the temperature started to rise to well over one hundred degrees Fahrenheit. The narrow winding road led down from a higher altitude to the lower elevation where Gambela rested. It was once again dusty, dirty, and very hot. If we kept the windows open, it would have been difficult to breath; but the dust seemed to enter through any small opening, so closing the windows wasn't much better.

I gave each of the team drinks from the water I had bought in Addis Ababa at the little convenience store. Maybe now they weren't questioning why I had purchased the case of twelve bottles. I was glad to do it, and even Abby accepted the water.

As we met trucks and other motorized vehicles on the road, the movement churned up the hot dust, making the visibility poor and any comfort non-existent. The girls looked miserable, and the doctors were probably asking each other why they didn't take a flight from Addis to Gambela.

****

We arrived at the outskirts of Gambela at 4:00 p.m.. The last three hours had been almost unbearable, and the dust on the road made all of us very dirty. We would need to take multiple showers when we arrived at the hotel.

We drove across the Baro River as we entered the city of Gambela. We could see people standing on sandbars, visiting, washing clothes, and engaging in other activities. A few people were also fishing. The river had a brown color to it.

We drove for several more blocks when Gabe turned his head and announced, "The downtown is straight ahead. Here is where you can shop."

All of the team came to attention and took note, as everyone had said that shopping was a priority in any spare-time activity. We passed an Ethiopian Orthodox church where we could hear a loud-speaker playing music along with speaking—very similar to the church in Addis Ababa. I might have to visit that church.

Abby was sitting in the front seat looking totally miserable. The hat I had given her was caked with dust. I could only imagine what her hair would have looked like had she not worn the hat.

We finally arrived at the Ethiopian Hotel. This would be our home for the next two weeks. A fence surrounded the grounds. There were two rows of cabins with many trees surrounding them. All of the trees were the same height, indicating that they were probably all planted at the same time as part of the landscaping.

Two guards were walking along the long driveway, each carrying a rifle with both hands, ready to use. None of our team commented or indicated any interested as we drove by them. I think everyone was hoping as I did that these guns would never need to be used while we were staying at the hotel.

The grounds were well kept, except for the roadway trash as we entered into the compound. The hotel must have a good groundskeeper. There were many small plants, but without flowers. It may not be the time of the year for the blooming of flowers in this part of Ethiopia. But, then again, I knew very little about flowers. I knew Abby liked them, and I would like to become more knowledgeable about them. Maybe I could find some for her in Gambela.

Gabe stopped Selasie in a parking area next to a sidewalk. We all got out and stretched for at least thirty seconds. Elizabeth started brushing the dust off of her clothes. All of the team, even our driver, followed with the same idea. We were soon creating our own cloud of dust.

We started to unload and clean the dust off all of the cases and bags. It took several more minutes. Gabe continued the job by cleaning the inside of Selasie, using a whist broom and beating on the seat cushions with his hands and fists.

"Hey, Gabe. You may want to take Selasie down to the river and give her a good bath." I suggested

"That's an excellent idea, Jack. You can come with me and keep the crocodiles away."

"Crocodiles! Are there crocs down there?"

"Yes there are. They sit and wait for you. Right now they're wondering where Jack is. I'll take you down there and you can greet them. Most of them understand English." Gabe had a good sense of humor and was going to fit in quite well with our team.

Cameron walked to the office and began the job of getting us registered. The team continued the dust-cleaning task. Cameron soon came back with our assigned cabins. "I have everyone all checked in. The nurses will stay in one cabin, the doctors in the second, our Sudanese brothers in the third, and Jack and I will share the fourth. There are two beds in each cabin. Here are your keys. Let's all meet back here at 5:00 p.m. for something cool to drink and a brief meeting."

I spent the next twenty minutes in the shower. It was cold, but once I got used to it, it felt good. The water in Gambela was just as good as the water in America for getting the dirt and dust off of a human body. When I had completed, I concluded that it was the best shower I had ever taken. I got dressed and was just leaving for the restaurant when Cameron walked in ready for his cleanup job.

"How's the water Jack?"

"Cold, but you'll get use to it."

"At least it runs today. Sometimes the water quits running, they advised me in the office. It's the same with the electricity."

"Best we shower when the water's running and we have light, I guess."

I walked to the restaurant, found a table. The two doctors and two nurses were already seated at one table. Samuel and James sat at another talking to a group of the Sudanese pastors. I sat alone, saving a seat for Cameron. The tables were in the same general area.

The Ethiopian hotel has an area that serves as a meeting place for people to visit, with a cash bar off to one side. There are lawn chairs, wooden benches, benches and seats made from concrete, and various small tables for the guests to place their snacks and drinks while visiting. I was told that this area was the hotel "garden lounge." I had the feeling that this would be the area to meet the guests of the world, which we were.

A man walked up to my table and spoke in an Ethiopian accent. "Can I get you anything?"

The man was in his fifties with a full head of gray hair, dressed in a white suit, black shoes and a black tie. He was our waiter.

"I would like a hot tea and a bottle of Ambo."

As the waiter went from table to table, the remainder of the team ordered the same.

"You people don't have to order what I ordered, you know." I said with a smile.

"It sounds good," Dr. Mike answered. "Wise choice."

"Make it eight hot teas and eight Ambos. We'll get the same for Cameron."

I glanced over at Abby. She was engaged in a conversation with Dr. Terry. Elizabeth and Dr. Mike were also having a discussion.

A feeling of jealousy came over me because I was not sitting there participating with them. I was feeling left out again, but I also felt inadequate to go over and join them. It was like I was from the other side of the tracks. They all had one thing in common—the field of medicine. Me? I was just an automobile mechanic.

Maybe it was time that I stopped feeling sorry for myself.

The waiter brought our drinks just as Cameron walked into the hotel restaurant. After a few minutes, the eight of us were engaged in four separate conversations, including Cameron and I. As I looked at everyone, I decided to try getting everyone focused on one topic.

I called our waiter over, put out my hand and we shook. "What is your name?" I asked him.

"My name is Moses."

"My name is Jack. What is your job and title here?"

The team suddenly ceased their talking and turned their chairs so they could see and hear the waiter speak. We were the only guests in the restaurant at this time.

"I am the head waiter, and I also supervise the restaurant."

"Can I ask you how you received the name of Moses?"

"Yes you may. That's a good question you ask." Moses sat down on a chair he pulled from another table.

"I come from the town of Bahir Dar in the province of Gojam. We lived on the edge of Lake Tana. When I was born, it was when Ethiopia was at war with Italy, and my family was afraid of the Italian army that was located in the town of Tana. My mother was pregnant with me, and my parents didn't want anything bad to happen. So my father took his wife down to where the Blue Nile River begins its flow southward. There, he made a hut for my mother in the woods on the shore and hid her. I was born about a week later. Since I was born by a river, my mother named me Moses."

"That is a beautiful story, Moses. Thank you! Then you are a Christian."

"Yes, I am, and my family also."

"How large of a family do you have?" I asked him.

"Three boys and twelve grandchildren."

"I have three boys, also."

"I must go now," he announced as he stood up.

"We'll talk later?" I asked Moses.

"Most definitely."

Moses disappeared into the kitchen and we all continued our separate group discussions.

****

We all finished our refreshments and started on our way back to our cabins. As I was walking through the garden lounge, Abby caught up to me. "That was a very interesting discussion with Moses. Thank you. I'm glad that you did that. He seems like a very nice man."

"Well, we now have at least one friend in Gambela. He may come in handy for information and favors. You never know."

"Jack, you have really changed, do you know that? I don't know you. Are you sure you're the same Jack Franklin I once knew and was married to for five years?"

"No, I'm not the same Jack Franklin. God is making me into a new person. The jury is still out on whether this change will be permanent. I'm a work-in-progress. Just keep watching."

As I was walking back to my cabin, it dawned on me that Abby was displaying two different personalities and behaviors—one when I was alone with her and a second when both Dr. Terry and I were in her presence. This was not the Abby I knew. It was the first time I sensed a struggle going on inside of her. Maybe only I could detect whether her behavior was "Abby One" or "Abby Two."

****

After unpacking my suitcase, I walked back to the hotel restaurant and decided to order some more hot tea from the waiter. Soon everyone came in, and it was time to order dinner. Moses brought menus, and we all sat quietly looking at the few items listed. I ordered the Nile trout. It was something familiar that I had eaten. Everyone else ordered the same. It was delicious, and the rest of the team voiced the same opinion.

We sat as a group and discussed setting up our clinic, which we would begin in the morning. It was a good session, and it got our team focused on one topic.

Dr. Terry and Abby sat next to each other. I tried not to look at either of them all through the meal and the after dinner session. Getting her away from him was going to be a difficult task. Of course, there was the possibility that God's plan was for Abby and Dr. Terry, not Abby and Jack. Maybe God would let Abby decide for herself, and He would abide by her decision. As a new Christian, the subject of God's will and how we determine or recognized it—or in most cases just accept it—captivated me.

"What does God have in store for Abby's life?" I asked myself. And could I change His mind if I wasn't in the picture? And what was God's will for my life?

In the weeks since I had become a Christian, I had studied the scripture passages pertaining to God's will in general, and what He wanted me to do with my life in particular.

I also knew that I needed to go back in time and make some things right, at least as right as I could. I couldn't undo a spilled glass of milk, but maybe I could go back and acknowledge the spill and offer to pay for the soiled carpet. My biggest spill was with Abby and our broken marriage. All of her tears and the hurt I caused my sons was a difficult topic to think about. But I was facing it and was now ready to deal with it head on. How I would do this was the challenge. God would have to direct me.

We finished our meal and planning session at 7:30 p.m. It had become dark outside, and I decided to explore the hotel courtyard with a short walk. We were on the other side of the world, and so far most things seemed to be the same.

The nurses decided to finish unpacking and turn in early. The doctors had set up their laptop computers and were busy entering the programs needed to collect data for our medical presence in the coming days. My Sudanese brothers were in the courtyard lounge meeting pastors and members of the Sudanese community. They were renewing old acquaintances and getting the latest news from Sudan.

Additional guards were posted around the perimeter of the hotel compound. I counted five of them. Two of them had rifles and another two had guns at their side. I spoke to a couple of them as I walked. They seemed to be friendly. Who knows, they may be of use in our mission at some point. I wondered who hired these guards—the hotel, the city of Gambela, or the government in Addis Ababa.

I decided to walk back to the garden lounge and write in my trip notebook. After a few minutes, the two doctors came and sat down at my table. The three of us struck up a conversation with a man who was a professional poacher bounty hunter from France. The

International Society for the Preservation of Endangered Species (ISPES) had hired him. He seemed very friendly and was sitting at the next table.

"I've never been on such a terrible road as the road to Gambela. I had to take two showers. I thought I'd never be clean again." He said. His opinion concurred with ours.

"I bet you have a lot of interesting stories to tell," Dr. Mike said.

"I guess I could write a book, and maybe I will someday."

"What cases or situations do you come in contact with in seeking out poachers?" Dr. Terry asked.

"I would say the largest number of cases involve wild animals that are killed for their gall bladder for use in quack medicines, believe it or not. The poachers kill the animal, cut out the gall bladder, quick freeze it, and leave the carcass to rot. What a waste! Only the vultures benefit."

"Do you ever catch any of the poachers?" Dr. Terry asked.

"Occasionally"

"What do you do with them?"

"Hand them over to the local authorities, where they are soon released after money is passed under the table."

"Doesn't that get you upset?"

"I guess so. But it may discourage others from getting into the poaching business, especially when they know that people like me are ready to shoot them. Occasionally, we have to shoot one of them. This news gets spread rather quickly, and it deters the poaching for a while. But it soon starts up again, and more aggressively than ever."

"What was your work prior to what you are doing now?" I asked.

"I was a lawyer back in England."

Elizabeth walked in and sat down at a table on the other side of the garden lounge area. I decided to join her and walked over to sit with her. "What's the matter, can't you sleep?"

"You guessed it, Jack. I'm still back on Minnesota time."

"How is Abby doing?"

"She's okay. I think she's having trouble getting to sleep, also. She'll probably be here shortly. She has a lot on her mind."

"My being on this team shocked her, didn't it?"

"Yes it did. It wasn't expected at all by her. It is absolutely amazing that the two of you would meet like this. I just wish she would treat you more in a Christian-like manner."

"Maybe if you had an idea how our marriage went, you would then realize why she feels that way about me."

"But why can't she forgive?"

"That's a tough question to answer. How long has she been seeing Dr. Terry?"

"Only for about a year."

"Is it pretty serious?" I asked hesitantly.

"Well, let me put it this way. He would like to get married on their way back to the United States, maybe in Egypt. She told me that he hasn't officially proposed to her yet, but he has talked about it. She expects it to happen on this trip, right here in Gambela."

"What does Abby think?"

"She has some doubts about Dr. Terry, but at the same time she sees him as a means of economic security for her and her boys. Added to that is the fact that she cannot believe that you are really the Jack she was married to for five years. She is unwilling to take the risk. All of this makes for a rather confusing situation. It's pulling her apart."

"I don't think our meeting in Frankfurt was by accident or chance. In fact, I believe it was God's doing."

"You are probably correct. Abby does seem to enjoy trading notes with you, Jack. Did you do this when you two were married?"

"Not really. I think it's a means of sharing thoughts with each other without the insertion of old animosities. Let's say it's communicating in a non-threatening manner. It's also a way for her to communicate with me without Dr. Terry listening in or his even being present."

"That's true."

"I can't believe I'm the same person, either. I told her that I'm a changed person. I can also tell you that I'm in love with her, and I will do anything to get her back, but only if she wants me. She's going to have to fall in love with me, also. I doubt if that will ever happen."

I turned my head and noticed that Abby had suddenly appeared in the lounge area, looking like she had just awakened. I don't think she heard any of what I had said; but if she did, it was okay.

"May I join this discussion?" Abby asked.

"Yes you may," I answered.

"I can't get to sleep, either. Back in Minnesota, I'd just be getting up for work."

"I think if we took a short nap after lunch in the hottest part of the day, maybe it would cure our jet lag. You girls will soon get accustomed to the lag."

I wasn't sure if Abby wanted to talk with me and I didn't want Elizabeth to leave. I decided to excuse myself and return to my cabin. I needed to write a note to Abby and give it to her in the morning. She may also be planning on answering my note from this morning. There were some painful things I had to say to her. Writing them would be a better way to express them, rather than voicing them. Besides, there was rarely a moment when I could talk to her alone.

"Ladies, let me say good night to you."

"Good night," both of them said at once.

I walked back toward the cabin. Tomorrow was going to be a busy day. As I was walking, James and Samuel saw me and asked me to join them.

"Jack, we need to tell you what we just heard from out pastor friends. It's news about what is currently going on in South Sudan." James seemed very restrained as he talked.

"More trouble?" I asked.

"Worse than that, torture worse than you can imagine, and it's getting close to the Sudan-Ethiopia border.

"Some of the pastors tell about one region of South Sudan where the children are being tortured while their families are forced to watch. The women are being raped, and those mothers with little babies are having their breasts ripped or cut off so they are unable to feed their little babies. It's awful. Only when our people renounce Christianity, do they let up on their persecution."

"I'm sorry to hear this. I just wish that America could do something about it. Very few people in our country know about it."

We continued to talk about the situation, with Samuel and James describing the methods used to scare the Nuer people from their towns and villages. I could see that I was going to have trouble getting to sleep tonight.

Would we see the evidence of any of this trouble while we were in Gambela? We would start to find out tomorrow.

CHAPTER 6

Wednesday—Day 6

I finally fell asleep at 1:00 a.m. and woke up at 6:30 from the racket caused by the wobbly fan in our cabin. Cameron continued to sleep. I quietly got my things together and walked out to the outside garden lounge area. I needed to re-write my note to Abby. It had to be perfect for her.

I completed the note just as Moses was opening the restaurant. The sign on the door said that the restaurant opened at 7:00 a.m. He was a little early this morning.

"Good morning, Moses. Did you have a good sleep?"

"I did, and how about you?"

"Once I fell asleep."

"The tourists do have that problem, especially the guests from America. That's why we stay open until 1:00 a.m., sometimes longer."

I walked into the restaurant and sat down at the same table I had used last night. It's interesting how we tend to sit in the same place when we go out to eat, assuming that we have our choice of seating. The same goes for where we sit in church. I am the newest confirmation of this theory, being a regular churchgoer for only the last six weeks.

I was about to have my first breakfast in Gambela. My appetite was not what it was only 72 hours earlier. The extreme heat was making me lose my desire for food, which was fine with me, as my body needed to shed some pounds anyway.

The restaurant would soon be filling up with various peoples of the world. The Ethiopian Hotel is the most popular hotel in Gambela. Moses told me that on any one night, there could be guests from as many as fifteen countries. Ie also told me that English was the most common language spoken, other than Amharic, spoken by the hotel management and staff.

Moses brought me the menu. It was one page with only a few of the most basic breakfast items: eggs, toast, pancakes, bacon, cold cereal, hot cereal, milk, tea and coffee. I ordered scrambled eggs, well done, and toast. A waiter brought my order in only eight minutes.

I carefully looked at my eggs. They appeared a little greasy. Also noticeable were many little pieces of some material that looked like greasy little maggots. I looked around the room for anyone observing me, reached into my pocket, pulled out my Swiss Army knife, and flipped out the little magnifying glass.

The little pieces in the eggs were one of two things: either maggots or finely chopped fried onions. After careful examination, I concluded that they were onions. I tasted the eggs, reached for the salt and pepper and added some additional flavor. Next time I would order them without onions.

My notebook needed to be updated with yesterday's happenings. It was absolutely amazing to me that I had bought this notebook specifically to record the trip's activities so I could send it to Abby. Then Abby herself shows up in Frankfort. I maintain my opinion—it was no chance happening. Someone else was involved.

I also had time to read the small thin New Testament I had tucked away in my notebook. In six weeks, I have read it through completely and was now back to Matthew. I was hungry for God's Word and now ready to put into practice that which I had read.

On her way to a table, and before the doctors walked in, Abby casually placed a folded note in front of me. I looked at it for a moment, imagining what the note would say while drinking my hot tea. I wanted to read it when Abby was not watching me.

The remainder of the team walked in over the next twenty minutes. They had used the extra time this morning to get rested up after the grueling ride from Addis Ababa. Elizabeth sat down at a table by Abby. The two doctors, Mike and Terry, soon joined them. Cameron sat at my table.

As the team was busy ordering their breakfast, I slowly opened Abby's note. It was her reply to my note at breakfast in Jima. I read it to myself:

> *Jack—I hate to discourage you, but Dr. Terry wants to get married when we return to the States, maybe even on our return trip. He has much more to offer me than you do. That might seem selfish of me, but I have three sons to take care of for the next 10-15 years, and you don't even have a job. Also, I still have my doubts about you. Do you blame me?*
>
> *You may be praying for a miracle, but it's an impossible miracle. You mentioned, "stealing my heart." I don't think you know the first thing about doing that. I think we should just work at becoming friends.*
>
> *—Abby.*

Her answer was about what I had expected. At least the note laid down some parameters to work in, and it formulated an objective for me to achieve. I would just have to work hard and be persistent. In the next fifteen days, I would need to be extra attentive and sensitive to the needs of others and, especially, to Abby. It would be natural for me, now that I had a main purpose for living—to serve the Lord. Closely behind was a secondary purpose for living—Abby—and to rebuild a relationship with her. God was going to help me.

It was a shame that I had thrown her away. When that happened, I was living only for myself. I thought the world revolved around me. As a result, our relationship had been broken. Some relationships that are broken just cannot be mended. This could be one of them. Maybe.

Everyone ate their first breakfast in Gambela and seemed to enjoy it. The hotel had exceptional tea and it was made very hot.

Cameron announced the first item on the day's agenda. "We need to go over to the Ethiopian Airlines office and get all of the bags of medical supplies. I'll take the two doctors and Gabe. We'll be back here in maybe an hour."

After breakfast they departed, and I quickly moved over to the table where the nurses were still sitting finishing their tea. I needed to give Abby my note to her. "I had an excellent sleep after we figured out how to set up Cameron's mosquito tent. I'm sorry you girls had to experience that awful ride from Gambela the last two days. How is your cabin?"

Elizabeth answered, "It's nice although the water comes out without much pressure."

"The fan in our cabin makes a clatter. I'm sure that the motor has a bad bearing. I may try to fix it." I handed a sealed envelope to Abby. "Here Abby, here is something that you have probably been waiting for. I'm sorry it took so long."

She took the envelope with a puzzled look and without saying a word. I walked out of the restaurant. Elizabeth followed. Abby was then able to read my note in private. Outside of the restaurant I sat down, reached in my shirt pocket, and took out a copy of the same note. I re-read it to myself.

> *Dear Abby—I need to say some things to you before going any further on this trip.*
>
> *First of all, attached is a sheet that shows what I owe you in back child support. If this is not correct, please let me know. One of my immediate goals is to make everything right with you financially. It will take me time, but I promise to clear up my debt to you. As proof that I intend to keep this promise, I have enclosed the title to my car, signed over to you. The car may not be worth much, but it's the only thing that I own.*
>
> *Next, I again want to ask you to forgive me for the many things I did to you during our marriage— there are so many. I started a list the day after I began my new life's journey, and I will give it to you*

soon. You may or may not care, but I need to do this. For now, if you will permit me, I will pile all on a giant hill and ask your forgiveness for the entire mountain range of iniquities. I would like to just burn the entire mountain range, but not without you lighting the match.

I also need to ask your parents for their forgiveness for the way I disappointed them. I may need to make a special trip to Tulsa to see them. Maybe they will not forgive me, and maybe you won't either. However, it is important that I go back into the past and attempt to make restitution for every wrong that I have committed. It is very important to me, and it is what God wants me to do.

When I return to the USA, I will need to have a session with our boys and ask for their forgiveness, also.

Please let me know if there is anything you can tell me that will help me in this process. —Love, Jack.

PS—Thank you for letting me send notes to you—I'm running out of notepaper.

****

It was about an hour later when Selasie came rolling into the hotel compound. We unloaded most of the bags of medical supplies into the doctor's cabin, leaving some in our vehicle for use at the clinic. The bags in the cabin were locked together with a chain and then chained to the beds. We may even need to hire a guard from the hotel to watch the cabin during the daytime.

We drove over to the church, arriving at 9:00 a.m. On our way, we drove past the Sudanese Nuer compounds. James pointed out a couple of the larger compounds. He also told us that the Sudan people made up forty per cent of Gambela's population.

My preconceived idea of the church was that it would be a good-sized steel building with windows and doors, all of which opened and shut. The roof would be made of a grass material or maybe wood shingles that overhung the edges to direct the rain away from the walls. There would be some type of bathroom or toilet facility, probably away from the building and in back. The sanctuary would have a wooden floor and seats or benches made of wood, and a pulpit sitting right in the middle. Finally, there would be a children's nursery for the mothers with little ones.

My vision promptly evaporated as we sat and looked at the church. We got out of Selasie and walked slowly toward the Gambela South Sudanese Covenant Church. There, sitting in front of us was a structure approximately 30 feet wide and 60 feet long. There were two doorways, both on the same side of the building, and three window openings, all on the opposite side.

The doorways were three feet by seven feet and the window openings an unevenly cut three feet by three feet. The uneven floor was dirt throughout the building, and there were no benches or seats. Three almost-straight, four-inch-diameter tree poles held up the corrugated tin roof. I continued my tour of the church, inside and out.

I saw no bathroom facilities either inside or outside of the building. I wondered where the people did their business—maybe at a nearby hut, in the bushes in back, or possibly down by the Baro River. But as I looked at the grounds surrounding the church building, I could see only an occasional small frail bush and a few almost-branchless trees. Maybe the people went to the bathroom before they came to church. I will eventually find out.

As we were standing there, I viewed what may be one of the most beautiful sights of this mission trip—tall Sudanese women carrying water on their heads. There may be nothing more graceful in all of Gambela or in Ethiopia.

The women range in age from teenaged to middle-aged, walking in single file, and wearing long, colorful dresses. The tall very black and beautiful women glide along the trail that leads to the Baro River. Their yellow plastic containers sit on their heads as they move like a Lincoln traveling over a newly tarred highway. When they come to a bump on the trail, their containers continue moving straight ahead with not a drop of the precious liquid being spilled.

None of our team had any experience setting up a medical facility in a foreign country—let alone operating one—so we didn't know exactly what to do. Dr. Terry and Dr. Mike were our leaders in this phase of the project, as Cameron had instructed them early in the planning of the trip. They had done some reading on the subject of third-world clinics and had been in discussions with missionary doctors in person and over the Internet.

Our plan was to train and use some of the Sudanese pastors and women to help us treat the people coming to the clinic. Many of them had walked several days to Gambela for the opportunity to gain this experience. With this limited experience, these pastors and lay people could then open up their own clinics in the Covenant churches hundreds of miles from Gambela, in war-torn South Sudan.

The use of native personnel would have two additional benefits: it would make it easier from a language standpoint, and it would allow our mission team to have a little time off.

Our first patient was a man who had just broken his finger. James asked him how he broke it, and the man answered in the Nuer language. We were not as yet set up, but we couldn't turn the man away; so Dr. Mike began treating him as the others in our team worked at setting up the medical clinic.

The man had been hauling rocks using a cart when another Sudanese threw a small boulder and hit his hand. The ground had cushioned some of the impact; otherwise the injury would have involved several broken bones in his hand. Dr. Mike set the man's finger and placed a splint on it.

The original plan was to spend the first day setting up and then began treating people the second day. Our schedule would be to run the clinic from inside the church from 9:00 a.m. to noon, break for two hours during the hot time of the day, and reopen again from 2:00 to 6:00 p.m. This schedule would give us seven hours a day, but it would be subject to change depending on the caseload, the weather, and other factors. But our plan had taken a detour, treating a patient first and then setting up—on the same day.

We were also scheduled to make a few field trips involving mini medical clinics and education. We wanted to visit one or two refugee camps, but that may not work out as we did not have the required permission from the Ethiopian government or the United Nations officials running the camps.

As we began to set up, it was quite evident that we were lacking some basic medical clinic fixtures. According to the pre-planning of this trip, this was expected and to be worked out during our setup day. Cameron started to announce the items. "We need some more tables, for sure. We'll also need some chairs, wastebaskets, and—"

I interrupted. "Hold it a minute, let me write these down."

I hastily took out a small piece of paper from my pocket and began writing a list. Cameron continued.

"Also some basins for washing. We'll also need to build a fire to heat the water. Actually, boil the water. So we'll need a big pot or kettle."

Dr. Terry and Dr. Mike continued to add more items. Our two nurses added more things to complete the list. Cameron then asked James and Samuel, the Sudanese members of our team, "Where can we get these items?"

Samuel was quick to answer. "The chairs and benches we can get from the members of the congregation. They carry them to church services every Sunday. The rest of the items will be a problem. We'll have to get them from downtown."

Cameron then turned to me. "Jack, why don't you and Gabe take Selasie downtown and see if you can buy the other items. You'll need to do some searching and asking around."

"What about taking Samuel or James with me, also?"

"That may be more trouble than it's worth. The merchants are almost all Ethiopian and may not be as open to selling to the Sudanese. Most of the Ethiopian businessmen love American money and, therefore, love Americans with US dollars."

Gabe and I got into Selasie and took off. Gabe was somewhat familiar with the downtown and knew some of the merchants. I had no idea what kind of stores we would find or if they stocked any of the items on the list. After seeing the church, relative to my preconceived notion, I was prepared for almost anything in downtown Gambela.

****

Our trip downtown was a huge success, and we were able to procure all of the needed items. In the process, we met some very nice businessmen. They may come in handy during our stay in the city. Many of the items we tied on the top of Selasie with cord and rope we obtained from the merchants.

When we arrived back at the church, the rest of the mission's team was already at work doing what we came to Gambela to do—treat patients. We were starting one day early. It didn't take long for the news to get around. A group of at least one hundred people were waiting outside of the church. Many were children who were probably just curious.

After watching the line of patients move, it was quite obvious that some better system was needed in managing the flow of patients through the clinic.

We carefully drove Selasie toward the crowd, with Gabe doing his usual thing. The crowd took the hint and scattered a distance from where the line was entering the church. Our medical team temporarily ceased treatment and took a break.

We unloaded and set up the tables inside and outside of the church. We then arranged the tables and chairs in a manner that would provide some order in admitting patients to the clinic and in treating the hundreds of expected patients in the next two weeks.

Cameron and James would get the people into a line and get their first names and ages. They would write this information on a form that had two carbon copies, for a total of three copies—the original, one for the doctors inside and one for the patient. On the form would be written the patient's name, age, sex, the date, suspected ailments, what treatment was needed, and other pertinent information.

The patient would carry the original copy into the church and give it to one of the Sudanese translators working with the team, who would then give it to one of the nurses. The doctors and nurses would write notes on this copy as the patients received his or her treatment. We all hoped the doctor's writing would be legible.

The original copy would be used to place the information into a laptop computer by one of the doctors each night. The doctors would use the data for study and analysis when we returned to the

United States. In what form the analysis and the final report would be was yet to be determined by Dr. Mike and Dr. Terry.

Since there was no electricity inside of the church, one doctor and one nurse were placed by each of the two open windows. The patient was then treated, given medicine, and may be told to return in a day or so for further treatment.

This system went great for a while, but soon the line began to look like the back part of a snake pulling towards its head. Everyone wanted to be the next in line. I had an idea.

There was a coil of wire inside of Selasie. I bought some posts from a young couple building a hut near the church and pounded them into the ground using an axe also found in our vehicle. The posts were placed such that when we tied the wire to their tops, the result was a walkway around the entire outside of the church. Some of the Sudanese men gathered rocks and piled them at the bottom of each post, thus ensuring greater stability. I had one of the young women find some long, wide grass blades and tie them on the wire every few feet, in order to prevent people from walking into the wire.

James then told all the people to get inside of the walkway if they wanted to be treated. That worked great. We were starting to take control of the flow of traffic through our clinic.

Then I noticed that many of the patients needed only some ointment and a Band-Aid. Why send them into the church when Samuel and I could treat them? That is what we decided to do.

I had Gabe back up Selasie about 25 feet from the registration table and away from the line. James was instructed to send the next cut finger patient over to me for a squeeze of ointment and a wrap of a Band-Aid. We began calling these people the "squeeze and wrap" patients. I then showed a couple of the women volunteers how to "squeeze and wrap."

After I had treated ten people, mostly children, I asked James to fetch Abby for a minute. She came out, and I asked her to observe what I was doing. "Please let me know if I'm doing this right."

I just wanted to see Abby. I think she soon realized this.

"Jack, you make a great nurse. I'll see if I can get you a nurse's cap."

"No thanks. I love my Yellow Freight hat."

"You're doing fine, Jack. Where did you learn to do that?"

"Remember what I do best—fix cars. I am always cutting, bruising, and scraping myself."

"One suggestion Jack—make certain that you wash any infected areas with our antibacterial hand gel first. Then you can squeeze and wrap."

"Good idea, Abby."

"Just keep up the good work."

Abby continued to watch me for a few more seconds and then returned to her station inside the church.

I just heard another crack of the ice.

About 11:00 a.m., some Sudanese women walked in and gave each of us our choice between a bottle of Ambo and a bottle of Miranda Orange. A young boy had procured the cold bottles from some business and carried them in a cloth sack on his rickety bike. I would need to do some free repair work on that bike. This would insure more deliveries of the cold liquid refreshments during the hot and dry daytime in the coming days.

****

We continued to treat patients all morning and into the mid-afternoon with good results and a sense of cooperation and team-work. We also trained some of the Sudanese men and women to do various miscellaneous tasks. This freed the team to provide greater treatment to the more serious cases, and it gave the Sudanese volunteers some valuable experience.

Our next problem was the water situation. We had two women carrying water from the Baro River. Two of the Sudanese men then boiled the water over a fire fueled by dried animal dung. The smell produced by this fire was like nothing I'd ever smelled before. It wasn't long before we were running out of water.

Clean water would be critical to the clinic's success. Infected areas of the patients' bodies needed to be cleansed with soap and water. Just getting the dirt off the infected areas was using much of this clean water.

It was about that time that a man came riding up to the church on a motorbike and demanded that we cease operation.

"Why?" Cameron's asked.

"It's the Gambela law."

"What city law is that?"

The man never answered and took off on the bike.

It was about time to fold up the clinic for the day anyway, so we packed everything up and headed back to the hotel. It had been a not-so-good ending to a good first day of our mission medical clinic.

****

Back at the hotel restaurant where I was alone drinking my usual bottle of slightly chilled Ambo and a cup of hot tea, I asked Moses about the law.

"I don't think there is such a law, Jack. True, some of the officials make rulings occasionally, but not permitting medical treatment of people is stupid. Let me call my friend who works at the city office and I'll ask him."

As Moses left the room, the rest of the team came into the restaurant. They all ordered something to drink. They too were discussing this latest development. Cameron, since he was our leader, spoke up. "I'll need to go downtown and ask the city officials what the deal is. I thought the Sudanese pastors had this detail worked out for us. We'll need to make this a matter of prayer."

Just as he finished speaking, Moses came around the corner from the office. He walked over to where I was sitting.

"Hey, Jack, my friend says there is no such law or ordinance. He thinks it's someone connected with the city hospital or one of the clinics that is just jealous and wants you shut down."

Upon hearing what Moses had to say, the rest of the team came to attention and gave him a round of applause. I thanked Moses for his help, and he left to pick up and serve another order. Abby came over to were I was sitting and talking to Moses. "Jack, so what does it all mean?"

"It means that we'll be able to continue our clinic tomorrow morning. That man who came on the motorbike this afternoon was a big scare. No such ordinance exists. Someone is just harassing us."

I walked outside and spotted our cold pop boy on his loose bike. I called for him to come over to me. "Let me fix your bike, if you want me to."

"Yes, I like you to fix it. It's broken."

"What's your name?"

"Andrew."

"Hi, Andrew. My name is Jack."

"Yes, I know your name is Jack."

I carried the bike over to where Selasie was parked and began to work on it. Luckily, none of the bike parts had to be replaced. The boy was fascinated by my work and at times helped me by holding a wrench. I let him screw on some of the nuts, after which I made sure that they were just tight enough. We were finished in only twenty minutes.

Abby happened to walk by with Dr. Terry and watched as we were finishing up. They both stopped to watch.

"OK, Andrew, take it for a short spin and see if it runs right."

Andrew got on his bike and took off. Abby and Dr. Terry watched as Andrew continued his ride up the hotel driveway and back.

"Our boys could have used you to fix their broken bikes and toys had you been around. Maybe Terry can fix them," Abby commented.

I just watched Andrew ride the bike. Abby's comment didn't deserve a reply from me. Besides, what could I say? She was right.

They slowly turned away and walked to their cabins. My new friend had his bike in good working order.

****

Abby wanted to call her folks in the United States, and when the rest of the team found out, they too wanted to make calls. The doctors needed to make several calls, so Gabe took all of us to the Communications Center.

We all walked into the first floor of the two-story, gray-stone building, which housed a group of offices, including the Communications Center. People who didn't have access to a phone were able to make contact with the world outside from Gambela. They also could use the e-mail and fax services. Western Union had an office in the building, also.

I was the only one who didn't have anyone to call. Abby was going to make two calls; I assumed one to our boys and the other to her parents.

"Abby, can you do me a favor? If you call the boys, say 'hi' to them from me. If it is convenient, let me say 'hi' to them."

Abby didn't acknowledge my request. I didn't think she would. It was possible that my sons had forgotten about their father. They probably have met their mother's new friend, Dr. Terry. I decided not to press my request since it may put her in a difficult and embarrassing position.

On the ride back to the hotel, I sat quietly in the front seat with Gabe. Abby leaned up and whispered in my ear, "the boys are fine."

That's all she said. It was apparent that it was not convenient for me to talk to them, let alone mention my presence with their mom. My guess is that she didn't even mention their dad to them.

****

After dinner we all walked back downtown to shop. The walk was relaxing. Abby and Dr. Terry walked together. I felt uncomfortable whenever I came close to them or saw them.

I spent some time just looking in the small shops to see what was available. After running into the doctors and nurses on a cross street, I decided to walk back to the hotel and find something else to do.

On my walk back, I began to visit with an American man who worked for a computer company in England. He was very well dressed and about forty years old.

"What brand of computers do you work with?" I asked.

"We distribute special computers in the communications industry. What brings you to Ethiopia and Gambela?"

"I'm part of a medical team working out of a temporary clinic at a Sudanese church."

"What language do those Sudanese speak?"

"Nuer."

"Oh yes. They are the tribe that is being singled out in South Sudan by the northern government, aren't they?"

"That is correct."

"I understand that there is buying and selling of women slaves in Sudan. Is that true?" he asked.

"I've heard of a few isolated cases from some of the Sudanese Nuer that I am acquainted with. How widespread this practice is, I don't know, and it's mostly rumors at this state. I do know that a few organizations are trying to use the slavery issue as a means of raising and collecting money. Who knows what happens to the money."

"Are you going into Sudan during your stay?"

"There is one member of our team who may walk into Sudan to see his mother while we're here. I guess it depends on how the fighting is going or, more importantly, isn't going."

"What do you know abut what's going on across the border?" he asked.

"Not much. Only what I hear on the street. My name is Jack Franklin." I reached out my hand and he put out his.

"I'm John. How long are you going to be staying in Gambela?"

John wasn't going to give me his last name and I decided not to pursue it. I also began to wonder where this conversation was going.

"We'll be going back to the United States in about two weeks. It just depends on how long our medical supplies last. We may run out at the rate we used them today. We were only open for a few hours today and treated some 150 patients."

"That's good. You're doing some good work here."

We continued to talk as we walked back to the Ethiopian Hotel. As we entered through the compound, John handed me his card. I looked at it as we continued to walk.

"John Hinton. Thank you. Maybe I'll visit you at your office someday."

"I'm going right to my cabin. I wish you luck and maybe I'll see you in the garden here some other time."

"Do you travel much?" I asked.

"Only back and forth to England, sometimes to the States and Japan."

"Best wishes to you, John." He turned and walked toward the

cabin area.

It was only ten minutes later when the doctors and nurses walked into the garden café area. They were carrying plastic shopping bags full of their evening of shopping. They probably didn't want to, but they came over and sat down in the general area where I was sitting. Elizabeth finally spoke.

"Jack, we heard some news from Sudan. The war is getting close to the border. The person we talked to said that many people have been wounded, there is no medical aid, and many are dying."

"We'd better be ready to help them if they come into Gambela," I said. "The word will probably spread fast about our clinic, especially since we were treating patients in a Nuer church."

The shoppers decided to walk to the waiter and order some liquid refreshments. I looked over and saw my new friend just coming into the garden lounge area. He had gone to his cabin and was now going to do something else. I debated whether or not I should inform him of the war news. I decided it was best not to. Who knows what he may do with such information. I decided to not tell anyone since it was not our purpose to get involved with the war itself.

I walked back to the cabin and decided to turn in early. As I walked past the garden area, I saw Abby and Dr. Terry sitting and talking. Once again, this upset me and I tried to forget it.

Cameron and I stayed awake talking for some time about mission work, my future vocation possibilities, his wife's medical problems, and a variety of other topics. I could tell that his wife occupied much of his time, and it frustrated him that she was half way around the world.

We finally dozed off to sleep to the beat of the bad bearing in the ceiling fan.

I had a strange feeling as I was dozing off that the next few days were going to really be interesting. I would see Abby in the morning and I couldn't wait. If tomorrow would be anything like today, Abby's two personalities would manifest themselves in her comments and responses to me—being civil and nice, or being cutting and humiliating.

I preferred one, but would take either, just to see Abby.

CHAPTER 7

Thursday—Day 7

It had been another night of noise. The power and clanky ceiling fan went off at 3:00 a.m., causing us to listen to the young Sudanese boys practice various beats on their drums. The drumming was continuous and had to involve as many as four groups at one time. From under my mosquito net, I could hear that there were several compounds participating, and they seemed to be answering each other.

It is interesting to hear the various rhythms that the Sudanese develop and beat for hours on end during the evening, into the night, and not stopping until daylight first appears. Perhaps the drummers are sending secret messages to each other. The drummers are boys as young as eight years. What messages would they be sending? Maybe they're courting the girls in the next compound or county. Wouldn't this cause the boys tired parents to want to smash their kids drum in the morning—for two reasons?

At breakfast I met a man who was touring various countries and studying the coffee-drinking habits of various native peoples. His employer was an international coffee distributor. This man told me how coffee was discovered in eastern Ethiopia. It seems a sheep-herder noticed that his sheep stayed awake all night after eating coffee berries. The man dried a few of the beans and made a drink using hot water. He then stayed awake with his sheep and, thus, coffee had its beginning. After the man left, I sat and enjoyed more coffee and wrote in my notebook.

It was my turn to write a note to Abby. This was beginning to be an enjoyable routine and I hoped it would continue. For some reason she kept it going. I could only guess why.

Abby was going though a struggle in her life, and I believe it began when she met Dr. Terry. This conflict intensified when I appeared at the Frankfort airport. Dr. Terry wanted to get married, and something inside of Abby told her it would be a bad choice. Not because he wasn't a good person; he was very good and kind. She was not in love with him; rather she was in love with the financial security that would result if she did marry him. At least, that was my theory.

I reread the note I had written:

> *Abby—Our God is a God of impossible miracles. Some miracle will happen this day, especially with you working in our clinic. You are a special nurse. Other miracles will follow. Get ready for them. Get ready for the really big one in the near future.*
>
> *It's true—I have nothing in material wealth to offer you. But I have potential, and God is going to make something out of me.*
>
> *The only thing I have to give you is love and a new Jack. Is that enough for you? —Jack.*

I purposely ended my note with a question. This would ensure an answer from her tomorrow.

I walked over to Abby's table and left it for her to read when she had time. She and Elizabeth were sitting alone. The doctors were somewhere else, maybe still sleeping. They might also be meeting with other doctors who live or work in Gambela.

Abby reached down on the floor and retrieved a small package from on top of her notebook. She stopped me by gently grabbing my hand as I was preparing to walk away, then she handed the package to me.

"Here, Jack, I bought something for you last night."

I opened the red plastic bag and took out a pack of light blue note paper and matching envelopes. "Thank you, Abby. How did you know that I needed some? Don't tell me, I wrote it in a note."

"You can use them to write to the boys. I'll send them for you."

It was a piece of good news to start out the day. Abby seemed to be relaxed this morning. Maybe it was because Dr. Terry wasn't present. This further confirmed my theory about her behavior toward me. She was Abby One this morning.

The ice was definitely melting.

I walked over to the church and clinic by way of the Sudanese compounds. I wanted to start visiting the Sudanese people in their places of residence. The people that had come to Indianapolis were very friendly and hospitable. I was assuming that the Sudanese of Gambela were the same.

As I walked out of the hotel compound, the road to the left went to the Baro River, and the road to the right led to the Sudanese compounds. I turned right and walked at a slow pace. There were many people walking on the road this morning. I greeted all of them.

The air was filled with the various smells that are ever-present in Gambela. I wanted to try to identify them before I left the city. There is the smell of dust from the well-traveled unpaved roads, the odor of burning cattle dung, the pleasant aroma of food cooking in the open air, and several others.

After walking about two city blocks, making a right turn, and crossing a ditch, a path led down to a walkway with seven-foot walls on each side. The walkway is at least eight feet wide and the walls made of two-inch diameter tree poles tied together with grass cord. I wondered if this walkway had a street name. It looked quite long and I decided to name it James Avenue, in honor of my good friend who introduced me to the Sudanese people.

The smell of breakfast was prominent. Maybe it wasn't breakfast. Maybe they were starting of the main meal of the day—late afternoon dinner. Many of the residents said hello to me as I continued to walk. They had seen me yesterday as we were setting up for the clinic. I stopped to visit with many of them. The people spoke English in varying degrees, from very well to just a few basic greeting words.

The young boys and girls looked longingly at my bulging pockets full of chewing gum. Some of them had seen me give it out at the clinic yesterday, and the good news had gotten around. It wasn't long before I was in my pockets and dispersing Wrigley's gum.

I noticed one particular little boy who was playing by himself off by the compound fence. I walked over to him and gave him a stick of gum. He dropped his ball and quickly had the stick in his mouth.

"What is your name?" I asked him.

"David."

"How old are you?"

"I'm seven."

His English was good. Wherever he was attending school, his teachers were providing good language study. English was available to most Sudanese children in their schools.

As he turned to get the ball he had just thrown, I noticed that he had a bump and bruise on his left eye. In fact, his eye was almost swollen shut. I decided to investigate. Maybe he needed to have the eye looked at.

"What happened to your eye?" I asked.

"Nothing. I'm okay."

He wasn't okay. I decided to test him. "Tell me, did you get your ball caught in a tree and fall out when you tried to get it?"

"Yes."

"And you hit your eye on a rock on the ground."

"How did you know that?" he asked, amazed at my insight.

I had an interruption and needed to go, but I noted where he lived.

A Sudanese man came and led me by the hand to a woman who had a badly infected sore on her foot. She needed to get to the clinic but was unable to walk. I picked her up and carried her another two blocks on James Avenue, then onto some winding trails, through a thicket area, and finally to the church. Even though the woman was tall, she was relatively light in weight. She seemed to enjoy being carried.

Abby and Elizabeth were standing outside waiting for the doctors to come over from the hotel. Gabe and Salasie were running a shuttle this morning. A line of patients had gathered.

"Looks like you're a human ambulance this morning, Jack," Elizabeth said.

"She can't walk," I replied.

"Take her inside and we'll fix her up," Abby added.

I carried the woman inside of the church and set her on a table by one of the windows. Abby and Elizabeth gave the woman the medical attention she required. Even though the woman was in pain, she seemed to enjoy the treatment she was receiving from the two young nurses from America. I stood and watched as the girls worked. The woman had something lodged in the heel of her foot. I talked as the girls worked. "Abby, there seems to be a lot of cases of slivers and other things getting into the feet."

"Yes, and most of the time the slivers finally work their way out," Abby answered. "Sometimes, however, the sliver becomes caught under the skin and then infection sets in. If the infection gets too bad, it could get into the bone, and the person could lose their foot."

While the woman was sitting on a table, I placed a stick of gum in her mouth. She was missing a number of teeth. After chewing it for a few seconds, a huge smile sprang forth.

"That smile is worth the entire trip to Gambela—and seeing you nurses work, of course," I said with a huge smile of my own.

As soon as Cameron and the two doctors arrived, we had a short meeting and prayed. Cameron prayed for wisdom for all of us, especially the doctors and nurses. We then briefly discussed the water problem. The task of getting enough clean water to be used in our clinic was going to be the limiting factor in the success of our efforts to treat the people of Gambela in a sanitary manner.

I suggested that we have a special session of prayer. "Team— Let's ask for a miracle!" Since I suggested it, I began:

"Lord, we have a problem that needs Your special attention. We need a miracle and You will provide it. We need fresh clean water here at the clinic in order to treat our patients in a sanitary manner. But You know all that. Also, Lord, the Sudanese in this part of Gambela need good clean water. Somehow, bring this water to us and to Your people in this part of Gambela. Help them also to hear and respond to the Living Water. Amen."

A few other members of the team prayed and then it was on to treating people.

Abby approached me. "Where did you learn to pray so well?"

"From listening to my Sudanese brothers and sisters pray."

"But they pray in the Nuer language."

"I know, and from the heart, also."

****

At the lunch hour break, Gabe and I decided to drive down to the Communications Center and make a phone call. I needed to make a call to my church to let them know how we were doing and what to pray for. Abby asked if she could tag along, as she needed to call home also.

After we had completed our calls, I asked Abby and Gabe if they would join me for a bowl of soup and something to drink in the open dirt-floored Roma Café next door.

As we were enjoying our soup and cold drinks, a man walked in and sat down at the table next to us. He looked like a businessman or some type of a technician. The pocket computer he was carrying was a dead giveaway. He opened a briefcase and took out a manila folder filled with letters. I decided to strike up a conversation with him as Abby, probably for a variety of reasons, didn't seem to be in the mood to talk. There was no smile on her face today. "Are you a visitor in Gambela?"

"Yes, I am. But also I'm also here on business."

"What kind of business?"

"My company develops, tests, and markets equipment. I'm here to look for a place and a reason to test some equipment."

"What kind of equipment?"

"A water purification system."

I quickly looked at Abby and winked. Her eyes suddenly opened as they did when she first saw me at the Frankfurt airport. Her smile suddenly reappeared.

"It sounds interesting. Tell me about it and what kind of a place you need."

"Well, we have the system all ready to go right here in Gambela. However, we now need to locate a place to set it up. That is, of course, if the trip from Addis to Gambela didn't shake the equipment to death."

Abby and I quickly looked at each other.

"The water will be purified at the Baro River's edge. Then a pump will produce sufficient pressure to force the purified water from the river to some point at least two miles away. There it will be distributed to the people for their water needs. "Permission has been received from the Ethiopian government and the Gambela city council to place our equipment anywhere along the Baro River. All of the paperwork has been taken care of.

"We'll need to run the system for at least two weeks. After that we could leave the system and two technicians to run it for a year. Money for this particular system to run for a year has already been provided for by some private benevolent fund in the country of Canada."

The man seemed eager to talk about his company's system. He had a captive audience eager to listen.

"The system is designed for the third-world countries. People will come to Gambela from all over the world to see the system, watch it operate, have a drink of water, and maybe eventually buy one. We've incorporated the latest technology in water purification.

"What's most important is that there be a definite need in the place where we locate the equipment."

I closed my eyes and took a deep breath. What I was about to say to this businessman needed to be exact and convincing. I prayed for God to give me the correct words to speak and for the businessman to receive them in a convincing way. I reached over to the businessman with my hand. "I'm Jack Franklin and this is Abby."

"My name is Robert Hall. I'm originally from Australia, now living and working in the United States." We shook hands and now I was ready with the right words.

"I think I have the answer to your search and a giant opportunity for your company to do a great thing for humanity. There is a great need in Gambela for such a system."

"What do you have?" he asked.

"We have just set up a medical clinic in a Sudanese section of Gambela. Our critical problem is the availability of pure water.

Presently, we have to carry it two miles and then heat it to boiling before we can use it."

The businessman, in his 50s, quickly closed his briefcase and stood up. "My search is over. I think it's just what we're looking for. Let's go and have a look."

It didn't take long and we were headed back to the clinic to set up the answer to our prayer for a miracle—pure water from the Baro River. Gabe was amazed at the speed at which our prayer was answered.

"Jack, I can't believe that this is happening," he said.

"God provides. When we prayed back at the church, I fully expected God to provide the answer. The only question was when."

Abby was the next to express her amazement. "I can't believe that this is happening, either, Jack. It's a miracle!"

"We're going to see more miracles in the days to come. We just have to keep praying and trusting."

Abby didn't respond. She caught on to what I was referring to. I was sure of it. My note to her was timely, as was our stop at the Roma café and meeting our new friend.

Soon the man's company crew was setting up the water purification system about forty feet south of the church. It was truly portable. Two truckloads of yellow, coiled-up hose were run along the ground right next to the trail on which the Sudanese women carried water. A pipeline would eventually replace the hose. The businessman worked along with a city official to ensure that any neighborhood or racial altercations be worked out.

By 3:00 p.m. the system was working perfectly. There were three faucets mounted on a box the size of a coffin. Four company employees made certain that the equipment and controls were adjusted and working properly.

We needed to put up some signs to instruct the general public on how to receive the water. Gabe and I drove back to the hotel with James. We found some cardboard and using a set of marking pens I was given before I left Indianapolis, we made a total of twelve colorful signs.

Four of us worked on the project. We covered the signs with some plastic wrap that we received from Moses in the restaurant. A small crowd gathered in the hotel garden lounge as we worked on the signs. The signs had written on them:

Drinking Water

Washing Water

Cooking Water

The fourth sign had written on it:

Welcome to Living Springs.
'Let he who is thirsty come and drink of the water of life.'

There were three each of the four different signs—one in English, one in Nuer, and one in Amharic.

We drove back to the clinic and erected the signs using stakes given to us by the same couple building a hut next to the church. The team gave us a big round of applause. We ceased treating patients at the clinic long enough for Cameron to conduct a 10-minute dedication service. Then the water was turned on.

All three faucets—one on each end of the distribution box and one in the middle—contained the same quality of water. A small meter on each line measured the quantity of water flowing through that line. The company would monitor the data and record it for research, design, and marketing purposes.

God had answered our prayer for clean water.

****

At 4:00 p.m., a group of Sudanese men and women came to the clinic carrying a woman who had been shot by a band of enemy mercenaries three nights ago in a town some ten miles into Sudan. This confirmed reports were that the war in Sudan was getting closer to Gambela. I had noticed the presence of a greater-than-normal number of Ethiopian soldiers in downtown Gambela, along with army vehicles traveling across the Baro River Bridge.

The Ethiopian government did not take sides in the civil war in Sudan, as long as the war remained in Sudanese territory. It wouldn't take much for the war to spill over the border into Ethiopia and especially to Gambela. That was the last thing the Ethiopian government in Addis Ababa wanted. It also was the last thing the government in Khartoum wanted. The Sudan central government for years has denied being involved with the killing of Christians in the south.

At one time, Gambela was a part of Sudan, and the two governments were well aware of this fact.

The woman was treated for the gunshot wounds, given an antibiotic, and bandaged. The doctors removed several bullets and portion of bullets. Two of her bones had been broken.

We were now presented with a new problem: Where do we put this woman? She couldn't go back to her home; it had most likely been destroyed. This particular woman knew no one in the city and lacked money to stay at any hotel while she was recuperating. Furthermore, the church officials expected the influx of the wounded war victims to continue. The woman told our doctors that people traveling into Sudan had told her that a medical clinic existed at a church in Gambela. The news of our clinic could soon cause a rush of war victims to us.

Cameron then requested, from the pastors meeting in a compound next to the church, an emergency session concerning the war victim situation. He asked me to attend, to record notes of the meeting, and to give my input. Cameron seemed to have a lot of confidence in me—probably more than I had in myself.

The meeting lasted an hour and ended with the decision to place any wounded war victims in Sudanese homes. Most of the homes were within a few blocks of the church. A committee was appointed to oversee this arrangement and to report any problems. The church board would then take any action deemed necessary. This ministry was to begin immediately.

I suggested that while we were in Gambela, the doctors and nurses should make regular daily visits to the compounds to check on the more serious patients and those unable to walk to the clinic. This would keep the traffic of these patients, and those who were needed to carry them to the clinic, from interfering with the new patient flow.

****

The hot Gambela afternoon sun was getting hotter by the hour. I wished I had brought a thermometer from home. I began to wonder how Abby was weathering the heat working inside the church medical facility. I decided that I would see for myself.

As I approached her, I could see that she was red from the heat, with perspiration on her face. I was afraid that she might get overheated. In fact, all of the people inside looked hot. There was limited air flow inside of the church.

The cold Ambo-boy had just arrived and presented each of the team with a bottle of their choice—Ambo or Miranda Orange. He smiled at me as he looked at his newly repaired bike. For some reason, my bottle of Ambo was unusually cold.

I took the bottle in my hand and looked over to where the nurses were working. I walked over to Abby and fetched a clean towel lying on the supply table. After removing the bottle cap with my Swiss Army Knife bottle-opening blade, I carefully poured the entire contents of the bottle of Ambo onto the thick towel. Everyone stopped what he or she was doing and watched.

What was the Indianapolis Kid up to now?

The towel was soon dripping wet and cold. I then placed the towel in Abby's hands and slowly raised her hands up to her face. There was no resistance as my hands guided her hands. She understood what I wanted her to do—wash her face and cool it off. She did just that for the next minute. Dr. Terry stood motionless as he watched what I was doing and probably asked himself, "Why didn't I think of doing that for Abby?"

Abby then stopped washing her face for a moment and said in a belittling tone of voice, "Jack, isn't this a waste of your cold pop? I think the heat is getting to you!"

Her response wasn't what I had expected. In fact, I never expected her to say anything. Was she attempting a piece of humor, or was she trying to make me feel humiliated once again? It was embarrassing for everyone except Abby. I didn't say a thing but turned and slowly walked out. Everyone had heard her and responded with a motionless moment of disbelief at what Abby had just said to me.

Her comment proved my theory. It was not the real Abby who said what she had just said—it was Abby Two. Her words were uttered for the benefit of Dr. Terry. It seemed that whenever he was present, her actions toward me were negative. She was trying to make an impression on him by putting me down.

****

Once again I was feeling wounded and decided to walk downtown after the clinic closed. I stopped at the Roma Café. My appetite was non-existent, and about all I ate was a bowl of Ethiopian chili. The temperature was even hotter in downtown Gambela, and I drank two bottles of warm Ambo. Various hot pepper condiments in open bowls—some with flies hovering on the rims—were available to make the chili hotter, but I decided to not risk getting my stomach upset.

Afterward, I walked from the downtown area back toward the hotel. I made a couple of turns and walked up a road that looked like it led nowhere. I was looking for something that I had not seen in Gambela—flowers. Somewhere in this city there would have to be flowers growing, I thought.

After walking for about twenty minutes, I spotted what I was looking for. Inside a compound, growing on the edge of a group of bushes, was a large garden with a beautiful assortment of flowers. There were flowers of all colors, sizes and shapes. Many of them looked strange and unfamiliar; others, like the flowers back home in the United States.

I walked up to the flower patch, looked at and smelled a multitude of fragrances—all wonderful aromas. I got down on my knees to get closer to them. I couldn't believe that I was doing this. I was never interested in flowers. Was this normal?

A woman saw me kneeling and came walking over to me. "Are you praying or smelling my flowers."

"Both. Hi, I'm looking at something you don't see much of in Gambela—flowers. They're beautiful. My name is Jack Franklin."

"Thank you, and my flowers thank you."

She was a tall, well-dressed, stately Ethiopian woman. I had never seen an Ethiopian woman this tall. "Are you a tourist in Gambela?" she asked.

"Yes I am, but I'm also working with a medical mission team. We have a small temporary clinic."

"Would you like to have some of the flowers?"

"Yes, I would. But they would be for someone else."

"Your wife or girlfriend?"

"Both."

"Both? Can you explain how that's possible? It sounds very interesting and intriguing."

"She was my wife a few years ago. We got divorced and now I would like to win her back. But I'm not having much success. I believe that in God's sight we are still married. Right now she needs some flowers."

"That sounds like a story I once read in an Amharic romance novel. I think it occurs in every language. Just a minute and I will get a vase for the flowers."

She walked back into a hut. I looked around. She must have had money by the looks of her large compound. Everything was neatly arranged in the yard. There was even an area of green grass growing and some shade trees.

She soon returned carrying an empty vase filled with water, along with a man who looked like he was a servant or a groundskeeper. She spoke to him in a language that was different than Amharic. Maybe it was the Tigrigna language and she was from Eritrea. The man started to cut some flowers using a hand clipper. He apparently had done this many times before.

"Would you like to have something cold to drink with my husband and me?" she asked.

"I would love it."

She spoke to her gardener, and then led me into the compound hut where her husband met us. He was tall and wore a tan shirt, dark brown slacks, and a straw hat. "This is my husband."

He was obviously from either America or Europe.

"Hi, my name is Oliver Thomas."

He was most definitely British.

"Good to meet you. My name is Jack Franklin, and I'm from the United States."

"What are you doing in Gambela?"

"I'm with a medical mission team, and we're running a medical clinic out of the Sudanese Covenant Church about two miles from here."

"That's great! The Sudanese are a persecuted people. It's tragic what's happening to their people in South Sudan, isn't it?"

"What's more amazing, Mr. Thomas, is that very few people know about it."

"Just call me Oliver."

A Sudanese woman soon appeared with a large wooden tray filled with some bottles of Cola and Miranda, some hot tea, and glasses filled with ice. She set the tray down on a small coffee table and left the room. She apparently was the maid.

"Help yourself to whatever you wish and have a seat," Mrs. Thomas said. She then left the room.

"What do you do in Gambela?" I asked Oliver.

"I work for an oil company with headquarters in America," he said.

"What do you do for them?"

"I work in new development." He quickly changed the subject and asked, "How is your clinic going? They really do need medical help in this city, especially in the Sudanese quarters. Are you busy?"

It seemed that he didn't want to talk about himself or his work, or perhaps he was just more interested in what I was doing in Gambela. I answered his question.

"We have more work than we can handle. Once the word got out, we were swamped. The majority of the people and children are being treated for minor cuts and infections. But there are some more serious cases: broken bones, problem pregnancies, skin diseases, and things like that."

His wife came back into the room, sat down by her husband, and spoke. "By the way, I never told you my name. I'm Tebee. You may think that I am Ethiopian, but I am really Eritrean. I come from Asmara, the capital of Eritrea. I'm very interested in your story."

She appeared to be very curious by the look on her face, almost like she didn't believe me. My story was a little unusual and could only occur from a person going through a sudden change in lifestyle and behavior.

"I think it's getting more interesting by the day. I just hope my story has a happy ending."

"You say that you are trying to get back with your former wife, and yet you are bringing flowers to her. That means that she must be with you in Gambela."

"You are a very perceptive woman. You are also correct."

"Would you mind telling us the story? It sounds interesting," she said curiously.

"The short version is that Abby and I got married very young—as teenagers in college. We really never fell in love. Consequently, when life got tough we just grew apart. In the meantime, we had three boys."

"Are the boys with you?"

"No, but I wish they were. I've been a dad from a distance for the past five years." I paused briefly.

"Continue," Oliver spoke up.

"We got divorced, I moved back to my home in Indianapolis, and I went to work at an automobile service shop. Meanwhile, Abby became a Christian and her life changed dramatically. She never remarried and even kept the same last name.

"I tried to do something with my life, but things just never seemed to work out. I missed my sons and even missed Abby. But I was too proud to go back to her, and I felt she would never take me back.

"Then about seven weeks ago, it was my turn to have God turn my life around. I was well on my way to a life of drunkenness when I went to a basketball game one night. At that game I said to God 'I cannot live like I have been living. Do something to me,' and He did.

"Starting the next day I became involved with a Sudanese church and their needs. Two of them invited me to tag along with them to Gambela with a missions team. What I didn't know was that Abby was making preparations to go on the same trip from a different city.

"Then, all of a sudden, Abby and I met at an arrival gate in Frankfurt."

"You are kidding me!" Tebee replied. "That sounds really exiting! So how did Abby feel about it?"

"She was shocked! I think she has yet to get over it. Meanwhile, to complicate matters even more, one of the doctors on the team has been dating Abby, and he wants to marry her."

"My, my, this story gets even more exciting," responded Oliver. "So what is the situation now, Jack?"

"Well, I told her at the airport in Frankfurt that I wanted her back, but before we even thought about getting back together, I needed to show her that I have changed. She deserves someone much better than she had when we were married."

"Then I assume you have fallen in love with Abby," Tebee said.

"Yes I have, and I would like to have her fall in love with me."

"So I'm curious. When did you fall in love with Abby?" Oliver asked.

"That happened in Frankfurt about an hour after I met the plane. Unfortunately, she sometimes isn't very nice to me. I think she needs some flowers."

The gardener came in with the flowers and set them down in front of me. I needed to go as the team was about to meet for dinner at the hotel.

"Where are you staying?" asked Mr. Thomas.

"At the Ethiopian Hotel."

"Mengistu's old getaway home. I can tell you many stories about that place and about Mengistu."

I wondered how he knew so much about what went on in the government of a former dictator and about the situation in Sudan. I also wondered why Oliver wasn't at work. He was probably a student of current affairs and history, and perhaps he had the day off. But something told me that this man was more than what he appeared to be on the surface.

"Thank you for your hospitality and flowers. I need to get back to the clinic."

We shook hands and concluded our visit with an invitation from Tebee. "Please come back, everyday if you wish, and pick some more flowers. Just help yourself. And please keep us informed about the ongoing soap opera between you and Abby. We would like to meet her sometime. Maybe we can have both of you over for dinner some evening."

"That would be fun."

****

I walked back to the hotel with the flowers, covering them with a paper bag to protect them from the hot sun and prevent their getting wilted. There must have been a dozen different flowers in Abby's bouquet collection.

I began to wonder if Abby would accept the flowers from me. What if Dr. Terry were present when I gave her the flowers? I really didn't wish to embarrass her, but at the same time I needed to express my love and feelings for her.

I walked into the hotel restaurant and spotted the doctors and nurses at the table where they usually sat. I walked over without any hesitation. Abby was very surprised when I placed the vase of flowers on the table directly in front of her. She had a look of embarrassment on her face, probably from her earlier remark to me.

I interrupted the table conversation, "these are for you, Abby."

It was the first time I had ever brought her flowers—a very sad record for being married to her for almost five years.

"Thank you, Jack. Where in the world did you get such beautiful flowers in Gambela?"

"At a place on the edge of town. I had to walk several blocks to find them."

I didn't want her to express any additional feelings or comments in the presence of the other team members, so I turned and left for my cabin to wash up.

****

After dinner on her way back to our cabins, I met Abby carrying her flowers.

"Thanks again for the flowers, Jack."

"Abby, would you like to go downtown tonight? We can do some shopping and maybe have some refreshments."

Maybe this was not the time to ask her to go out with me. Maybe I needed to wait until we returned to Minneapolis. But I needed to do something before Dr. Terry got too involved with her. She waited for what seemed like a full minute to answer my simple question as we continued to stroll.

"You mean you're asking me to go on a date with you?"

"No...Well... Yes, I am."

"You're not giving up, are you?"

"No, I'm not, nor will I give up."

There was another pause. She finally turned to me and smiled. "Maybe another time. I have something planned for tonight."

"That's fine, and maybe I shouldn't be doing this on this trip."

"Thanks again for the flowers. I was beginning to wonder if any existed in the city."

"There aren't many people who raise flowers in Gambela. At least that's what one of the waiters told me."

I turned to walk to my cabin.

"Hey Jack, I need to say something to you. I'm sorry for the comment I made this afternoon when you used your cold Ambo to cool my face. It was nice and cool, but what I said to you wasn't very nice—it was very cold and hurtful. I seem to have a problem with that, with you don't I?"

"That's all right. I guess I may have embarrassed you, even though I didn't mean to. I just wanted to do something nice to you, and at least you got cool. That's all that counts."

"You know, I am really confused. I have two men after me, and I don't know what to do. What should I do, Jack? Or maybe you're not the best one to ask, seeing as how you are one of those men."

"Let me give you some advice, dear Abby. Do what God wants you to do. Fall in love with one of them, then the choice will be easy."

"What if that person is not you?"

"Well, I'll just have to take that chance. God's will and your happiness are more important. You'll have to make that decision. I need to warn you, however, that I will be working very hard to impress you and win you. I may even have to change God's will."

With that answer I turned and walked to my cabin.

****

About 11:00 p.m., I was sitting in the garden lounge, enjoying the relative coolness of the African breeze, when I happened to look toward the hotel compound gate. I could just barely see two people walking slowly toward the hotel. As they came closer, I recognized the walk of one of them—a woman. It was Abby's walk. I could identify her walk from a mile away. Who was she with? The dim lights made it difficult to see. It was a man. As they came under one of the dim streetlights, I could see that it was Dr. Terry. They had been out together.

I didn't wish to be seen by them. It might be embarrassing for Abby.

Dr. Terry stayed at the entrance to the garden lounge area while Abby walked to the hotel office, presumably to get any phone messages. As she came out, she momentarily stopped and looked straight toward where I was sitting. I could feel her stare, as I was purposely looking down. Maybe she wouldn't recognize me. But she did. I know, because she suddenly changed directions and walked quickly back to where Dr. Terry was still standing.

Maybe the doctor would be the best person for Abby after all, and maybe it would be better not to ask her out again on this trip.

I decided to sit and pray—pray for my sons, for the team, for the Sudanese in Sudan, and for Abby. I asked God to give her wisdom in the decision she had to make.

I also asked God to give me more wisdom to know what to do in my continuing effort to win her heart back.

CHAPTER 8

Friday—Day 8

 The roosters of Gambela produce a most unique sound. They are all over the city and run freely, even in the downtown district. Aren't roosters supposed to be all penned up in a building or fenced in a contained area? Not in Gambela. They are free to roam the entire city covering almost every block. So when they start their racket, you can hear every rooster within a radius of a mile or more from where you are standing—or in my case, lying and writing at the same time.

 They begin their daily clamor at exactly 5:00 a.m. and do not stop until they have awakened everyone, including the tourists in Gambela. If you are fortunate enough to be awake when the Sudanese boys are practicing their drums at this time of the morning, the sound becomes cock-a-doodle-do with a beat. For our team, this ensemble has become one of Gambela's identifying features. If your cabin has a fan with a bad bearing, as ours has, you may miss this unique sound. This morning the fan is once again lacking electricity.

I arrived at the hotel restaurant just after Moses opened up at 6:30 a.m. I continued writing in my notebook for a half hour and then decided to write a letter to each of our three sons. I would mail them later or have Abby include them in her next letter to the boys.

At breakfast I glanced over to where Abby and Elizabeth were sitting. Once again, I could have moved over to sit with them, but the two doctors would walk in and then where would they sit? They seemed to always sit together at hotel restaurants. They form an informal group, and that's okay because of their professional association and their work at the clinic.

But I still had this feeling of jealousy as I looked at Abby and them sitting together. I kept asking myself if God approved of this type of jealousy.

Abby stood up, walked over, and dropped a note in front of me. I opened it and began to read as she was returning to her table.

> *Jack—Love may be important, but what's wrong with financial security? You had your chance. If you were me, would you provide you a second chance? Maybe money is not the most important thing in the world; but when we were married, it never seemed to concern you. It's a new game, Jack. —Abby*

At least this note gets down to the real reason for Abby's attraction to Dr. Terry. Maybe she's in love with another guy—Dow Jones.

I decided to change the subject and send Abby a different message this morning—one that contained some meat and potatoes. A sheet from my yellow legal pad provided the start. A "Have A Great Trip" card from inside my notebook provided me with a straight edge. It took me 20 minutes to complete. As I was working on it, Cameron and the two doctors walked in and sat down.

When I had finished, I folded the sheet of my work and wrote: "To Abby and the boys." When Moses made his next trip, I motioned for him to come over to my table. "Can you take this over and give it to Abby."

"I will, but I think it's about time you two sat together. Even I can tell what's going on between you two and the doctor."

"Thank you, and I agree. I hope that will happen soon, Moses."
Abby took the note from Moses and opened it.

"What is it?" Elizabeth asked, "or isn't is any of my business."

"It's a drawing of a portable Hot Wheels race track. It's to our boys and me. Jack built one of these one time in our garage."

She passed it around the table for everyone to look at. Abby then looked over at me, folded the note and placed it into her small case. Maybe she thought it was a dumb idea. But, then again, I would hope that she would bring it home to our boys. That's what was important to me.

I had the design memorized and decided to build one somewhere in the Sudanese community for the children. I would need to find the material for it and then invite the neighborhood boys and girls to race Hot Wheels cars. The opportunity would definitely present itself at some point during our stay. In one of my bags was a box containing 300 brand new Hot Wheels racecars—25 pounds of them—waiting to be distributed among the little kids of Gambela.

****

On our way to the clinic, the doctors wanted to visit the Gambela City Hospital. We had heard many things about the Gambela hospital, most of them not too complementary, and wanted to see it first hand. The doctors, Gabe, James and I made the trip—a short distance from the Ethiopian Hotel. None of the team knew what to expect.

The complex had a fence around it with an open gate, and there was one guard standing to one side. Gabe spoke to him in Amharic. We drove through the driveway and parked the car. At first I thought I was looking at several chicken houses. This couldn't be a hospital, could it?

We walked into what supposedly was the office. It looked like the interior of an old gas station in rural America. No one was there except for an elderly man.

"Anyone here?" Terry asked.

Gabe translated into the Amharic for the man.

"No, everyone is gone for two hours."

We decided to walk down the hill and give ourselves a tour.

As we approached one of the buildings, we could see a Sudanese man sitting on a bench with a woman lying on her side beside him. A little child was standing on the ground and nursing from one of the woman's breasts. Her arm was wrapped up crudely, and it was obvious that she had been seriously injured.

James asked the man what happened and then translated his answer back to us. The man spoke with in very scared, depressed, and exhausted voice.

"We've just walked to Gambela from Sudan. The KNM attacked our village three evenings ago and shot many people. Some were killed and many were injured. We lost our little boy. A soldier just walked into our home and shot him in the head. I was able to wrestle the man to the ground, and in the tussle the gun fired and shot one of the soldiers. Then they shot my wife. We were eating a meal."

The woman's arm was wrapped using a piece of cardboard for a splint and a clothesline rope to hold her arm in place. The bullets had probably broken her arm. She was either unconscious or asleep with her head resting on her husband's lap. The man continued telling their story.

"I hurriedly buried our little boy and wrapped my wife's arm so the bleeding would stop. Then we took off for Ethiopia where we would be safe and maybe get some medical help. I had to carry both my wife and little girl at times. Once we got into Ethiopia, some rides on trucks were available. Otherwise, my wife would not have made it. We have been walking and riding for nearly twenty hours."

Noticing their weak condition, Dr. Mike asked the next question. "How long has it been since you have had anything to eat?"

"Many hours. We walk from our town in Sudan for at least a day, and then all night. Maybe 20 hours. Some Ethiopians along the road gave us a little something to eat."

"Let's look at your wife's arm," Dr. Terry said.

He began the tortuous task of unwrapping the woman's arm. I watched with horror as the mutilated arm was exposed. The arm had been broken in several places with much of the flesh gone, exposing the bare bone. It was painful just to watch Dr. Terry gently unwrap her arm. The woman was in great pain and barely conscience.

"If she were in the United States, she would need months of hospitalization and then many more months of skin grafting. We can't leave her here. The hospital probably will not help her at all since they have no money."

The doctors made the decision to take the woman back to the clinic and treat her there. As her husband was carrying the little daughter and helping his wife up the hill to our vehicle, she started to fall. I was close by, so I caught her, picked her up, and carried her to Salasie. Every move I made caused a grimace on the woman's face from the pain she was experiencing. I placed her gently in the front seat and the rest of the family in the back seat.

I had a bag of trail mix and an energy bar in my camera bag. The food gave the couple some instant energy and brightened their awareness.

We arrived back at the clinic where the woman was given immediate treatment. The doctors did the best they could, given the seriousness of her injury. Much of the flesh on the upper part of her arm was missing. All the doctors could do was to stitch her arm together and set her broken bones.

I walked back to Selasie, slowly sat down leaving the door open, placed my hands over my face, and started to weep. The combination of the heat and what I had just witnessed was too much for me to bear. The sight of the woman's mutilated arm, the look of despair and hopelessness on the husband's face, and the thought of the little girl having witnessed her big brother's murder, got to me.

Abby came outside for something and saw me sitting in our vehicle. She walked over with a puzzled look on her face. "Jack, what's the matter?"

I paused for a few seconds and then briefly related to Abby the story of the family as I continued to weep. As I was telling her, Abby also began to tear up. She reached in and took my hand. We both stayed in that position and quietly finished expressing our emotions.

"I really shouldn't do this. This is not Jack. Do you ever remember me crying before?"

"No, but it's okay for you to cry, Jack. Furthermore, it proves to me that you really have changed. You really do have some compassion."

Abby and I walked back into the clinic just as the doctors had completed the woman's treatment. She was eating some trail mix, as Elizabeth was feeding her, while at the same time nursing her little girl.

The husband placed his wife and little girl into the front seat of Selasie, and we delivered the family to a Sudanese compound where another family would care for them in the coming days.

This ordeal had put me in the mood for some more flowers. I asked Gabe to drive me over to Oliver and Tebee's flower garden so I could pick a couple more flower bouquets. Since my new friends had given me blanket permission to take whatever flowers I needed, I wanted to honor their invitation and put the flowers to good use.

As we drove into the compound, I could see that Oliver and Tebee were not at home. I used two empty Ambo bottles in which to place the fresh bouquets of various colored flowers. My new friends had just planted a huge variety of new plants in a freshly dug up portion of their property. I wondered where they got all of the fresh plants. On top of the soil I saw what looked like dried, chopped cattle dung. Everything had been just watered. It was no wonder their flowers grew so beautifully.

On the return trip, we stopped at the Sudanese compound and gave the injured women one of the bouquets. She had fallen asleep from her exhaustion and from the effects of the medication. I just left the bouquet of flowers on a small table by the mat she was lying on.

We drove back to the church where the nurses were sitting at a table treating a little girl. I set the flowers in front of Abby. "Thank you, Jack. Again, they're beautiful."

She pulled out one of the flowers and gave it to the little girl. I pulled a stick of gum from my pocket supply, unwrapped it, and placed it into the little girl's mouth. I bent over and gave the little girl a kiss on the cheek.

I wanted to give Abby a kiss also, but this was not the time or the place. I wondered what her reaction would be if I did. She may either try to stop me or love it. I didn't want to risk it—maybe sometime later.

James and Samuel told me that Cameron and Dr. Mike had a bet going to see which one gained the hand of Abby—Dr. Terry or myself. My Sudanese friends didn't tell me who was betting on whom. I wondered what the amount of the bet was. Maybe the prize was an ice-cold bottle of soda pop, which would be impossible to find in Gambela.

Abby walked over and spoke to Gabe. "At noon, can we go down to the Communications Center? I need to make a couple of calls before it gets too late in the US."

I decided that I would tag along for the ride and to see what was going on downtown.

****

The rest of the morning's schedule was filled with patients receiving treatment for the same types of ailments and wounds as we had encountered over the past three days. Every once in a while, we would come across some new kind of disease, affliction, or injury. The doctors were always anticipating the unusual.

One old man wondered if we had anything to restore the hair that had "waved good-bye" from his head several years ago. Dr. Mike tried to explain to the man that baldness was a worldwide problem and that thousands of people in the United States spend a lot of money for hair replacement, wigs, and various hair-restoring operations and medicines.

"Just try to live with it," Dr. Terry concluded.

I quickly went out to our vehicle, retrieved a new baseball cap, brought it back inside, and placed it on the man's head.

One man came crawling to the clinic. He had no legs below the knees. The reason for his visit was to have the team look at his eye. It had swollen shut, and infection was very evident. Dr. Mike said that he probably received the infection from the ground, since his hands were constantly touching the dirt of the Gambela streets. As soon as I saw the man, I had an idea.

I excused myself for a ten-minute break and ran down to the Sudanese community on James Avenue. I remembered that I had seen something as I walked the previous morning. I approached a small hut and knocked on a post. A man came to the doorway and he immediately recognized me.

"Sir, I'm Jack from America and I want to ask you something."

"How can I help you?" he asked.

I was in luck as this man spoke English.

"The other day when I came past your hut, I couldn't help but notice what looked like a pair of artificial legs on your floor. May I look at them?"

"Yes you may."

He reached over a few feet inside his hut and grabbed the artificial legs sitting at the exact spot where I had seen them. "Here you are."

He handed the metal and plastic legs that had obviously been manufactured in some other country, probably the United States. I looked at them for a moment, looked at the man, and spoke: "Is anyone using these?"

"No. They belonged to my dad, who had his legs deliberately shot off in Sudan. He got them from a Christian medical organization based in Kenya. The organization just happened to be in the town when my father was shot. They gave them to him to use when his legs had healed. He used them for about two years and then he died of a disease. I've been meaning to give them to someone who could use them. Unfortunately, my dad was a very tall man and the legs were designed for a short man. As you probably notice, my Sudanese brothers are all normally tall people."

"We have a man at the clinic right now who could use these legs. He's short."

"Then you may have them. I'll pray for that man who receives these legs."

I thanked the man and ran back to the clinic. Abby and Elizabeth had just finished bandaging the legless man's eye.

"What was wrong with the man's eye?" I asked the nurses.

"He had a foreign object stuck in it and it had infected."

The girls then noticed the pair of legs I was holding. They looked at the man, the legs, and then me. "Go for it, Jack," Elizabeth whispered.

I carried the man outside to Selasie and I sat him down on the passenger side of the front seat with the door open and his stubs protruding out. Within a few minutes, I had the artificial legs attached to his legs. They were just his size. Now we needed to find him a pair of crutches to aid in his walk. I remembered that two days ago, a severely injured man, who had come from Sudan and died in one of the Sudanese huts, had used a pair of almost-new aluminum crutches. They, along with the remainder of his personal belongings, had been left at the church. I walked into the church and fetched the crutches.

As the man placed the foam tops under his arms, I began the simple task of adjusting the crutches to his height. Soon the man was walking around Selasie with a big smile on his face. He had only the one eye with which to see, which inhibited his depth perception and walk to some degree, but he managed.

I led him into the church walking past the doctors and nurses. The four of them began to applaud, with everyone else soon joining in. It was one of the high points of our trip to see this man now not having to crawl on the ground.

I called Samuel over to ask him a question. "Find out what happened to his legs?"

Samuel and the man talked for a few minutes. The conversation was full of intense emotion and hand and arm movements. At one point, both of them had tears in their eyes. After they had finished talking, Samuel gave the man a hug and said good-bye. The man thanked me for helping him and took off toward James Avenue. Samuel watched him walk away, turned to me, and began to translate what the man had said.

"Here is what he told me: 'The militia from the north came into our village one morning and began to raise havoc with the people. They surrounded the town so no one could escape. Then they proceeded to shoot people at random. They even shot little children.

"'They selected ten men and began to chop off one arm and the opposite leg of each person. After they chopped them off, using a tree stump for a chopping block, the ten men were left to bleed to death or stop the bleeding somehow themselves. I tried to help one of the men, and the militia shot both of my legs above the knees. They shot many times until there was only skin and flesh holding my legs to my body. I managed to survive.'"

After Samuel related the man's story, both of us just stood and looked at the ground, trying to envision the horrible bloodshed.

****

It was noon and time for our normal one-hour lunch break. Abby, Elizabeth, Gabe, and I drove downtown. We were soon at the Communications Center, the two-story brick building on the edge of Gambela's business district. The place was busy with people making telephone calls.

There are three phone rooms, not much larger than the normal telephone booth. The rooms have doors, but with no fans or air-conditioning; it becomes very hot inside, especially late in the afternoon.

Abby sent me over to the Roma outdoor restaurant to order some cold drinks while she and Elizabeth made phone calls to their parents. Abby was going to call our sons and quite possibly didn't want me around. Twenty minutes later they walked over and sat down at the crude folding table where I was sitting. I then handed Abby the three letters I had written to our sons at the restaurant before breakfast. "Can you send these with your next letter home?" I asked her.

She took them and placed them in her purse. She never mentioned her phone calls.

While we were enjoying our drinks at the Roma Cafe, a fight broke out. The combatants were four Sudanese young men from the Dinka tribe, who had been drinking. The fight seemed to be fair, two against two—starting out with fists in about the center of the table area. We were closest to the action, and I quickly moved Abby and Elizabeth to protect them from any fight spillover. Other people also moved from their tables and against the walls of the restaurant.

The conflict suddenly began to escalate! The participants were so drunk that they were soon fighting one another. The action then moved to the street in front of the restaurant. It also progressed to the weapons stage with all four men taking out an assortment of knives. They would have seriously injured each other were it not for the police arriving in a Jeep and stopping the fight. One of the men had a nasty cut on his hand. I asked the police if Abby and I could treat the man before they took him to jail. Otherwise, the man would receive no treatment.

The police approved but then walked over to the Jeep with the other three men, loaded them in, and drove away. The cut man was left for us to take care of. I wondered why the police did that. They possibly didn't wish to be bothered with having to take him to the hospital.

The nurses and I put on rubber gloves and proceeded to fix the young man's wound on the back of his wrist. All of the needed supplies were in Abby's purse. The young man was exhausted from his fight and was about to pass out from the effects of whatever he had been consuming. His condition made him easy for the girls to treat.

"This wound is almost like yours, Jack. What did happen to you?" Abby asked.

I remained quiet.

"You're not answering, Jack. Why won't you tell us?"

"Someday I'll remember exactly what it was that happened, and then I'll tell you."

After treating the man's wound, we laid him under a large shade tree off of the street where he fully passed out or fell asleep. We got into Selasie and took off for the clinic. It had been an interesting noon break—a working lunch.

****

Back at the clinic, the team had a long line waiting. The lines continued also at the Living Springs. The spigots were designed to shut off when not engaged, which was never for very long—both day and night. This ensured that no water would be wasted. The rumor that free, fresh drinking water was available was getting around, and many other ethnic peoples were now using the facility. It was also adding to our caseload, as people waiting in lines would look their bodies over and try to find some physical ailment to be treated.

One of the cases that came through the line was a woman with a toothache. One side of her jaw and face was greatly swollen and she had a high fever. Her painful condition was audible, as well as visible. After examining her, Dr. Mike confirmed that it was a bad molar and determined that if she didn't get help soon, she might die if the infection spread into her brain.

Normally, when this type of situation happened in the African culture, there was no treatment or method of safely pulling the tooth. If they did pull the tooth, the methods were so archaic that the result was something worse than the toothache. Dr. Mike asked Samuel about it.

"Once, my uncle back in Sudan had a similar tooth problem. One of the townspeople used a hammer, a small chisel, and a small knife in attempting to extract the tooth. The result was a broken jaw. The man got the tooth out of my uncle's mouth; his jaw was deformed for life. My uncle talked funny for the rest of his life and could not chew properly for a long time."

"So how can we safely pull the tooth out of her mouth," Abby inquired of Dr. Mike?

"We need pliers of some type that will enable us to not break the tooth and yet keep a firm grip. I have no such animal in my collection of medical tools. We really should release the infection, but we have no drill that small."

Meanwhile, the woman continued to lay on the ground by the church door with a high fever, groaning and talking out of her head. It was quite disturbing to the people. I all of a sudden remembered something. "I have an idea, Dr. Mike. In my auto repair tool kit that I brought along, I have a small grip plier that I think is what you are looking for. It's really a vise grip, and it allows me to unscrew a small nut or bolt that has been jimmied, or when a standard wrench is not available."

"Let's take a look at it. Do you have it here?"

"It's back at the hotel. I'll quickly go get it."

I had Gabe take me back to the hotel where I grabbed the wrench. In 10 minutes, I was back at the church and gave the wrench to Dr. Mike.

"Jack, this is exactly what we need."

"How about if we cover each finger of the wrench with a piece of rubber glove to cushion the grip and to keep it clean?"

"Good idea, Jack. Wash the wrench well with alcohol."

Dr. Mike led the woman outside behind the church to an area where there was plenty of sun to see into her mouth. We laid her down, and Dr. Mike gave her a shot of something that soon put her to sleep.

"Jack, put on some rubber gloves and hold her mouth open. You'd better put on two pair of gloves."

I then sat down against a dead tree stump with the woman's head between my thighs and carefully opened her mouth. Dr. Mike set the grip by using the adjustable screw. He tested the grip by gently wiggling the tooth. He then loosened the grip, readjusted the tool, and tried the grip again. "Get ready Jack. I think this setting will hold the tooth firm."

"I'm all set," I assured him.

By this time a crowd had gathered to watch Dr. Mike pull the tooth. Cameron had his video camera going and was getting all of the action on tape.

"Here goes!"

There was a quiet twisting noise as the tooth came out with a thud-like suction sound. The quiet crowd suddenly groaned as they momentarily empathized with the woman, imagining her pain. The entire tooth was intact. The infection also came out, which Dr. Mike soaked up with a wad of gauze. The stench was awful! Dr. Mike then placed some gauze into the opening where the tooth had been.

"Jack, hold this firmly with your thumb until she wakes up. We need to stop the bleeding. I need to get back inside the clinic."

I sat quietly, pressing the gauze in the woman's mouth. Her family was nearby watching me. There was a bucket of clean Baro River water by my side. I took my clean handkerchief, dunked it in the water, and wiped the women's forehead and face. Her young daughter came over, took a washrag, and began to give her mother a sponge bath on her arms and other parts of her body. The woman had apparently suffered from the infected tooth for many days.

She soon regained consciousness with the fever having quickly gone down. Dr. Mike gave her a shot of antibiotic; Elizabeth gave her some Tylenol and an extra drink of water. The woman then stood and slowly walked home with the aid of her husband and family.

The whole family was relieved from the pain.

****

The clinic closed at 5:00 p.m., having seen a record number of people. Dr. Mike picked up the stack of patient forms so he could tabulate the results and enter them into his laptop computer. His goal was to write a report and maybe publish an article in a medical journal. We were all to supply him with photos of patients and other pertinent subjects.

Since the fresh water system had become such an integral part of the clinic, many photos were taken of the system itself and of the lines of people waiting to receive fresh water. These photos would also be in the report.

When we returned to the hotel, I asked the nurses if they would like to walk down by the river before dinner. I didn't feel comfortable or confident asking just Abby to accompany me but both of the nurses might accept my invitation. They did.

The Baro River not only provides water for the town of Gambela, but also it serves as a meeting place for various groups. There are women on the shores washing clothes with their children close by swimming. The men aren't far away and are usually fishing for anything that can be caught, including small crocodiles.

Many tourists are also at the river at all times of the day. People who own cars drive into the shallow part of the river onto the sand bars and wash their cars, taking advantage of the free water.

The Sudanese people are not allowed to work in Ethiopia. This forces the people to create their own enterprises. It is interesting to see the various capitalistic ventures that are present in the Sudanese sections of the city. We saw many of these enterprises as the three of us walked on the road along the river. One man was selling mangos and various coffees. Another man had a supply of fairly straight tree branches that he sold for a variety of uses. Further down, a woman was with her children making and selling handmade jewelry. Much of the commerce was done with currency, but there was also some bartering done.

Elizabeth suddenly decided to go back to the hotel. "You and Jack continue your walk, Abby. I need to get my laundry before Moses goes home."

I'm not sure that was the real reason why Elizabeth terminated her walk. All three of us realized what was going on. Abby and I continued the walk.

We strolled along a swampy section where an elderly man was standing in water and mud, stabbing a spear into the ground. He was apparently fishing for some kind of mudfish. He had already caught three of them, which he proudly displayed to us.

"What kind of fish are they?" Abby asked him.

"Luth," was his answer. I wondered how they tasted.

We continued to walk toward the church where we could then head back toward the hotel.

"Abby, I have been thinking about going back to school when I return to the United States. Maybe I will continue my engineering studies at the University of Minnesota. What do you think?"

"Do you think you can hack it? Engineering is a tough subject."

It wasn't the encouraging answer that I was looking for. Abby didn't think too much of my previous brief academic career, and she was basing her comment on that first attempt. After a short pause, I responded by changing the subject, which was very noticeable. "I wonder how many people have received water at the Living Springs. I need to ask the engineers."

Abby suddenly realized what she had said to me and that it wasn't very kind. "Forgive me Jack, for that comment. I didn't really mean it."

I wondered why she had said it then. I should have asked her, but I didn't. I continued the discussion. "My only problem is the financial part. I have no money in savings."

"Maybe you can obtain some financial aid," Abby suggested.

"God will provide. If He wants me to go, He will make it possible."

We continued to talk as we walked to the hotel compound. This was probably the most time Abby and I had spent talking with each other since we drove to Tulsa the weekend we were married ten years ago. I wanted this time to last as long as possible, so I purposely slowed our pace. I also purposely decided on a detour by turning and walking on James Avenue through the Sudanese compounds.

The ice continued to melt—slowly.

"How are the boys doing in school?"

"They're progressing very well. Jack Jr. has a slight behavior problem in class. He talks too much. But he has a good teacher."

"With the name like Jack, what can you expect?"

"He'll be okay."

We were soon at the hotel and entering the garden lounge area. Abby all of a sudden stopped. "I need to go to the office."

She turned and walked away. When I entered the garden lounge area, I saw the reason Abby left in a hurry. The doctors were sitting and drinking some coffee. Abby didn't wish to have Dr. Terry see us together. I understood, but I didn't like it.

****

The team had dinner at the hotel restaurant and engaged in a good discussion about how we needed to be preparing to accept and treat more war victims. Cameron concluded the discussion. "There is the danger of getting more than we can handle. And, of course, where are the victims and patients going to go after we leave? The flow from Sudan will continue, and someone will need to continue our work."

I decided to enter the discussion after remaining silent for most of the hour.

"I would guess that by now the word has spread into the war area among the Sudanese and the KNM that we are here to treat the injured. The Sudanese may start to come to us in droves. Worse yet, we set ourselves up for possible terrorist acts by the enemy. Our facility could be bombed with us in it. Maybe it's a good thing that we are going to leave in a week."

It was quiet and everyone seemed to agree. We were all contemplating such a tragic occurrence.

We broke up at about 8:30 p.m. and everyone went back to his or her cabin. I decided to stay and write in my notebook. After about ten minutes, an older Chinese gentleman appeared at my table.

"May I join you?"

"You may. My name is Jack Franklin."

"I'm Sing Lu. I couldn't help but overhear you group's discussion about war. That's a really sad situation over in Sudan, isn't it?"

I wasn't sure the reason for this man's interest in this subject and why he wanted to sit and talk about it. He may be in need of social contact while drinking his beverage. He had just been delivered another drink from the bar.

"It's a sad thing, all right, and as usual the women, children and elderly people seem to suffer the most."

"I understand you have medical clinic. Is that correct?"

"Yes. That is correct." I nodded.

"Where do you have the clinic?"

"About a mile from here."

"What do war victims say about what's happening over the border?"

"The only feedback we get is the stories of how they became injured."

"Let me give you my card. I work for a pipeline company. We are attempting to lay line from the Southern Sudan oil fields into Ethiopia."

I suddenly began to see where the conversation was heading. "I'm awfully tired, so if you'll excuse me, I will go to my cabin and get a few z's."

"Let me know if I can help you with your medical mission work."

As I began to leave I started to wonder how his company could help our clinic and what exactly was his interest in the war. I turned toward him and added a parting comment: "The best thing you can do is to use your company's influence to stop the killing of people in South Sudan. You and I both know that one of the reasons for the slaughter of innocent people is to facilitate the exploration and drilling of oil, along with the desire to force a religion down the throats of a strong Christian ethnic group."

The man was suddenly quiet. He knew exactly what I was talking about. I turned and walked to my cabin and went to bed.

CHAPTER 9

Saturday—Day 9

My day started at 5:00 a.m. with the electricity once again going out, the roosters calling all hens, and the young Sudanese boys pounding their tight calfskin-covered drums to death. This morning, however, the young boys had a different beat. It reminded me of the rhythm in an early 1960s rock-and-roll tune. My dad had a huge collection of mid-century popular music, along with his old Jack Teegardin recordings.

We usually had the choice of listening to the noisy fan or the roosters and drums. The switch on the fan gave us that choice. Not this morning—it was only roosters and drums.

At 7:00 a.m. I was alone in the restaurant and ready for breakfast. After I had ordered my usual well-scrambled eggs and burnt toast, Moses sat down and gave me a brief history of the Ethiopian Hotel. He seemed quite eager to tell me.

"It was built by the former head of the Ethiopian government, Mengistu, to serve as his getaway spot. He had a special cabin built, the only one with air-conditioning, and it was always reserved for him. It's right next to the cabin where you are staying, Jack. His staff was always on call and sometimes traveled with him.

"The restaurant had a special area and table that was reserved just for him and his family. It's right over there in that corner with the four posts surrounding it. When he was in the restaurant, the entire place was evacuated unless he had guests, of course. When guests were present, there were sometimes as many security guards as there were guests. Mengistu had people who wanted to harm him, and it was sometimes difficult for him to tell his friends from his enemies.

"I was one of his special aides and on call day and night," Moses continued. "I would taste the food before he ate it to make sure it was okay, and I even did much of the cooking and baking for him. He and I got along just fine, and he especially loved my pancakes. I didn't always agree with his policies and politics, but that's another story.

"There were always guards around to protect him. A couple of times someone attempted to assassinate him here, but they were soon subdued and never seen or heard of again."

"Were you ever in any danger?" I asked him.

"Only from some of the other staff. They often displayed an open jealousy toward me. Everyone tried to get as close to Mengistu as they possibly could. I think they figured that being close to the leader would shield them from any of his brutality.

"On one occasion, I remember, a couple of the guards tried to frame me by placing some poison in the food that was cooked for Mengistu. These guards thought I had cooked the food on that particular day, but I was ten miles from the hotel. I returned just in time and was asked to taste the food.

"I saw right away that the color of the food was not quite right and I informed Mengistu. He made one of the guards eat a whole plateful. That particular guard had placed the poison in the food, and within an hour he was lying dead on the floor. They took the other guard out in back and shot him. I think the guards figured that I would taste the food, give it to my boss, and then we'd both die.

"Like I said, I didn't always agree with what the man stood for, but I did what I could and stayed alive. When he fled the country, I stayed low for a few months, resurfaced here at the hotel, and started work under a different boss."

We were interrupted. Moses had to get back to his work as people were starting to enter the restaurant.

At exactly 8:00 a.m., Abby walked in and sat down at my table across from me. This was the first time she had sat with me for any meal on the trip. The only possible reason for this was that she either would soon move to her table, or the doctors were not coming for breakfast this morning. She handed me a note and I set it aside.

I had my belt off and was busy making another hole with a blade of my Swiss Army knife. With no scale around, I wasn't sure how much weight I was losing.

Moses walked up to us, took Abby's breakfast order, and walked into the kitchen.

"Jack, you're losing a lot of weight, aren't you?" She said it in a complimentary tone of voice.

"It's about time, don't you think?" Abby started to answer, when I interrupted her. "You don't need to answer that."

"Well, I was just going to say that this is the place to lose weight. I don't mean the restaurant here—rather Gambela. The hot African days do wonders for a weight-loss program. I've lost a few pounds myself."

"We lose our appetites in this weather. By the way, Abby, don't lose too much; I like you just as you are. You look great!"

"Oh, really?"

"Yes, really! You're more beautiful than ever."

Abby just smiled and never responded to my complement. I hoped that she would just remember it later.

We continued to talk, and soon Moses came with Abby's breakfast. Abby bowed her head and prayed silently. I closed my eyes until she had finished.

"I wonder what exciting things will happen today. I have trouble just keeping up with writing notes in my notebook."

My words hadn't finished echoing in the empty hotel restaurant, when one of the Sudanese men from a compound near the church came running in. He announced the first crisis of the day. "Come quickly! Many victims from the war in Sudan are at the church. They've just come from Sudan."

Both of us stood up. I quickly fastened my belt and began to head for the door. I had completed my breakfast and was about to depart anyway.

"Abby, see if you can find Gabe and have him get Selasie ready to go. He should be sitting in the garden lounge area. I'll get the doctors. Then run and get Elizabeth."

Abby quickly left with her breakfast still warm on her plate.

"Moses, will you please cover this plate with foil so I can take it with me and give it to Abby?"

"Sure, and I'll send some plastic tableware with it and some hot tea. I like Abby. She is a good woman. Don't you agree, Jack?"

I just smiled. Moses knew my feelings for Abby.

I hurriedly walked outside and ran to the cabin where Dr. Mike and Dr. Terry were still sleeping. My shout of the urgent news from outside the cabin window got them up and ready within minutes. I then raced back to wait for Gabe and Salasie. I sat down, opened Abby's note, and read it.

> *Jack—Thanks for the flowers. I love flowers. Where in the world are you getting them? Some of them I have never seen before. It's nice to have someone bring me flowers.*
>
> *Jack, I am praying that God will help me to just be your friend. I trust that this will satisfy you. God has other plans for my life—plans other than what you may be thinking. —Abby.*

I walked back into the restaurant and picked up Abby's still warm plate of eggs and toast, covered with foil and sitting on the table. Moses had placed them on a tray along with a container of tea, some tableware, and a napkin.

It was only a matter of minutes and everyone was in our vehicle, with Gabe racing toward the church. I could only imagine what shape the victims would be in. *Would there be only men, or women and children also?* I asked myself. Maybe there would be some wounded older people. James and Samuel should already be at the church, and they would serve as translators.

I reached up and gave Abby her breakfast. She looked at me for about five seconds, and I wondered what she was thinking. Then she took a sip of the tea. Everyone thought that it was my breakfast that I was carrying.

"You'll need the food for energy, Abby."

Abby began eating without any hesitation.

Dr. Terry just looked out of the window and said nothing. He was starting to worry. I had news for him; his worries were only beginning.

As we approached the church driving on the long, bumpy, dusty driveway, we could see a crowd standing and looking at people lying on the ground and up against the church's outside wall. Three of the victims had apparently been transported on crudely made stretchers, possibly all the way from Sudan. I made a quick count. There appeared to be at least 25 victims—men, women and children. Two of the victims were lying off to the side. They appeared to be dead, and someone would soon need to cover or remove them.

We jumped out of Selasie and began to administer first aid. The doctors picked out six of the victims they determined to be critical. They had gunshot or pieces of metal still in their bodies and would require surgery. They were carried inside. Some were placed on what tables we had and the rest on mats on the dirt floor.

Two of victims were children. Another ten had gunshot wounds that were not life threatening. The nurses gave them first aid and the doctors performed some minor surgery and the stitching up of their wounds. Most of the victims had to be treated outside, since there were too many to bring inside. An audience of people continued to watch. We worked as fast as we could, attempting to finish before our regular clinic was to open.

The doctors called for one of our Sudanese women to come inside and translate. One of the six inside the church was about to die and wanted to say something.

As the victims were being treated, James asked two of the men what had happened. One of them did the talking and Samuel translated:

"We were having a community singing and prayer service when we heard planes coming toward us. We all knew what was going to happen. Only last week we had been having drills to see how fast we could exit the crowded church. This drill was for real. The women with small children were the first ones out by the two doors. Next to exit were the men, some leading one or two older people and one leading a blind women. Two people were crippled and crawled out. The young boys and girls jumped out of the three windows.

"It took us only about thirty seconds—our record time. We scattered in all directions so that it might confuse the pilot. If a bomb were dropped, only a few of the congregation might then be directly hit. The plane would also shoot with machine guns.

"There were two planes and, unfortunately, two bombs were dropped: one directly on the church and the other a short distance from the church. This hit resulted in several deaths and injuries. The other bomb completely destroyed the emptied church. The pilots were smart enough to not make another pass at the church. We have some of the Nuer forces with guns close by. They could move in almost immediately and are very skilled at shooting down planes."

Our team continued treating the victims and was able to save all of them but the one. Three more had already died by the time they reached Gambela and the clinic. They were taken out to a small graveyard under a large tree in back of the church and given an immediate funeral and burial, attended by many of the Sudanese community.

I walked quietly into the clinic, gently took the hands of our almost-exhausted nurses, and led them to where the burial service was being conducted. The Gambela Sudanese Covenant Church pastor was just finishing up, and a group of men had just completed digging four burial holes. Everyone stood motionless after the elderly Sudanese pastor said "Amen."

I began singing "What A Friend We Have in Jesus." The nurses joined me in singing but soon stopped when they became overcome with emotion. A few in the crowd joined me as the nurses' singing dropped off. I heard the song sung in both the Nuer and English languages.

This was not a happy event for our team or the Sudanese community. I wondered how many times this scene repeated itself in Sudan in the past fifteen years. How many of our martyred Sudanese brothers and sisters are there that never had a graveside service?

****

Our next crisis of the day was also serious; we were running out of medical supplies. Our caseload was much greater than expected. Cameron sent me on a mission to find and buy whatever I could. The doctors and nurses made up the list of items.

Gabe and I were soon on our way to downtown Gambela. I had been given a generous amount of money for just this purpose from a man in our church in Indianapolis. He had the foresight to know that we would run out of supplies. He said, "God told me to do this. And He will direct you on how to use it."

We drove to a long row of small businesses on a side street. It could take me several hours just to find the needed supplies, and then I would need to negotiate the prices. There were the normal questions: Could we find what we needed? Would we be able to get the required quantities? Did any such supplies even exist in Gambela? I was ready for several hours of shopping.

I walked up to a small business selling jewelry and clothing. Two young Ethiopian women were out front busily sewing using old-fashioned treadle sewing machines. I had no idea where to begin, but this looked like as good a place as any.

The young man standing in front of me was an Ethiopian in his mid-twenties. He appeared to be the manager or the owner of the business, or maybe both. He spoke to me in English. "May I help you?"

The man was well-dressed and seemed to be very much in command. His store was neat and well-stocked with a wide variety of items that the local populace and tourists apparently purchased.

"I'd like to buy a necklace for my girlfriend. Something with a turtle" I answered him.

He turned, led me down the main aisle to near the back of the hut, and showed me a big box of necklaces. After digging around, we found one with a jade-green turtle. I picked it up and examined it closely like I was a jeweler. I used my Swiss Army knife magnifying glass to examine the necklace even closer. I had no idea why I was looking at it or what I was looking for. But he didn't know that.

"How much is it?" I asked.

"30 birr."

"How about 20 birr?"

"27 birr."

"25 birr?"

"Done. You have made a good choice for your girlfriend."

"I think Abby will like it."

I gave him his choice of Ethiopian birr or a crisp five-dollar bill. He seemed pleased as he took the American currency.

"Can you help me with another matter?" I asked.

"What do you need?"

"Medical supplies. You know, tape, Band-Aids, ointment, rubber gloves, etc. They have to be clean and in closed or sealed cartons."

"How much do you need?"

"Probably more than you have."

I pulled out a wad of 25 fresh new birr bills as an enticement to share the best information he had. He took the money, fondled it for a moment, folded the bills, and carefully placed them in his shirt pocket.

"Follow me. A business friend of mine has a big building on the edge of the business district. I saw a pallet of medical supplies just the other day. Let's take a walk."

He spoke some instructions in Arabic to an assistant, and then we left.

We walked several blocks with Gabe following close behind, driving Selasie, so as not to lose us in the busy crowd. Soon we were standing by a big building with the businessman knocking at a side door.

"Oh! One thing—don't ask my friend where he acquired the supplies. Okay?"

"You got it, man." The businessman winked at me.

The door soon opened. The two businessmen shook hands and spoke in the Amharic language. They talked for a bit, presumably discussing the supplies. My merchant friend then turned and spoke to me. "How much money do you have? He wants to know."

"Tell him I first want to see what he has to sell."

We all walked to the back of the large building and stopped at two plastic-wrapped pallets of medical supplies sitting on the dirt floor. The writing on the side of the boxes was in French. I began to unwrap the pallets and examine the various boxes. Some I opened to see if the supplies were fresh, clean and not too far out-of-date.

"Ask him what he wants for everything."

The two businessmen talked for a few seconds. Then silence. Finally they started talking again. They both turned and faced me. The warehouse businessman spoke.

"4000 birr."

"3000 birr," was my reply.

"3500 birr," he countered.

"3200 birr."

"3200 birr? Okay—but take everything."

The price was about $400 in US dollars—just what my friend in Indianapolis had given me. I reached into my pocket, retrieved the money, and gave it to the businessman. I also gave the store manager an added tip for his good work. I would imagine that my contact received an additional tip from the warehouse businessman.

Soon we were loading the supplies into and on top of Selasie. It was more than we needed, but at the price we agreed on, it was a steal. My thought was that if we didn't use all of the supplies during our clinic stay, we could send them into South Sudan in the form of first-aid kits to be used by the churches in treating people coming to their medical clinics.

Needless to say, the rest of the team was relieved when all the cartons were unloaded at the church. Gabe was proud of himself. Cameron thought it would be best to place an extra guard as a precaution against possible pillaging at night. This included possible sabotage by an enemy whoever that might be.

I walked over to where Abby was administering first aid to a head-wound patient. After a few seconds, she looked up at me. I whispered to her. "Abby, I need to give you something."

Abby stopped and looked at me momentarily. My immediate thought was that she may have the idea I was about to give her an engagement ring. That would be nice, but at this point in our renewed fragile relationship, I know what her reaction and answer would be.

"Why do you need to give me something? What is it?" she whispered back with a skeptical look on her face.

"Don't worry, it's not what you might think it is."

"Good. What do I think it is?"

I didn't answer. She glanced at me with a puzzled look.

"When I was fishing for medical supplies today, I bought something, using the purchase as bait to obtain information. I told the shopkeeper that I was buying it to give to my girlfriend. I bought the item, and you're the only girlfriend that I have. Unless I give it to you, I'll be guilty of telling a lie."

She again looked at me with the same doubtful stare and then looked at my clenched fist. I took Abby's hand with my other hand, opened it palm up, and emptied my fist. It was the necklace with the glistening jade-green turtle. I had taken off the "Made In China" tag.

"It's beautiful. Thank you. I've been looking for a turtle of some sort in Gambela. I've started to collect them."

"You're welcome. Just think of it as one of the perks of the trip and knowing me. If you don't want it, give it to someone. I'll understand."

She continued to look at me with a serious intent look. Maybe she didn't believe my explanation. After she had placed the necklace in her pocket, I turned and left the clinic.

****

After the clinic closed, we all went back to the hotel, cleaned up, and gathered for dinner. We shoved three tables together and sat as a group. The discussion was again about the treatment of the patients from the war. The doctors hadn't been prepared for this kind of medical treatment, especially one requiring a leg amputation and two with severe burns. I really didn't care for this subject of conversation as I was eating my usual Nile trout and American fries. It didn't seem to bother the doctors and nurses, as this was normal table talk for them. At least they didn't discuss festering wounds and colostomies.

As we were about to leave, two of the Sudanese pastors walked in with a look of concern on their faces. It seems that their meeting on church business had ended at an impasse with much confusion and a shouting match.

The issue was the question of where the responsibility of Christian education of the children rested within the individual congregations. The two alternatives were: 1) Christian education as taught in the church, and 2) Christian education as taught in the home. The committee couldn't agree.

I looked at the two leaders, looked at Abby, and then spoke. "I have a possible solution. Have the committee meet here at 9:00 p.m. tonight. I will lead the meeting."

Cameron suddenly looked at me with a degree of doubt on his face. I could read his mind. "What does Jack know about church matters?" he seemed to be asking.

My suggestion was made to calm the unsettling behavior of the committee. I was hoping that by the time of the meeting, all involved would have cooled off. No one had a better idea, so everyone agreed.

I turned to Abby. "What are you doing for the next two hours?"

"Nothing, really. What do you need?"

"Come with me. I have a task for you."

We walked to where Moses was in the kitchen.

"I have a favor to ask of you, Moses," I said.

"I'll see if I can do it. What is it?"

We discussed the plan—the action and timing. Then I hurried to my cabin to get some of the groceries I had bought in Addis Ababa at the little grocery store. I walked into the kitchen where Abby and Moses were talking. Moses also called his wife and invited her to join in the project.

****

At 8:45 p.m. the group began to trickle into the restaurant. I had arrived early, pushed tables together, and set up the seating so each person could see all others who would be gathering. We essentially took over the restaurant. Our entire team was there, along with the pastor's committee and a few of the Sudanese community leaders. We all sat down.

All eyes were focused on me; I had called the meeting and, therefore, was expected to conduct the session. I wasn't quite sure what the discussion would entail, but I did know how it was going to start and end. I stood up and cleared my throat. James served as translator, although only two or three of the pastors didn't understand the English language.

"We are gathered here to discuss the opportunity of educating the Sudanese children in the area of the Bible and God's plan for their lives—a very important topic. But before we talk about it, we have another task."

I had their undivided attention. Everyone was wondering how an ordinary car repairman could solve a church administration problem half a world from Indiana.

"Tonight we have, right here in Gambela, a world-famous woman, a special guest, and an expert in an American tradition. In fact, she is here in this room right now. Abby, will you stand up."

Abby stood up and smiled as I started everyone applauding. She had become a favorite of the Sudanese community, especially among the young women and children.

"Abby has made something in Moses' kitchen, and she doesn't know what to do with them. So I have asked her to show you what she has made and let you suggest how to dispose of them."

The smell from the kitchen was stimulating everyone's salivary glands. The Sudanese in attendance had no idea what I was talking about. From the looks on their faces and their longing glances toward the kitchen, they were anticipating something out of this world. The smell was intense and permeated the entire restaurant complex.

Abby walked to the kitchen and returned balancing a 36-inch diameter aluminum tray above her head. She had a big smile on her face as she strolled to the tables.

"Abby, tell us what you have prepared."

"Peanut butter cookies," she answered!

"And not just any peanut butter cookies," I continued. "Folks, they are Abby's Peanut Butter Cookies."

Dr. Mike, upon my queue, spoke up. "What do you mean you cannot find a place for those cookies? Pass them down here!"

"Abby baked 80 cookies and there are twenty of us sitting here. How many is that for each of us? Can someone do the math? Who has a calculator? Crunch the numbers, somebody."

One of the committee shouted out, "That's four each."

"Brilliant! Let's eat."

For the next few minutes the group passed the tray to each other around in a circle and proceeded to consume all 80 of the cookies. The Sudanese had never tasted this American tradition: peanut butter cookies containing a generous amount Planter's Party Pack Cocktail peanuts brought from America.

The atmosphere was almost religious, similar to when communion is served. As the cookies were being served, everyone was quiet except for the chewing and the smacking of lips. Moses was busy hauling coffee, Ambo, and tea with which to wash the cookies down.

As the last cookie was taken from the tray, I stood up. It was time for me to make my next move—the pitch they all had been waiting for. I had no idea how I was going to get from the cookies to solving the impasse with which the Sudanese pastors were faced. I only knew that God had allowed Abby to use one of her special talents and allowed the group to have some fun.

"Now, it seems to me that the solution to the stalemate that your committee finds itself in is working together—maybe even compromising. Maybe each side will need to give a little. Maybe you should do both options. James, you can take it from there."

As James was translating my words to the group, I motioned for Abby and Elizabeth to come outside. When we arrived outside in the garden lounge, we sat down on lounge chairs.

"Abby, your cookies have always been the best. Now you have baked them in Africa. Thank you. I think I'm going to order a hot tea. Do you ladies want anything?"

Elizabeth responded, "That sounds good."

"Me too," Abby added.

I called the waiter over and gave him the order for three hot teas.

"Are you girls having a good time in Gambela?" I figured it was a good question to ask them. I was sure that Abby had continued to share with Elizabeth all of what was going on between the two of us. Or, more accurately, all of what was not going on with Abby and me, which I wished was going on. Abby responded first.

"The days of this trip have been the most challenging of my life.

Each day there is something new to put in my diary, and they just keep getting more exciting."

"It's the same with me," Elizabeth answered. She then posed a question to me. "Jack, what are you going to do when you return to the United States? What kind of work are you going to do?"

Her question seemed to have been asked for Abby's benefit rather than mine. I took a swig of tea and waited a few moments before answering. "There are several options that I have been thinking about. However, my first priority is to move to Minneapolis, unless Abby objects to that."

"Why would I object to that? But, then again, why not Indianapolis?"

"My number-one objective is to be where I can see my sons every week. They are my top priority. Beyond that, I have been thinking about more school. I never finished my schooling in engineering, but, then again, God may want me to just be a great auto repairman. God has a place for me somewhere."

"Doesn't God have an exact special plan for each of us?" Elizabeth questioned.

I thought for a moment and said, "You know, I always used to think that was the case—that God had an exact plan for us. But since I have become His, I feel differently."

Abby suddenly had a puzzled look on her face. "What do you mean, Jack?"

"Well, even before I became a Christian, I always thought that God had some master plan in heaven for each of us, along with dates, places, people—what car we should buy, what we should order for dinner, and so on. Now, I think that what He really wants from us is our attention and availability. If that condition exists, and we truly believe in Him, then God can use us wherever we are and in whatever we do. I can fix cars to the glory of God, or you nurses can give shots to the glory of God, if we are truly in tune with Him. Agree?"

"Agree," they both answered.

"I have a few talents and abilities, but I never used them in my former life. But more than having talents, I am now on hand to do anything on a second's notice. It's called availability."

Abby wanted to ask me a question. I could see it on her face, even though it was very dark and only a low-wattage bulb was illuminating the garden lounge area.

"Jack, are you sure you are the same Jack I was married to for five years? The Jack I once knew was the complete opposite from you."

"Let me put it this way: I'm the same Jack on the outside, but a different Jack on the inside. God has re-created me, fed me nice pills, sent my mind to the cleaners and caused me to want to serve Him."

We chatted for another thirty minutes, and then the nurses decided to go to their cabin.

"If you don't mind, I'll walk you to your cabin." I volunteered.

"That's fine," Abby answered.

We walked out of the hotel garden lounge and onto the sidewalk leading to the cabin area. It was dark, and again there was only a single low-wattage light bulb high on top of a utility pole. Everyone was either in their cabins or at the hotel restaurant and lounge.

As we approached the group of cabins where the members of our team were staying, I saw a man slowly approaching us. I suddenly had a funny feeling that something was about to happen. I pulled the nurses closer to me with my outstretched arms. Abby and Elizabeth wondered what was happening. I spoke softly to them. "Ladies, let me walk you right into your cabin."

"Why?" was Abby's response.

"Just let me do it."

We soon were upon the porch of the cabin and into where Abby and Elizabeth slept.

"Do either of you have any mace or hair spray?" I asked in a whispered voice.

"I have some hair spray and some spray deodorant," Elizabeth whispered back. "Why?"

"Okay here's the deal. I think that guy outside the cabin was about to rob me."

"Really! What makes you think that?" Elizabeth asked.

"He was acting very suspicious and strange, he has no business in this area, and I saw him at the store today. He probably saw me take some money from my pouch."

"What should we do?"

"You girls go to the back door, quietly walk outside, pick out some rocks, and move to the two sides of the cabin—one on each side. I will go out the front with a bottle of spray in each hand and walk toward the hotel. When you hear me say 'DOGS,' start growling like a big Doberman. If he comes after me, I will spray his eyes. You girls then come running, throw rocks at him and scream at the top of your lungs. The guards will then come running." I then added, "also, pray girls!"

I think the girls thought that I had finally gone over the edge. What if the man has a gun?

My exit from the nurse's cabin was cautious. The next thing that happened was scary. The young fellow approached me as I was walking to the hotel office. I turned around and confronted him.

"Can I help you?"

He stopped walking and stood there. Maybe he didn't understand me.

"Do you want something?"

"Yeah! I want your money."

I held up the spray cans and shot some in the air.

"Well, I hate to tell you this, but what little money I have on me belongs to God. If you take my small amount of money, you'll be robbing God. You don't want to do that, do you?"

I took a step toward the young Ethiopian in his early twenties and quickly looked to see that the nurses were in place at the sides of the cabins. They were.

"Something else you should think about. If you attack me, you will get sprayed in your eyes, also. My lady friends will scream, shriek, and throw rocks at you. Then Zappo! You'll have the hotel guards here within thirty seconds. That will be followed in another thirty seconds by two huge DOGS with very sharp teeth, racing at you at forty miles per hour and lunging at your behind with the intent on having an early breakfast."

"Growl! Growl!"

The nurses started barking. It sounded remarkably authentic.

I could see that this fellow was not prepared to encounter what I had just described. It wasn't long before he was heading out of the cabin area like a jackrabbit being chased by a bunch of dogs—real ones!

I turned to Abby and Elizabeth and signaled to them that it was all over.

They just stood at the two sides of the cabin looking scared while watching the man as he disappeared into the night. I needed to do something that would assure them that they would be safe throughout the night. I walked to the driveway where the hotel guards usually congregated. Three of them were just coming on duty. After talking to them and explaining what had just happened, one of them accompanied me back to the nurses' cabin where he was to stand guard all night. The girls had not moved.

"Good night Abby and Elizabeth, sweet dreams."

I walked back to my cabin. As I was tired from the heat, I was able to fall asleep right away.

CHAPTER 10

Sunday—Day 10

Our clinic would be closed on Sundays so the Sudanese could have their worship service at 9:00 a.m. and Sunday school at 11:30 a.m. The doctors and nurses had been working hard in the heat for the past four days, and we all needed the extra rest and relaxation.

One of the nurses and I were scheduled to conduct a three-hour clinic after lunch on the main street close to downtown Gambela. Cameron thought it would be a good way to reach other ethnic groups of the city. He hadn't decided which one of the nurses would accompany me. My hope was that it would be Abby.

I was awake at my usual 5:00 a.m. time and attempted to get a few more winks. It proved to be fruitless as I only lay in bed thinking about Abby. I would see her in just a couple of hours and couldn't wait.

I wondered how much she was thinking about me. Maybe she was thinking only about Dr. Terry. Or maybe she was thinking about both of us. I know which one of us she favored, but I was still praying for a miracle to happen that would cause her to change her mind and heart.

But how would I support her and our boys? I had no money, no job, and no assets. Dr. Terry had all of it—everything a young woman would want. It hurt me to even think that maybe it was God's will for Abby to marry Dr. Terry.

I suddenly had a strange feeling that something dangerous was about to happen on our mission trip. In fact, the feeling was of several dangerous occurrences. I also had a sense of comfort, knowing that God was going to be present at all times protecting us. This caused me to become sleepy and I dozed off.

I had a short dream. I dreamed that I was walking down a crowded street in Addis Ababa, when I encountered an old man walking toward me. He walked straight at me, glaring with his penetrating brown eyes. I was scared!

The old man stopped about three feet in front of me and spoke in plain English. "Do you love Abby, Jack?"

"Yes I do, sir."

"How much do you love her?"

"How can I explain? I love her very much!"

"Would you be willing to give up your life, to save her life?"

I stood motionless, not able to speak.

"Well, would you be willing?" he asked again.

I just stood frozen, not able to answer.

I woke up with a jolt! I never answered the man's last question.

My attempt to fall asleep, continue my dream, and answer the question proved futile. What was the meaning of this dream? Was it some premonition of ominous tragedy? What was going to happen in the next few days? I was almost afraid to get out of bed.

****

At 7:00 a.m. I decided to walk down by the river to see what the activity was. The morning air was very still, cool and refreshing. The traffic of people and carts to the river was heavy this morning. As I walked along the road and trail, many of the people I passed recognized me from the clinic and the Living Springs water distribution center.

The Ethiopian Hotel compound has a high fence around the property for security reasons. This requires one to walk an extra half-mile to get to the river. I could have climbed over the fence on the backside of the hotel compound, but this would surely bring out the security guards—maybe even the dogs. I hadn't seen any yet, but it wouldn't surprise me if there were a few hidden in some dark back room.

The riverbank was active this morning with many women washing clothes. It is considered improper etiquette to walk too closely to this activity as many of the women had their clothes off down to the waist. Why they do this, I'm not certain. It may enable them to splash the water and cool off that part of their body as they scrub and rinse.

I visited with a group of tourists from Texas who were also staying at the Ethiopian Hotel. They had also traveled from Addis Ababa to Gambela on the same rough road, and they were now on their way to northern Ethiopia. They had driven their vehicle onto a sandbar and were busy washing it with the free Baro River water.

I took some photos of the river with some children swimming and playing on the edge of the water. I walked further down the river and spotted a small crocodile lying on a large rock. I wondered if any of his large relatives were close by.

There are many stories of people—especially small children—being eaten by the crocs in this part of the river. The crocs wait camouflaged by the brown, slow-flowing water and strike at some unsuspecting victim. Many times, the stories go, the victims would lose one or more of their limbs. Other times they would disappear completely. The stories involved mostly children. I suppose that many of these stories, although tragic as they may have been, were slightly fabricated and embellished to make them more exciting— but maybe not.

****

The team met at 8:00 a.m. for breakfast. On my way in, Moses handed me a note. It was from Abby, who was already seated at her usual seat with the doctors and Elizabeth. I took my seat at the table and slowly opened the folded note and read it to myself:

> *Jack—Thanks for last night. You made me feel like a million dollars. The cookie idea was great. I had a couple of the cookies myself. Moses and his*

wife helped me make them. Now I have to teach the
Sudanese woman how to make cookies. Thanks a
lot—Abby
          PS————————

She had started to write another sentence but crossed it out. I could only imagine what it was—maybe something good.

The ice was slowly turning to water.

Cameron came in and sat down with me. He looked tired. I could tell he was worried about his wife back in Denver. Added to that worry were the problems the Sudanese churches were facing in Ethiopia and in Sudan. The medical clinic seemed to be giving him little concern, as it was running smoothly.

"Cameron, how did the meeting go last night? What was the outcome?"

Cameron suddenly came alive! "Jack, you cannot believe what those cookies did for the committee. It was as if the committee had taken some happy-get-along-with-each-other medicine. They voted unanimously to teach Christian education to the children both at home and at the after-church Sunday school. This will be something new for the Sudanese, as they normally don't have any organized Sunday school back in Sudan. The cookies apparently were the catalyst that was needed. Abby's peanut butter cookies glued them together. Thanks, Jack!"

I glanced over to the next table and saw the doctors and nurses listing to Cameron, with Abby smiling.

"By the way Jack," Cameron continued, but in a whispered voice directed at me, "Abby will go with you downtown to run the mini-clinic this afternoon." He winked as he informed me.

As I was walking out of the restaurant, Moses caught up with me. "Jack, you might want to be a little cautious if you venture downtown today. Rumor has it, that a couple of rival street gangs are going to do battle."

"Thanks for the information and warning, Moses."

****

The church service was scheduled for 10:00 a.m. The medical mission team was to have a role in the service with Pastor Cameron giving the message and James translating. We were all seated on chairs, in a corner at the front of the church.

Each of us gave a greeting from our representative churches in America to an overflowing crowd. Many people were sitting outside against the church and under the nearby trees. The other members of the team had written out their messages for the benefit of the translator. I was last to speak and did so without notes, with Samuel translating.

I told the audience of my recent conversion, how God had changed my life, and how I became acquainted with the Sudanese people through James and Samuel. I also told them that God had a special plan for my life and that He would reveal it to me in the coming months.

I never mentioned my ex-wife, Abby, or my sons. Abby never mentioned them or me, either. I did mention that I had not lived a very good life in my former days and that I had made many bad choices.

I then prayed for the Sudanese people in Sudan, that God would help them through the persecution they were enduring, and for the ongoing United Nations' peace negotiations involving the conflict in southern Sudan.

The Sudanese women's choir sang with my drummer friends accompanying. I recognized most of the beats and rhythms. Most of the song melodies I recognized as being old hymns of the faith. The ladies' group was made up of older teens, as well as mothers and grandmothers. They were all dressed in long red gowns, and wore caps.

After the church service and just prior to Sunday school, I handed out gum to the children. I also found the drummer boys and shook hands with them. Some of them were not more than eight years old. There was even one girl who took a turn at playing her homemade drum.

Many of the men and women became children for a few minutes while they also retrieved a stick of Wrigley's Spearmint chewing gum. The distribution of colorful gumballs from a plastic zippered bag to about 100 children was the entertainment of the day.

The little children, some of whom had no clothes on, knew just how to get a gumball, then circle around and get a second and third. One little boy had four in his hand. They were experts at doing an end-around. A crowd gathered to watch.

For some reason, the children chewing the gum abruptly became noticeably active. It was almost like they were getting "high" from the gum. I later asked Dr. Terry about it. He said that the sugar in the gum might have been their first nourishment of the day and that the sugar served as a rush to their bodies.

Abby walked up to me when I had run out of gum and was finally alone. "Jack, I never heard the full story about your conversion. It's a marvelous story."

"Well, I have wanted to tell you about it, but the opportunity never presented itself."

"What you really mean is that I have never given you the chance to tell me," she admitted.

"Yeah, but I can understand why. I would like to tell you more sometime."

"Maybe soon."

****

We drove downtown to the Roma Café next to the Communications Center and had some food. None of us ate much as we were still satisfied from our late breakfast only a few hours earlier. James and Samuel ate most of what was ordered. If any of us became hungry in the afternoon, we could eat an energy bar or some nut and raisin mix that many of the team members had brought with them.

After lunch, some of the team members made some calls back to the United States at the Communications Center. I imagine Abby made calls to our sons and maybe her parents. I wondered if she had told her folks about me being in Gambela.

We all went back to the hotel to have a short rest. I stayed awake fearing I would have another dream. It had been on my mind all through the Sudanese worship service. At some point I needed to tell Abby about my dream.

****

Abby and I drove to the downtown area to set up our treatment center out of the back of Selasie. We would conduct the clinic for three hours or until we ran out of patients. We had no permission to conduct a clinic in this part of Gambela, nor did we ask any official if it was permitted. It was worth the risk to give it a try. There were some rumors going around that we were ignoring the Ethiopian citizens. We never turned anyone away from our clinic, no matter what their ethnicity was. Although our mission was to the Sudanese people, the team made the decision to open up our medical mission to the general public of Gambela, if only for a few hours. The only resistance that we anticipated was from the hospital and the private clinics. This shouldn't be a problem, however, as the people that we were going to treat were those who lacked the money to seek treatment in these other facilities.

The doctors and nurses had set up the mobile clinic in the back of Selasie just after the clinic at the church had closed yesterday. We had all of the medical supplies that we figured we needed. I made sure that we had an adequate supply of chewing gum. I even had some of the soft bubble gum for the elderly men and women who lacked the teeth to chew. They would then be able to "gum the gum."

I was glad that Cameron had picked Abby to conduct the clinic. It would be the first time in many years that we would be alone together doing something constructive for a few hours. We now had a common goal—to administer some relief from pain and suffering, and to distribute chewing gum to a few individuals in downtown Gambela, Ethiopia.

As we were setting up, Abby paused for a few seconds, and then turned toward me. "Jack, I never realized that you could speak like you did in church this morning. You didn't use any notes, did you?"

"I spoke from my heart. I don't need any notes for that."

"Well, I was proud of you. I wish our boys and my parents could have heard you."

I suddenly felt a blast of hot air pummeling an already melting ice wall.

Our first patient was a young girl about twelve years old. She had a large sore on the front of her right leg that had infected, and flies were not only covering the wound but also swarming around it. Layers of buzzing flies were sitting on the wound waiting their turn to lay more eggs.

"Jack, can you put on a pair of gloves and help me?"

I did, and then I helped the dusty, mud-caked little girl up onto a 2 x 10 board in back of Selasie, with her legs over the bumper. I had made the seat just for this clinic.

"You just tell me what to do, and I'll do it Abby."

She stopped for a moment and gave me a doubtful look. "Are you sure about that? Do you realize what you just said?"

"Hard for you to believe, isn't it?" I grinned.

Abby retrieved a full bottle of Bactine from the supply case. The young girl had a crusted-over sore about two inches in diameter just below her knee. Abby poured a generous amount of Bactine into the wound, which caused the flies to depart immediately. I looked at the girl's face and she looked back at me. She wanted me to think that it didn't hurt, but I could see tears welling up on her lower eyelids. But those same tear-filled eyes told us that she trusted both Abby and me.

"Just hold her leg still while I clean it out, Jack"

The next step was painful for both the girl and Abby. I looked away, but I turned back occasionally to peek at what was going on. With a Q-tip soaked with some more Bactine, Abby began the tedious task of cleaning out the dirt crust that had covered the scab. It took at least two minutes to carefully clean it out. Some of the eggs had hatched into tiny maggots.

Half way through I reached into my pocket and pulled out a package of gun. I carefully pulled off the wrapper and gave the gum to the little brown-eyed girl. A big smile was the result! The pain was worth the gum, and it seemed to also ease Abby's concern for the girl. Just to see the smile from this skinny patient was worth the trip downtown.

The wound was now cleaned out and it emerged a crimson red, contrasting with the dark skin of the young girl. It was the size of a silver dollar and, because of her skinny body, extended half way around her leg. Abby covered the exposed wound with an antibiotic ointment. A piece of gauze was then placed on the wound and secured with some tape.

I lifted the girl off of the back end of Selasie and placed some additional tape around her leg in two different places on the bandage. Abby looked at me. "That's a good idea. The bandage will stay in place longer. Where did you learn that?"

"From watching you bandage up our boys when they cut themselves."

"That's right, I did do that several times. I didn't think you were watching back then."

I was quiet for a moment, trying to think of how to respond. "Abby, you were a good teacher. Sometimes the student wasn't always paying attention—sometimes he was."

I looked up and saw a man standing close by. He had apparently been standing there for some time. His voice and words told me that we were not welcomed. "Who gave you permission to do this? What are you doing here?"

I slowly walked over to the man and looked at him in the eye for a few seconds. I wanted to be as non-confrontational as possible, yet forceful. He was waiting for an answer. Maybe he thought that I was going to slug him.

"That little girl gave us permission. She needed our help. If she asked *you* for help, would you give it to her? I'm sure you would."

The old man didn't say a word. He just stood there, like he was wondering what I had just said. He may not have understood my comment and question. Then he spoke in an official tone of voice. "You need some official permission. Taxes have to be collected."

"On what we are doing, there are no taxes. It's free. Is there any tax on something that is free?"

The man stepped back as Abby walked in front of him in a manner that indicated that he was in our way, which he was.

It was then that I noticed a woman standing ten feet behind the man. She was wearing the traditional Ethiopian white dress with part of it wrapped around her head. I looked down and saw that she had a sandal on one foot and the other foot wrapped up with a white cloth. It appeared that something was wrong with her foot. Was this woman the man's wife or maybe a daughter? Maybe they didn't know each other. Did her foot need attention? Dare I ask her? I decided to take the risk.

I walked over to the woman, pointed to her foot and asked her if we needed to look at it. The man answered, "Yes." They were acquainted.

I took the woman's hand and led her over to our vehicle. The man followed and just stood there and watched. The woman sat down on the back of Selasie. Abby placed her leg on a wooden crate, and unwrapped her foot. It had swollen to twice its normal size.

The foot was bad. Abby and I talked while the woman sat there absorbing all of the attention. The man, who had by this time let it be known that it was his wife we were treating, suddenly became very supportive at what we were doing.

"How long has she had this infection?" Abby asked.

"For about two weeks," her husband answered.

"I think I see the cause of the infection," Abby announced. "You have a giant sliver in your heel. We'll need to get it out. I am going to dig it out with a sterile needle and tweezers. Jack, you hold the leg and foot still. But first, let me wash the foot."

Abby then asked the man to embrace his wife while the extraction took place. Since Ethiopian men usually do not touch their wives or show emotion in public, this was a difficult thing for her husband to do. But Abby's request to the man was firm and persuasive. He took hold of his wife.

It was only a few seconds later and a good-sized piece of wood was pulled from the bottom of her foot with a tweezers. The purulence came next and was not pleasant to look at. The man hugged his wife tighter as he looked away and Abby squeezed the woman's foot. From the look on the woman's face, the relief was immediate. As Abby was putting on some antibiotic ointment and dressing, the woman spoke to her in the Amharic language.

"What did she say?" I asked.

The man was quiet for a moment and then spoke. "She…she said 'If I could get my husband to squeeze me that tight everyday, I wouldn't mind having a sliver every day.'"

Abby and I looked at each other, both realizing that we had just witnessed more than the extraction of a sliver. This occurrence may have done more for their marriage and relationship than a dozen bouquets of flowers.

I invited the man to bring his wife over to the church and clinic in a couple of days, and Abby would change the dressing. He then asked an assistant to stand watch over our street clinic to make sure no interruptions occurred. As he was leaving, he gave me his official card. He was a member of the city government.

We worked on patients until 5:00 p.m. The downtown clinic was a success and we made many new friends, many of them being local Ethiopians. The bad news was that we could have treated many more patients. We ran out of time and would need to repeat our mobile clinic on another day before leaving Gambela.

We were packing up and just about to leave when we heard and felt an explosion across the street. Both Abby and I looked and saw a small car on fire. Then there was another explosion within the same car only seconds later.

"Abby! Quick! Throw everything in Selasie and let's get going."

We were out of there inside of thirty seconds.

"Jack, shouldn't we stay and see of anybody needs medical attention."

"That explosion was probably a diversionary blast. The big one will come next, when a crowd gathers."

I stopped our vehicle at an intersection about four blocks from where the explosion occurred.

"Are you sure about another explosion, Jack?"

"Here, take the binoculars and look."

Within ten seconds a second blast occurred. Even before the sound of the explosion reached us, Abby jumped in her seat. She quickly moved over and grabbed onto me.

"Jack, I was looking right at where that one went off. Let's get out of here! That last explosion was right on the edge of the street."

We were soon on our way back to the hotel.

"Abby, let's not say anything about this."

"What is it all about, Jack?"

"Moses told me that there are two rival ethnic gangs operating in downtown Gambela. His friend on the city council must have told him. He said they were expecting some activity this weekend. My guess is that the car blown up belongs to one of the gang members."

"Jack, how did you know that there was going to be a second explosion?"

"That's the way terrorists operate. They plan for an explosion to attract the onlookers to a seemingly safe spot and then have the big one go off. That's how most of the people get their injuries."

"That means that one of the opposing gangs probably was gathered where we were. Do you realize that some of the people we treated this afternoon could have been members of one of those gangs?"

"That's right!"

"So, now what do we do?" she asked.

"Nothing. We'll let the Lord sort it all out. We came, we treated, and we left—in a hurry. Just write good notes tonight."

"Yes, I will."

"One other thing. Like I said, please keep this from the other members of the team. It's quite enough that only we get scared out of our gourds."

****

Cameron and I had dinner at the restaurant with a pair of retired part-time missionaries passing through on their way to Kenya. Their names were Norm and Ruth McKay, and they worked as part-time missionaries three times a year in areas where there were particularly troublesome situations. They had some good stories to tell. It wasn't long before the rest of the team had turned their chairs and were listening intently. The pair loved to talk, with the wife doing most of it.

As we were eating our dinner and listening to the missionaries' tales, a young man came into the restaurant. He handed a note to Moses, said something to him, and just stood off to the side. Moses walked over to our table and handed me the note. I slowly opened and read it:

> *Jack and Abby—You are invited to dinner tomorrow evening at 6:30 p.m. Our driver will be there to pick you up about 6:00 p.m. Please come—Oliver and Tebee Thomas.*
> *PS—Please send your reply back with our driver.*

I refolded the note and wrote:

> *Oliver and Tebee—We'll definitely come—Jack.*

I then wrote on the bottom of the note:

> *Abby—This will be a good chance to have some excellent food. I know these people. —Jack*

Everyone was wondering what was going on. I handed the note to Moses, he brought it to Abby and she read it. She glanced at me with a questioning stare. It was a date for us, only we didn't arrange it. Oliver and Tebee were doing some arranging and matchmaking.

Abby handed the note back to Moses and he delivered it back to the driver. The driver then left the room and everyone continued listening to Norm and Ruth, our dinner entertainment.

****

I decided to walk downtown and do some shopping. It was already dark and maybe not very safe, but the road was wide and had many people on it. None of the team wanted to go with me. They apparently had other plans. I needed to look for some materials to build a Hot Wheels racetrack.

My effort was not in vain. I found a shop beyond the last shop on a side street that had almost anything that the people of Gambela would need for building or repairing a shelter or small structure. The place was Ethiopia's version of The Home Depot, only they didn't take credit cards.

I bought some straight pieces of plywood about six inches wide and eight feet long; some shorter pieces of the same material; some long, straight pieces of _" x _" wood; and an assortment of bolts, nuts, screws and nails. I purchased all of the material for 200 birr— a good price. The owner was glad to part with the material.

I also bought three small imitation ivory crosses for my boys.

I had no vehicle to haul my construction material back to where I planned to set up the racetrack. Gabe had taken the doctors and nurses elsewhere. I found some loose twine lying on the street, tied everything securely into a nice bundle, tied one end of the bundle to my belt, and proceeded to walk two miles. Since the main roads in Gambela are without hills, the task was relatively easy. The noise caused everyone to look at me. It was hot and I needed to stop occasionally and rest. One stop was at a restaurant for a bottle of Ambo.

As I continued my walk, I soon caught up with a frail elderly woman carrying a large bundle of branches on her back. She was just like the women I had seen when we drove from the Addis airport to the hotel the first day we were in Ethiopia. We greeted each other as I passed by her. She smiled, revealing her toothless mouth.

****

About 9:30 p.m. I sat outside of the restaurant drinking some hot tea. I struck up a conversation with a UN official. He and his associates were traveling throughout Africa gathering information on the spreading AIDS epidemic. They were pretty well inebriated.

"I just came from Kenya yesterday and heard tell of a near tragedy in the jungle involving a bunch of people. Seems a small car was traveling down a road, when an extended family of lions appeared. The lions just stayed put, and the driver decided to drive over one of the cubs to continue the journey. The occupants of another car said they saw the whole thing as they were waiting also to pass on the road.

"The cub being run over so infuriated the adult lions that they attacked the small car. They tipped it over and over until a door opened and two of the people rolled out. The people managed to run back to the other car and quickly jump in. The car sped away.

"But that wasn't the end of the story. The adult lions tailed the escape car until they met up with a group of elephants crossing the road. The lions quickly ceased their pursuit of the car and waited for the elephants to vacate the area. The driver of the car, seeing an opportunity to retrieve the rolled-over car, circled back. Everyone quickly got out and tipped the car right side up. It was only moments and the two cars were once again racing down the jungle road."

This story seemed slightly inflated, but it was entertaining.

My two drunken friends finally decided to turn in. They had a long drive in the morning. I decided to stay and write in my notebook.

I wrote about my morning dream, what it may mean, and about our mobile clinic. The explosion that we witnessed had made us realize that danger was also sometimes just across the street.

I hurried back to my cabin, as it had started to rain.

My time to win Abby's heart was growing shorter. If some incident didn't happen to jolt her soon, my opportunity would be lost forever—to a rich doctor. My praying for Abby and our boys caused me to become sleepy, and it wasn't long before I turned out my night lamp.

I felt relaxed. God was in the room with me. He had given us another exiting day.

CHAPTER 11

Monday—Day 11

It was my turn to write a note to Abby. She and the rest of the team were using the cool morning to get a few extra moments of sleep. After witnessing the car explosion yesterday, I was even tempted to stay in bed. It especially scared Abby and she might want to remain inside her cabin.

Tonight was when Abby and I would be going over to the Thomas's for dinner. I was a little nervous about the whole thing. I think Abby was also a little uncomfortable because of what Dr. Terry might be thinking about her going. The whole team knew about our arranged dinner date, and it was surprising that Abby agreed to go.

I decided to face the world and the day and jump out of bed. Hot tea would be a refreshing way to start the day. Cameron was just waking up as I was leaving the cabin.

"Hey, Jack, remember that we have a busload coming from a refugee camp this morning."

"That's right, that should be interesting. Will they be all Sudanese?"

"I would guess so, but I don't know for sure. Our churches at the camp are coordinating the trip, but they may include other ethnic refugees."

"We'll be ready for them."

At the restaurant I sat in my usual spot and opened my notebook.

I knew what I wanted to say in my note, but I didn't know how to say it—or rather write it. While I was trying to collect my thoughts, an older gentleman came into the restaurant and sat down at the next table. He looked to be of retirement age, and he appeared very unhappy about something. Maybe that's the way he was. I needed some conversation to start the day and maybe it would help him to cheer up. "How are you this fine day?" I asked him.

He turned to me and gave me a look like I shouldn't be talking to him.

"I am fine and I think it's going to be quite hot today," he answered.

By his accent, I could tell he was from a European country.

"How hot was it yesterday?" I asked him.

"I heard that in the downtown area of Gambela, it got up to 43 degrees Centigrade."

"What would that be in Fahrenheit?"

"Somewhere around 110 degrees," he answered.

"Can you believe that yesterday afternoon I saw some people actually using sledgehammers on the main street of Gambela to break large rocks into small ones, and in this heat? I'd have to be insane to do that."

"Well, that's probably all of the work they can get," was his response.

Are you a tourist or are you here on business?"

"I am just passing through on my way to Kenya. How about you?"

"I'm with a group that is conducting a medical clinic for about fourteen days. We're from America."

"I'm from Switzerland. What kind of a medical clinic do you have?"

"Well, we are really members of a church group and are using our vacation to help ease the pain of the sick, afflicted, and wounded in Gambela."

I looked at the man when he all of a sudden became quiet. I sensed that I had hit some raw nerve. "Are you part of some Jesus freak group, trying to save the world?" he asked.

I needed to be careful how I answered his question. The man

had just jumped out of the circle of rationality. "Lord, give me wisdom and some good words," I prayed silently. I was ready with an answer.

"As a matter of fact, we are here to provide some very needed medical help. Have you ever been to any of the Sudanese compounds to visit the people? There is almost zero help for anyone who comes down with a case of malaria, dysentery, or breaks a leg—let alone the common cold, bruises, ingrown toenails, or a young mother-to-be having trouble with her pregnancy.

"Yes, I do happen to be a Christian, and yes, I am doing it for the glory of Jesus. I don't know if that answers your question or not."

"It does," he curtly replied.

That is all he said. He opened a notebook he had with him and began to write.

I grabbed a piece of paper from my notebook and began my note to Abby. I now knew the words to use for what I wanted to write. My confrontational friend had just inspired me.

> *Abby—I want to let you know what I'm going to wear tonight for our dinner engagement at the Thomas's. I will wear a pair of tan slacks and a light blue short-sleeved shirt. I will also wear my new wing tip black shoes. I am not dressing up for our hosts; I am dressing up for you.*
>
> *Also, in order to not cause you any embarrassing or uneasy moments, I will introduce you as just "Abby." If you wish, I can use your maiden name, Olson. Just let me know sometime today. Just relax; we'll have a great time.*
>
> *Have a great day. I am looking forward to tonight. — Jack*
>
> *PS—I am keeping copies of my notes, and of yours. They will be the most valuable part of this trip in 50 years, other than my memories of you. —Jack.*

I had just finished the note when the nurses came walking in.

They sat down at their usual table and grabbed the one-page menus. I looked through the windows and saw the two doctors in the hall heading for the restaurant. I quickly got up, rushed over to Abby, set the note in front of her, and rushed back to my table. The doctors then walked to the table to join the nurses.

Dr. Terry noticed Abby reading my note. He could see that it was the same light blue paper and envelope as were the others. Why in the world would she read it in front of him? A possible reason— she may want him to see it.

It wasn't long before Dr. Terry was talking to the medical table about the trip back to the United States. His discussion was directed toward Abby. I watched out of the corner of my eye and listened carefully. He mentioned Egypt, the country he was planning to stop and visit for a few days. It wasn't difficult to conclude what his purpose was for stopping there, and I was beginning to fear that I might have already lost in the race.

My mind was preoccupied with the thought of going on the dinner date with Abby in about ten hours. I was hoping that Abby's mind was in a similar state and that she was thinking about me. But, I needed to focus on our work at the clinic instead of Abby, no matter how difficult that would be for me. That's what we were in Gambela for.

****

The work at the clinic was becoming routine as more and more people were being treated. The good news: news of free medical aid was spreading beyond the outskirts of Gambela and beyond the Sudanese ethnic community. The bad news: In a few days we would be leaving, and there was no one to take our place. Maybe we could propose a permanent clinic to the Covenant people back in the United States. But that would take a lot of time, money, and people.

The free water lines were also adding people to our patient numbers. There was no doubt that the two free-of-charge services were a complement to each other.

With the additional cases coming in from beyond the city limits, new and rare diseases and infections were being treated. The doctors had their computer files with them and were kept busy after hours studying the tropical diseases and their recommended cures. The trip had inspired them—especially Dr. Mike.

About 11:00 a.m., we were visited by the expected busload of patients from the Nelu refugee camp. Most of them were what Dr. Mike called "exciting routine" cases for the clinic—none was life threatening. The Band-Aid only cases were left at the refugee camp where some treatment was readily available. Any critical cases would need to be treated at the refugee camp, as the drive to Gambela would probably result in their death from shaking or dust inhalation.

Cameron had negotiated a deal with the Nelu camp director, once it was determined that we were unable to visit the camp. Our only purpose was to treat some of the people. It was agreed that the camp vehicles would provide transportation to Gambela for the patients if we would provide treatment at our clinic.

There were some broken bones, some foreign-object-in-the-body-causing-infection cases, and many pregnancies. These later cases were brought because Dr. Mike was a very good obstetrician. We enlisted extra Sudanese women to handle the extra work that was required with the pregnant women; many of them were young women not over 16 years of age.

The most excitement was when a young pregnant girl had her baby as Dr. Mike was examining her. The little Sudanese baby boy could now grow up to say that he was born in a church.

****

Dr. Terry was beginning to grasp the seriousness of my desired relationship with Abby. He could see the notes that Abby and I were passing to each other, and he knew that she and I were invited to the Thomas residence for dinner this evening. He probably felt that his relationship with Abby was being threatened. It was, and this is the way it would continue. I was in hot pursuit of her. She knew it, Dr. Terry knew it, and the other members of the team knew it. Most of all, God and I knew it.

All the while this soap opera was going on, we continued our work as a team, not letting the romance triangle interfere. Cameron continued to watch us for any problems, as he had warned us at the Frankfurt airport.

Abby continued to put on an occasional act when both Dr. Terry and I were in her presence. I guess she was trying to make us all believe that she was still not as warm to me as she was to Dr. Terry. Everyone was seeing right through this pretense. I continued to be friendly with Dr. Terry. He was both my Christian brother and my competition.

****

I left the clinic early to get ready for my dinner date with Abby—or, more accurately, the dinner invitation to which Abby and I were invited. She didn't know that our hosts were playing matchmaker, and she seemed very curious who these people were.

On the way back to the hotel, I stopped and purchased some Mangos from a young Sudanese boy. I met him as he was pushing his wobbly wheelbarrow full of mangos to the compounds.

When I arrived at the hotel, I walked into the restaurant and sat down. Moses had the day off and his assistant was in charge. I ordered some hot tea and asked the assistant to bring me two plates. When he returned with them, I began to peel four mangos, slicing the fruit onto one clean plate and piling the peelings on the other clean plate. The fruit was refreshing and I ate every fifth slice. What a mess.

A mango needs to be peeled and eaten in a special manner. The largest blade on my Swiss Army knife provided a good peeling tool. As it is peeled, the fruit becomes increasingly slippery. My left hand was used to grip the fruit, but not too hard. The fruit might pop out of my hand and splat onto someone or something on the other side of the room.

Once peeled, I cut the mango into slices until I got down close to the pit. The flesh binds to the pit similarly to how a pineapple sticks to its core. After peeling most of the flesh off and by gripping the core with both hands, the flesh can be eaten off—again similar to the pineapple. The mango slices are best eaten with a fork, since the juice makes them messy.

The waiter brought me some more hot tea as I was eating. The Ethiopians love paperwork. Or maybe the government requires it.

I have noticed that every transaction is filled out in triplicate. Even when I come into the restaurant and order a bottle of Ambo, the procedure is the same. The waiter writes the order down on the order tablet. He then takes it to the desk where a man writes the order in duplicate. That makes three copies: one I receive, one the hotel gets, and one the government eventually obtains. I am guessing that that is the way the copies are distributed.

There are very few calculators, cash registers, or computers in sight. Apparently, the entire economy is run like this. Even at the airport branch of the Ethiopian bank, a receipt was handwritten in triplicate. The Ethiopian people and the Sudanese people are ambitious; and if this archaic system could be scrapped, the economy would increase rapidly.

****

At exactly 6:15 p.m., I walked from my cabin toward the cement seats in the hotel courtyard. As I walked along the sidewalk, I heard a cabin screen door shut behind me. I looked back and saw that Abby had just come out of her cabin.

She was wearing a long white dress and black shoes. Her hair was flowing in the warm Gambela evening breeze. As she came closer, I could see that she was wearing the jade turtle necklace I had given her.

Abby looked beautiful—dressed perfectly for the anticipated evening. She wore just enough makeup, and her blue eyes sparkled in the setting sunlight. My heart skipped a beat or two, and I promised myself that if I ever were fortunate enough to once again claim her as my own, I would make her the happiest woman in the world. She was almost to me when she spoke. "Jack, you know that Terry is not too happy that you and I are going out tonight. He tends to be a little jealous."

"You should tell him that he doesn't have the corner on jealousy, in this situation. Like my high school band director used to tell us when we were about to perform in a contest, 'A little competition is a good thing and severe competition is a blessing.' Just tell Dr. Terry that it's some people I met the other day who invited us. I only mentioned your name to them as being the person to whom I was bringing flowers."

"I suppose."

"What did you tell him?" I asked.

"I told him that Jack met some people who invited you and me out for dinner."

"There you are. You'll love these people."

"I also told Terry that we would be discussing our sons and a few other subjects of mutual interested. And I told him that this wasn't really a date."

"The mutual subject wouldn't be back child support payments, would it?

"How did you guess?"

"Just lucky, I guess."

"He wonders how you will ever get caught up."

"I see. Well, I want you to know that I've been waiting for this moment for the last 24 hours. I also want you to know that I am very nervous and have been all day, if that means anything to you. I made all kinds of little mistakes and wrong moves all day long. I kept thinking about you. Gabe even asked me if I was all right."

Abby looked down and smiled. She may have momentarily enjoyed the attention, even though it meant that the eventual decision between Dr. Terry and me would be that much more complicated.

A big white car soon rolled into the hotel compound and slowly drove to where we were standing on the sidewalk. I walked over, opened the back door, and let Abby get in. Just before I got in she looked at me and said, "Jack, that's another first for you—opening the door for me."

As we were driving out of the driveway, I turned, stared at her in her white dress.

"Abby, you look great!"

She started to say something, and I immediately interrupted with, "I know, that too is another first."

"I'm sorry, Jack," she apologized.

"That's okay. I deserve it and I'm still learning. This should have happened ten years ago."

"You're doing just fine. But I still think you are someone else. You still have the same body, but what you do and say—it's not the same you."

I let Abby dwell on that thought and comment as I looked out of the window.

As we entered the Thomas's compound, I asked the driver to stop long enough to let me pick out a nice flower for Abby.

"So, this is where you get the flowers," she said as I handed her a beautiful orange poppy. "I've wondered."

As we exited the car, the Thomas's came out to meet us. We got out of the car and stood face to face with our host and hostess.

"Abby, I want you to meet Oliver and Tebee Thomas. This is Abby."

I didn't go any further with the introduction. What would I say, "My ex-wife, the mother of our sons, the girl that I threw away"? My new friends already knew almost all there was to know about Abby and me.

We walked in and the Thomas's led us to a sofa that was covered with a beautiful large brown animal skin. It looked like a bearskin. I wondered if Mr. Thomas had shot it, maybe in the back yard.

"Can I offer you a drink from our bar," Mr. Thomas asked?

I needed to answer this question very carefully—for both Abby and myself. Abby didn't drink; I couldn't and didn't want to.

"No thank you. Abby and I only drink Ambo, Miranda Orange, coffee, or tea. How about a bottle of Ambo and Miranda Orange for Abby and me."

"I'm assuming that you two probably do not drink any alcoholic beverage."

"That is correct."

"I respect that."

Abby turned to me and mouthed the words, "Thank you."

The dinner was steak, American fried potatoes, and corn-on-the-cob. The potatoes were cut into cubes and perfectly browned. Since corn was out of season, I wondered where they obtained it. The dessert was an African-style cream cheese delight covered with a cherry sauce.

The Thomas's had a chef who fixed all of their meals. What in the world did Mr. Thomas do to enable him to afford such luxuries? Maybe our conversation would reveal the answer to that question.

We talked for a while, our conversations covering many topics. Abby seemed to be enjoying herself. While we were waiting for our dessert, I decided to ask a question that had not been answered at my first visit with our host and hostess. I turned to Oliver. "Tell us, how did you two meet?"

Oliver was puffing on a pipe that he had just lit. "It's a long story. Are you sure you want to hear it?"

"Yes, please tell us."

"Well, I was teaching high school math in Addis Ababa and had Tebee as one of my students. She had been driven out of her native Eritrea because of the fighting in the capital, Asmara. I was about 24 at the time, Tebee was 18, and she and I were seeing each other. It was a case of the student falling in love with the teacher."

Tebee broke in. "Ah, correction. It was really the other way around. Oliver just doesn't want to say it, or maybe doesn't know how to say it."

Oliver continued. "Anyway, the Ethiopian army appeared in our school one day and commenced to shut the place down. Since I was from England, they gave me the choice to leave the country or join the army and fight the Eritrean army—Tebee's people.

"I disappeared and resurfaced in Khartoum, Sudan, a week later. I made contact with Tebee through the British Embassy. She then wrote a letter to me and asked me to return to her. She said in her letter, 'I want you to come back to me—we need to finish our algebra.' I believe those were her exact words."

Oliver paused and reached for some more tobacco. It was Tebee's turn to talk. "Oliver wrote a letter back and told me 'If you want me, then you'll have to come to me.' So, guess what! I walked to Khartoum—over desert, through forests with snakes crawling on the ground, with wild animals all around, and with all kinds of regional and tribal warfare going on. I almost thirsted to death, roasted to death, and starved to death, all the while dodging bullets and spears. But I kept going."

"You must have really been in love with Oliver to do that," I said.

"How far was it?" Abby asked.

"About 400 miles. It took me two months. If you think I am thin now, you should have seen me when I reached Khartoum. If I stood sideways, I appeared like a line; or better yet, I was like one of the lines on a UPC sticker," she laughed.

"Then what happened?" Abby asked.

"You'll have to come back tomorrow night and find out. Just kidding," Oliver joked.

He had a keen sense of spontaneous humor.

"We were married in a small chapel at an abandoned mission located on the Nile River. I went to work for an American company in Khartoum, and then a few years ago we moved here to Gambela."

Just then, a telephone of some type rang from the next room. Oliver stood up with an unexpected jolt! "Excuse me. I need to answer a phone."

He walked into the next room and shut the door. I turned to Tebee and asked the question that I was itching to ask. "Tebee, what does Oliver do?"

She looked at me for about five seconds, took a drink of her tea, and cleared her throat. "You know, Jack, I am not really sure. I do know that he has a very secure and secret job with an American communications company. Beyond that I don't know, and he has told me it is best not to ask. I have some idea, but I would rather not say."

Tebee and Abby talked together about the furniture in the Thomas's living room, while I sat and paged through a magazine sitting on the coffee table. After five minutes, Oliver walked back into the room. It was time to change our discussion to some other subject. Tebee asked the question, as she turned to Abby. "Tell me, you two, how are your sons?"

Abby looked at me, suddenly realizing that I had given the Thomas's at least part of our story. "Well, I don't know how much Jack has shared with you," she said. "We have three boys in Minnesota. They are wonderful sons and they're fun to have."

There was an embarrassing pause as all of them waited for me to speak. "I want to be honest with you good folks and tell you that

Abby has raised our boys in a very wonderful manner. I haven't been around them or her in the past five years, but I wish I had been."

I stopped at that point, my voice starting to weaken. If I continued, I would probably lose it. It was very embarrassing. The next question by Tebee was the icing on the embarrassment cake. "Tell me, what would it take for you two to make another attempt at marriage and in raising your family?"

Abby sat there not wanting to reply to Tebee's question. I didn't want her to be placed on the spot, so I finally answered.

"The truth?" I asked.

"The truth," Oliver answered.

"It will take a miracle. A miracle on the magnitude of Jesus turning the water into wine, of God delivering Daniel from the lion's den, and of two people finally deciding to fall in love with each other."

I never looked at Abby as I completed my answer.

"Well, I think we had better get back to the hotel and get some rest. Abby has a very important date with a swarm of patients at the clinic tomorrow, and I need to take a little trip."

Oliver unexpectedly became interested. "What trip? Where are you going?"

"Somewhere I would rather not say."

"You are going into Sudan, aren't you?"

I just looked at Oliver and didn't say a word. How did he know that?

"Be careful," he added.

"Well, thank you for your great hospitality and the flowers," Abby said.

The chauffeured car brought us back to the hotel, returning us at 10:00 p.m. We both stood and watched as the driver and car slowly exited the hotel compound and then disappeared out of sight.

Abby turned to me and asked, "Jack, where are you going tomorrow?"

"Abby, I just cannot tell you now for a reason I will explain later when I get back."

"Okay, but you won't be in any danger will you?" she asked with a concern in her voice that melted my heart.

"Abby, our God is a god of protection and safety, as well as miracles! He will protect us."

"Us? Who is going with you, Jack?"

"God will be with me, if you must know."

"You're evading the question."

"I know."

"Well, I need to pray for your safety," she said.

"Thank you."

She seemed to be somewhat satisfied with my limited answers. She also seemed interested in my safety and even me, more than ever before.

I could almost feel the wall of ice between us falling to pieces, melting, and the water flowing slowly away.

"Abby, can…can we sit and just talk a bit?"

"Sure. The coffee that we drank during dinner at the Thomas residence was a little too strong, and it's going to keep me awake half the night anyway."

We walked over to two lawn chairs under the big mango tree and sat facing each other. "Can I ask you a question?" I asked.

"Shoot," Abby answered.

I wanted to tell Abby about my dream, but I was afraid of what her reaction would be. She may even think I made up the dream.

"What's going to happen when you get back to Minnesota? What do you want to be doing five years from now? Maybe they are not fair questions for me to be asking."

"No, they are good questions. I ask myself the 'five year' question almost every day. First of all, I want to raise our sons in the best manner possible. That's my main task for the next few years. When they leave for college or find work, I'll keep working, probably doing something in the medical field, I guess. At one time, I even thought about becoming a doctor."

Abby sat in the chair in deep thought looking toward the cabins. Then she looked at me and then to the ground, and she added in a whisper, "And I'd like to get married again, also."

There was a pause, with the sound of the trees being blown by the wind along with background noise coming from the hotel bar.

"What about you, Jack? What are your plans?"

"I want to return to Minnesota, find a job, and help you raise our sons. Now, that may entail being a weekend dad, but I want to be there. I'm not going to ask you how that makes you feel. I'm also going to get caught up on my child-support obligations.

"I'll need to find a new church, a place to live, and a support group. A group like: 'Fathers who Made Poor Choices,' or 'Divorced Men who are Now Christians and Who Wished They Could Go Back and Start Over' or how's this one: 'Ex-husbands of Beautiful Ex-wives who are Working at Growing Up, Finally'?"

Abby just sat there, slowly breaking out with a smile. Then she looked directly at me. "If I hadn't been with you tonight, Jack, I would have to conclude that you've been drinking."

"May I tell you about a dream I had the other morning?

"You may."

Just then Dr. Terry, Dr. Mike, and Gabe came driving in Selasie into the hotel compound. They had probably been shopping. Abby suddenly stood up. "Jack, I had a good time. We need to get some sleep. Good night."

She started walking toward her cabin. I followed her at a distance. The doctors were just starting their walk to their cabin. As Abby was about to step onto her cabin's front porch, I turned and spoke. "Abby, remember, our God is the god of miracles."

She stopped, did not turn around, and then opened the door to her cabin. "Good night, Jack. Thanks for the evening."

I walked into my cabin and found Cameron asleep. It had been a nice evening with Abby but with an abrupt ending. She and Dr. Terry were still involved with each other.

I asked God to give me wisdom and direction in the coming days as I pursued Abby. I also asked Him to keep me in His fellowship and in fellowship with the other team members, and not let me lose my focus on helping the Sudanese.

Tomorrow would be a big day for James and me. We would be traveling into the country of Sudan, where he would visit his childhood home. James had told me that we could expect anything.

CHAPTER 12

Tuesday—Day 12

James and I were up at four a.m. and ready for our trip into Sudan. He had not seen his mother and family for over ten years, and he had communicated only twice with his village through third parties. An uncle who recently had arrived in the U.S. told him that he had heard that his mother was still alive. This was only a rumor, however.

It would be a risky trip. No permission had been asked of or granted by any of the governments of the United States, Ethiopia, or Sudan. For certain, the Covenant Church would look very negatively on such an excursion. No one on our mission's team had talked about it openly, although it was known that James had not seen his mother and wanted to. It was then expected that he might try to make the trip, unannounced.

What everyone didn't know, or at least so I thought, was that I was going with him and, we would be using Gabe and Salasie as our driver and transportation to take us almost to the border. James and I gave Gabe the choice to stay in Gambela and I would drive, or he could go with us. He wanted to drive.

Cameron was not aware of my making the trip, and it could result in my being sent back to the U.S.A. when he did find out. I weighed the benefits and potential consequences and decided to make the trip. To be with and help my Christian Sudanese brother was well worth the risk.

Moses came in early to fix us a breakfast. It was not necessary, but since I had become his good friend, he chose to do so. I had told him that I would be traveling to a "dangerous area" and that it was to remain a secret. He knew where I was going.

It puzzled me how my new friend Oliver Thomas knew where I was going. Maybe he merely guessed Sudan as my destination, but he said it in a positive tone of voice accompanied by a "be careful" expression.

As we were eating our scrambled eggs and toast, Abby unexpectedly walked into the restaurant. It was little wonder she'd found out about the trip, after our late-night discussion at the Thomas's. Maybe she just couldn't sleep; she looked tired.

"Abby, what are you doing up so early? You need your sleep."

"I couldn't sleep, Jack. The one thing that you and James need right now is prayer. I'm going to pray for you two."

"Thank you. That's a good idea. We'll need the prayer."

We stopped eating and put down our forks.

"I won't take long," Abby said, as she sat down at the end of the table next to both of us. She took our hands and we all bowed our heads.

"Lord, we ask You to protect James and Jack as they journey into Sudan. Send down Your guardian angels to protect them. Be with Gabe as he drives Selasie. Keep Selasie in good working order as he travels over the rough roads. Be with Jack. Protect him and give him energy as he walks with James. We pray that James's mother will still be alive and in good health. Help us at the clinic today as we treat your children. Bless our boys back in Minnesota. Amen."

I squeezed Abby's hand extra hard all through the prayer. Before she left the restaurant, she handed me a note. I placed it in my pocket. I would read it later.

I would like to believe that she showed up just for me. However, I knew better. She was doing it as a concerned Christian sister. I was her Christian brother as well as her ex-husband and the father of her children.

Gabe was going to take us to a point about a mile from the Ethiopian-Sudan border. We would walk into the country of Sudan to James' village, stay for a few hours and then head back. James knew the region well.

The visit would be short, since James was afraid that someone inside the village may be a spy for the KNM and our lives would then be in danger. If that happened, we may not have a chance to get out of Sudan safely. The village of Somagowa was only ten miles inside the border, and it would take only two hours to walk each way, assuming we had no delays or roadblocks.

Our forty-mile trip to the border went smoothly, taking only two hours. The road was good, but winding. Just before the border, Gabe found a spot for Selasie in a wooded area where it would not be spotted from the road or from the air. Anyone finding it would do so accidentally.

We all got out, James and I packed our backpacks, and Gabe locked up Selasie. We then walked a short way and found a hiding place for Gabe along the road under some bushes. He had a gun to protect himself from the wild animals and snakes.

"I'll wait for you guys right here. We'll see you at six p.m.," he said.

"What will you do all day, Gabe?" I asked.

"I'll use the knife you gave me to carve something for you, Jack."

"Gabe, if we don't return this evening or by early tomorrow morning, don't wait for us any longer. Drive back to Gambela alone," I instructed.

"You guys will return," Gabe said confidently.

James and I took off walking at a speed that would ensure that we could be in Somagowa in two hours. Each of us was carrying two bags filled with medical supplies and food, in addition to the items on our backs. In one of his bags, James had some personal items for his mother. The KNM had shot his father in 1993, and he wanted to visit his grave, which was located just outside of his boyhood village.

As we were walking, James told me how the enemy was recruiting young Sudanese men to raid villages and shoot women and children. The KNM would pay these young mercenaries with money, food, or even young imprisoned Sudanese women. This was starting to make it difficult to know who the enemy was.

Our walk went smoothly for the first six miles. James, having traveled by foot in this part of Sudan for years, had a talent for determining the distance traveled. He could also accurately estimate our speed. I never doubted him, although I had no means of measuring either distance or speed.

Some three miles inside the border as we rounded a bend on the road, we encountered a family of baboons who had stopped on the road to socialize. The baboons took up the entire width of the narrow road. On each side of the road were deep gorges, making it difficult to travel around them. For the moment, we were stuck in the traffic—a baboon roadblock. The baboon family was sitting almost motionless. As long as we maintained a short interval, we figured we would be out of danger.

"What do we do now, James?"

"I'm not quite sure, but I have an idea. My father said he was in a similar situation one time. Let's just lie down on the road and pretend that we are sleeping. They should stop looking at us and move on, I hope."

"You're kidding, of course, aren't you James?"

He wasn't. James dropped his bags and, using one of them as a pillow, lay in the position of sleep with his head and eyes toward the baboons. I did the same, placing my head next to his and facing the same direction.

"Close your eyes, Jack. Baboons may have good eyesight."

"This is nuts, James"

"Quiet, Jack, they may think you're not sleeping. Maybe the baboons have super hearing, too."

We lay motionless for about a minute.

"I think they are attracted to your white skin, Jack. Maybe they want to eat you instead of me." We were now whispering.

"James? Are you okay? Should you be on some medication?"

"I'm fine, Jack"

While we were waiting for the baboons to move, James pulled a shocker on me. "You know, Jack, this situation doesn't concern me. Even the fear of running into enemy soldiers doesn't concern me. What really is on my mind is something that I have feared for several years, ever since I got married in Gambela."

"What are you talking about, James?"

"It's the possibility of running into my wife's family when we get there. You see, in my culture a wife is bought with a number of cows. When I got married, the going price was twenty-four cows. That's what I agreed to pay to my wife's family. But I only sent the equivalent of twelve cows to her family in Sudan, and now I'm afraid that my in-laws will find me and want the other twelve, or the equivalent in US dollars or Ethiopian birr."

"So, what will happen if you don't pay the other twelve cows?"

"They may come to America and take my wife back. They may even place the dreaded curse on my mother, or even on me or my family."

"You're kidding! Do you believe in all of that curse business? That's not for Christians. That's a bunch of baloney!"

"Unfortunately, some of the heathen tribal customs have stuck with us. Some of the Christians refuse to do away with those practices and superstitions. They've crept into our American-Sudanese society."

"Just tell your in-laws to go fly a kite. Where is love in your culture? Where is common sense?" I asked.

James just laughed quietly.

"James, tell me, is the price for a wife always twenty-four cows?"

"Not always. It could be more, sometimes less."

"Who determines the price?"

"The girl's family—the price is actually negotiated."

"On what is the price determined?"

"The girl's beauty has something to do with determining the price. But mostly it is the size of the girl's family, since each uncle gets a cow or two."

"Who determines the degree of beauty?"

"The girl's family, also."

Our plan worked. We lay for five minutes, and finally the baboons moved down into the gorge and up into a bunch of trees a short distance from the road. We slowly got up and walked quietly up the road. As we passed where the family of baboons had been resting, we increased our walking speed in order to make up for lost time.

"Yup! They were looking at you and salivating, Jack. You may have a chance, however, since the adults usually let the younger family members feed first."

"James, I think the heat is getting to you."

We walked for two hours in the early African morning sun. As we walked, we passed many species of wild animals, birds, and an occasional snake. We talked as we walked, stopping occasionally to rest and have a drink of Ambo.

As we approached the village of Somagowa, James stopped walking and looked around the countryside. We were next to an open area with two huge trees that had been untouched by the fuel robbers. He was looking for his father's burial site.

"I think that's it over there, Jack."

We walked over to where several large stones surrounded one of the huge trees.

"My father is buried somewhere under one of these rocks. Several people told me this when they came to the refugee camp I was at in 1994. Let me take a couple of photos."

"Here, let me take the photos and you stand among the rocks," I suggested.

James was quiet and just stood there. I wondered what he was thinking—maybe of how his father had been killed. The government soldiers sometimes tortured their victims and then shot them. We continued on the road toward the village.

"James, you let me run your camera and then your mom and you will be on all of the videos."

"Good idea, Jack, that is if my mother is indeed still alive and living here in my hometown. I have many happy memories of this place from my childhood and youth."

We arrived at James's village of Somagowa at about 10:30 a.m. Since it had been ten years since he had seen his mother, he was not sure what she would look like. "Famine, as well as age, does strange things to a person's physical appearance."

"Tell me about it, James. I'm living proof of that. I think I've lost 20 pounds in Africa."

James stopped and asked a man sitting on a rock where his mother lived. The man knew his mother.

"They live on the other end of town," the man informed us.

"Then she is still living?"

"Yes, she is."

James was relieved. We continued to walk.

"How large is Somagowa, James?"

"It was 500 people when I left ten years ago. The war, famine, and the refugee movement in and out of the town probably have modified the population considerably, so I have no idea how many people live here now."

We walked to the opposite end of the town and stopped just outside of a compound where a woman was grinding grain. She was holding a stone with both hands and moving it back and forth upon another, much larger, flat stone. James and the woman did not recognize each other. He again spoke in the Nuer language and translated it into English for me.

"Do you know where Martha Amok lives?" he asked her.

"Yes, just a minute."

The woman walked into the compound and soon returned with an elderly man. The man spoke.

"Who are you and why do you want Martha?"

"I am James, Martha's son from America. I've not seen my mom since I left ten years ago."

James and the man shook hands. They remembered each other.

"She has talked about you many times. Before I tell her that you are here, I need to tell you something that you may not know and that may upset you."

"What is it?" James asked.

"Your mother is blind."

"Blind? What happened to Mom? Some disease?"

"No, the soldiers came soon after you escaped and burned her eyes out. She will tell you the story. Your mom has asked that no one tell her son, James, if they ever meet him."

James was quiet and seemed both saddened and somewhat angered by his facial response.

The man and woman led us into the compound and to a small hut. The woman then went inside and soon led out a bent-over, frail, blind woman to us. It was evident that she had once been a tall woman.

"Mom?"

James' mother stopped walking and stood at attention on the

dusty earth. She was barefoot. "James? I hear James, my son."

"It's me Mom. I've come to see you and to tell you about your grandchildren in America."

James and his mother hurried to each other and embraced. James was soon crying. His mother was also crying but had no tears. Her eye sockets had healed almost over the entire openings. They sat down on a bench and began talking. James translated everything his mother said into English.

"What happened, Mom?" James suddenly stood up again and turned to me. "Before you tell me, I want to introduce you to my friend from America. This is Jack Franklin. Jack, this is my dear mother."

Martha stood back up, I took her hand, kissed it and then shook and squeezed it hard.

"James, your friend is a Christian too, isn't he!"

"Yes! How did you know?"

"I can tell whenever a Christian comes close to me. The Spirit within me tells me. My eyes may be gone, but not my mind and heart. I have lost my eyes, but I can see with my heart."

"Mom, do you mind if Jack videotapes our conversation? I want to show it to your four grandchildren when I return to America."

"Please do. I want them to see their grandmother. I will give them a greeting, also. It's so good to have you here, Son."

"Tell me the story of what happened."

Martha sat down on the bench. James sat beside her, and I continued to stand facing them and running the video camera.

"I want to tell you, Son, but I am afraid that you will feel bad. If you will just keep in mind that whatever suffering I have been through has been to the glory of God."

"I need to know, Mom, and your grandchildren need to know. People in America need to know. Some people in America don't think that there is a war in Sudan or that the Christians are being persecuted, tortured, and killed. The Christians in America need to know so that they will continue to pray for you and our Sudanese brothers and sisters."

James' mother took a deep breath and began to talk. "Son, soon after you were taken away and escaped to Ethiopia, the soldiers from the north came to our village again looking for you. They came to me and asked where you had gone. I told them you had gone on a journey. I told them that you wanted to get married to a young woman in Gambela, that she had moved there, and that I didn't think you would return.

"This angered them greatly. The head of the soldiers then asked me to renounce Jesus and Christianity. I told him, 'I will not renounce my Jesus.' He asked me three separate times to curse Jesus. I repeatedly told him that 'I love Jesus and I am willing to die for Him, like He died for both you and me.'

"This made the leader furious. The soldiers grabbed me and lay me down on the ground. I could see a soldier coming with a hot iron.

"They burned my eyes out, one at a time. I still remember hearing the sizzling sound, smelling my own burnt flesh, and feeling the spit as my captors spat on me. The pain was intense at first. Then my head began to throb and finally I passed out. They say my screams were heard over the entire village.

"Once I had passed out, I was repeatedly raped, according to the people who were forced to watch. My Christian brothers, sisters, and townspeople have all been wonderful in helping me."

James put his hands up to his face, covered it, and began to weep. He was feeling the pain by just listening to his mother retell the story. At that point, Martha stopped talking. She was waiting for James to regain his composure. I stopped the video camera.

I walked outside and let James and his mother talk and have some time alone. I sat down in the hot sun and reached into my pocket for some gum. The note from Abby came out with the gum. I opened it and read it to myself:

> *Jack—I think Dr. Terry is going to ask me to marry him in Egypt on our return to the States. I might accept his proposal. How often does a woman get the chance to marry a doctor? I want to do it, but yet I'm confused. I wonder what God wants me to do. Maybe you and I will just have to be good Christian friends. I need some wisdom. Please pray for me. —Abby.*

I was afraid that this might happen. Maybe it was God's will. I just may have to change His mind. There was a segment of good news that wasn't in the note—she never mentioned any love she had for Dr. Terry. The attraction to him was strictly economic. On that issue, I would never have a chance. Time was getting short.

I walked back into the hut. Both Martha and James had regained their composure and were once again talking and laughing.

"Son, tell me about my grandchildren. How many are there and what are their names? Do you have any photos?"

"I do, but how can you see them?"

"I can feel the pictures and you can tell me about each one."

They spent the next thirty minutes looking at family photos, talking, laughing and having a good time. James translated some of what he and his mother were saying.

"What do you do all day, Mom?"

"Oh, I have many things to do—I help with the children, teach the children on Sundays, and I compose songs."

"You do? Can you sing one for me?"

James's mother immediately started to sing a song. The music was a combination of a traditional hymn and the Sudanese style of music. Only the drum accompaniment was missing. The language was Nuer, of course. She had a beautiful voice that was lower in pitch than most of the Sudanese women. After she had completed two verses she again spoke to us. "Many of the hymns the missionaries taught us were written by a blind woman in America. Did you know that, Son?

"Yes I did."

"Her name was Fannie."

She sang a few of the more familiar songs. At the end of each song, James would give me the title and some of the words. Most of them I knew from my youth when I attended the Baptist church back in Missouri.

The man and woman then fixed us a meal of injera with sheep, goat and some other kind of animal meat. I didn't ask what creature the meat was from and didn't want to know. I just pretended it was Iowa beef. The injera was the best I'd ever eaten. It did not have the sour taste.

"Can you stay overnight, Son?"

"Sorry, Mom. I'm not exactly the favorite visitor in Sudan at this time. Our enemies may have a bounty on my head, and nowadays you can't tell who your enemies are.

"You are right there, Son."

Our visit went by fast and it was soon time to go. We spent several more minutes taking more photos of James and his mother. She gave greetings to each of her grandchildren as she held each of their photographs, and to the Sudanese Christians in America.

Finally, they embraced each other, and I did likewise, as we said goodbye. I felt like I had embraced the very hand of God. She was a remarkable and Godly woman. I had a story to tell to Abby and my boys. This would be another on my list of trip highlights. The list was getting longer.

We were soon walking through the town and on our way back to Gabe and Salasie. As we walked, I took some more photos and video images of the town and its people—especially the children. James stopped and greeted many of the people, some he remembered from his childhood.

When we were about two miles up the road, two young Sudanese boys who spoke English stopped us. They informed us that there were enemy soldiers up ahead and it was unsafe to travel. We decided to camp until sundown and travel by night. Some bushes along the road gave us good cover.

The sun went down early and fast. At 6:00 p.m. we took off when it was almost dark. We had flashlights with us, and we made slow but steady progress. James knew the way, even at night. The landscape hadn't changed in the ten years of his absence.

We walked as fast as we could, talked infrequently, and listened to the nighttime Sudanese sounds. In the background was the faint sound of guns going off. We encountered many wild animals, most of them a safe distance from where we were walking. According to James, there were lions, hyenas, deer, many small rodents, and very likely snakes of all sizes and kinds. Both of us prayed quietly as we walked—James in the Nuer language and I in a frightened English.

"Sounds like they're bombing again, Jack. Must be nighttime. The government troops usually strike at night."

"James, do you think there will ever be a peaceful Sudan again?" I added.

"Probably not—not until the Prince of Peace returns. It seems like the war and killing never stops in southern Sudan."

By the time we reached Gabe, it was 9:00 p.m. and he was calmly waiting for us. James and I were soon relaxing inside Selasie from our long walk, and traveling back to Gambela on the winding road. Gabe drove very fast as we wanted to get back before the hotel closed. Both of us needed to pick up our laundry and were dirty, tired, hungry and exhausted. Maybe we could get some food at the restaurant.

It wasn't long before both James and I were fast asleep.

Halfway home, I woke up and looked in the back seat. James was still asleep and seemed to be at peace. He had seen his mother. She was fine and happy, and so was he.

In addition to what we had experienced at Somagowa today, there was what James didn't experience—he never encountered his relatives. He was happy for that, even though he never mentioned it to me. Twelve cows would be free to roam in America or in Africa, at least for a while.

James finally woke up as we came to the edge of Gambela. He remained very peaceful. He was normally very talkative, but tonight he was absolutely quiet. He had just experienced one of the saddest yet happiest days of his life.

When we arrived at the hotel at 11:30 p.m., Abby and Elizabeth were sitting alone on the concrete benches waiting for us. As soon as I opened the door of Selasie, Abby was right there.

"Jack, where have you been? What happened? I have been worried about you. I've been sitting here praying for you."

"What about me? Weren't you worried about me?" James asked.

"Yes, James, I was worried about you, too."

"Have *we* got a story to tell you, Abby! It will be one that I can share with my children and grandchildren someday. It's a long story and we'll tell you later."

James came up to me and gave me a very large Sudanese hug.

"Thank you, Jack, for coming with me. You risked your life

walking into Sudan with me to see my mom. I will always remember you for this."

"I wouldn't have missed this trip for all the Ambo and injera in Ethiopia, and someday we'll get your mother to America."

He next turned toward Abby. "Abby, Jack is a very special person, I hope you know and remember that. I'm praying for both of you, but I'm not going to tell you what I'm praying. I'll let you guess that."

Abby took a deep breath, smiled, and responded with, "I know that, and thank you." Her happy look suddenly turned to an expression of worry.

James and I ate some Nile perch and fried potatoes, along with some Ambo and hot tea. Abby and Elizabeth sat with us and told us about the mission team's day at the clinic. It had been another very busy day.

"You and James were missed, and we could have used your help. We had another busload of patients come in from another refugee camp, with many pregnancy cases. I think we should have brought some birth control pills with for the wives of those who stay in the refugee camps. They're multiplying like rabbits."

"What else is there to do in a refugee camp?" James responded.

James stood up and announced, "Well, my fellow team members, we need to get some sleep. We have a big day ahead of us again tomorrow, so I think I will hit the mattress." Abby and I said "good night" to James as he headed for his cabin.

I thought about the note that Abby had given me this morning, and I know it was on her mind. I wanted to say something to her about it, but something told me that it was not the right time. I decided to bring up some other subject in order to converse. "Abby, how are you doing? How are you feeling? How is the African heat treating you?"

"Hey, one question at a time! I am fine, I feel great, and the heat sometimes gets to be a little too much, especially after just coming from Minnesota in February. I'm glad you asked. I just loved what you did for me the other day with the bottle of cold Ambo. I didn't think so at the time, but now I think it was very kind. Again, I'm sorry for what I said."

"Well, maybe I'm making up for missed opportunities. There'll be more, I hope. After today, I realize that the little things we do or don't do in life are important. They will come back to us eventually—with joy that we did them, or sorrow because we missed an opportunity and didn't take the time to do them."

"This is true."

"Well, I need some rest, too, after walking for several hours in the Sudan desert. I'm going to say good night; but if you will permit me, I'd like to walk you to your cabin."

"You may. Thank you."

As Abby and I walked to our cabins, I took hold of her hand, held it, and squeezed it. She did not return the squeeze, for whatever reason. We were soon in our individual cabins.

The note I would give to Abby in the morning would probably be the most important note I would ever write. It had to be perfectly written and to the point. I stayed up late writing it over several times until I had it correct.

CHAPTER 13

Wednesday—Day 13

M oses opened the restaurant door at 6:30 a.m., as I was sitting in the garden lounge waiting for him. The sky was cloudy, after having produced a severe thunderstorm during the early morning hours. I was just glad that the storm hadn't occurred while James and I were walking through the Sudan countryside. That would have been a muddy mess.

I wondered if the church and clinic or water distribution facility had been damaged. Our medical supplies were in one corner of the church with a guard watching them closely. If any serious damaged had been done by the wind, he would have made it known soon after. No news was good news.

"I see that you are early up as usual, Jack," said Moses with his customary smile.

"Yeah. I guess I just can't wait to get started in the morning. I just hope I am able to continue this enthusiasm when I return to the United States."

"That was quite a storm this morning, wasn't it?"

"To tell the truth, I heard it but slept through it. I was really tired."

"On my way to work, I saw where many trees were blown down by the storm in the downtown area of Gambela."

I sat down in my usual restaurant spot and began to write in my notebook. I had so much to write about after the experience yesterday. The short reminder phrases that I had written could be used to expand our trip into a full-blown story. This is the only way I could keep up with the continuously unfolding events, especially when many of the details were so vital to the story.

This morning it was difficult to write about anything. I was very nervous about my note to Abby, which I had carefully placed in my pocket. Should I give it to her at breakfast or later in private? Maybe now was not the time. Yet I just had to give it to her today, and I hoped that she would come to the restaurant alone or with Elizabeth only.

At 7:15 a.m., everyone else showed up at the restaurant. The doctors and nurses sat down in their usual place. How would I give my note to Abby in an inconspicuous manner or without embarrassing her? I waited for a bit, drank my tea, and tried to think of how I could get it into her hands. Maybe I'll just wait until later in the day; although this was the time we usually passed notes to each other.

I ordered my usual breakfast and gave the menu back to Moses. As I was looking outside, my eyes happened to glance at the ledge of the window. There was a Bible sitting there within my arm's reach. It was Abby's Bible. She must have left it there yesterday.

I glanced over at the rest of the team to see that no one was watching me and quickly placed it on my table. The Bible was in a carrying case and was zipped closed. I carefully unzipped it and placed my note to Abby inside the Bible in such a way that she would get the zipper caught when she tried to zip it closed.

I paged through Abby's Bible. There were photos of our boys, of her and Dr. Terry, of her parents, and of her at work. Noticeably missing was a photo of me. For a moment, I began to feel sorry for myself, until I realized that these were placed in her Bible prior to her meeting me in Frankfurt. How could there be any photos of me? She more than likely had burned any she had soon after our divorce.

When Moses brought my breakfast I whispered to him, "Moses, would you just place this Bible by Abby? Tell her she left it on the window ledge yesterday. Don't mention my name."

Moses picked it up and walked over to the table where the doctors and nurses were engaged in a discussion that had everyone's attention. I watched out of the corner of my eye as he handed the Bible to Abby. She was elated! "There's my Bible—I've been looking for it since yesterday! I thought I had probably left it here at the restaurant. Thank you, Moses!"

She took the white nurses' Bible and started to close the zipper. The note got in the way, just as I had planned. She took the note, opened it and read it. Everyone was busy talking and barely noticed what Abby was doing. I had the note memorized. I closed my eyes and read it in my mind:

> *Abby— I believe that God wants you to consider another option—me.*
>
> *Can you possibly find it in your heart to love me? If and when you do fall in love with me, will you remarry me?*
>
> *I need you. I am in love with you, and I want to make a second attempt at being your husband and the dad to our children. Take some time to decide, but don't take too long. I am praying that you will say yes.*
>
> *I am praying that something will happen that will cause you to make the decision that God wants you to make. —Jack*

Abby carefully placed the note back into the envelope and neatly tucked it in about the middle of her Bible. She zipped up the case very slowly. She momentarily looked over at me. I wasn't looking directly at her, but could feel her head turn. Then she rejoined the conversation at her breakfast table.

She had received my message and proposal, and now she needed to make the second most important decision of her life.

****

The clinic opened at the usual time with the line already formed at the door of the church. Everyone was in his or her place five minutes before our scheduled opening time.

The lines at the Living Springs were also long. It was apparent that the distribution of water had gone on all night. People were coming from all over Gambela to get pure water. The engineers had done an excellent job of designing this system. All those standing in line able to, were reading the Bible verse on the signs that we had placed on a pole in all three languages—"Let He Who is Thirsty Come and Drink of the Water of Life."

The morning was routine with nothing unusual occurring. One man had an epileptic seizure while standing in line at about 10:30 a.m. The doctors knew exactly what to do and the man seemed to understand, as if their procedure had been performed on him many times before. Afterwards, he was a little embarrassed, which showed that even the people of the Nuer tribe in Africa reacted like any other ethnicity of people in similar circumstances. I walked over to the man and gave him two sticks of gum. It brought the expected smile to his face.

The reason the man was in line today was to have the doctors examine his hands. The KNM thugs had cut off his thumbs some six months ago in South Sudan. I motioned for Samuel to come over to where I was standing. "Samuel, what happened to his thumbs?"

Samuel walked over to the man and asked him the question. They chatted for a while, and then Samuel returned to where I was working. "Jack, I told him that you would share his story with the people of the United States."

"I'll do that." I assured him.

"The militia forces cut off his thumbs when he wouldn't renounce Christianity. They killed the rest of his family as he was forced to watch. He sometimes wishes that he had also been killed. He thinks the mercenaries wanted him to suffer with the memory of what he had gone through and of his family being killed. The severed thumbs will continually remind him for the rest of his life."

What remained of the thumbs was healing well, according to Dr. Terry and Dr. Mike.

What was striking about this man was that he didn't seem bitter about what he had gone through. Rather, his demeanor was remarkable and was a reflection of God living inside of him. His horrible experience had made him stronger spiritually.

My question of why these people were so spiritual strong had just been answered—suffering for their faith.

****

For lunch we all decided to go downtown for something to eat. Gabe brought us to a restaurant that was neatly tucked away, in an alley. The name was "Injera Heaven." He knew exactly where it was, and Samuel and James had also eaten there several times in the past. Gabe said the food was very good, and he had never heard of anyone getting sick.

We all ordered injera with sides of goat, lamb, and another baked animal, the identity of which the waiter either didn't know or didn't want to tell us. We also asked for a side order of spicy rice— and I mean spicy. It took two bottles of Ambo to wash it down. My mouth felt like a hot stove.

We all ate our fill and relaxed in the hot sun. The doctors dozed off while the Sudanese talked rapidly and loudly. Later, I asked James what they were discussing. He told me that this was the area that flooded one summer from a tributary of the Baro River that flows through town. Some crocodiles worked their way up the river and onto the streets of Gambela. The government provided a bounty for anyone who killed one. Several men and children were eaten by the crocs during the weeklong flood.

Maybe the unknown meat we ate with the injera was roasted crocodile.

The restaurant had several cats running around and chasing the local tropical birds that were landing to eat the scraps of food dropped during mealtime. "Hey, waiter, I don't see any dogs running around here," Samuel commented.

"Well, there were a couple of strays running around here a few days ago, but somehow they disappeared," the waiter responded.

Samuel's facial expression suddenly tightened up and he quickly looked at the empty plates where only a few cleanly sucked bones remained. Then he looked at each one of us. The doctors had suddenly awakened, just in time to hear the conversation about the dogs.

"Woof! Woof!" Samuel barked. "We have just consumed Lassie

and Rin-tin-tin."

The rest of us gagged and reached for the drinks we were consuming.

"Time to returned to the clinic," Cameron announced.

I needed to make an announcement while I could get the team's attention.

"Hey, guys! Can any of you come over to the Sudanese compounds this afternoon after the clinic closes and give me a hand with a fun project? I'll be going there right after we close." I was about to tell them about the plans for the Hot Wheels race when Dr. Terry interrupted me.

"Sorry, Jack, I need to make a couple of phone calls downtown at the Communications Center. I need to call my stockbroker in Minneapolis before he leaves his house for work. If I have time, I'll stop. Abby, why don't you come with me?"

Abby thought a while and then responded favorably with a nod of her head as she looked at Dr. Terry. Elizabeth then piped up. "Jack, I'll help you."

We piled back into Selasie and headed back to the clinic. I was hoping that I would have more interest from the group. But Elizabeth and I could handle it, along with some of the parents of the children.

****

The mission medical team was very busy during the hot afternoon session, and the caseload didn't allow for any of us to get any type of a break. I was busy running short errands, restocking the medicine bins, carrying fresh water, and passing out gum. The gum seemed to be as important a commodity as the medicine.

I also did some repair work on the church roof from damage caused by the early morning windstorm that had gone through Gambela. One of the other churches in the area had some spare pieces of the corrugated roofing that was the same size.

A man with a severe case of rash on his body was one of our patients. Our doctors were stumped and needed more time to research the rash. They suspected that he had picked it up from some type of tropical weed. The man was asked to return in two days. He was given a tube of a cream ointment to keep the rash from getting any worse, and to help keep it from itching. Apparently, his scratching was making it spread even more.

During the evening, the doctors would be able to access a telephone line in the hotel office in order to obtain medical information from over the Internet. They also conferred by telephone with the doctors in their St. Paul hospital, as well as other hospitals around the USA.

A woman whom Dr. Mike determined was about to give birth to triplets walked into our clinic. She had walked all the way from just across the border in Sudan. Dr. Mike advised her to find some relatives and remain in bed for the duration of her pregnancy. Everything seemed to be normal with her, as well as the three little ones inside her. The woman's husband had been missing for two months from his SPLA regiment inside Sudan. She believed that he was somewhere in a South Sudan prison.

A little Ethiopian boy with a crooked leg from birth limped into the clinic at mid-afternoon. After examining the leg, Dr. Terry said that an operation was needed, but the necessary equipment and facilities were unavailable. This was heartbreaking for everyone, especially the boy's parents. "Maybe we can bring him to Minnesota and get his leg corrected in the near future," Dr. Terry suggested.

The peak of the afternoon came when another pregnant woman's baby decided to come into the world right in the clinic. The birth came easily and soon the little Sudanese girl was crying and lying on her mother's chest. The woman spoke good English and voiced her only concern, "What should I name the baby?

I was close by, so I quickly and quietly walked over to where she was lying on the table. I leaned over and whispered in her ear, "Name your little girl Abby—A-b-b-y. It's the name of the nurse who helped you deliver your little girl. Abby—A-b-b-y."

"Abby is what I will call my baby! A-b-b-y!"

Everyone seemed somewhat surprised except Abby, who had seen me talking to the woman. Cameron took a photo of nurse Abby, little Abby, and the mother.

****

After the clinic closed, Elizabeth and I headed for the Sudanese community to put the finishing touches on the Hot Wheels race-track I was building. All I needed to do was set one end of the 60-foot track on some barrels and find a support for the middle. The track was sitting on a small hill, which provided a natural downward slope for the event. The track had two lanes.

At 4:00 p.m. we were ready to go. I sent out seven little boys and girls to locate other boys and girls in the neighborhood. I needed 300 children to each receive a brand new Hot Wheels car. "Bring back anyone who would like to have a race car. You'll get one, too."

The little children scattered, one of them completely bare-naked.

Elizabeth would be stationed down by the finish line. I would make certain that the starting line ran smoothly. Some of the Sudanese dads were recruited to help with crowd control and to make certain that the lines were orderly.

I estimated that we could conduct three races each minute, or approximately 150 races each hour. I had 300 Hot Wheels cars to distribute. So if everything went smoothly, we could let each child race at least twice during the two-hour session.

Within thirty minutes, there was a mob of little kids around the track. The children also brought their parents and older sisters and brothers. Had it not been for the fact that the racetrack was sitting on an incline—thus providing easy viewing—the crowd would have become unmanageable. A few of the Ethiopian children and parents also showed up.

The cars were not handed out to each child until it was time for their race. Once they received them, I told the children to hold on to their cars—they would only get one. If they wished, they could trade with each other. They were to have an adult help them write their name or initials somewhere on the car. Sharp pointed red ink markers were provided. When I had packed the cars in Indianapolis, I had placed a small piece of masking tape on the bottom or top of each car for just this purpose.

The race went off without a hitch. There was no formal

competition, other than each particular race between two cars. No prizes were given out—just fun. The parents were almost as fascinated by the cars racing down the track as were their children. There was plenty of cheering.

At 6:00 p.m., Gabe and Selasie returned with the two doctors and Abby. They were on their way back to the hotel and decided to stop at the Sudanese compounds to see what we were doing. They all got out and walked over just as the race was concluding. Abby walked up close to me. "Jack, why didn't you tell me you planned to do this?"

I didn't answer. I looked at her and Dr. Terry. "Can you two help me pass out gum?"

Both Abby and Dr. Terry suddenly became willing volunteers.

The race had concluded. The racetrack remained for the children to race their cars for the next several days or weeks, or until the racetrack broke or wore out. Everyone seemed to have had a good time. I had James take a video of the race. I walked over to Abby and handed the video to her. "Here, can you give this video to our boys?"

"I'm sorry about not being here, Jack. Yes, I will show it and watch it with them."

****

We were all invited out to a family compound for dinner a few miles from the hotel. Sudanese cooking was something I had not yet tasted. Maybe we were going to have Ethiopian food prepared and served by the Sudanese. As far as I could determine, the two ethnic groups ate basically the same food.

I was once invited over to James's apartment in Indianapolis for noon lunch, but on that particular occasion his wife served Kentucky Fried Chicken. Some of the women did bring various dishes of food to one church potluck. I had a taste of a couple of them, but I'd never learned what they were or if they were indeed traditional Sudanese cuisine.

The entire mission team was invited to attend. Also invited were some of the pastors who had just completed the prayer conference and would be heading back to Sudan—some in the morning, others in a few days. All were heading back on foot, with some of the pastors walking for two weeks to get to their homes. One particular group of five would be traveling on foot for three weeks and each carrying two bags of medical supplies.

By the time we arrived at the compound, it was completely dark. Gambela's proximity to the equator causes it to become dark very fast once the sun sets. It was somewhat difficult for the team to navigate with all of the people and not much light.

We were treated as royal guests. The men of this compound and other invited church leaders were all sitting on 15-inch-diameter logs that had been arranged into a square. The women were all gathered around three separate kettles with steam pouring out. The fire was burning intensely, fueled by dried cattle dung, wood, or other burnable material. The children were running around, playing, laughing, and having a good time.

I had been told that when the Sudanese refugees came to my church in Indianapolis, the first Sunday in the church nursery was chaotic. The infants were not wearing diapers or underpants and the subsequent "happenings" sent many of the nursery workers into a high orbit. There was gossip and complaining for at least two weeks before it quieted down.

However, there were some nursery workers who became instant nursery heroes and took the floor messes in stride, knowing that each cleanup was a step in reaching out to these newcomers to America. During the week, some of the nursery workers took the time to explain "hygiene in America" to the Sudanese mothers. They taught the mothers how to purchase and use underpants and diapers from Kmart.

Our host and hostess brought out eight steel folding chairs and placed them in a semicircle facing the fires and the log seating section. The air was filled with a combination of smoke and road dust, and the motionless Gambela air made the odor from the fires even fouler. But these dear people are used to it, as much as we in the United States are accustomed to the diesel smell of the buses and trucks.

Our team chatted about the day's work at the clinic. We discussed the rapid use of the medical supplies. "If Jack and Gabe hadn't found those supplies downtown, we would be in tough shape," Dr. Mike commented after a short discussion of the topic.

"Jack, you're a good man," Dr. Terry added. "I'm glad you came on this trip."

This was the first compliment he had paid me. I wondered if he really meant it, as it had been quite obvious to the other members of the team that he and I were after the same woman. I think he thought he had the girl won. He might have thought that, but I was running as fast as I could to the finish line. He was going to be a little surprised—maybe.

It wasn't long before the meal was ready to be served. This was going to be fun. There was not sufficient light to see the food, other than the fires, the stars, and an occasional motorized vehicle traveling 400 feet away on the road. How were we going to see to eat? I questioned to myself. Exactly what were we going to eat? I was sure the other members of the team had the same questions.

We were escorted into a large hut, to an almost-round 6-foot diameter low table made from a 4-inch thick tree trunk slab. We could just barely see it as we were asked to sit down on the floor. There were cushions placed on the floor around the table and cloth napkins on the table.

Cameron asked the question, "How did they cut that slab and what kind of tree is it?"

Dr. Mike added his observation. "Look how uniform the slab is. That had to be one big saw."

A very tall Sudanese woman walked in with a large, clear pitcher filled with what looked like fruit juice. She handed a stack of paper cups to Elizabeth and motioned for her to pass them around the table. The tall woman then walked around the table filling each cup with juice. I tasted my cupful. It was a mixture of several juices.

Three large bowls were set on the table. Candles were finally brought in to provide some light. The entire team was instantly relieved. In the middle of the table was placed a plate of injera.

Cameron prayed and we began eating.

We all ate of the various dishes on the table—not much, but at least a portion of each. I motioned for one of the women cooks to come to our table. "James, ask the woman the names of the food what we are eating." I figured that this would be a diplomatic approach to learn what we had just put into our stomachs. One of the women spoke and Samuel translated.

"A sheep was slaughtered in your honor and has been cooking slowly most of the day. It is on the large plate. You are also eating a Sudanese form of American goulash. It has three kinds of grain in it, several chopped vegetables, and some meat. There is also fish from the Baro River. The third dish is a no-name salad made from herbs, nuts, hot peppers, and a lettuce-type of plant. There is also the traditional injera, with which you are all familiar. The last item you were served was an okra lamb stew."

We all commented that the food was very tasty. Since everything was cooked or boiled, the chances of getting food poisoning was kept to a minimum. We tasted little portions of each of the Sudanese dishes, which made the women happy.

A woman came out with dessert. Abby and Elizabeth each ate a few bites. Dr Terry decided also to have a taste. I declined, as did the remainder of the team.

After dinner, Samuel brought the cooking ladies out and we all gave them a round of applause. We then went around the circle and gave them our names, a short greeting and what we did back in America. Samuel and James took turns translating for us.

I was the last to speak and decided to continue the discussion on a different topic.

"Tell me ladies, do your men ever carry water for you from the Baro River?"

After James translated, there was a flurry of quiet talk among the ladies. I must have asked a sensitive question. A woman answered and James again translated. "Not usually, unless no woman is available in their home or all of the women are sick. The man may even have a neighbor woman or relative carry the water."

The next question was from one of the ladies and was directed at me. "Are you married?"

This was not the question I wanted to answer. First of all, I was married, but not any longer. Secondly, my ex-wife was sitting six feet from me. Finally, would they understand if I told them the truth, that all of this had happened prior to my becoming a Christian seven weeks ago?

My hesitation was awkwardly long. I made a quick look at Abby and she was looking at the ground. I also began to worry about how whatever I said would be translated.

"Let me answer your question like this—I have made many mistakes in my past. I once was married to a very beautiful and gracious woman. Then I divorced her. It was a big mistake and it was before I became a follower of Christ. In getting divorced, I threw away a very precious jewel, a piece of gold, a beautiful and fragrant rose."

After the translation, I stopped for a moment and thought about what I should say next. The crowd was very quiet. They were obviously very interested in this question and were waiting for me to continue. "God is still working with me to rebuild my life, and I will rely on His will."

The woman then asked another question, even more embarrassing than the first. "Is your first wife married again? Would you like another wife?"

All of the women joined in a chorus of laughter. Could it be that they had an eligible Sudanese woman for me?

"No. My ex-wife has remained unmarried, and no, I would not like to have another wife," I responded.

Another woman came back with another question. "Would you consider getting remarried to your ex-wife?"

What an embarrassing question for me to answer! How should I answer? Should my answer be for the woman, for Abby, or for the rest of the team who knew of the triangle soap opera going on between Abby, Dr. Terry, and me? Or, maybe I should just let my heart speak.

"Yes I would, but that's up to her. I may not be good enough to remarry her. I don't have any cows to give her family."

This answer brought on a chorus of laughter. The women seemed to understand that I meant I was lacking in material wealth.

"Are there any other questions for the other members of our

team?" I asked, hoping the questions directed toward me would cease.

A woman sitting to one side directed another question at me. She started to speak, paused, stood up, and started over. She spoke surprisingly good English, and Samuel needed only to translate into the Nuer language.

"I need some advice. The Khartoum Militia captured my husband three years ago. We had just gotten married and we had no children. I have heard that he is in a prison in northern Sudan, but I don't know that for sure. He may be dead. My question is this: should I get remarried, or should I remain as is and true to my husband, knowing full well that he may never return?"

At this point the woman sat down.

The crowd, which by this time had grown to over 100 people, once again became silent. This was followed by a swarm of quiet whispers. The question apparently was the subject of considerable community gossip about the woman. The question was also one that was even more embarrassing for Abby and me.

I wondered how in the world I got to be the expert on Sudanese marriage, divorce, and remarriage out of the clear blue. Why was I being singled out with these questions? I prayed an express prayer, took a swig of my warm bottle of Ambo, cleared my throat, and started to let words flow out of my mouth. I had no idea where I was going with my answer.

"You have two options, which you have already stated: One, get divorced and find another husband; or, two, remain as you are now.

"If you get remarried and your first husband returns, then you have an additional problem—which husband do you choose? What does the law say? What are your customs? If you choose your first husband, what do you do with your second husband? What happens to all of the cows?

"In preparation for deciding what to do, maybe you could find out through the two governments, Sudan and Ethiopia, if your husband is still alive. Maybe the answer will be that he is dead. Give the process a year or two and then make your decision. Above all, ask God to give you wisdom.

"Tell me, is your husband a Christian?" I asked.

The woman stood up again and spoke. "I have some question about that. He may or may not be. I don't know."

She sat down and I pondered this additional ingredient into the set of circumstances.

"Let's suppose that your husband is not a Christian and that he is alive. Now let's further suppose that you get remarried. Who will pray for your husband to become a Christian? Who will pray for his protection in prison?

"If, because of your praying a lifetime for your husband and your remaining unmarried, he becomes a Christian, would it not be worth it?"

The woman shook her head affirmatively.

"Does anyone have a question for our doctors?"

I sat down and the question and answer session finally turned medical. I looked over at Abby and she was staring at the table.

****

On the way back to the hotel, Abby became very sick. The dessert that she and Elizabeth had eaten might have been spoiled. At this point it was only affecting Abby. She continued to be sick for the next two hours. Our two doctors gave her some medicine, but it would not stay down. Even the Ambo she drank would not stay down, which meant that she may soon become dehydrated. On my way to the restaurant, I stopped at the hotel courtyard, sat down, and prayed for Abby.

I mentioned Abby's condition to one of the Ethiopian waiters at the lounge. He wanted to know what she had eaten. I described it as well as I could remember.

"I have just the answer for you. My mom made a tea and gave it to us whenever we got this food poisoning from eating that particular dish. It's the herbs or mushrooms that are making her sick. The tea is made from the root of a small tree that grows down by the Baro River."

"Will you help me make some of that tea," I asked?

"Yes, I will."

The waiter was just ending his shift and we went to the river.

Using a flashlight we found the small tree, dug up a root, and brought it back to the hotel. After washing it good, the waiter used a sharp knife to scrape the root, make a mash and finally dry it in a kitchen oven. Using a clean piece of cloth, I made some hot tea.

I brought the tea to Abby and drank some myself to show her that it would not be harmful. Within 90 minutes she was sleeping soundly. I continued to pray for her.

She needed to be well in the morning to make a trip with Dr. Terry and Gabe. I wasn't pleased that she and Dr. Terry were making this trip, but it was necessary and they would be doing the Lord's work.

Before I went to sleep, I prayed that God would quickly heal Abby of her sickness and order events to His will and glory. I fell asleep.

CHAPTER 14

Thursday—Day 14

W e had a big surprise at the breakfast table. Moses brought in a message left at the hotel office. During the night Gabe had taken off for an undisclosed location for a couple of days. This was okay, however, since we had told him he could do it because our team now had an alternate driver—me. Gabe left Salasie in the parking lot for us to continue using and left the keys in the hotel office in an envelope. We all assumed that he might be staying with a friend in Gambela or another town close by. He was well acquainted with many people in the area.

I ordered some breakfast and began writing in my notebook. So far our trip to Africa had been more exciting than I had ever dreamed. It had been filled with great opportunity to achieve my initial goal—that of helping a hurting world. The goal probably sounded altruistic and even self-serving, but it was my goal.

Being a new and much changed person, I needed something toward which to direct what limited talents God had given me in a manner that was pleasing to Him. After Gambela, I needed to find a new vocation to serve the Lord. But who knows. Maybe God wanted me to remain an auto mechanic; I could tune engines for the glory of God.

My trip goal had been somewhat modified after meeting Abby in the Frankfurt airport. Since this meeting was not by chance but rather by divine design, I now had a companion goal—pleasing

Abby. How exactly this would all come to pass had been the on-going adventure of the past two weeks. I will just try to please the Lord in whatever I do and try to accept however He orders events in my life.

It was just a few minutes later when Abby walked into the restaurant. She sat down at my table, which seemed a bit unusual. She normally sat at the table with the doctors and Elizabeth.

"I feel fine this morning, Jack. What was in that tea that you gave me last night? Maybe we could market the stuff in the United States and make a fortune. I just barely remember you helping me drink it."

"It was from a tree root that grows down by the river. One of the waiters told me about it. We found the tree, dug it up, scraped the root into a pulp, dried the pulp in Moses' oven, and made some tea—all in less than an hour."

"Once I fell asleep, I slept like a log. Thanks for your concern, the tea medicine and tucking me in. I hope that no one else gets sick from whatever I ate last night. Elizabeth is still sleeping."

"It was the dessert you ate, Abby."

"Then I'll bet Terry and Elizabeth get sick, too"

"Well, I've got extra root pulp to make some more tea for them if that happens," I reassured her.

"By the way, thank you for the note and your proposal."

That is all Abby said about my wanting to marry her. Her comment was like she didn't think it was important. But she did mention it; that was significant. I decided that I wouldn't mention it any further at this time. At least she now knew my feelings and intentions, and it gave her a clear-cut decision to make—Dr. Terry or me.

"Jack, I had a talk with James about your trip to Sudan. He showed me some of the video on his camera and told me about his mother. Both he and I cried when we were watching it and listening to Martha's story. I would liked to have met her. What a sad but at the same time happy story."

"She is a very godly woman. For sure, you will meet her in heaven—maybe sooner if James can bring her to the United States."

Cameron walked in, sat down at our table, and ordered come coffee. "It looks like you are feeling fine, Abby. However, Elizabeth and Dr. Terry are now very sick. It seems that they also had a bite or two of whatever caused the food poisoning. Jack, you'd better make some more tea."

Abby was quick to comment on her earlier prediction. "I knew they would get sick. I wonder why the dessert affected me so quickly last night. When I left the cabin a few minutes ago, I thought she was asleep—but maybe she wasn't."

"I'll make some more tea and take it to Dr. Terry. Abby, you take some to Elizabeth."

I walked to Dr. Terry's cabin with a cup of hot tea. He was lying on his bed groaning.

"Hi, Jack. My stomach's a mess. I guess I got whatever Abby had last night. How is she feeling?

"She's fine this morning. Here, have some tea. This will make you well."

"What is this stuff?"

"It's a home remedy made from a tree root that the Sudanese use to cure upset stomachs. Abby drank some last night and now she's fine. Here, I'll drink some to prove it's okay."

I poured some in another cup and drank it to prove it was perfectly safe to drink. I handed Dr. Terry a cupful and told him to stay in bed until the sickness was gone. He might have thought I was attempting to poison him, but most likely that was not the case.

"Thanks, Jack. I'm also having a problem with my back. Do you have anything for that?"

"Not really. Maybe some bed rest?" I suggested in my most "doctorly" tone of voice.

"Just kidding, Jack. Although, my back really is starting to give me some trouble from bending over those tables at the clinic."

"Maybe you should be sitting on a chair more."

Abby brought some of the tea to Elizabeth. She too was reluctant to drink it, but Abby talked her into it. Elizabeth could see Abby's remarkable recovery from her previous night's gastronomical disorder and eruption.

****

Now we had a problem. Abby and Dr. Terry were scheduled to go with Gabe to a small village beyond the Gambela National Park soon after our clinic closed for the afternoon. They were to conduct some first-aid training for the Sudanese and deliver some medical supplies. They were to travel west out of Gambela toward the Ethiopian/Sudan border, drive to the village of Yelwah almost on the border, and stay overnight. They were then to return in the morning.

Cameron and I met back at the restaurant and discussed the trip and who would go in place of the people now unavailable.

"Jack, you'll have to drive in place of Gabe. Abby can handle the training alone, with your assistance, of course. You'd better get packed and all set to go. Leave about the time the clinic closes this afternoon; maybe before, if we aren't too busy. You'll need to make sure you get to the village before it gets dark. Samuel has a map drawn up showing the location of the small town."

"Sounds good, Cameron. I'll make sure that Selasie is all gassed up and ready to go. How are the roads up there?"

"Supposedly good, but who knows for sure? This sickness sure does put up a roadblock in our plan, but somehow I believe God is in it."

There were some dangers in making this trip since we would be only a few miles from the war area. Cameron figured it was worth the risk, however, since there were a lot of hurting people in this village because of the war. Wounded people were coming into the small village every day and hiding in the compounds. Fearing that the Khartoum militia would attack the village, some of the wounded and their families hid in the nearby woods.

The war had not yet spilled over into Ethiopia, but the Ethiopian military presence in Gambela indicated that the Ethiopians were monitoring the border activity for just such an incursion. The KNM didn't want that to happen, since the Ethiopian army would then drive them back up to the north and leave a safe haven for the Sudanese Christians.

We were not expected to treat any injured at the village. Our task was to take several bags of medical supplies to a makeshift medical clinic and teach some of the people how to treat wounds. My assignment was to get Abby there and back safely. The total weight of the medical supplies was around 200 pounds, all of which I purchased from the downtown businessman.

The drive was supposed to take about two hours—a distance of 40 miles. The roads were supposed to be good. Of course, that's what we had been told about the road from Addis to Gambela.

****

Our clinic opened with only one doctor and one nurse. Samuel and James worked as nurses, and Abby did the work of Dr. Terry. I recruited another Sudanese man and woman to help with the in-take registration. Everything seemed to go smoothly, and our one doctor and one nurse being ill provided the opportunity for the Sudanese to receive some clinical experience. It also gave Samuel and James some on-the-job training as nurses, which was what they were planning to be in a few years. One of the young Sudanese mothers helped with the pregnancy cases. She spoke very good English.

The soda pop boy continued his three-times-a-day delivery of fairly cool refreshments. After the last delivery of the day, I walked over and checked out his bike. One of the nuts on the front wheel had become slightly loose and needed tightening.

I walked to Selasie, fetched a spare adjustable wrench that I had in my toolbox and walked back inside the clinic. I gave the wrench to the young lad and told him to tighten the nut.

"Now, you may keep the wrench. When I leave Gambela in a few days, you can fix your own bike."

"Thank you, Jack!" he grinned.

Abby was standing close by and intently watching us. I looked at her as the delivery boy was preparing to leave the inside of the church. I wondered what she was thinking. I could only guess as we never have time to talk about it.

****

At 3:00 p.m., Abby and I prepared to leave for our overnight trip. The team gathered in a circle at the clinic and joined hands as Cameron prayed.

As he was praying, I remembered the dream I had. The question that the old man in the dream asked me had been on my mind almost constantly—"Are you willing to die for Abby?" Was the dream some sign of a coming disaster? If so, what, where, and when would it happen? All during the prayer, I had my eyes opened and fixed on Abby.

I answered my own questions: I was willing to do whatever was necessary, at any time, and at any place, to preserve her life. My love for her had become that profound. I felt this way, even though I knew that her feeling toward me was not mutual and may never be. Abby was, foremost, my Christian sister. But in God's sight, I believe we were still married. In either relationship, I needed to protect her from whatever dangerous situation may take place.

As Cameron got near to the end of his prayer, Abby suddenly opened her eyes and looked intently back at me with the feeling that someone had been staring at her. We continued to look at each other until Cameron finally said "Amen," a period of 10 seconds.

We packed a dozen bottles of water, several bottles of Ambo, some trail mix, and a few energy bars. Since we were not sure of our sleeping arrangements, we loaded up our mosquito tents, blankets, and pillows from our cabins. Abby also brought some cans of bug repellant.

As we left the church and drove on the road leading to downtown, Abby was quiet. I sensed that something was on her mind, and I was pretty sure I knew what it was.

"Abby, I need to say something to you. We need to keep our minds focused on this trip, so let's not discuss our relationship. It's very much on my mind. I'd love to talk to you about it, and we will at some time soon. But, right now, we have an important mission to think about. So if you don't mind, and I'm quite sure you don't, let's discuss other things as we drive. Is that okay with you?"

"That's fine, Jack. Thank you! You are so thoughtful and understanding."

We took off out of Gambela, crossing the Baro River at exactly 3:30 p.m. The road was not too bad for the first few miles, but then it became almost impossible to drive on—covered with rocks, potholes, and even fallen trees. The road was narrow in long stretches and just barely wide enough for vehicles to pass each other. Dust was mixed in with the rocks; and because our speed was only 30 mpr the wind caused the dust to sometimes catch up with us. It was nerve-wracking, but we had no choice. We needed to get to the village before the sun went down.

I decided to begin a new subject and "talk shop."

"Abby, I wonder if there's support in our Covenant churches for a permanent medical clinic in Gambela."

"Well, I think if a medical clinic were in Gambela, there would be many professional medical people in America that would love to take off a month and work in it. They could even bring their families, especially if they could stay at the Ethiopian Hotel. And if they would volunteer every four to six years, it could be staffed on an ongoing basis. It would just be a matter of scheduling. What do you think, Jack?"

"It would also provide a place where the youth groups in our churches could go for a mission trip."

"Maybe we could suggest and organize such an ongoing mission outreach."

"Abby, I wish to nominate you as the chairwoman of the Gambela Covenant Medical Clinic Board," I said with determination and authority. "How does that sound?"

"Sounds like work. I can have the tea concessions."

"The big obstacle would be from the Ethiopian Government. It wouldn't take much political or religious opposition to have the clinic shut down." Then I changed the subject and asked, "How does your stomach feel, Abby?"

"I'm fine. My stomach's fine."

"I wonder how Elizabeth and Dr. Terry are feeling."

"They're probably eating a full meal by now."

"It's interesting how this mini trip has worked out for you and me."

Abby didn't comment."

****

It was about 5:30 p.m. when Selasie suddenly began to sputter.

He was losing power, as if he wasn't getting enough gas. I was an expert at identifying a car's ailment from the sounds underneath the hood. Our vehicle finally came to rest at the bottom of a hill. We were still a few miles from our destination, according to our hand-drawn map.

I turned off the ignition and it became unusually quiet. I sat and looked at the steering wheel for a few seconds and then turned and looked at Abby. We were deep in Africa, on a strange road, with car trouble.

"What is it, Jack?"

"I don't know, and it isn't going to be good. It's the fuel pump or somewhere in the gas line. It sounded like the gas just quit flowing. I'm going to get out and take a look."

We both got out of the vehicle and looked around. We were in a heavy jungle area which was divided by the recently constructed road. There were weeds and vines all the way up to the edge of the rough and rocky road. The jungle was thick, and I could only imagine the kinds of wild animals lurking within to devour us.

I opened up the hood and removed the air cleaner cover from over the carburetor. I could see that the motor was not getting any gas. However, the air filter was still clean from our stop on the way to Gambela from Addis Ababa. That eliminated that possible cause.

"What are we going to do, Jack? Can you fix it?"

Just then, a large truck drove by and interrupted Abby. The truck was piled high with sacks of grain of some type. There were four men in the cab of the truck and six Ethiopians riding on the sacks of grain. Soon it was gone, leaving a huge continuous cloud of sickening dust.

"What do you think is wrong?" Abby asked.

"I'm going to crawl underneath and have a good look at the gas tank and gas line. You get inside in case another car or truck drives by. We need to find the problem fast; it's going to get dark very soon."

Abby jumped back into Selasie and I crawled underneath. It wasn't long before I was able to determine the problem: A rock must have rocketed up from the tire with such force and with such accuracy that it crimped the gas line and cut off the gas flow. The crimp was in a difficult place to reach.

I heard another vehicle coming up the road. As it came closer, it began to slow down. I quickly crawled out from under Salasie and stood up. When the driver saw me, he started to speed up again. I opened my door and jumped in. Had we not been in the vehicle, the driver and his riders may have attempted to rob us.

"What is it, Jack?"

I could tell from Abby's voice that she was scared.

"Here's the deal, Abby. I need to make a repair to the gas line underneath. When that's done, we'll be able to travel on. That's the good news."

"So what's the bad news?"

"The bad news is we'll have to wait until morning to make the repairs. The crimped section of the gas line is in a very hard-to-get-to location. I'll need all the light I can get, and it'll probably take me more than an hour to repair. In about thirty minutes the sun will go down, and it gets dark almost immediately. If we work on it here on the road, we will be sitting ducks for a robbery, or even worse."

"So, what do we do tonight? Where do we stay?"

"Abby, guess what. You and I will be sleeping right here. Except, not right here."

"What are you talking about?"

"An abandoned vehicle on this road is an invitation to be burglarized. One could expect nothing to remain until morning. They may even try to pull Selasie down the road with a chain or a rope, or even a thick strong vine."

"But we'll be inside. They wouldn't do anything then, would they?"

"They may kidnap us. That would be even worse. Selasie is expendable—we're not."

"Shhh—Jack, Selasie will hear you."

"You're right. Sorry, Selasie."

"So what are we going to do?"

"We need to get Selasie off of the road."

I got out, walked to the edge and then up and down the road. I was looking for a spot to move Selasie into the jungle. The sun was about to set; and once it set, the combination of our proximity to the equator and high forest density would make our location shadowy within minutes, followed by complete blackness.

"Abby, we're going to have to move Selasie in among the trees. I'll give you a push and you steer. When I give the signal, turn the steering wheel clockwise as sharp as you can. When you feel Salasie hit the brush, straighten out the wheel and let him keep moving so that the front of Selasie is about six feet beyond the edge of the brush."

"Jack, I don't know if I can do that."

"You'll do just fine. I have all of the confidence in the world with you," I assured her.

Abby stopped and looked at me. "You know, that is the first time you've said that to me."

"I'm very much aware of that fact; but, rest assured, I'm not just trying to get on your good side. I mean every word of it. You can do it."

I moved to the front of Selasie and pushed. Abby gripped the steering wheel and looked right at me. I had made a mark on the road to tell me when it was time for her to turn the steering wheel. Selasie was on a slight roadbed incline, which made it easy to push and establish some momentum.

Our vehicle moved faster and faster down the slope. At the precise moment, I gave Abby the signal to turn the steering wheel. She turned it perfectly, and the speed of Selasie provided enough momentum to back it into the jungle brush so that is was almost out of sight by at least three feet.

I walked down the road toward our vehicle, squeezed into the brush, opened the door, shook Abby's hand, and crawled in. Abby slid over to the passenger side.

"You did brilliantly, Abby." She beamed. "Now, we need to do one more thing before it gets totally dark."

"What's that?" she asked.

"We need to cover the front of Selasie so that no one can see him from the road. Also, I need to cut down the growth underneath so we don't have to do it in the morning. We still have enough time before the sun goes down."

"Here, Jack, put on some of this bug repellant. It'll keep us bug-free for the rest of the night."

"A good idea. Abby, you're a genius!"

"No—I'm just following good health procedure. Here, let me put some on your neck and shoulders, and you do the same to me."

It seemed like we took longer to apply the repellant to each other than really was necessary. I enjoyed it and I hoped Abby's thoughts were the same. But maybe it was my imagination, or just wishful thinking.

We both worked fast and furiously for the next ten minutes. I sawed bush branches off with my Swiss Army knife saw blade, and Abby pulled and piled them onto the front of Selasie. When we were done, we both jumped inside and shut the door. It was now completely dark outside—and even darker inside. I hung my tiny flashlight by a string on the mirror for use during the night.

I grabbed a bottle of Ambo, opened it with my knife bottle opener, and gave the bottle to Abby. She took a big swallow, followed by another and another. Finally, she gave the bottle to me. I drank the remainder.

"We will need to keep the windows shut to prevent the mosquitos from entering. Other than that, we'll just have to talk. Are you okay, Abby?"

"I'm fine, as long as you're here."

At that moment we both had the same idea. For the next ten seconds we were locked in an overdue embrace. It was the first time in years this had happened. It was spontaneous and real. There seemed to be a great measure of forgiveness that flowed from and to both of us. Maybe it would lead to more.

The wall of ice had crumbled to the ground, was fast melting, and soon to disappear.

As I was closing the window, I stopped and everything was quiet. I heard something out of the open window.

"Shh!"

"What is it Jack?"

"I hear guns!"

"Guns? What do you mean, guns?" Abby asked, noticeably alarmed.

"It's dark and I think they are attacking the Sudanese villages again."

"Who's attacking what villages?"

"The Khartoum militia—the militant thugs. I was told they are in this area. I was also told that the Nuer forces are engaging them more and more every day."

Abby became very still. Then all of a sudden, she started to shake—just a little at first and then with increased intensity. At first I thought it might be the effects of food poisoning from the previous day still lingering in her body. Dr. Mike had no idea what the poison in the food was and was unable to determine it, since there was no laboratory to check any culture.

I took Abby in my arms and just held her. It was then that I realized that her shaking was from her being hot, the feeling of being stranded, and being just plain scared. I had to do something to take her mind off of the situation that we were both in.

Here we were, in the jungle in Africa, our vehicle broken down, hiding from potential robbers on the rough road, and a war going on only a few miles away. No wonder Abby was shaking. I felt the same anxiety.

"You're scared, aren't you Abby?"

"I'm petrified, Jack," she said as she started to sob. I needed to do something to calm her down. I never thought we'd get into a situation like this.

"I have an idea that will take our minds off of the situation we are in. We're going to be here for the next ten hours. Let's make the best of the time—one that will be memorable. Let's pray and then we'll sit and talk about anything that you want to talk about. When you run out of things to talk about, then I'll talk. At some point, one of us will fall asleep."

"For whom do we pray? Us?" She asked.

"For our sons, for our mission, and yes, for each other and ourselves."

"That sounds like a great idea."

"But, we need to whisper," I answered.

"Why?"

"The mosquitoes, the wild animals, and the people walking on the road, may all hear us."

For the next hour, Abby and I took turns praying for each of our three sons, for each other, for our mission, and for the Sudanese. After that we talked about Abby's parents, her work, Cameron and the problems that his wife was having, and a variety of other topics. One topic led to another. We sat close to each other and whispered.

We started at about 7:30 p.m. and continued until 10:30. I looked at my watch. We were all talked out. The time seemed to fly by.

"Jack, may we talk about your proposal?"

"If you wish."

"I need some wisdom. I don't know what to do. You seem to have wisdom. Can you give me some?"

"No, but God can. Ask Him. Abby, I made a promise with God after I met you in Frankfurt—I wasn't going to let anything interfere with our mission trip. I was going to remain focused on what we came to do. Having said that let me say this: I cannot go through one hour of the day without thinking about you. But as great as my desire for you may be, I cannot change your heart. I cannot interfere with what you and Dr. Terry may have planned. I will only say that you need to make sure that your decision is based on love and not on economics or the stock market. I can't give you dollar bills—only love. That's all I want to say on the subject."

Abby was quiet all of a sudden. She knew what I was talking about. She placed her head on my chest. "Thank you, Jack."

There was a noticeable pause for a couple of minutes. I finally looked at Abby. She had fallen asleep. The whispering for three hours and the sudden relative coolness inside Selasie made her tired.

A peace suddenly surrounded us and there was a sense of protection—like what a baby must feel being in a mother's arms. God was with us inside Selasie. His angels were protecting us. I could feel it.

I also sensed that this feeling of peace and protection was going to be needed for what we may face in the morning and during the day.

I was ready for anything, especially with and for Abby.

CHAPTER 15

Friday—Day 15

Abby slept from 11:00 p.m. until 7:00 a.m., and I from midnight until 5:00 a.m. Then I was wide-awake and for two hours I sat with Abby in my arms, her head resting against my chest. Did she realize that she was so close to me? She might have, but she probably also figured that the alternative was to be against the passenger door, which was locked, but next to the jungle outside. I wanted to believe that she felt comfortable in my arms for another reason; she was falling in love with me.

During my sleep I could hear motorized vehicles driving by. The wild animals, rodents, crawly things, and people walking on the road, all provided sound to my short dreams. Since we were concealed solidly within the thick Ethiopian forest and with the front windshield covered by branches, it remained very dark inside Selasie. The sky may have been clear during the night and early morning, but I was unable to verify it.

Abby woke up as I had just finished removing the branches from the front of our vehicle. I looked at my left watch—it was 7:15 a.m. Our jungle camouflage of Selasie had been successful. I crawled back into the driver's seat. Abby was stretching and yawning.

"Good morning, Abby. Did you have a good sleep?"

"I had a wonderful sleep. Where am I? Never mind, I just remembered. What time is it?"

"It's 7:15 a.m."

"What is our next move, chauffeur?"

"We're going to fix the crimp in the gas line. I'll need you to hold the flashlight and hand tools to me. But first, let's eat some breakfast. Do you want your eggs over medium or well done?"

"I want them well done—like yours."

"Hey! You remember."

"Of course I remember how you liked your eggs, and you still do."

"You've noticed." I said, moderately surprised.

"Yes, and you've added Ambo and hot tea to your breakfast items. When did you start drinking tea? You never did when we were together, Jack."

"Time goes on, people change and new habits form. I began when I first saw you drink tea at the McDonald's in Frankfurt."

"It's nice that you copied me, but why?" Abby asked.

"I'll let you figure it out. Let's have an energy bar, some trail mix, and a bottle of Ambo."

"Sounds good."

I bowed my head and began to pray. Abby reached over and grabbed my arm with both of her hands.

"Lord, only You know what this day will bring. We are going to trust You to bring us protection, good health, wisdom, and especially courage, as we first fix Salasie's gas line and then go on to the other tasks of the day. Continue to be with our mission team back at the clinic and our sons in America—Amen."

"Amen, Jack."

We began eating what would be our main meal until we returned to Gambela, whenever that would be. There was a possibility that our hosts at the small village would provide us with a meal, but we weren't expecting it since their own food supply may not be enough to feed their own people, in addition to the war victims.

"Can you fix the car, Jack? Don't answer that, I know you can."

We continued to talk while we ate.

"It shouldn't take over an hour to fix the gas line. Then we can be on our way. How long will your first aid class be?"

"About two hours, without a question and answer session," Abby answered.

"Will you have someone to translate for you?"

"They're supposed to have a Sudanese pastor by the name of Paul who will translate from the Nuer into English, and vise versa. I just hope his English is good."

"How do you feel this morning, Abby?"

"I feel fine. I was really scared last night, wasn't I?"

"Yes you were. I was too, if it makes you feel any better," I assured her.

"Well, I'm just glad I wasn't driving alone. Thanks for being here, Jack."

"I wouldn't have had it any other way—for all of the injera in Ethiopia. It'll be another highlight of our trip."

"You mean that we'll be experiencing more and greater happenings?" she asked.

"Yes indeed."

"How do you know?"

"I dreamed it." I answered.

"Oh! Now we're into dreams, are we? Tell me about it."

"I can't just now, or it will scare the pants off you."

"Then you better not tell me. Maybe later."

We finished our breakfast and I was about to exit Selasie, when Abby suddenly took my arm. "Jack, let's put on some more mosquito repellent before we get out. There may be some little creatures where we are about to crawl—some crawling or flying bugs."

"I think it will repel any snakes, too."

"Thanks, Jack! I needed that!"

Abby and I helped each other put repellent on our arms, face and hands. I reached into my pocket for my knife and felt a pack of gum. I opened a pack, gave a stick to Abby, and took one for myself. We had no way of brushing and refreshing our teeth and the gum would have to serve as our morning dental hygiene.

We both got out of Salasie and crawled underneath. I had a small automobile repair kit that I had put together a few years ago for just such a time as this. I never dreamed I would use it half way around the world.

Using a miniature hacksaw, a piece of plastic tubing that fit tightly over the gas line, and some electrical tape, I was able to make a good splice. It was in a difficult place to get at, and it would be a temporary fix until I could do a more permanent job later. Abby was my assistant, handing me the tools I needed and holding the small powerful flashlight. The repair job took less than two hours.

"This didn't take as long as I thought it would. It's possible that we may have been able to fix it last night, but I wasn't sure. I'm glad we waited, Abby. We had some very special moments together that I will always remember, no matter what happens between you and me. God was in our midst last night."

"He indeed was," Abby responded.

We were soon traveling on to our destination, only a distance of five miles. The directions that Samuel had given me to the village were not real clear, with many jogs and turns. The village was off the main road, and at times it seemed like we were traveling in circles. I just hoped we didn't get lost when we exited the town.

When we arrived at the village, the people were waiting for us with the women singing as we drove into the compound. The Sudanese pastor, David, introduced himself to us.

"We were worried about you last night. We figured something had happened to your vehicle or that you had gotten lost." Pastor David spoke good English.

"We did have some mechanical trouble, but Abby and I fixed it."

I unloaded the bags of medical supplies, and we carried them into a large hut that was serving as a clinic. There were many injured people lying on the dirt floor, rugs and grass.

There would be no notes passed between Abby and me this morning. It was Abby's turn. She needed to answer my marriage proposal. My offer to Abby only hours before was very timely. I was more in love with Abby than ever before after last night. I felt that she had some feeling for me, also. God was at work!

There was a real struggle going on inside of Abby. It could be that Abby was trying to determine a way to give me a negative answer. I was afraid that she had already made her decision to marry Dr. Terry.

If only I had saved all of the money I'd spent running around before I became a Christian, then I would have something to offer Abby. I didn't even have a job when I returned to the States. I'm sure this was weighing heavily on her mind and a big factor in the decision she was contemplating.

The name of the village was Yelwah. I'm not sure if it had a meaning in any language. It was difficult to estimate the population of the town, but it appeared to be very small and, according to Samuel, was normally peaceful. But today the atmosphere was tense. Even the birds seemed to be chirping a different and somewhat subdued song. The anticipation of a possible attack on these unarmed people was very evident.

Yelwah was just inside Ethiopian territory. Most of its citizens were Sudanese, with a few other ethnic peoples mixed in with its population.

Abby began her class in "First Aid and the Treatment of Gunshot Wounds" soon after we arrived. The latter topic was really Dr. Terry's expertise. The class was composed of twenty men, women and young people. Pastor Paul translated from English to the Nuer language, and vise versa when it became necessary. His English was very good.

I used the extra time to check over Selasie. I took photos of the small village and its people and of Abby teaching her class. Abby was good at teaching first aid, and her students seemed attentive and eager to learn.

There were many wounded people in the village; and although I was not required to treat anyone, I had the time. I used my own first aid kit, which I'd brought along. The people were lying or sitting on a grassy area next to and inside the clinic hut. Some of the wounds were not easily treatable, and I had to pick and chose the easy patients who needed only cuts covered with ointment and a Band-Aid. They were all supplied with Jack's special medicine—a stick of gum. For some of my patients, this was probably the best first aid I could give them.

A little Sudanese girl took my hand and led me to another close-by hut where four adults were lying on the ground, all with high fevers. In looking at their wounds, it was apparent that the fever was caused by gunshot still in their bodies. I was in the hut looking at the wounds when Abby walked in. She had just completed teaching her crash class.

The little girl took both Abby's and my hand and led us over to a corner of the hut. There, lying on a rug on the ground, were twin girls about the same age as our small tour guide. The little girls had been shot in the legs and shoulders. They both appeared to be unconscious. "Pray for them," the little girl pleaded as she begun to cry.

It was more than Abby could take, and she started to weep as she hugged the little girl. I prayed for the twin girls as Abby knelt down and examined them to determine the extent of their injuries. My prayer was short.

"Abby, we need to bring these people back to Gambela to our clinic. If we don't, they will die for sure, won't they?"

"Yes they probably will, but do we have room for them? The people in my class told me about them"

"We'll make room," I answered her.

With help from some of the men, we carefully loaded the two men, two women, and twin girls into Selasie. They were very fragile, thirsty, and probably hungry. Abby also recognized this condition.

"Lets give them a drink of Ambo and see if they will eat a piece or two of an energy bar."

Our patients were dry and appreciated the liquid refreshments. The energy bars seem to perk them up.

"Jack, the townspeople warned me, we need to be careful on our way back to Gambela. The war is beginning to spill over into the border area, and the KNM are in a hostile mood.

I asked the Sudanese pastor, some of the townsmen and women, and Abby to join hands around Selasie while I asked God for healing and protection. I also asked God to keep the six people alive until we arrived at the clinic in Gambela, where the gunshot could be removed from their bodies. Abby squeezed my hand tightly for the entire duration of my prayer. I sensed that she was once again worried and had a feeling of threatening danger. I did too.

We found a bucket of river water that had been boiled and cooled overnight. Abby would need to move from patient to patient cooling off their bodies with a wet towel. Some of the war victims were barely conscious.

A thin, elderly Sudanese man wearing a gray hat, green shorts, a white tee shirt, and using a walking stick hobbled up to us. He was barefoot. He slowly placed his hand on my head, took Abby's hand, and prayed a short prayer in the Nuer language. I asked Pastor Paul what he had prayed.

"His prayer was quite interesting. He asked God to send down seven special angels to protect you. He asked specifically for seven angels and repeated it three times."

I thanked the elderly gentleman and shook his hand. In his hand I placed a Swiss Army knife, and then slowly closed his hand around it. He opened his hand as he looked down at the shining new red-handled knife. He looked at me and smiled.

It was time to go. We bid farewell to our new friends and drove off. As we exited the town of Yelwah, I turned to Abby. "Abby, are we having a good time yet?"

"Jack, we are having a meaningful time, and that's good. I can't think of anywhere on earth I'd rather be than here. I'll be glad when I get back home, of course. About the only thing we haven't run into yet is a big snake."

"We have a few days to go. Maybe snakes are next."

"Thanks!"

"Now I know why God wanted me to come to Africa. At least one of the reasons."

"What's that?"

"To be your chauffeur. I just hope I can find my way home."

On our way out of the village, I must have taken a wrong turn. I was very quickly lost and at a point where I couldn't find my way back. I tried but only became even more lost. Within five minutes, I started hearing the faint sound of guns out of my opened window.

Suddenly I realized we were in Sudan—I was sure of it. I said nothing to Abby, and I don't think she even sensed that we were lost. She was busy with her patients, washing their faces and bodies with water in an attempt to lower their high temperatures and trying to get some bottled water into them. It was difficult for her to maneuver inside Selasie.

All of a sudden a plane flew over us, not very far above the car. I quickly drove off of the road, through a ditch and into an open field of grass.

"What was that noise, Jack?"

"We need to get everyone out as soon as possible. Next time they will shoot at Selasie and probably kill all of us."

"Who will shoot at Selasie?"

"The militia thugs from the Khartoum government. That was their plane that just flew over us."

"How do you know it was their plane?"

"Who else would be flying a plane a few feet over our heads in this remote part of Sudan? I don't think they have any crop dusters here."

We drove through the field, found a large tree, drove under it, and carefully, but hurriedly, removed our critical patients onto a grassy area of ground. I then drove Salasie 200 feet further under another larger tree, parked it and ran back to the patients and Abby. The long grass was hiding our position.

"Jack, maybe they won't come back."

"Don't count on it—they'll be back."

It took only two minutes, and we heard the sound of the same plane coming closer and closer. They saw Salasie and fired. Incredibly, all of the shots missed our vehicle. They were either very poor shots or God somehow deflected the bullets. I tend to believe the latter.

We continued to sit quietly with our patients. It was hot and not yet noon. Today it would be a scorcher in Sudan. But the way things were unfolding, we may not be in Sudan much longer. We could all soon be in heaven. I was scared, but not as much as I would have been had I not gone to a basketball game some eight weeks earlier. I was no longer afraid of dying, just the painful moment or two in getting to that point—or merely thinking about it.

We frantically sat waiting for something to happen, desperately hoping nothing would. But that wasn't to be. Within five minutes, two trucks were sitting between Salasie and us. The doors burst open and eight semi-uniformed men along with their leader got out. They were dressed in gray shirts, black pants, and red berets.

They quickly had Selasie surrounded with their rifles pointing at him. These men were all a lighter-skinned Africans, except for one very black Sudanese. The group had apparently recruited a member of the Nuer tribe. I wondered what they were giving him in return.

Maybe they had his family held hostage with the threat of torture.

One of the militia walked over to Selasie, opened the door, and looked inside. After he saw that there were no people inside, he said something to the militia leader. The leader looked around and suddenly spotted our group hiding in the grass. Within a few seconds, they had us surrounded. The leader spoke. "Americans! Stand up!" His English was good, like a person educated in English.

Abby and I quickly stood up.

"Everyone stand up!" he repeated his command.

I quickly responded to the leader's demand in a clear but frightened voice: "These are patients that we are taking to Gambela to be treated. They can't stand up. In fact, they are almost dead. What do you want with us? We are not your enemies."

"We intend to kill you—all of you."

Abby quietly gasped and quickly grabbed my arm!

My heartbeat immediately accelerated. I was terrified! I quickly asked God to calm me down. I didn't know how to respond to a death threat, but I needed to respond promptly and boldly. I took a slow, deep breath and suddenly recalled my dream—the answer to the old man's question that I had not answered at the time. Within seconds I had calmed down and felt a sudden sense of confidence and purpose. I faced the militia leader.

"Well, let's talk about your wanting to kill us. Our patients are very sick and may die anyway, so to shoot them would only put them out of their misery. They won't suffer and that's not what you want. Isn't that what you people are all about—inflicting pain and suffering on Sudanese Christians?"

"You're right. So we'll just kill you and the woman and let the others just die. Or maybe we'll just kill you and take the woman with us to be a slave—maybe even our slave. She should bring a good price."

I took Abby's hand and squeezed extra hard. She was trembling. I placed my arm around her and pressed her tightly to me. She seemed to relax a bit.

I suddenly had acquired a new boldness, resulting from a reservoir of stored up prayer. I was feeling it flooding down upon me.

God was with me, and I could physically feel His presence and power. I looked squarely into the eyes of the leader of the band of mercenaries with my arm tightly around Abby.

"So let's talk about that, also. Let me inform you that this woman is a very famous nurse from the United States and is on a medical fact-finding mission to Africa. Her name is Abby Olson and I'm her driver. Our officials in Gambela are expecting us to return before noon today. If she doesn't return, they may send in many men to find her."

"Why is she so famous? I've never heard of her."

"Have you ever heard of Mother Teresa?"

"Yes, I have. She's not Mother Teresa. Mother Teresa is dead."

"I know that Mother Teresa is dead. She lived in India, among other places. Miss Olson, here, is from the United States, and she is the Mother Teresa of Minnesota. Haven't you ever heard or read about the great things Abby Olson is doing in Minnesota and in parts of the rest of the world? And now she's doing good work in Africa. I think you should be glad for her work. You're African, aren't you?"

"I'm African, but I'm not impressed."

"Also, if our officials come to get us and find any evidence of violence, they will spread the news on CNN. Then all the rest of the media will catch the news. Next, the whole world will know what the Khartoum National Militia is really doing in South Sudan— killing Christians. Do you want that?"

The part about CNN was a little far fetched, but it sounded good. The pockmark-faced enemy leader stood expressionless for a moment, like he was contemplating what I had just said.

"No, we don't," he replied to my question.

"Then I suggest that you take me and leave Miss Olson to care for her patients."

"Hey! I'm giving the orders here. Are you a Christian?" he demanded to know.

"Yes, I am."

"If you renounce Jesus and Christianity, I'll let all of you go."

"No! I will not renounce Christ or Christianity. In fact, Jesus is here with us."

"I don't see Him. Where is He?"

"His Spirit is standing in front of me and is in me."

The leader stepped back and spoke to one of his men. Then he turned, walked over to me, and hit me on the side of my head with the back of his hand. A ring on his finger caused a cut on my cheek. Reaching up with my hand, I felt blood. I retrieved my handkerchief and pressed against the wound.

"Okay, you come with me. Your nurse friend, Mother Olson from Minnesota, can get going back to Gambela with her patients."

I took Abby's hands in mine, looked directly into her eyes, and spoke to her for the benefit of the soldiers and their leader to hear.

"Good-bye, Miss Olson. You'll have to drive the vehicle back to Gambela. You should have no trouble. Just stay on the main road. Say good-bye to everyone from me."

I winked at her, gave her a quick embrace, and kissed her on the cheek.

Abby just stood there with a white, blank look on her face. She couldn't believe what she had just heard me say and the meaning of it—that I was willing to take her place and be murdered for her. What was in my heart for Abby, had just came out of my mouth.

I whispered to her, "Quick, Abby, put two Band-Aids on my cheek."

The leader of the mercenaries stood there permitting Abby to proceed. She reached for her medical supply kit inside her bag, selected two large-sized Band-Aids, whiped off my blood with her shirt, and gently applied them to my still-bleeding wound. As her hands touched my face, I could feel them trembling.

The dream once again came back to me. I could almost see the old man standing in front of me. My answer to him was clear in my mind and was about to happen.

"Get going!" the militia leader blurted out.

"Abby, you'll need to get going, quickly."

We needed to get the patients into Selasie. I walked back to our trusty vehicle, got in, and drove it to where the patients were lying on the ground. I got out, turned to the soldiers, spoke, and made motions. "Can you fellows help us get these patients back into our vehicle?"

"Jack, what are you doing? Why does this have to happen?" Abby whispered in an almost hysterical tone of voice.

"Abby," I whispered back, "Pray! Pray! Pray! Tell our patients to pray hard. God will get us out of this. He has more work for you and me."

"But what if God doesn't save you and you are killed?"

"Then God will be glorified, I'll get to see Jesus that much sooner, you'll have something good to tell our boys about their dad, and you'll go on living your life."

Abby looked over at me and suddenly was overcome with emotion. Tears streamed from her lower eyelids down her cheeks. I again whispered to her, "Abby, don't cry over me. I'm just your driver. They may see your concern for me and kill you along with me."

The mercenaries helped load the patients back into Selasie. Abby climbed into the driver's seat and I started the engine. She turned to the patients now sitting in our vehicle, some of whom were unconscious and the rest with high fevers.

"Pray! Pray hard!" she said.

The militia led me over to their trucks and laid their guns on the ground. Abby sat in the driver's seat with the motor running. She was preparing herself to witness the most gruesome act that she would ever see—the taking of a human life, possibly by means of some type of torture.

I looked over at her and saw that she was now praying, her head resting on her folded arms in the open window of Selasie.

Everything suddenly became quite. All that was audible were African birds flying and chirping in the air, oblivious to the violence that may be about to take place.

My entire life flashed before me. It was like a giant mural hanging in the sky. Then for a split second I became light-headed and my mind went blank, probably from a combination of the heat and fear.

The militia soldiers took out their knives. I had never seen such an assortment of wicked-looking instruments in my life. They were obviously handmade torture weapons, probably used many times in the murder of many of my Sudanese Christian brothers and sisters.

With my heart racing I again looked over at Abby, probably for the last time. She was still praying, with her folded hands still resting on the door. The KNM leader was waiting for her to drive away. The atmosphere was tense. Something was about to happen.

I was ready to die. Not just an ordinary death, but also possibly a slow and extremely painful death—like thousands of the two million Sudanese Christians who had died before me. I was ready to "meet my Maker," like the secular world sometimes phrases it. I could feel God's presence as I stood waiting for something to happen.

Maybe this was God's way of providing Abby with the solution to her dilemma of whom to choose for a new husband. God would permit me to go to meet Him. At the same time, I would be able to provide the ultimate proof of my love for Abby.

But I didn't really believe that I was about to die. I was sure that God would get us out of this predicament. He had more work for me to do down the road, and I wanted to do it. More than that, I was available to do it. He would just have to produce a "ram in the thicket." I remembered that from a story taught in my Sunday school days as a child.

The eight soldiers stood there waiting for their leader to give the attack signal. Maybe the mercenaries would get some sadistically emotional high from the cutting of my flesh. They seemed to be excited. I saw the very presence of evil as I looked at their eyes.

The leader walked over and took out a whip from a box attached to one of the trucks. He slowly strolled over to where I was standing. The handmade whip in his hand was obviously used as a tortured weapon. Each of the four plastic ropes had a piece of sharp steel fastened on the ends. I knew what was coming next, and I fearfully anticipated the impending pain.

I looked at Abby and she was now almost in hysterics, having momentarily ceased her praying. I felt sorry for her having to go through this ordeal. I wished that she would just drive off.

The leader stood ready to hit me. "Wap!" The hit was in the area of my lower back. I felt the steel cut through my light blue tee shirt and into my flesh. The only reaction I showed was grimacing from the pain. The leader drew back for another hit. My eyes returned to Abby. She was now looking at something in back of me.

Then something amazing happened. All eight of the soldiers

and their leader began struggling with themselves and their sharp weapons. It wasn't long before they were accidentally cutting themselves and each other. There was an atmosphere of mass confusion. What in the world was happening?

I quickly glanced over at Abby. She had stopped praying, had a smile on her face, and had her arms up in the air outside of Selasie's window. She quickly stepped out of the driver's seat and onto the ground. She was now clapping with her hands. I wondered if she had gone crazy or if maybe the heat had gotten to her.

The militia leader stood there with a frantic look. He drew his handgun and began to fire randomly, hitting nothing. He soon ran out of ammunition. The leader unexpectedly gave the command for everyone to get back into the trucks. Soon the small contingent of mercenaries was gone from the scene.

I stood there for a few seconds, not believing what I had just witnessed. I ran back to our vehicle, hugged Abby, jumped in, and hastily prayed out loud, "God lead us back to Gambela safely!"

Abby ran around to the other side, got in, and we drove off. She sat quietly with her mouth wide open. Finally, she couldn't contain herself. "Jack, who were those men and where did they come from?"

"I don't know, but they are all gone now, and I hope their trucks are a long way from here. Those thugs looked mean! Did you see those sadistic knives? I wonder how many people they have tortured or killed with those knives?"

"Jack, I don't mean the militia soldiers, I mean those other men."

"Abby, what other men are you talking about? They were a bunch of murderous thugs."

By this time we were back on the main road. I had my sense of direction once again.

"Jack, you didn't see them? There were seven of them. I counted them. They just appeared from nowhere—seven tall and very black Sudanese men."

"Abby, what on earth are you talking about?"

I was quiet for a moment. Abby wasn't speaking clearly and must be having a post-stomach-ache delusion of some sort.

"Jack, you must have seen them."

"Abby, let me tell you what I saw. You then tell me what you saw."

"Okay, I'm listening," she said.

"I saw seven soldiers try to cut themselves and each other to pieces. Then, their leader shot his gun in rapid fire, running out of ammo. Finally, they all just climbed back into their trucks and left the area. Now, what did you see?"

At that point, we passed the driveway to the village of Yelwah, where we had been only an hour before. It was obvious that we had taken the wrong turn when we left. We were now on the right road to Gambela—another answer to prayer.

"Jack, here is what I saw: "Eight soldiers and their leader surrounded you. They dropped their guns, drew out their knives, and were set to kill you. The leader started to whip you, applying only one swipe.

"Just then, seven tall Sudanese men wearing yellow tee-shirts ran from in back of the trucks and started to wave their hands like they were directing the final passage of Beethoven's Ninth Symphony. They must have caused confusion in the minds of the soldiers.

"The leader drew his hand gun and fired at the seven tall Sudanese men until he ran out of bullets. His gun clicked several times. He then gave the command and the militia jumped back into the trucks and took off. The seven Sudanese men walked toward the wooded area and just disappeared."

I looked at Abby and didn't say a word as I slowed our vehicle. She wondered what was wrong. I finally stopped Selasie and turned to her. "The prayer of the old man, back at Yelwah, what did that old man pray?"

"What?"

"When the man with the green shorts prayed, what did he say?"

"He said, 'Lord, send down seven angels to protect them,' or something like that." Abby's last words slowed and her stare at me became frozen.

"Abby, you have just seen seven of God's angels. You are positive about what you saw?"

"Yes I am."

"Seven?"

"I counted them twice, Jack."

"You must be a very special person, Abby. I didn't even see them."

We embraced each other in joy for a short while. Our joyful session was interrupted by a little voice in the back seat. "Can I have some Ambo?"

We both broke out with laughter. Abby gave both of the little girls a drink of Ambo.

"Jack, move forward and let me see if the whip hurt you."

I moved forward against the steering wheel to let Abby examine my back. She pulled up my tee shirt.

"Uffda, Jack. There are cuts on your back, and I need to put something on them. One can only imagine the bacteria on that whip."

"Let's wait until we return to Gambela."

"No, you let me put some disinfectant on them and stop the bleeding. Here, keep your shirt up and face the door. The cuts are on your lower back, and they need a stitch or two."

Abby applied a generous amount of Bactine to the cuts with a cotton ball, which stung slightly. Then she applied a large Band-Aid over each of the four cuts, even though they had not stopped bleeding.

"Here, Jack, place your back against this towel on the back of the seat to soak the blood and help stop the bleeding.

"Abby, you've experienced a very rare occurrence today— seeing angels from heaven. Do you realize the importance of that?"

"Jack, I experienced something much more important and meaningful today than seeing angels. *You* are the special person. Are you aware of what you just did for me? Do you know what happened today?"

"Yes, I do. I just got my butt beat and my face slashed!"

"You offered to give your life for me. That's something that every girl dreams of. How many girls have had that happen to them? Why would you do that? After the way I have talked about you on this trip, sometimes ignoring you and making you feel small."

I kept looking out the window at the road and didn't give her an immediate answer. When she had finished putting the medical supplies back into her first aid kit, I turned to Abby. "I think you know why. I love you. Now you know the extent of that love."

She turned her head straight ahead, looking at the road. She had no response as we once again took off for Gambela. What had just happened was about to make Abby's decision more difficult than ever. We both sensed it.

"Jack, who is going to believe us when we tell them what happened today?"

"Our sons will. My friends will when I tell them. Most of all, you and I will believe it because it happened to us. Others may not believe us."

"If I can remember all of it."

"Abby, take this tablet and pen and write down every detail you can remember from the time we left the village of Yelwah until now. Write what you saw, how many, the times, the atmosphere, what everyone was wearing, what everyone said, etcetera. Write everything that you can possibly remember. I will do the same tonight."

****

We arrived back at the clinic at 3:00 PM. Abby and I sat in front of the church for a moment, quietly reflecting on what had happened in the past few hours. I reached over, took Abby's hand and began to pray:

"Lord, we give You all of the glory for what happened today. Thank You for being with us and sending down Your angels to protect us. I thank You for letting me be with Abby on this trip and for the opportunity to let me prove to her that I really do love her. Help us to know how to share this story so it will give You all of the glory.

"Be with the critical patients in the back seats of Selasie, and may Your healing hand be upon them—Amen."

I tried to release my hand from Abby's, but she continued to hold mine tightly for a moment. Her eyes were fill with tears, but without her smile.

"Now, let's get medical treatment for our friends in the back," I abruptly said.

We unloaded our patients and Dr. Mike and Dr. Terry immediately began to remove the bullets and administer antibiotics. From the clinic, the patients were moved to some of the compounds close to the church. The doctors and nurses would need to make more house calls in the next few days, prior to our leaving.

Once our critical patients were removed from the clinic, Abby led me by the hand over to an empty table, carefully took off my tee shirt and began further treatment of my wounds. Two of them were deep, and Dr. Mike stitched the cuts as Abby assisted him. He also gave me a couple of injections.

Dr. Terry noticed us and walked over to where we were. The rest of the team also decided to take a break and join us. Dr. Terry asked, "What happened to you, Jack?"

"Jack will tell you later," said Abby.

Abby turned and walked out to Selasie where Gabe was waiting. I soon joined her and we headed back to the hotel restaurant where we had a late lunch and rested for a two hours.

****

I woke up at 6:00 p.m. My back was sore from both my stitched-up cuts and from driving in a forward position on our trip back to Gambela. I quickly fetched some items from my suitcase, and walked to the restaurant. Moses was there and I gave him the items along with some special instructions.

As I entered the restaurant at 7:00 p.m. for dinner I asked Moses, "Is everything in place?"

"Yes it is. Everything is all set."

At dinner Cameron came to me. "Jack, I received this note at noon today. I have no idea where it came from."

"What did it say?"

"Here, I'll read it—it's short.

Jack in danger in Sudan—8 + 7 men involved—vehicle returning to Gambela.

"Is that it?"

"That's all there was to the note."

"Let me keep it."

After dinner, just as everyone was ready to leave, I stood up and made an announcement. "May I have your attention, please? Since this is one of our last nights in Gambela, I thought it would be nice to celebrate. But what do we celebrate? Surely, we cannot celebrate the work we have done these past two weeks—there's so much more to do. What we have seen and heard about what is going on in Sudan is something to actually grieve about."

I took a few steps toward the kitchen. "Moses, come out with something to celebrate!"

Moses suddenly appeared with a birthday cake, complete with lighted candles. He carried it over to where Abby was sitting and set it on the table in front of her.

"Happy birthday, Abby," Moses said with a big smile on his face.

Abby was shocked.

"Oh, my gosh! I forgot it's my birthday today. Jack, where did you get the cake?"

"Someone from my church sent the mix with me. The candles were provided by Moses."

We sang "Happy Birthday" to Abby, ate the entire cake, and had a good time. James and Samuel sang a Sudanese birthday song.

Neither Abby nor I said anything about what had happened. However, the rest of the team sensed that something miraculous had happened during the day. Abby and I would need to tell them. They had seen the cuts on my back and were very curious for an explanation.

****

After what had happened in the past two days, I wasn't sure if I was ready for any more excitement. The heat, the stress, and the driving of Selasie had rendered me physically and emotionally exhausted.

What had happened today was something that I would never choose to go through ever again. At the same time, I was glad that it had happened to me. It spoke very loudly to Abby.

My Christian relationship with Abby had grown. We had become a team to do God's will, if only for a few days. Now, if only I could convince Abby to extend that teamwork to a lifetime relationship, and in a romantic manner! I thought she might be close after today. She knew of my love for her.

Her bitterness toward me seemed to have vanished. The wall of ice had melted completely. Now she needed to be convinced that a lifetime relationship with Dr. Terry might not be the best option for her and our sons. My biggest fear was that she had already promised to marry him.

I prayed that something would happen quickly that would finally convince her to break any promise to Dr. Terry, turn her heart toward me, and give me another chance.

CHAPTER 16

Saturday—Day 16

The night was peaceful, and once I fell asleep I had a good rest. I must have slept at least eight hours. If the usual Gambela night and early morning sounds had been present, I was totally unaware of them. Since my back was still sore from the whip cuts and Dr. Mike's stitches, I had to sleep on my stomach. Maybe that's the reason for my restful night.

Nightmares should have filled my night. I couldn't believe I was able to rest without thinking about almost getting murdered inside of Sudan. God had protected us and I was spending some time thanking Him when He put me to sleep. That was 10:00 p.m.

The experience that Abby and I had been through starting 24 hours earlier somehow seemed insignificant compared to what our Sudanese friends had gone through for decades. True, we had the scare of our life. But we were not harmed, other that a few whip cuts on my back and a ring slice on my face. A debate was going on inside of me whether or not I should even tell my Sudanese friends about what happened to us in their country.

I could only speculate what the eight KNM mercenaries and their leader told their buddies after their encounter with seven of God's angels. They are probably just now sending a communiqué to "be on the lookout for seven tall Sudanese men wearing yellow tee-shirts—stay clear of them!"

I decided to make my way to the restaurant for some breakfast, although I wasn't very hungry. The coffee Moses brewed would taste good, and it would be a good way to start out the day.

Moses had become my best friend living in Gambela. Maybe he and his family could visit America some day. Our friendship could extend across the sea, and we could become life-long friends.

"Hey, Jack! I missed you yesterday. Where did you go?" Moses asked as I walked into the restaurant.

"I had to take a little safari a few miles from Gambela."

"Was your trip successful? Did you have a good time?"

"I would say that our trip was successful, yes. And yes, we did have a good time—maybe too good. It was exciting—maybe too exciting."

"Did you get to see much of the countryside, Jack?"

"As a matter of fact, I was able to see more than I really wanted."

Moses knew where Abby and I had been.

"What'll you have this morning?" he asked.

"I think I'll have some very well-done scrambled eggs, without onions, a cup of hot tea, a pitcher of hot water, and a cup of coffee."

"That's what you have every morning, Jack. Does your order ever change?"

"One morning I ordered a cup of coffee, a pitcher of hot water, a cup of hot tea, and well-scrambled eggs, without onions."

"That's the same order, only backwards."

"I know and I just love the way your chef fixes the eggs and how you fix the coffee."

I had just finished ordering when I looked toward the entrance. Abby was walking in with Elizabeth. They strolled over to my table, and Abby sat down across from me. Elizabeth reached down, took my hand, and kissed it. Then she gave me a big hug. "That's for saving my friend Abby's life yesterday—not only saving it, but actually offering your own life to save hers. What a story!"

Abby had apparently been talking to Elizabeth and had told her all about our ordeal in the Sudan countryside. I expected her to do that, since Abby said she was going to enter all that she could remember into her laptop, and Elizabeth was probably present.

"Well, Elizabeth, let me tell you about Abby. She is a real

prayer warrior. You need to kiss her hand, too. She saved my life. I don't think I have ever been more scared at any time in my entire life. But all of a sudden, God gave me a boldness that is not humanly possible in such a situation. I attribute my state of daring to prayer—with Abby doing the praying."

"Well, you two should talk. I'm going to the other table and have some nourishment."

Elizabeth walked over to her regular table and sat down. The two doctors were already seated and had ordered breakfast. Dr. Terry looked over at us and wondered why Abby was not sitting at his table and was talking with me instead. He had no idea what had happened on our medical trip to the border of Ethiopia and Sudan. Maybe he thought we had some unfinished business to take care of concerning our trip.

On the other hand, he had to know something was brewing between Abby and me. I could feel it, especially by Abby's answer to Dr. Terry's question at the clinic about what had happened to my back.

"First of all, Jack, I want to thank you for the cake last night. I'd forgotten about it being my birthday. That was very thoughtful of you. I didn't think you remembered."

"Well, we can remember things if we really want to. Birthdays are important. Besides, you deserved it after your nightmare yesterday. I just hope I can share your birthdays for the rest of your life, as well as our sons' birthdays."

Abby looked at me for a moment in deep thought. Then she began on the other subject that was very much on both of our minds. "Jack, I sat down last night and typed out in detail what happened yesterday. I can't believe it. Was it a dream? No person is ever going to believe us when we tell our story. I stayed up until 2:00 a.m. telling and retelling Elizabeth what had happened. At first she thought I was telling her a big tale. The more I retold the story, the more she believed me."

"I think only Christians will believe it. Maybe we should keep it quiet for a while, at least until we arrive back in the United States."

"I think you're right, Jack," Abby stated.

"Abby, I want you to know I'm glad you were with me yesterday.

You inspired me to try to get us out of that mess. I know that God was the person who really got us out alive, but you were there, Abby, and you have become my inspiration."

She looked at me for a few more seconds, smiled briefly, and then looked over at her usual table where Dr. Terry was sitting. Her facial expression gradually became solemn.

"Life sometimes gets complicated, doesn't it? The choices we have to make are not always easy."

"Follow your heart, Abby. God will cause something to happen that will make the choice easy."

I let her sit and think for about a minute. Neither of us said anything as we stared in opposite directions.

"Thanks for your understanding, Jack," Abby said, finally breaking our silence.

"Let's join the others," I said as I suddenly rose up from my chair. "I've changed my mind. We need to tell the team what happened while it is still fresh in our minds. They need a full report of our trip, and especially, what happened on the second day."

We pushed the tables together and had a short meeting, and Abby and I related the full story. The team sat quietly as first I, and then Abby, talked. We were already late for the opening of the clinic day, but Cameron also thought it would be best to relate our brief incursion into Sudan. Cameron was busy taking notes.

We told them about our trip to Yelwah, about the old man praying for us, and about him asking God three times to send us seven angels. We told them how God had delivered Abby and me, how He permitted me to talk with confidence and firmness to our captors, and about the angels who appeared as Sudanese men fighting for us.

"What was really evident to me was the fact that once I got through the initial being-scared-out-of-my-wits stage and had asked God to deliver us, my fear was completely gone. I talked to the soldiers in a calm, bold, and confident manner."

"What do you think happened to you?" Dr. Mike asked.

"There was no doubt that God put the calmness and boldness in me. It's probably the same thing that happened to Daniel when he faced the lions or when David was about to slay Goliath. Who knows? Daniel and David may have initially been shaking in their sandals like I was shaking in my boots.

"But I really think Abby was the real warrior, daring to pray calmly and with great faith in the midst of such imminent danger. I also felt an additional force. I believe it was from others around the world and their prayers—like you folks. There had to have been a reservoir of prayer for the Sudanese Christians that all of a sudden produced a giant flood. Abby and I were the recipients of that stored up prayer. I could feel it."

I glanced at Dr. Terry. He had become quiet and was staring out of the window.

"We were definitely praying for you," Dr. Mike responded.

"How did it feel to sleep in Selasie for twelve hours in the jungle and in the midst of wild animals and a war going on?" Elizabeth asked. "What did you do to occupy your time?" Abby quickly answered these questions.

"I don't know about Jack, but I was scared like I've never been scared before. We prayed for a couple hours, talked and talked and talked, and then fell asleep."

Cameron then asked the most probing question of the session. "Jack, were you really willing to give your life to save Abby's?"

I didn't think Cameron would ask such an embarrassing question. I was ready to answer it. He was asking the question for the benefit of Dr. Terry—and especially Abby.

"Yes, I was. Anyone else? I don't know—maybe not. But for Abby, yes, indeed."

"Why?" Dr. Mike asked.

I couldn't believe that Dr. Mike would ask why. I was being put on the spot. I wasn't prepared to give all of the reasons, especially the most important one—at least in front of the rest of the team. But maybe I should.

"There are several reasons. One of them is the fact that Abby is the mother of my sons, and they need their mother probably more than they need their father."

I paused for a moment wondering what my next words should be. Maybe my pause would cause the cessation of this line of questioning. The team took the hint. Cameron came to my rescue. "Well, I think that should do it, and it would be best if we kept this story quiet, at least while we're in Gambela. The main reason is that the three involved governments would never allow us to be going into Sudan. Our church surely wouldn't look at it too kindly, either. On the other hand, not everyday do we see angels.

"And that brings me to another reason. A person who claims to have seen angels is sometimes viewed as being a holy person or as a certified nut case. Our Sudanese friends may even try to make Abby into a saint. They can do that after we return to the USA if they wish, but not while we're here.

"I'm sure that all of you will be sharing this story when you return to your churches. Just make sure you retell it exactly the way we've heard it this morning. Abby has detailed it on her laptop. Maybe she will print out a copy for each of us," Cameron concluded.

"I need to share one more thing." I paused while every one quieted down. "I think we need to make sure we give God the glory whenever and wherever we relate this story to people. He is the One who delivered Abby, me and the patients throughout the day."

"I agree, Jack," Cameron responded.

As we were talking, Moses came in with a message for me. I opened the envelope and read it. It was a telegram from my media friend I had talked to in the airport in Addis Ababa. He wanted me to call him in the U.S. He wanted to know if I was the person who had come upon an accident on the freeway near the airport in Indianapolis on February 16. He said that the man on the video looked just like me. It seems that "a person happened to be standing on a footbridge and got the entire rescue segment on video. He missed only the actual car rollover itself."

The note concluded, "I remembered the hat that you were wearing had 'YELLOW' printed on it and Not everyone has a Yellow Freight hat."

I folded the note and placed it in my pocket.

****

I walked over to the church through the Sudanese compounds and visited with many of my new friends at their places of residence. Once again, my little friend David was playing by himself. I walked over to him, reached down, and shook his hand.

"How are you doing, David?"

He was sitting on the ground playing with his very dirty ball. As he got up, I could see that he was hurting. "I'm fine," he said in a nearly inaudible voice.

He wasn't fine. He was wearing a white shirt full of holes. I looked closely at it and noticed that there were a couple of small red bloodstains that had soaked through. I could see bruises through two of the holes in the shirt. I had an idea that I would find him in this situation, and this time I decided to get fully involved.

I lifted up the right side of his shirt. He jumped away from me, but not until I saw that he had apparently been hit several times on his little back.

I quickly left him and ran over to the church to get James, Samuel and Abby. I wanted a nurse to be there as well. We walked back to the compound to where David was still playing. James walked up next to David. "Can I see the marks on your back?"

"No."

"How did you get those marks?" James continued.

Little David remained quiet, looking away from us. I pulled out some gum.

"How about some gum for a look at your back?"

"No!"

"A whole package of gum?"

David waited for a brief moment and then reluctantly agreed. Five sticks of gum were more that he could resist.

It was quite obvious that someone had beaten the little boy several times with a rigid object, tearing the flesh. It had probably been done with a branch of a tree. There were also places where old wounds had healed over. I turned to James and Samuel and said, "Someone is using this young man for a whipping post. Do you know the parents?"

"Yes, we do," James answered. "This is a difficult situation for the Sudanese. This type of thing goes on occasionally and is frowned upon, but the community leaves it for the parents to handle. Therefore, it is hardly ever brought up and almost never resolved."

"That doesn't make it right," Abby added.

"No, it surely doesn't. So, Jack, I wonder what the best way to handle it would be," James said.

"Let's start by taking the boy and his parents over to the clinic and have the doctors examine him. Abby, take little David's hand, and we'll walk over to his home."

James knew the parents since they all came from the same town in Sudan. We took David over to his home and confronted the parents. James spoke in the Nuer language and translated into English for the benefit of Abby and me.

"How did David get these marks on his back?" James asked the little boy's father.

David's father at first denied what was clearly a case of child abuse. He was an elder in the church, and this fact made it a very touchy situation. I spoke up. "Let's all go over to the clinic and have the doctors look at David's back."

The wife stood nervously in the background and just looked at the ground, indicating that she knew fully how the marks got on little David's body. The father suddenly became very edgy and tried to give reasons for the marks on the boy's back. None of us paid any attention to him. Meanwhile, the mother began to cry.

We all walked over to the church. I went inside and informed Dr. Terry and Dr. Mike of the abuse situation. They left the church and took David and his parents into a small open hut some 100 feet away. James went with them to translate for the doctors. Samuel, Abby, and I stayed in the church and continued discussing the abuse situation.

"What will happen next, Samuel?" I asked.

"The doctors will meet with the elder board and the parents and give them a report. Then some action will be taken. I'm scheduled to give the sermon next Sunday morning. Guess what I am going to speak on! I just need to organize the Bible verses that pertain to what I will say about abuse."

"Little David needs to be protected from his father's frustration," Abby suggested.

"I'll make sure that a young couple stays at their compound for the next few days." Samuel said.

"Both the father and mother need some heavy counseling,"

Abby added. "She may also be abused but is not telling anyone. Unfortunately, this is something I see all too often in my line of work."

****

We could see the lines of people waiting for fresh water at the Living Springs. The water purification system and supply was more than sufficient to handle the needs of the people within a one-mile radius of the church and even beyond. Since the flow continued 24 hours a day, many people were now scheduling their trips to the fountains during the night. This made for shorter lines during the day.

The engineers were continually monitoring the water's purity, the flow, and usage. They also watched the clinic and the patients as they were waiting for treatment. On many days, the engineers would conduct tours for visitors from other third-world countries who were interested in obtaining a similar system for their town or country. Our clinic was a stop on this tour. Many of the potential buyers said that the clinic and the water distribution system worked very well as companion ministries. We agreed.

****

Saturday at the clinic was no different than any other day. In fact, we seemed to be busier. Our method of moving the cases through the clinic had been a success and was very efficient, thanks to the hard work of many Sudanese men and women volunteers.

Most of the patients were new, with almost everyone having an ailment or physical problem that was common and easily treatable. Some of the adults and children merely wanted to have their wounds re-bandaged and more ointment applied on their cuts, scrapes, or infections.

Some of the children just wanted another stick of chewing gum. Fortunately, my 5,000 sticks of gum had not yet been exhausted. Had I not developed a method of identifying the "gum patients," my supply would have run out. Many of the young boys and girls were just out grazing for more gum. I had their number.

****

It had been unusually hot during the day; and when the clinic closed at 5:00 p.m., we all voted to get something cool to drink. Gabe drove all of us to Eman's restaurant in downtown Gambela. Eman, who pronounced his name as "E-man," was a 60-year-old Ethiopian. His name was short for Emmanuel—"God is with us." His restaurant wasn't very big, but was always clean and well staffed. At any given time, there were all ethnicities of people eating and drinking. Eman had somehow found a way to keep his beverages very cold in hot Gambela.

Although this establishment had good food, it was noted more for its bar. This didn't make me feel comfortable, and I was certain it made Abby feel very ill at ease.

Abby and Elizabeth were seated together on a short bench. The doctors were sitting close by on lawn chairs. Abby was particularly quiet and in deep thought. She had not yet answered my marriage proposal, and I could tell that it was weighing heavily on her mind.

Cameron told me that Dr. Terry had finalized his proposal to Abby. His proposal was accompanied by a time and place in an Egyptian hotel in Cairo. Since he was from a family of considerable wealth, and had communicated this fact to Abby several times, she was under much pressure to accept his proposal. She needed to give Dr. Terry an answer, also.

I only wanted for Abby to be happy and for God to have His will accomplished in the lives of everyone involved. She had asked everyone's advice, including mine, and now the decision was hers and hers alone. I had given the matter over to the Lord and promised Him I would trust His will.

We all ordered something different. I decided to mix Ambo with Miranda Orange soda pop. The nurses stuck with the Miranda Orange only. Cameron and the Sudanese ordered Cokes.

The doctors surprised me, and maybe others on our team, by each ordering a bottle of Ethiopian beer. My personal view of the good doctors doing such a thing was not positive, since I'd had a problem with drinking in my past. If the doctors knew this, they may not have ordered the beer. It was their business, of course; but because this was a mission trip, I felt it was inappropriate for them to do so. They apparently thought differently.

I glanced at the other members of the team to see what their reaction was. Abby was noticeably disturbed by Dr. Terry and Dr. Mike's action. She and Dr. Terry looked at each other. The look from Abby was not positive. For some reason, Dr. Terry seemed to not care.

We consumed the drinks as if we had lacked liquid for days. The waiter soon came back and took an order for another round. I ordered some hot tea to drink. The doctors were the last to reorder and decided on another round of the same beer.

I decided to make a statement. The doctors had no sooner voiced their order when I spoke out to the waiter, "Cancel my order!"

I stood up, said nothing, left five birr for my share of the beverages, and quietly and quickly exited Eman's restaurant. My departure was noticeable and it spoke a thousand words.

I walked down the crowded street until I came to a small shop selling grains and many different coffees, all of which were displayed in open sacks lined up on the ground. I bought three small bags of different Ethiopian coffee beans to take back to the U.S. and roast in an oven. As I walked out of the shop, I noticed Abby walking toward me. She was trying to catch up to me. "I've been looking for you. May I walk back to the hotel with you, Jack?"

"You may. I would be honored."

We started walking and I took Abby's hand. She held mine tightly. Her grip was communicating a message—like she was angry and confused.

She didn't say a word all the way back to the hotel. Her pace was slow and I followed. It was a long way back—very hot and dusty—and the animal and human traffic seemed greater than normal. At about midway to the hotel, I stopped at a restaurant in a small hut to get a bottle of Ambo. We shared the cool liquid and continued our walk.

We passed many people, some of whom we recognized from the clinic and in our visits to the Sudanese compounds. Abby wasn't in the mood to do any greeting, so I did it for the both of us.

I think Abby's bubble had just exploded. She had made a decision weeks ago that she would marry Dr. Terry. Now she was questioning the wisdom of that decision. There had been a battle going on inside her mind. I knew that the conflict also involved her heart.

We were soon at the hotel courtyard. I walked her to her cabin and said nothing. The walk back to the hotel had been very hot and exhausting for both of us. She walked into her cabin and shut the door.

I went up to the hotel and sat down on one of the lawn chairs in the garden lounge area. The waiter approached me and asked if I wanted something.

"Give me Diet Pepsi and a hot tea."

"Sorry, we don't have any Diet Pepsi."

"That figures. We're in Ethiopia, aren't we?"

"Could you send a bottle of Ambo and a bottle of Miranda Orange to cabin eighteen? Make sure they are as cold as possible. Just bring me a tea. But bring the Ambo and orange to cabin eighteen first."

"Right," the waiter responded.

Abby needed to drink some liquids.

Even before the waiter brought my tea, Cameron and Elizabeth walked into the garden lounge and decided to join me. I found two more lawn chairs and set them around a table. Cameron opened the conversation by asking the obvious question. "Were you a little upset at the doctor's imbibing?"

"To say the least, yes, I was. But I think Abby was even more upset."

"She was *very* upset," Elizabeth joined in.

"Let me tell you something about Abby's background. She comes from a family of teetotalers. Her great-grandmother was a member of the WCTU, the Women's Christian Temperance Union, back in South Dakota. She was a leader in that movement for many years. Abby had a Sunday school teacher who gave her the secret of 'never becoming an alcoholic.' He told her to never take the first glass. This is why she never drinks alcoholic beverages."

"You're kidding us," Elizabeth responded.

"She never told you that?"

"Come to think of it, she's never ordered anything but Diet Coke when we've been out to eat. I do remember we were served wine at a hospital social function last year. She set the glass aside and drank water instead. At the time I never thought much of it. I suppose that when she and Dr. Terry have been out to eat, either out of respect or for professional reasons, he never orders any wine or other strong drink. Maybe she never told him about her total abstinence."

"You don't drink, either, do you, Jack?" Elizabeth asked.

"That's correct. I did eight weeks ago, but I will never again take any alcohol to my lips. I had a problem with it in my former life, and now I have three boys to set an example for."

"I guess now you and Abby really are a pair," Elizabeth said.

She stopped speaking and suddenly looked at me.

"That's how I am praying," I responded. "God will have the last say. He causes things to happen."

"What do you suppose is on her mind right now?" Cameron asked.

"I think she may be rethinking her future plans as we speak." I said.

"Maybe tomorrow will tell the story," Elizabeth added.

CHAPTER 17

Sunday—Day 17

The day started out with a scream and a bang—literally. We were all sleeping soundly at 3:00 a.m. in our cabins. A violent storm had whipped through Gambela at about midnight and the power had gone off. Our windows were open, and the air was now still. The clatter from the noisy fan was not keeping us awake, the rain had silenced the Sudanese drums, and it was not yet time for the roosters to start their morning racket—"calling all hens of Gambela." It was nice and peaceful.

First there was the scream! That woke me up in our cabin. It may have also awakened the other team members and nearby hotel guests. The scream seemed to come from some female guest next door.

The next sound was a volley of yelling in the Amharic language between a man and a woman. An object hitting a window and the breaking of glass was quickly followed by a shot from some type of gun.

It was only a matter of ten seconds and the sound of boots hitting on the concrete walkway was heard. The stomping was getting closer and closer, coming from many directions, until they all stopped next door. I unzipped my mosquito tent and carefully peaked outside the screened window. I could see six hotel security guards with guns aimed at the cabin next door.

Inside the cabin another object was thrown and hit its mark. The two people then started fighting again, this time with greater hostility.

The security guards quickly broke into the cabin and led the two combatants away. Cameron was now wide-awake.

"What's the noise about, Jack?"

"We can only imagine what the story is. Maybe the man and woman are husband and wife who can't agree on the dividing of household duties in their home. Or maybe the man and woman were about to carry out a business deal and it went south."

Cameron laughed and rolled over for more sleep.

My sleep until 5:00 a.m. was on and off. The drums once again began to pulsate north of the hotel compound, and the roosters had now begun their morning ritual. Things were back to normal.

****

At 7:00 a.m. I was at a table in the hotel garden lounge. I had ordered my usual coffee and was beginning to write some notes in my notebook when Abby appeared at my table. She sat down next to me and gently took my arm. I sensed something was on her mind. It may have been what happened at Eman's restaurant last evening.

"Jack, let's you and me drive out to the airport and pick up something. It may have already arrived at 7:00, or may be arriving at 8:30."

I wondered what it could be. Maybe the doctors had ordered some special medicine for the clinic. Maybe Abby's parents had sent something for her. I stood up, grabbed my coffee, and walked with her out to Selasie. She held onto my arm with both of her hands. Something was definitely on her mind. She had not grabbed onto my arms like this since we were students walking around the campus at the University of Minnesota, before we were married.

"Here are the keys. I got them from Gabe."

We drove out of Gambela toward the airport, some ten miles away. Abby slid over and was sitting next to me. The road was straight but very bumpy. We drove without either of us saying a word for about two miles.

A few deer were grazing in the fields along the road. As I looked at them, I wondered how the deer had managed to escape the hungry Ethiopian hunters and the occasional lions that made their appearance in this part of Ethiopia.

"Jack, can we stop here for a few minutes?"

"Sure." I didn't question why.

She opened her door, walked around to my side, opened my door, took my hand, and led me to the side of the road. We stopped and she opened her small purse, gracefully retrieving sheets of paper. I recognized them.

One was a detailed listing of the back child support owed to Abby and what it would be in the future. The other two sheets stapled together was a list entitled, "The many sins and failings I was guilty of during our marriage." Both sides of both sheets were filled. I remembered the last words I had written in bold letters on the bottom of the second sheet. "ABBY, PLEASE FORGIVE ME!!" The list had been written in the past two weeks, and I had given it to her only two days ago.

"Here, hold my purse for me, please."

Abby opened both sheets and crumpled them together into a tight ball. Then she reached into her purse and took out a new book of matches. Slowly, she ripped out a match, lit it, and held it to the crumpled ball of papers until it was well afire. She finally dropped the flaming ball to the road and watched it consume for a few moments. Then she turned to me. With tears starting to well in her eyes and her voice breaking, she started to speak.

"Jack, I am going to forget that these things ever happened. Can you find it in your big heart to forgive me for not forgiving you when I first read them?"

I drew her close to me and whispered in her ear, "Yes I can. I will forgive and forget all of them."

I stood there and held Abby who was now crying. She cried like I had never seen her cry before. It was like she had stored up years of hurt, turmoil, grief, and bitterness, and now it was being released. I continued to hold her in my arms as I looked at the smoldering ashes on the ground.

As we were standing embracing each other, traffic continued to pass by. I watched the drivers' faces as they had slowed down to see what was going on. They were probably wondering what our story was, but I think they may have had some idea—or, at least could formulate a good scenario.

"Let's move Selasie, Abby. "

"We'd better get going; we might be late."

"Late for what?"

"You'll see. And don't ask any questions."

We jumped into our trusty vehicle again and took off on the airport road. After we had driven for a mile, Abby suddenly broke the silence.

"Jack, I've made the decision to accept your proposal to get remarried."

There was a sudden slight change in Selasie's stability as I jerked my head to look at Abby. I began to mumble something when Abby interrupted me.

"Let me explain something to you. When I first became a believer, I began praying for the day when you too would become a Christian and we would then get remarried. This is why I never remarried. But somewhere along the line, I stopped praying for this to happen and for you.

"Then I met Terry about a year ago, and I started to see dollar signs. I began to relive our years of marriage with all of its disappointment, heartache, grief, and poverty. I think I was trying to justify my not praying for you, and I attempted to put you out of my mind.

"If Terry had not been in the picture, I would not have been so hostile to you when we met in Frankfurt. I was trying to cause you to return to the United States from the airport that same day. I'm sure you were well aware of that, and it was the cruelest thing I could have done to you. Just think of how different our trip would have been if you had gone back home that day. You have been such an enormous asset to our team.

"After Frankfurt, I decided to see if you could fulfill your desire to prove yourself to me. I figured it wouldn't happen, and I even hoped you couldn't. This would then justify my desire for Terry with his money.

"I had no idea you could accomplish that challenge as you have done during our short stay in Gambela. The big finale was when you almost gave up your life for me trying to prove your love for me. I am ready for you and you may have me."

"So, Abby, tell me, why do you want to marry me?"

"The answers are simple. I have fallen in love with you in the past two weeks, I need a husband, and our boys need their dad. That's three reasons for wanting to marry you."

"Do you think they will accept me?" I asked a bit hesitantly.

"They have told me on the phone that they want you to come home." She smiled and then continued. "What happened last night at Eman's restaurant was the final wakeup call for me. Dr. Terry asked me to marry him about two months ago. My mind and pocketbook told me to say 'yes,' but my heart kept saying 'no.' I don't love him, and last night confirmed that God's will is for me to marry the person I have fallen in love with on this mission trip— Jack Franklin."

I stopped Selasie in the middle of the road, and Abby and I had another brief moment, with the traffic moving around us. We then traveled on.

"What do you think your folks will think of me? Will they want to see me?"

Abby began to smile, some tears still on her cheeks glistening in the early Ethiopian morning sun. "Why don't you ask them?"

"When?"

"In about thirty minutes."

"Where?"

"At the Gambela airport."

"You're kidding me, Abby. Why are they coming?"

"They just wanted to see their daughter in Africa."

We continued to talk and travel to the airport, arriving at 8:00 a.m. The next surprise Abby had for me was just as big. We were sitting in the open hut that served as the waiting area.

"There's another reason why my folks are coming," she said with a smile.

"What reason is that?"

"Jack, I want us to be remarried in Gambela."

"Where?"

"In Gambela."

"But where in Gambela?"

"In the Sudanese church."

"Are you serious? Why not wait until we get back to the U.S. and have a big church wedding?"

"There are many reasons, but the biggest one is that we will be remarried when we arrive home to our sons. This will send a very important message to them."

I looked at her and smiled.

"I agree with you. What else do you have up your sleeve?"

"You'll just have to wait, Jack," she grinned.

The airport was out in the middle of nowhere. It had been a major airport during the previous Marxist regime. The old Soviet Union had made its presence here, and looking around one could see that they had suddenly abandoned the airport. There was old equipment in the weeds, rows of vacant barracks, and a driveway that was worse than the road to Gambela—if that were possible.

Ethiopian Airlines from Addis Ababa was on time, and the unloading was fast and efficient. Rumor had it that Ethiopian Airlines was among the best in the world. Watching the plane come in and unload confirmed that rumor.

Abby had apparently communicated to her parents the 180-degree turnaround in my life, my presence with the medical mission team in Gambela, and who knows what else. It had been almost seven years since I had seen or talked to them. They were the best in-laws that a person could ever ask for. I had let them down and was nervous about meeting them once again.

I let Abby run to her parents, and she embraced both of them. Her tears may have been for the way her life was coming together, a delayed reaction from the hair-raising experiences she had been through in the past few days, or the joy of seeing them once again. Maybe it was all three.

I had nothing to worry about. Fred and Mabel Olson accepted me with open arms, like I was a Christian brother or maybe their prodigal son-in-law. Abby had definitely been talking to her parents about me on the phone. Some of it must have been good. I walked over and embraced both of them. Abby joined in the family hug and we stood in silence while the rest of the passengers walk around us. Abby's father finally broke up the family gathering.

"Jack, guess what!"

"What?"

I was ready for anything from my ex-father-in-law.

"Do you know that all of the major networks have run a video of you? They are searching for you. You've become a national folk hero, especially on police and rescue shows."

Abby stopped and look at her dad as we kept walking toward the airport baggage building. "What's the deal, Dad? What is it all about?" Abby started walking again and then spoke to me. "Jack, what happened?"

"I have no idea. It's nothing."

Abby's father suddenly looked at me. "Nothing, Jack? You say nothing? You only saved six people from a horrible burning death! I wouldn't call that nothing."

"What are you talking about, Dad? What was on that video?"

"Our son-in-law, the father of our grandsons, traveling on a freeway on February sixteenth, comes upon an accident, gets out, uprights a rolled-over car, and pulls two adults and four children from the car—all within seconds of the car exploding. Someone close by got every second on clear video. They figure that the probability of catching an event like that on video is almost zero. The amateur cameraman just happened to be there. He probably sold the video for a fortune and is still selling it."

"How do they know the person was me? It could have been any number of people." I said.

"The video showed you driving off. The police traced the car license number to you. Some reporter who saw your face on TV called the police and said he'd talked with you at the airport in Addis Ababa. When the police talked to him and then saw the video, they concluded that you didn't cause the accident but rather aided in a manner that was heroic. You were on all the network news programs and in many newspapers in the United States and the world.

"But instead of hanging around for the publicity, you decided to get to your plane and disappear for three weeks."

"Jack, that's where you received your wrist injury, isn't it?" Abby asked.

"Yes, and maybe I'll talk about it later. But right now, your parents are here and that's more important."

****

When the four of us arrived back at the hotel, I helped my former and future in-laws get settled in their cabin. Abby and I showed them everything about the cabin and informed them of all of the health concerns.

The new attraction between Abby and me was obviously apparent to Abby's parents. They were both standing in the doorway, watching us holding hands and smiling. I looked at them for a few seconds and they looked at me—like I was some kind of stranger they had just met. I really was.

"I can't believe you're Jack," my father-in-law said.

"Neither could I," Abby responded.

I walked over, put my arms around them, and pulled them toward me. Abby walked over and joined us.

"This is a good time and place to say something to you Mom and Dad. I would be so happy if both of you would forgive me for causing your lovely daughter and you folks so much disappointment and heartache for so many years."

Fred answered, "We forgive you, Jack, and we want to tell you that this is an answer to years of prayer."

"This makes us very happy," Mabel added.

"I know. I have really felt it, especially in the past eight weeks."

"Now, Jack, how about providing us with some of the same excitement that you have shown our daughter for the past two weeks," Fred said excitedly.

"How did you find out about it?" I asked.

"The phone calls. Abby has been giving us a running account of what has happened in this latest romance."

I looked at Abby with a puzzled expression then turned to her parents.

"You haven't heard the latest wild experience. We'll talk about it later, but let me just give you a small hint; three days ago, your daughter actually saw seven of God's angels."

"What?" was Mabel's reply?

"Let's all go on a walking tour of the river area. Abby and I will show you the famous Baro River."

We walked along the road leading from the hotel to the Baro River. I wanted to let them pick some of the mangos if we could find any. Most of the trees had been picked over by the Ethiopian and Sudanese street vendors. Some of the mangos were high up in the tree and would drop overnight. I would look for one or two of them, or pay a young Sudanese boy to climb the tree and fetch one.

We talked as we walked, with Abby repeating the story of us getting shot at and almost killed in Sudan. I interrupted her occasionally to give the Olsons some commentary of what we were seeing on the tour. They too marveled at the beauty of the Sudanese women carrying water.

"The number of women transporting water to the Sudanese compounds near the church has been reduced drastically thanks to the Living Springs water purification system. Yet there are a number of the women still carrying water. Maybe old ways are hard to give up in Africa, as well as America," I told my tour group.

We were all looking up into a tree when we suddenly heard a woman's panicked scream! It was coming from the bank of the river. We all hurried over and saw a woman who had been washing clothes on the edge of the river. I immediately could see what the story was.

One of her children, a little girl, had a bloody right arm. Her hand was missing. The woman was running and yelling in the Nuer language, pointing to a spot on the shore of the Baro River. We quickly ran down to where she was running back and forth. I spotted a group of crocodiles off the shore lying still in the water with the tops of their backs and heads barely visible.

It was evident from the way the woman was ignoring her handless daughter that a more tragic incident had occurred. A crocodile had taken her other child. She was yelling historically in the Nuer language. I couldn't understand a word she was saying, and there was no one who could translate at that moment.

Soon a crowd of Sudanese women hastily made their way to where the action was taking place. I grabbed the crying handless little girl and moved her away from the shore. Mabel comforted the mother, as I took out my handkerchief.

"Abby! Quick! Stop the bleeding of the little girl's hand with my hanky!"

Abby made a tunicate and applied it to stop the profuse bleeding. One of the Sudanese women took the girl into her arms. My attention turned to the missing child.

"Fred! See if you can find any evidence of the missing hand. I'm going to see if the crocs got any of the other children."

Fred was joined by Abby in searching up and down the shore for the little girl's hand. After about a minute, I turned to walk up the riverbank when Abby suddenly yelled out, "There's a child in the water! She's alive! The crocodile has the child in its mouth!"

I quickly prayed. I think everyone did. It was probably one of the shortest prayers in the history of prayer.

"Abby, stay there!" I yelled out.

"Fred, walk slowly down the river about ten feet from shore. Maybe the crocodile will release the child and come after you. It's our only hope. Just stay away from the edge of the water."

Fred looked at me like I was out of my mind, but he started to walk slowly down the river. The crocodile took the bait and released the child. It had started moving slowly down the river toward Fred, thinking an adult Norwegian would be tastier than the little Sudanese child.

"Fred, move away from the shore very slowly," I instructed.

Meanwhile, several young Sudanese men came with clubs and long sticks. They had been close by and were probably aware of the presence of the crocs.

"Abby! It's your move. Quickly run in and grab the child. Be careful—watch for any other crocs. You fellows give her some protection."

I hoped the boys understood my English.

Abby was brave. She strolled unhurriedly into the water, reached down, carefully picked up the stunned boy, and quickly ran out of the river. The Sudanese men by this time were throwing their sticks and clubs trying to taunt the several crocodiles. They hastily swam away.

"Fred! Grab the little boy and carry him back to the clinic. I'll carry the little girl." I turned to another young boy and asked, "Do you speak English?"

"Yes, I do," he replied.

"Run as fast as you can to the Ethiopian Hotel and get the two doctors from America. Tell them to get to the church as fast as they can. Tell them Jack said so."

The skinny young man, with nothing on but white shorts, took off running like a deer chased by a lion. He ran in a straight line through the muddy swamp area filled with river water—the shortest way back to the hotel.

Fred and I also ran across the same swampy area. Our boots sank into the mud as we ran with our valuable, crying loads. To run around the swamp would have taken an extra five minutes. My father-in-law was in good shape, and we soon made it to the church where the clinic was.

In five minutes Gabe came racing down the street with his horn blasting to clear the road of people. He was once again in his element. A crowd had gathered in addition to the people waiting in line for water. The news of the crocodile attack had spread like wildfire through the Sudanese community, probably via the women carrying water.

By this time, Abby and her mother had made it to the clinic, along with the family of the two little children. All of them were panting out of breath from rushing the two miles from the Baro River.

The doctors proceeded to perform emergency surgery on a table outside of the church. The inside of the church had been cleared away for the Sunday Sudanese worship service. Abby's parents watched as the doctors performed the surgery, assisted by Abby and Elizabeth.

The little girl's missing hand was never found, and the doctors made the decision that they could not wait for it. They sewed the arm shut just above the wrist in order to stop the bleeding. The little girl's brother had only a few marks on his body from the teeth of the crocodile. The crocodile must have handled the little boy like she was one of her babies.

I walked up to my in-laws and shook their hands.

"Thank you for your heroic and timely assistance. I'm sorry our tour was interrupted. We'll continue it later."

"Jack, I said I wanted some excitement, but, my goodness, not this much!"

"As a family, this is probably the most excitement we'll ever have—we four, that is. Abby and I set the record for excitement the other day in Sudan."

The Olson's recognized Dr. Terry and greeted him as he helped Dr. Mike with the surgery. They had apparently met at some time in the past year. Abby walked over and watched with her parents but said nothing to Dr. Terry.

Abby took my hand. Any close relationship between Abby and Dr. Terry, romantic or economic, had been terminated.

****

At 10:00 a.m. we were at the church waiting for the Sudanese Sunday morning worship service to begin. The worship began with a prayer service in the Nuer language. James stood by and translated some of the prayer for Fred and Mabel. At the end, Samuel asked Fred to pray in English, with Samuel providing the Nuer translation.

The little boy and girl lay in their parents' arms sleeping, one of them from the medication and the other one from the trauma of being in the crocodile's mouth. The mother then stood and prayed a passionate prayer. Many people were crying. I asked James what the mother was saying.

"She was thanking God for sending people from America to save her children. She was also asking for God's protection, for the healing of their bodies, and for God's protection for the people in Southern Sudan."

****

After church, Abby and I gave Abby's parents a tour of the Living Springs water distribution center and the Sudanese compounds along James Avenue. They were most impressed by the friendliness of the Christian Sudanese community.

"These folks are a very strong and proud people, aren't they, Jack?"

"You caught that, too, didn't you. Once you hear of some of the persecution they've been through, you quickly understand why they are such spiritual people. Almost every Sudanese Nuer family has suffered some atrocity, murder, or injury inflicted by the government from the north."

****

In the afternoon, we had Gabe give the four of us a tour of Gambela. We stopped at the Oliver and Tebee compound and had tea. I pick out two unusual flowers for Abby and her mother. The women stayed outside in the garden area, while we men sat in the main hut discussing Fred's work in the United States.

I didn't bring up the work of Oliver as I was still unsure exactly what occupied his time. I had an idea it was connected with some type of intelligence gathering. I just wasn't sure for which government. Maybe it was strictly industrial intelligence work. I might find out before I leave, or I might even have a chance to ask him.

Dr. Mike and Elizabeth were conducting a mobile clinic at another location in the city. This location was the home of an unusually high number of pregnant women, many of them very young. We dropped Abby and her mom at the mobile clinic where they assisted. Fred and Mabel were making good use of their time, the first day of their visit, along with a little excitement.

****

We all met at 5:00 p.m. for dinner at the hotel restaurant. Abby, her parents, and I sat at our own table. The remainder of the team sat together in another section. Moses seated us at the Mengistu table surrounded by the three pillars. I had Moses once again share his connection with the exiled dictator of Ethiopia.

After dinner, Abby's mother spotted a piano in the hallway and wanted to play it. I asked Moses if she could. He gave his approval and asked some of the hotel employees to move it to the dining hall. Mabel then entertained us for thirty minutes with beautiful piano music. One of the keys was out of tune, so Fred looked in the piano bench, found a tuning wrench, and proceeded to tune the bad key.

This had been an eventful day, and this was a perfect way to end it. I was hoping that the two remaining days in Gambela, culminating with my remarriage to Abby, would be peaceful.

I couldn't have been more wrong.

CHAPTER 18

Monday—Day 18

O ut of force of habit, I was waiting when Moses showed up to open the restaurant. He quickly made coffee and brought me a free cup to sample. The sky was clear, there was no breeze blowing, and it had all the signs of being a beautiful day in Gambela. I felt relaxed this morning with only minor discomfort from the four wounds on my back. I credit nurse Abby for her care in treating them. She was now going to be my nurse for life.

Moses's first cup of coffee was the best he had made in the two weeks of our visit. I was on the second cup when Abby and her folks came walking into the garden lounge area.

"Good morning, everyone!" I greeted them.

"Good morning, Jack," was the response in unison.

We walked into the hotel restaurant and proceeded to order breakfast. Abby prayed, asking God to bless the food, the team at the clinic, our boys in Minnesota, and the healing of my back. The breakfast conversation started with a discussion of the previous day's rescue of the little Sudanese boy and girl from the crocodiles. Abby then turned to her parents. "I wanted Jack present when I told you, Mom and Dad, what our plans are for our wedding. Of course, it will not be exactly a wedding, since we officially did that in Tulsa ten years ago. We will merely be renewing our vows."

"You want to get remarried in St. Paul, don't you?" Mabel asked, anticipating Abby's next words.

"No, Jack and I want to exchange our vows right here in Gambela, tomorrow afternoon at 4:00 p.m."

Fred and Mabel suddenly became quiet. They looked at Abby and then at each other. The look on Abby's face reflected an expected negative response from her parents.

"Why, here?" they asked"

"The main reason is because Jack and I want to be remarried when we return to our sons. But, there is another reason. Let us explain to you.

"While most young girls dream of having a wedding in a huge church with majestic décor, the best music available, and an elaborate dinner at some country club, Jack and I have chosen to have our wedding in a humble church in Africa with a dirt floor, no permanent seating, no electricity, and no running water or bathrooms." It was my turn to say something.

"Abby and I have come together here, we have fallen in love with each other here, and here is where we have had a ministry beyond our wildest imagination. God is definitely here with the Sudanese. We have seen Him perform miracles in Gambela, the greatest of which will be our broken marriage healed."

Abby's father then broke in. "Abby and Jack, you two are absolutely correct. We agree, and, in fact—we will pay for the wedding, or whatever you call it when this sort of thing happens."

Abby got out of her chair and gave her mom and dad a hug. I did the same.

We continued to talk with Fred and Mable about many topics and then branched into a discussion of the wedding details. Since Abby's mother had never had the chance to plan for her only daughter's first wedding, she was now given a second chance to do it. She and Abby would plan the entire event, and that was fine with me.

I gave Gabe instructions to drive Abby and her parents to various places in the afternoon to find and buy some things for the wedding. I would stay and help with the clinic.

After breakfast the four of us walked over to the clinic, going by several of the Sudanese compounds along James Avenue. Many of our new friends greeted us, and we introduced them to Abby's parents.

Her parents were already well known in the community for their heroic deed just 24 hours earlier involving the little Sudanese brother and sister. One man asked Fred if he was "going to take on more crocodiles today."

"I've had my fill for a lifetime," was Fred's response.

At the clinic Cameron and the two doctors put Fred and Mabel to work. They helped with some of the older patients, assisting them as they walked, taking care of patient's children, and giving people drinks of cold water from the Living Springs.

The clinic was scheduled to shut down at noon on Tuesday. This would give the church people time to set up for our wedding, which was scheduled for 4:00 p.m. I hoped everything would remain quiet for the next thirty hours.

****

About 11:00 a.m., Cameron came running from the direction of the hotel. He was almost out of breath when he got to me. This type of physical exercise was not good for a man his age. Whatever the reason for his haste I figured it must be important. He handed me a note. I read it out loud.

> *From the USA— Word has been received that five Sudanese pastors have been kidnapped and are being held about 40 miles from Gambela, just over the Ethiopian-Sudanese border. Reports are that the pastors and their kidnappers are just outside of the town of Gallor in an abandoned building. They were walking back to Sudan after a church conference.*

"Where did you get this note?"

"A young boy brought it into Moses about thirty minutes ago."

"Who would kidnap them, Cameron?" I asked.

"I don't know, but my guess is it's our KNM friends again. The leader of the kidnappers is asking one million dollars for their safe return."

"Where did that information come from?"

"That's another note. It was left at the office of the Ethiopian Hotel," Cameron added.

"Who left it there?"

"The night clerk doesn't know. He found it sitting on the counter tied to a rock this morning just before he ended his shift"

"From whom are they asking that kind of money?" was my question.

"From the Sudanese Covenant church."

"Are those people crazy? What have they been smoking?"

"They must be crazy—the Sudanese churches can't even pay their own pastors."

"What should we do? What can we do? Cameron, this is terrible. Those mercenaries will kill them in seconds and for little or no reason. They're butchers."

"I know. But we really can't do anything because they're in Sudan and we, as representatives of our church, have no permission to enter that country. If we did, it may create some type of international incident. It would get us into a heap of trouble with our church leaders, as well as with three separate governments. But someone needs to try rescue them."

"Someone not directly connected with the Covenant church," I said. "Someone who might be just attending the Covenant Church?"

"Something like that."

Cameron winked at me in almost slow motion. I wasn't sure what the wink was for or if it had any meaning at all. Maybe it was Cameron's signal to go get the kidnapped pastors. If that was the meaning of the wink, than Cameron was putting a huge amount of confidence in me.

Cameron was right. Someone needed to try the rescue. For sure, no money was available for any ransom, and no force of any kind could be assembled from any of the countries involved to plan and execute such an incursion. If the pastors were American citizens or Ethiopian citizens, than a force could possibly be formed to go over the border and rescue them. But they were only Christians from South Sudan.

"Tell me, Cameron, if someone were to go in and try to rescue them, would someone else be willing to organize a prayer-support group?"

"You bet that would happen—a world-wide emergency prayer group!" Cameron exclaimed.

I turned my head away and continued the conversation.

"Explain something to me, Cameron. How in the world was this information obtained with such detail, and why are we probably the first ones to receive it? Don't tell me. We are the closest to the action."

"Something like that."

"So many questions: who is collecting and sending this information to the United States? Who is sending it back to us? And how can they know what is happening with such precise detail? A lot of unanswered questions, don't you think?"

"It does seem strange, yes. I don't have any answers—just more questions, like you."

Just then, Abby walked up to us. We gave each other a kiss and a brief intense hug.

"Abby, I need to talk to you." I said.

Cameron, seeing that I wanted to talk to Abby alone, turned abruptly and went inside the clinic.

"What about, Jack?"

"Abby, I need to go with Gabe for a little while. I may not be back until late tonight. It's just on a routine mission of mercy."

"Where are you going, Jack? Not again!"

"I'll be okay."

"It's not okay, Jack! You're going somewhere where you'll be in danger again, aren't you? Isn't putting your life in danger three times enough? You did it in Indianapolis, you did it in the alley in Addis Ababa, and you did it the other day in Sudan. I don't think God expects you to do it for the fourth time."

"I need to run an errand that will take a few hours. But don't worry; I'll be back soon. You and your folks can have a good time planning our wedding. Okay? Just tell everyone to pray for us."

"Pray! You know, Jack, that the word 'pray' from you is a code word for 'Lord, get us out of this mess,' and that means Jack is about to put the man I love in harm's way.

Where are you going?"

"Gabe and I are going to pick up five pastors."

I gave her another quick kiss and a huge hug. "Be good! Abby, I love you dearly!"

I turned and ran to our trusty vehicle.

"Jack! Jack!!"

I quickly jumped into Selasie and instructed Gabe to take off. I wasn't going to tell anyone where we were going, not even Cameron. But he knew. Gabe would find out in a few minutes. Everyone else, including Abby, would know shortly—once Cameron announced the prayer request, the news of the kidnapping spread, and I became absent. The connection would be made quickly.

"Gabe, let's go back to the hotel. I need to get some items before we take off. How much gas do we have?"

"We have enough in the tanks to drive at least 150 miles. We have another 10 gallons in cans—enough for another 150 miles. Why? How far are we going?"

"Actually, not that far. We're going into Sudan."

Gabe momentarily slowed up as we turned the corner going into the hotel compound gate. He looked directly at me. "Are we going to be in danger, Jack?"

"Well, I don't really know yet. Maybe. But, I do know this: Whatever happens, God will be with us. And many people will be praying for us."

"Good, I need some more excitement in my life."

At the hotel I had Moses supply me with adequate clothes to make me look like an Ethiopian sheepherder. This disguise may come in handy.

After we picked up a few other items from my cabin, we headed for downtown. I found some additional items at the store warehouse where I had bought the medical supplies. We headed out of Gambela traveling northwest. I turned to Gabe and gave him the good news by asking him a question.

"Gabe, do you know where Gallor is?

"Yes, I do. I've been there many times."

"Good, because it's where we are going."

"It's just inside of Sudan—not a very big place."

We were going to the town of Gallor, a small South Sudanese village just over the border from Ethiopia. It was a town where one of our Sudanese Covenant churches was located. The church building was no longer there, having been mysteriously blown up by enough explosives to destroy a large ship. The congregation met in various secret locations in the woods surrounding the town. I had met the pastor in Gambela and he had given me the details and history of that Sudanese-Nuer language church.

As we were driving, I once again began to wonder how it was that Cameron received the news about the kidnapping of the pastors. Also there was the question of why. Why would someone try to obtain money from some 250 churches that couldn't even supply their pastors with salaries?

The mercenaries may be running out of money to fund their genocide operation. But that didn't seem probable since they were being supplied indirectly with oil money from some of the Western oil companies. This money was going directly into the killing of the Sudanese and clearing of the towns where the oil wells could be placed. This fact was well known. The militia forces were also being supplied with war materiel from many other countries.

There was another possibility for the kidnapping and for demanding of ransom money. Maybe a group of KNM soldiers was seizing upon an opportunity to obtain some cash for themselves. It was about the only logical answer to this puzzling question, and one that was credible.

The Ethiopian government didn't allow the Sudanese people to work in Ethiopia, but they were allowed to operate small businesses. Many of the Covenant churches in the United States were providing seed money to form and fund various enterprises and community projects in Ethiopia and Sudan, and especially in the area around Gambela. The projects were being initiated in the hopes that the Sudanese church could develop these ventures into moneymaking enterprises and, thus, become self-sustaining.

Some of these projects were working out quite well while others were not, and a few had become like "pounding sand into a rat hole." Many of the Sudanese knew about these failures and considered them to be only money-eating projects. It is possible that this information had become common knowledge of some Sudanese traitors within the KNM, some of whom had friends inside the churches. Maybe a few of the KNM militia had decided to obtain some of this cash for themselves through kidnapping, thinking the ransom money was readily available.

We needed to be careful that we weren't spotted by any of the militia as we approached Gallor. It would be expected that they might be parked along the road. On the other hand, there was little traffic—only a few trucks, animals pulling carts, and some cars containing tourists.

I needed to give Gabe some instruction and information as to what to expect. "Gabe, we are going to try and rescue five Sudanese pastors who have been kidnapped."

"Kidnapped by whom?"

"I don't know and I have no idea exactly where they are. Supposedly, they are in a wooded area south of the town of Gallor. The message said that they are in some abandoned building."

"When my family lived in Gambela," Gabe said, "we sometimes traveled to Gallor to have picnics, so I'm familiar with those woods. There used to be a park there where we went on holidays. I think there's nothing left but some old buildings. Maybe the pastors are hidden in one of those buildings."

"That's where they probably are, Gabe," I agreed.

"I know the area quite well in that part of Ethiopia and over the border into Sudan. I used to chase girls around there."

"What do you mean 'chase girls' Gabe? That's an American expression."

He never answered—just grinned.

The road was again dusty, rocky, and rough, just like all of the roads leading into and out of Gambela. It again made me long to return to the freeways of America.

"Gabe, tell me when we are close to the wooded area and the town. Meanwhile, I'm going to catch a few minutes of sleep."

I dozed in and out of sleep. I felt bad about leaving Abby and her parents to plan the wedding. However, how much could I add to the planning? It was a woman's thing. They knew what they were doing, and all I needed to do was to show up.

The two-hour drive took us almost to The Ethiopian/Sudanese border. Gabe pulled over to the side of the road. "The woods are only one mile down the road, Jack."

"Can you find a place to park where Selasie will be out of sight?"

"Let's drive off the road and into this grassy field. We'll find a place."

Gabe was a good driver. I didn't think so when we first left Addis on our way to Gambela. I take back all I ever thought about his driving. But it still scares the living daylights out of me when I think about his driving toward a crowd of 200 people going 40 mph!

We stopped under a huge tree with overhanging branches. We were now completely hidden. Gabe had a knack of finding these spots.

"This is perfect, Gabe."

We exited Selasie and I dressed into my Ethiopian clothes that Moses had given me. They were a little baggy, but it was all he had.

"Hey! How do I look?" I asked as Gabe had his back to me.

"Now what, Jack? Hey, you look great! Where are your sheep?"

"One of us needs to walk into town and find out what is going on. You'll have to do the snooping as you speak Amharic. Do you know anyone in town?"

"Yes, as a matter of fact I do. I know an old man who runs a small engine and car repair shop. He's also a farmer and may still be in business. I'm told that he grows some illegal drugs in the woods. Maybe he can provide us with some information."

"Gabe, I have some two-way radios that I brought with me from America. Believe it or not, they actually work—up to two miles. We'll need to have a set of signals to communicate with each other. Here is a list I wrote down. We'll use a tapping sound—like your knuckle on the walkie-talkie—like this."

I showed him how to tap and the resulting sound on the other walkie-talkie.

"Did you get those at Radio Shack?"

"As a matter of fact, I did. How do you know about Radio Shack?"

"I saw an ad in *USA Today* advertising Radio Shack."

"Let's go. I'll walk with you until we get to the wooded area.

We'll find a place to meet."

We were soon at the spot we dubbed "home" and where we would meet and exchange information. I prayed briefly and bid Gabe farewell. He took off down the road leading into the town, a distance of about a half a mile. I began to make my way slowly through the woods to the see if I could find any sign of life—the human kind.

It was about an hour later when I heard a tapping on the walkie-talkie. Gabe had found out some information. In my hour, I had seen nothing other than a den of snakes and a pack of wild dogs—from a distance, of course. Several people walking on a main road leading into the town also greeted me. They spoke to me in Amharic, thinking I was an Ethiopian sheepherder. My disguise was a success.

On my way back to "home," I did spot the abandoned buildings at the park that Gabe was talking about. There were three of them. The report was at least correct about the buildings.

We met back at home base where I found Gabe excited.

"My friend is still operating a repair shop and guess what! He's been repairing a vehicle that could be owned by one of the kidnappers."

"How does he know that?"

"There's some of the pastors' stuff in the trunk. My friend is 'Mr. Snoopy' and he looked into one of the bags. It contained several Bibles and songbooks in the Nuer language. The fellows who own the car are not Christian. In fact, my friend said that if they knew there were Bibles in the car, they would go berserk—probably burn them. My friend says that the men are from the northern part of Sudan."

"How many kidnappers are there, Gabe?"

"He says there are only two that have been into his shop. They apparently have two vehicles. I'm guessing that there is at least two more guarding the five Sudanese pastors at the abandoned buildings."

"Did your friend see the second vehicle?"

"Yes, and guess what! It has an automatic gun mounted on the back."

"That adds a new factor in this situation. This could get messy and we have no guns or weapons." I paused briefly then said, "We need to find out which building the pastors are in, how many guards there are, and what paths lead through the surrounding woods and back to Selasie. It's my turn to go snooping. Did your friend say how long before he's finished with the repair job on their car?"

"He's waiting for parts to be flown in from Addis to Gambela. Then he'll need to drive to Gambela and get them."

"Gabe, you look around while I go snoop in the buildings in the park area. See if you can find an alternate route out to the road to Gambela. If the kidnappers follow us, we may need to try and lose them at some point. It may become useful in case we need a quick getaway. Also, drive Selasie back to home and hide him."

"Okay. Sounds good. I'll find a couple of routes."

"Here's some paper. Draw a map. We'll meet back here in thirty minutes."

"How in the world did you find out where the kidnappers were hiding?" Gabe asked.

"That's the same question I've had since Cameron told me this morning. I don't know and neither does he. All of the information that he had was delivered to him in a note."

Gabe and I took off going different directions.

There were three buildings in the abandon park. They were probably used for storage when the park was in operation. The woods and tall grass provided enough cover to effectively move around. My disguise was my backup cover. If any of the kidnappers spotted me, they would think I was an Ethiopian sheepherder looking for my lost sheep—at least that was my hope.

I approached the largest building, found a busted-out window, and crawled through it very cautiously. It was a window to one of the rooms within the building. I very carefully opened the door of the room and looked into the main part of the building. It was obvious that there was no one inside. There were two more doors at the other end.

Exploring the other two buildings was my next task. One had been originally painted blue and the other had been white. Both had faded after years of neglect, and there was the smell of decaying wood.

I crawled through the weeds toward to the back of the white building. There was the wooded area about twenty feet away. This would be our quick getaway.

As I was moving around, I wondered why I was doing this. Eight weeks ago I would not have lifted a finger to risk my life for any kidnapped pastors in Sudan. But this was why I failed in my marriage to Abby. I didn't care for anyone but myself. Maybe God was punishing me for my past iniquities, but I knew that wasn't true.

Tomorrow I would remarry Abby—if I made it back alive and on time. The marriage would be a result of a miracle, no less a miracle than the parting of the Red Sea or of Jonah being preserved in the belly of the whale. To me, Abby and me falling in love with each other after a failed marriage was nothing short of a miracle.

This present situation needed some heavy prayer. I trusted that many people would be praying back in Gambela and even around the world. What I really should have done was bring Abby with me to just sit in Selasie and pray. Maybe some more angels would appear—other than Abby, of course.

Now I had to find out where the pastors were being held. I continued to crawl in the tall grass to the back of building. I listened carefully. I could hear talking inside. The language was different— maybe Arabic.

A window in one of the back rooms was open, and I crawled very carefully through it. The noise level inside was such that my quiet entry went unnoticed. I crept to the open door and peeked inside the main room of the old warehouse.

There they were, the five men, sitting with their backs to the wall and towels around their heads. I assumed that their hands and feet were tied with some type of rope. A single low-wattage bulb provided me just barely enough light to see them. They appeared to be sleeping or, at least, resting.

There were two guards with high-powered rifles only twenty feet from the pastors. They had no uniforms on and seemed to be relaxing. This was also a good sign—they may even fall asleep at some point. They were wearing pea-green tee shirts and shorts and looked as if they were members of a soccer team. But soccer play- ers don't usually carry guns.

In order to rescue the pastors, I would need to get the guards out of the building—if only for a span of a few seconds. I could unbind the pastors and lead them out of the building and into the woods. I would need to find a route through the woods and back to where Gabe and Selasie would be ready to go. That was Plan A. I hadn't thought of Plan B or C yet.

Before I left to return to Gabe, I needed to let the five pastors know that they were about to be rescued, or at least that an attempt would be made to rescue them. I pulled out my tiny high-intensity pocket flashlight and pointed it at one of the prisoner's heads. I blinked the light twice. I did this twice for each of the other pastors. If the towels around their heads were not a tightly knit material, maybe they would see the blinking lights. I had no idea what signal I was sending them with two blinks of light.

The guards didn't see the light, nor did they see or hear me. Their conversation was continuous and loud. The static from a radio playing some African popular music provided additional noise cover.

I crawled back out of the window and walked to home base where Gabe was waiting for me. On the way I was able to map a path from the abandoned buildings to our home base. It was getting late in the afternoon. We decided to wait until dark to execute our plan of attack.

Gabe had found an indirect and confusing path from home base to the main road. Between the two of us, we drew a map of the area, detailing our two escape routes. A yellow legal pad provided writing material. We made two copies of the map—studying them carefully for some time.

About 8:00 p.m. I had our rescue plan prepared. Gabe and I went over it several times, got our watches synchronized, and secured what we needed to get the job done. We had no weapons; but by using the element of surprise, our plan would work effectively without their use. God would see to it.

At 9:00 p.m. I told Gabe it was time to go.

"I hope this works, Jack."

"Let's pray before we go."

"Lord, guide our movements and clear our minds. Confuse the enemy. Amen."

We took off.

As I was walking to the abandoned buildings, I couldn't keep my mind off Abby. I would imagine by this time she and her folks would be frantic and very worried. We were supposed to be married at 4:00 p.m. tomorrow afternoon, and we probably wouldn't be back in Gambela until morning. I just hoped they would understand.

My first task was to get the pastors free from all bonds. My observation earlier in the evening didn't reveal if the kidnappers used rope, vines, or duct tape on their hands and feet. Whatever the material, I assumed my knife would cut it. I had a wire cutter just in case they used a material a knife wouldn't cut. If I could get one of the pastors untied, he could untie another and so on.

I approached the building area crawling carefully and quietly through the tall Sudan grass. I moved freely in back of the white building, since all of the guards were either inside or out in front. As I looked inside the building through a missing board, I saw more light. The room was now lit up with an additional bulb, enabling me to see the captive pastors more clearly. There were three guards sitting around a table playing some type of game—maybe cards.

How was I going to get my five Christian brothers free? Any movement inside the room would possibly create some type of noticeable moving shadow. There was also the chance of the floorboards creaking or even breaking. The building was old and deteriorating from lack of upkeep.

The pastors were sitting against the back wall of the building. I moved to a point on the other side of the wall where I estimated them to be. Using my flashlight, I spotted a loose board near the ground. One single nail was holding the board to the building. If I pulled on the board and tried to force the nail out, it might make a screeching noise loud enough to cause the kidnappers to investigate. Maybe, by using the board to force the nail in the right manner, it would just bend. I tried it. It worked.

With the board now hanging off to the side, it created an opening about five inches by thirty inches. The light from my flashlight revealed two sets of bound hands. The hands had been tied behind the prisoners, and the kidnappers had used rope.

I needed to let one or both of the pastors know that I was outside and was a friend trying to free them. If I touched their hands, they may become scared and groan. If I grabbed their hands, they may think they were in the jaws of some giant Sudanese-Christian-pastor-eating rodent. Then they would make an even louder sound.

I had an idea. In my pocket I had three crosses made of fake ivory that I had bought at a shop in the business district in Gambela. They were for my three boys in Minneapolis and would be souvenirs for them from my trip. The crosses were about all I could afford.

I took one of them out and very carefully placed it between the fingers of one of the pastors. The fingers took the cross and fondled it until he knew what it was. I now had the attention of one of my Sudanese brothers. I very carefully placed in the same set of hands one of my many Swiss Army knives opened to the large blade. He grabbed it with his fingers. In the process, I let him feel my fingers.

Using another knife, I carefully cut the rope binding his hands. His hands were now freed. I did the same to the other set of bound hands, giving him a cross and a knife and then cutting the rope on his set of hands. Now two of them were freed. I needed to rely on the two of them to free the hands and feet of the other three.

From my shirt pocket I pulled out a note wrapped in a small flashlight and secured with a rubber band. I placed it into one of the sets of hands. I was trusting that he would be able to read the note without alarming the guards. The note was in English:

> *Don't worry—God is with you. Free your hands and legs. Leave the towels on your heads. Be ready to escape to Gambela. Signal when you are ready.*
> *—Jack Franklin, a servant of God.*

I needed to give them at least ten minutes to finish the job freeing their hands and legs.

I knew for sure that God would get all of us back to Gambela safely. Nothing could keep Him from having Abby and me get remarried tomorrow in Gambela. If He had other plans, I would have to convince Him otherwise.

Meanwhile, Gabe was hopefully ready to do his part in the rescue attempt. He was getting ready to set up a diversion to get all of the guards out of the building for just thirty seconds. Our plan would work only if all of the guards were outside the building and away from the captive pastors.

A snap of a finger suddenly caught my ear! It came from the set of hands I had just freed. I crawled over from the weeds and grabbed the warm sweaty hand. The huge hand latched firmly onto my entire hand and wrist. He squeezed mine like it had never been squeezed before. My encounter with this hand told me that all five of the pastors were ready to go.

I gave three more knives to the first pastor, who, I hoped would hand them down to the others. Now all five of them had weapons. There was the possibility that this rescue could turn violent, and the five Sudanese brothers would need something with which to defend themselves. My desire was to not have any violence. The Sudanese Nuer tribe is a peaceful, non-violent people. But I also knew from listening to their personal experiences, that they could do battle if they needed to, especially if their opponents were influenced by the forces of evil.

I walked away from the building and, using my walkie-talkie, gave the signal to Gabe to commence the fireworks. If everything went according to plan, there would be two of them, thirty seconds apart.

The first explosion went BOOM!!.... WOOMPH!! It was produced by a stick of dynamite placed next to an open gallon can filled with gasoline. We were able to buy both items from a store in Gambela before we left.

I quickly got down on my knees, pressed my ear against a knot-hole, and listened for the sound of the guards running outside. I had no way of knowing if all of them would exit, but I had to take that chance. I heard a lot of talking among them and the sound of them running to the door. Then quiet.

I quickly attempted something that I had no idea if I would be able to do. I ripped three more boards off the wall. I asked God to give me the same super-human strength that He had given me when I tipped over the Honda on the freeway in Indianapolis. The boards flew off, probably more the result of their rotting, weakened condition than from God's doing. But I still give Him the glory—after all,

He created the decomposing process in nature.

My pastor friends began to crawl out of the large hole even before the last boards were thrown behind me. As they exited the room, the towels flew off of their heads.

"Follow me," I whispered quietly.

There was a second explosion—VOOOM…VOOOM! This one was designed to further divert the guards' attention for as little as five seconds while we made our way to the wooded area and to our escape path.

It was only a five-minute run to Selasie. I led the way, using my one flashlight. Gabe had used a shorter route and was in our trusty vehicle with the motor running when the six of us arrived. We all jumped in and Selasie took off. I sat in the front seat and the rescued pastors sat in the back seats.

I looked at my current-time watch. It was almost midnight. The kidnappers would surely be on our trail in minutes, if not seconds. Gabe raced down the road leading away from Gallor with great haste. This stretch of the road was the smoothest Gabe had driven on in the past two weeks.

"I hope we don't run into any families of baboons or elephants, Gabe."

"I'll just drive right through them."

"I don't doubt it a bit."

"Jack, does my driving scare you?" he asked with a slight grin.

"Just a tad." I answered slowly.

The kidnappers must have had a second vehicle ready and were soon in hot pursuit of us. They must have known the same shortcut that we were taking. Gabe spotted them in the side mirror as they rounded a curve on a downhill stretch of the road. How did they get on our trail so soon? It didn't worry me. We had the best old-road driver in both Ethiopia and Sudan—Gabe.

We were safely on our way back to Gambela. The rest of the journey would be smooth. Maybe we could even get some rest.

It wasn't to be.

CHAPTER 19

Tuesday—Day 19

I glanced at my watch again—it was 12:01 a.m.

My bed at the hotel seemed like a happy dream—I longed to be in it. *When I return to the United States*, I promised myself, *I'm going to sleep for at least a solid week*. Then I realized that when I returned to the U.S., I would be a newlywed—or, more correctly, a newly re-wed—with no job. My sons would need a great deal of my attention. Sleep would have to wait.

I should have disabled the kidnappers' second car. Why didn't I think about that? Once I got under the hood, I could have rendered it inoperable in ten seconds, using a pair of wire clippers. The car could have even been unrepairable, except for an expert auto service man or woman. I knew exactly what to do.

It was possible that our pursuers had some radio communication with their KNM buddies hiding along the road. If this were the case, we could soon have a small army attacking us. There were reports that this area was infiltrated with the enemy.

I turned around and helped two of our released pastors finish getting free from the remaining restraints of rope. They never had time to remove them completely. They had merely cut the rope securing their feet and hands together. The kidnappers had used several knots. I introduced myself.

"I'm Jack. Is everything okay?"

One of them spoke in English. "We are fine. The Lord is with us. How did you find out about us being kidnapped?"

"That's a mystery to me. Somebody in Gambela wrote us a note. Where the note came from—I don't know. Do you know anything?"

"Not a thing!" shouted one of the pastors in the way back seat above the noise. His English was also good. "We are fine and God has sent you to free us."

"How were you fellows kidnapped?" I asked. A third pastor answered.

"We were walking along the road, just over the border, when a truck stopped and seven rough-looking characters jumped off and surrounded us. Their leader, an eighth man, told us to get on the truck. They blindfolded us and took us to the abandoned building."

"Why don't you pastors continue to pray? We're not out of the woods—er—Sudan yet."

"What do you mean 'out of the woods,' Jack. We are nowhere near a woods right now," Gabe responded.

"That's just another American idiom, Gabe."

"Jack, I'm just staying ahead of their vehicle. They must have a driver as crazy as I am," Gabe admittedly said.

"Fat chance," I mumbled.

"What did you say?"

"Fat branch there."

"Yeah, I just missed it."

We drove for another ten minutes. The Sudan moon was almost full, providing us with some extra light to navigate the road that Gabe was taking us on. I decided to open the windows occasionally in order to give our vehicle and its contents some fresh air. The churned up dust wasn't much better.

It seemed that whenever I opened the window, another world appeared. The warm air, jungle sounds, and distinct odors gave me a sense of the real Africa. The only closer sensation I could experience would be if I were outside the car, standing still in the night with nobody around. I didn't care to go that route in sensing the "real" Africa.

All of a sudden, Gabe drove into the ditch and through a bunch of bushes.

"I know of another route to Gambela. It involves using some

back roads and dried-up riverbeds. It's going to be a little rough and it'll take us more time to get back, but I hope to evade the kidnappers and any of their buddies that may be in the vicinity."

Gabe suddenly stopped and turned off his lights. The pursuing car raced past the spot where we had left the road. It would not be long before they realized we were on a different route.

For the next three hours, Gabe took us on a winding ride that I will never forget. He drove in and out of ditches, over grassy fields, and on roads that were covered with a variety of obstacles.

I pointed my flashlight out of an opened window to view the night scenery as he drove. There was an extensive collection of wild animals at every turn. It was difficult to see what the beasts were, but their eyes were reflected from the flashlight and from Selasie's headlights. The eyes that were visible told me I was glad that I was inside a moving vehicle. They also told me that I had better keep praying for Selasie not to break down.

Samuel had told me that some of the animals in southern Sudan had escaped or migrated south into the country of Kenya because of the war. However, this section of Sudan appeared to contain many wild African animals.

My back was still sore from the stitches Dr. Mike had given me after our trip to Yelwah and into Sudan. I got some relief by sitting away from the seat cushion.

My five rescued friends in the back seats continued to pray and talk among themselves in the Nuer language. They may have been praying more for our driver than for protection from their kidnappers. I used my flashlight to shine on and view their faces. I recognized all of them from the prayer conference.

"Gabe?"

"Yes, Jack?"

"Have you driven on this route before?"

"As a matter of fact, many times."

"I thought so."

"A few years ago when I lived in Gambela, I smuggled some of the Sudanese out of Southern Sudan over to the refugee camps. I made several trips. I developed this alternative route so the authorities wouldn't catch me."

"That was very humanitarian of you, Gabe."

"Not really, I did it for money."

"How do you know if you are on the right path, or making the correct turn, or not heading for some ravine?"

"I have this certain sense, a natural talent to know where to go."

"Oh, really?"

"I don't have a clue, but it's fun."

"Gabe, where did you pick up the American idiom?"

"What's idiom? I just listen to the people I drive."

"I thought so."

There were many times that we had to get out and do some clearing of trees and fallen rock. At one point, Gabe just drove through and around them like he was driving on the road filled with potholes from Addis to Gambela.

He also drove on one dried-up riverbed. There was only one spot on the river that contained water, with a host of animals gathered around drinking. Gabe just drove around them and continued on his way. One time, we got stuck and everyone had to get out and push.

Most of the time we were on old roads and trails that were very treacherous. Gabe seemed to know exactly where to drive. God had to be guiding him—it was a miracle in itself.

At about 4:00 a.m. we entered a small village that put us back on the main road to Gambela. I recognized it. We were still in Sudan, however, and it wasn't long before Gabe sounded an alarm. "Our buddies have spotted us! And they have companions. I see two sets of headlights. Hang on! We're going to fly!"

The kidnappers and maybe other members of the militia had been waiting along the road; and as soon as they spotted us driving past, they were once again on our tail. Gabe had at least a one-mile lead on them by the time the pursuing vehicles were at our speed. They were also starting to use guns.

"Everybody get your heads down. We're almost at the border, and I'm going to try make it," Gabe yelled out.

The windows were open and the bullets whizzed by.

"Gabe, how far are we from the border? Will there be any protection for us there?"

"Maybe five miles. Maybe there will be some people there. The road is a little smoother. Notice I said a *little* smoother."

Some of the bullets hit their target by the sounds from the back of our vehicle. Luckily, the gas tank was not where it would be easily hit. Selasie had steel belted tires that would make it somewhat difficult for a bullet to penetrate. Gabe had begun to drive in a serpentine manner, dodging both the potholes in the road and bullets from the guns.

"Hey, guys, guess what! Looks like we have company ahead of us, too."

Gabe suddenly again turned sharply into the ditch and drove into a grassy plain. He drove for two miles, shut the lights off, and drove for another mile.

"I hope I don't hit anything or drive into a big pothole or some deep cavern. If we drive into a family of lions, get ready to be eaten."

"Do you know where you're going, Gabe? What are you doing?"

"What I am trying to do is to lose our friends. My hope is they will not try to find us. I've been in this field."

"Did you chase girls into this field, too, Gabe?"

"I don't remember, but maybe."

We soon drove behind two large trees, turned around, faced the direction from which we had come, and stopped. Our lights were still off. The full moon had aided us as we traveled in the dark.

We could see our pursuers driving on the road. They suddenly stopped and just sat there. I found the binoculars and had a peek.

"Looks like they just had a conference. Hold it! They are now going into the ditch and are coming this way. They must have seen our trail in the weeds."

"What do we do now, Jack?"

"There is only one thing we can do. Just stay here and wait for them to drive past far enough so we can drive back to the road without them seeing us. We'll just have to pray that God will blind their eyes to seeing us."

"You pastors do some praying. Pray in the Nuer language. I'll pray in English, and, Gabe, you can pray in the Amharic, Tigrigna, or Arabic. You might try all three. God will understand you."

We all began to pray at once. The car sounded like the day of

Pentecost, whatever that sounded like. I remembered hearing that story in Sunday school and reading the Acts account of it a few weeks ago. I had never heard Gabe pray before.

I cheated and peeked while I was praying to see if our buddies were getting close to us. It wasn't long before they passed on each side. The big tree had provided a good camouflage.

"Looks like they're lost, Gabe."

"It won't be long before they'll be turning around, driving back, and looking in the other direction for us," Gabe commented. "One of them may even come close to these trees. I think right now one of the vehicles is just driving in circles.

"Shhh! Stop praying for a second. I hear something." I could hear the sound getting closer. It sounded like a plane. My heart sank. "Here we go again—another plane attack. This time the bullets may not miss."

"Jack, what's that sound?" asked Gabe.

"It's the sound of a plane of some sort."

"We are sitting ducks, Jack!"

"I don't think it's a plane," I observed. "It sounds like a helicopter."

The sound soon became deafening. It was hovering about twenty feet above the ground and about two hundred feet in front of us. Then some lights came on. I looked and saw a helicopter landing directly in front of us. It was a big one. Someone got out of the chopper and began running toward us. I recognized the run, but I couldn't believe my eyes. "It's Abby! What is she doing out here?"

"That chopper is going to rescue us, Jack," yelled Gabe.

I got out of our vehicle and ran to Abby. "Abby! What are you doing here?"

"Jack! I just knew that you would make it. I'm the co-pilot, can't you see?"

I took Abby's hand and ran back to Selasie.

"Let's get everyone into the chopper before our buddies find us."

"Jack, you guys take the chopper. I'll drive Selasie back to the hotel in Gambela."

"But you'll be killed, Gabe."

"I'll make it. I'll have a head start. I know a few more shortcuts to Gambela."

We all quickly boarded the helicopter. I was the last to board. Abby sat down in the co-pilot's seat. "Abby! What are you doing here?"

"I told you, I'm the co-pilot. Can't you see?"

Abby and I embraced each other, as the large helicopter took off. There was a short period of time when everything seemed to stop, except for the whirling of the helicopter blades and the sound of a few well-planted kisses. The five Sudanese pastors recognized Abby, and they sat and watched us—then applauded. Within seconds we were in the air. I looked down and saw Gabe driving Selasie in the dark with only the moon to light the way.

Looking back, the two pursuing vehicles had stopped and I could see the firing of guns up toward us. Within a few more seconds, we were completely out of range and there was no chance that any bullets would hit us.

"Abby, why are you here?" I asked.

"I'm here to rescue you."

"So Abby, where did you get the chopper?"

"When you didn't return to the hotel, I got a ride over to Oliver and Tebee's compound. I told him about your attempting to rescue the pastors. He somehow knew all about it, made a call, and within minutes a chopper came down right in their compound and took me away.

"I was worried that the pilot wouldn't know where you were, but he seemed to know exactly where you were. He was in communication with someone at all times."

"But you were putting your own life in danger, Abby."

"You bet I was, and I'll do it again if I have to. You are well worth every risk a girl could possibly take."

Our pastor friends seemed to relax. They began to talk excitedly among themselves. Gabe's ride had scared them, probably more than the kidnapping. Now they were safe inside a helicopter. It was the first time any of them had ever had an airborne ride.

"Do you have any peanut butter cookies?" one of the pastors asked.

Abby quickly turned around and smiled. "Sorry, I need to make some more."

"They were the best thing that has happened to me in many years," the pastor said.

My saintly friends in the back of the helicopter would begin their return trip home once again to Sudan, after getting something to eat and drink in Gambela. Southern Sudan is where their families are, where their ministry is, and where dangers and life-threatening situations are ever present. I turned around. "Hey, you pastors may want to consider an alternate route when you start for home again."

Daniel, who seemed to be their leader, spoke up. "I think you are right."

It was difficult to imagine how they could continue to preach the Christian gospel message in a place that has such an anti-Christian atmosphere. Only God could cause them to continue—and with such zeal.

I started to think about our rescue. How in the world did someone know about us? I began to wonder if there was more to this than just a simple kidnapping and ransom situation. It was almost as if some type of communication network was at work connecting the various involved parties: the spying on the mercenaries, someone in Gambela, someone in some other part of the world—maybe America. I had a strong feeling that my new friend Oliver Thomas was involved.

Maybe the CIA was at work using a satellite camera. How else would they have known our movements or the movements of the kidnappers? If that were the case, then someone in Gambela had to have a direct line to the CIA somewhere in the world. I had an idea who it was.

I decided to ask a few question of our pilot. He was a man in his fifties and wore civilian clothes. "Did you have any trouble finding us?"

"Not really," the pilot responded.

"What did we look like on the satellite screen?"

The pilot turned to me, looked for a few seconds, and then spoke. "Just a few dots—but you were moving. Your driver must be nuts."

"Gabe? Yes, but he is good at what he does."

Maybe the American government was interested in the Sudan conflict after all. They had to be. The number of deaths due to the KNM and their brutal genocide endeavor may have no equal in the last half of the twentieth century.

I wondered if the satellite camera had picked up the seven angels that Abby saw the other day in Sudan. According to the note delivered to Cameron, it did. How would an angel look from 50,000 feet?

We were soon approaching Gambela and the hotel compound, this time from the air. A crowd had gathered along each side of the driveway leading up to the Ethiopian Hotel. We landed in the fenced-in area where cattle were once kept for Mengistu and his staff, according to what Moses had told me.

As we stepped out of the helicopter, the crowd applauded and the Sudanese were singing. The young boys were banging on their drums, providing accompaniment for the choir. Cameron was there, and he and one of the Sudanese pastors led a prayer of thanksgiving. After he had finished, Cameron came up to me. I wasn't quite sure what his reaction or comments would be.

"Good work, Jack. I had a note delivered to me at 5:30 a.m., telling me that you were safely over the border and that Abby was with you. Tell me Jack, what was that all about?"

He handed me the note, which I read and then stuffed into my pocket.

"Cameron, what's going on here?" I asked. "Who's writing all of the messages, and how did the chopper pilot know where to go?"

I think I knew, but there wasn't time to explain my theory.

"I honestly don't know, Jack. Something tells me that someone is following our activities at every turn."

Abby and I walked with my arm around her toward the hotel. She held my free hand tightly with both of hers.

I looked for Abby's parents, expecting them to have given up on me. I spotted them making their way through the crowd. Abby and I walked toward them. We all embraced and just held on to each other.

"I am going to handcuff you to me for the rest of the day!" Abby declared.

"I'm sorry for not telling you where we were going," I answered.

"No, you're not."

****

This was to be one of the most important days in Abby's and my life. Much prayer had been offered to make this day finally come together.

But it was also a happy day for the five Sudanese pastors. They could now start their journey to their homes in South Sudan once again. They may decide to stay in Gambela and rest for a day before beginning their long walk in the hot sun. They may attempt to catch a ride on a grain truck as far as the border. It was very difficult for a non-believing person to imagine why these men of God would want to go back to a land where two million of their people had been killed because of their Christian faith.

Today would also be the last day for the medical clinic. The mission team would be starting the clinic at 8:00 a.m. and running it until noon. This would give us time to dismantle and then to set up for the afternoon wedding.

Abby, her parents, and I walked into the restaurant for breakfast. Moses was there and served us a special breakfast. He made a special pancake for me. "This breakfast is on the house for all of the mission team." Moses declared.

"Thanks, Moses."

"I'm going to miss you people."

"We're going to miss you too, Moses. Why don't you bring your family to visit us in the United States?"

"Maybe we'll do that. But it takes a lot of money to make a trip like that."

Dr. Terry walked in and took his seat at his usual table, from which Abby was noticeably missing. After he had ordered his breakfast, he stood up, walked to our table, and stretched out his hand to me. "Jack, I just want to say that you are the best example of a Christian that I have ever known. Please forgive me for embarrassing you in Eman's restaurant the other night."

He then turned to Abby.

"Abby, I want to apologize to you, also. I had no idea that you felt the way you do about using alcoholic beverages. It never dawned on me."

"Thank you."

Abby didn't say another word.

"Best wishes to you two in your marriage and for a lifetime together."

Dr. Terry and Abby had apparently had a long talk. Maybe the talk occurred while I was gone on the rescue mission.

After we had finished breakfast, we sat in the garden area and talked about the wedding and what was going to take place. My absence for the past 24 hours left me uninformed as to what to expect.

"Jack, I need to check your wounds. Mom and Dad, you may leave if you don't care to see where Jack was cut."

"On the contrary, we want to see what wounds our son-in-law received in rescuing our daughter," Mabel said.

Abby lifted up the back of my shirt and pulled off four bandages. She examined each cut, one by one, and carefully placed on fresh bandages she retrieved from her bag.

"They all seemed to be healing nicely."

Abby suddenly became teary eyed and started talking with a quiet and broken voice. "When we get home, I will show these wounds to our sons and tell them the story of the seven angels and how their dad offered his life for their mom. Their father can tell them about how he almost got burned up along the freeway. I need to look at that cut also."

Abby took my hand and showed her parents the well healing cut on the back of my wrist. She placed a Band-Aid on it also.

"I know what my grandsons are going to tell their dad when they hear these stories," Fred said. "They are going to tell their dad to stay home."

"Yes," I replied, "and how many grandfathers are there who can tell their grandchildren about fighting crocodiles?" I added, as I took my father-in-law's hand and shook it.

****

The wedding was supposed to start at 4:00 a.m. In the relatively short time that I had been acquainted with them, I had become familiar with of the Sudanese tendency to not be on time for meetings and social functions. Cameron said that this was an African cultural thing, but some of the Western people had the same habit.

I left for the church at 2:15 p.m. I had managed to get a couple hours of sleep in the late morning—enough to get my energy back after staying up all night.

I was dressed in Fred's tux that he had brought from America. We were about the same size. I walked through the Sudanese compounds. The residents looked at me in my tux and knew right away that I was the one getting married. All of the little children came and held out their hands for gum. Some of them still had their Hot Wheels cars I had given them. Many of the people came up to me and greeted me with handshakes. Many of them were also dressed up in their suits and colorful clothes, and would also be attending the wedding.

Fred and Mabel had planned all along to come to Gambela to visit their daughter. Abby and her folks had also planned on a wedding; but until I had appeared in Frankfort, they were tentatively planning on it being held in Cairo, Egypt. Abby had changed her mind and decided to give me the second chance. Now they would see their daughter get re-married in a church in the western tip of Ethiopia.

As I came close to the church, it was apparent that a great many people were planning on attending the wedding. It was as if all of these people had some "very best" clothes sitting in their compound and huts, just waiting for an occasion to wear them.

The contrast I observed as I walked was astonishing. Along with the well-dressed people waiting for the festivities to commence were little children with nothing on. I became worried about the possibility of having photos taken with this contrast in the background. Then I remembered this was their culture.

I had told Abby and her parents that I wanted just a small wedding. But, I also told them that they should do what they wished and that I would approve. Just so that it was a brief humble wedding.

As I approached the church, I could see that Abby and her mother had been to visit the Thomas flower garden. There were many kinds of native as well as imported flowers. The entire outside of the church was lined with boat-shaped baskets of flowers.

Abby's father had arranged for someone to set up a sound system for the wedding. There was a speaker set up outside the church up off of the ground. A portable system generated power for the sound system and lighting inside of the church.

Many candles were placed at various places inside of the church. A temporary platform was brought in for the ceremony. Members from the congregation brought benches to provide seating for the guests. Sudanese men carried in large rocks and set them in rows, providing more rows of seating. The church was now ready for the big event.

This may be the largest social event ever held at this church. I was told that only once a more important gathering had been held in the past. There was a 24-hour fasting prayer meeting held in 1999, where a packed church prayed passionately for their suffering Christian brothers and sisters in South Sudan.

Abby and I were to walk down the aisle together. It would be the second marriage for us, and we felt that we could break with tradition. Both of us felt that we were still married in God's sight; it would be a matter of renewing our vows. There would be, of course, some type of formality needed back in the U.S. to make the marriage once again legal.

Our walk was to begin at a small hut near the church. Tall green grass was cut from the bank of the Baro River and placed on the pathway where we were to walk. We would then enter the church using the side rear door and walk up the center aisle to the front. I was watching for Abby to appear. She never told me what she was going to wear, but she would be very beautiful in any attire.

She finally came walking up the pathway that led through the same compounds that I had just walked through on my way to the church—James Avenue. From where I was standing in the hut, I could see her at least six city blocks away. People were walking with her, especially the young girls.

Her beauty seemed to emerge from within her and flow outward. Since meeting the Sudanese people in my congregation, I had learned that some people have an inner beauty that far outshines any outward beauty they may or may not possess. Abby's beauty flowed from within her and multiplied.

I reached in my pocket and pulled out three notes. I had stuffed them there in a hurry when getting dressed. The first note was the invitation to Abby and me, to attend a dinner at the Thomas's—our first date in Gambela. The second note was the message Cameron gave me concerning the kidnapping. The third was the note given to Cameron early this morning.

I suddenly stopped walking and compared all three notes. They were made on the same colored paper using the same computer font. Mr. Thomas had written all three notes. He had to be the unknown link in the mystery communications network. Maybe he was an agent for the CIA.

Abby was wearing a long floral-print gown with a white hat. She looked amazing. Everyone was quiet as she walked past the gathered crowd. They all recognized her as the nurse who had come from America to treat their cuts, wounds, sicknesses and give them a big smile. She had also taught some of the Sudanese women how to make peanut butter cookies.

Soon she was at the door of the hut. I smiled at her and she smiled back. We both were aware that we had already been participants in a miracle just a few days ago—God saving us from the seven knife-wielding KNM mercenaries. But the healing of our broken marriage was going to be an even bigger miracle.

As we both stood waiting by the open hut, an amazing thing started to happen. People whom the team had treated started coming to the church. Especially noticeable were the victims of the war, many of them being carried on their homemade stretchers and some using crutches. After some fifteen minutes, it seemed like an ocean of people were approaching the church.

Abby and her folks had extended a general invitation to the Nuer-speaking Sudanese. Special invitations were sent to some of the Amharic-speaking Ethiopians and English-speaking people of Gambela. Many of them were also starting to surround the church.

Samuel and James recognized the potential problem of crowd control and began to discuss this situation with the church elders. They, in turn, began to fan out and ask the people to be seated on the ground in small groups. This would keep the people from crowding in closer just to get a better view. The majority of these people probably had never seen an American wedding ceremony.

I looked and saw Cameron with a strange woman. He walked up to me and introduced his wife, who had come to Gambela to visit her husband.

"Ruth had been secretly planning to visit me here in Gambela all along," Cameron announced to me. "She just never told me about it. Jack, I have my own miracle. Thanks for praying for us."

The marriage ceremony was to be in three languages—Nuer, Amharic, and English. It would take a while for each sentence or phrase to be translated. According to my specific instructions, God would be given prominent recognition in arranging this marriage— or remarriage—and we needed to give Him the glory for everyone to observe and hear.

Some of the Ethiopian people were present. The city government official was there with his wife, whom Abby had treated in our Sunday afternoon downtown clinic. Some of the businessmen whom I had bought various items from were there, as well.

As we were walking up the aisle, I spotted Oliver and Tebee Thomas. They were standing next to the aisle. I reached into my tux pocket, grabbed all three of the notes and handed them to Oliver. The reaction on his face was very telling. He was an agent.

"Hey, Mr. Thomas—great work—thanks!"

The five rescued pastors were at the wedding. As we passed them walking up the aisle, they stopped us and wanted to shake hands with both of us. One of them reached into his pocket and brought out the two ivory crosses. I looked at them for a moment and placed them inside of my pocket, alongside the third one. I would now be able to give them to my sons in America. A story would be told to my sons, and maybe daughters, about the crosses—one that they would tell their children.

We walked a few more steps and I turned my head to see who else may be in the crowd. As I turned from one side to the other, I did a double-take. There standing on the end of the row was my media friend whom I'd met in Addis at the airport currency exchange bank. I wondered what he was doing here?

Moses and his family were standing in the front row. His wife had on a very colorful dress, and was adorned with glittering jewelry. He had two boys and two girls, all grown.

The little girl and boy whom our family had rescued were present. Abby stopped and reached into the aisle to touch the heads of the two Sudanese children. She was blessing them. Their parents beamed.

David, the abused boy from the compounds, was there with his mom and dad. They were next to the aisle. The father looked down as if to say, "I am so sorry." I took his hand, shook it, and gave David a stick of gum.

I looked through the open doorway. A table was set up outside of the church where people could place gifts for us. None of them was wrapped. There were all kinds of items. The gifts were truly from the heart, as many of these people could barely afford their daily sustenance. Abby's parents had agreed to get them shipped back to Minnesota.

The Nuer singers and drummers provided music. Mrs. Olson had worked with them and taught the Sudanese women's chorus a song in English.

Unknown to Abby or me, Cameron had added an extra section to the service. At the end, just before I kissed Abby and before we were introduced to the gathered crowd, a vow-renewal service was conducted. Since the majority of the people in attendance had their marriages arranged, God may have not played a prominent role in their marriage ceremony. Cameron asked all those who wished, to stand with their spouses and join hands. They then repeated a marriage vow to each other. Cameron especially wrote the words for this occasion and with all of the ethnic peoples in mind. All three languages were used and there were at least fifty couples standing. It was the most moving part of the day.

****

We had a dinner at the hotel. The dining area was packed with guests and the crowd extended to the outside area. Baked Nile trout was served with Ethiopian fried potatoes, candied yams, and a mango pecan desert.

Gabe came to us and presented Abby and me with a wrapped gift.
"Well, aren't you going to open it?" Gabe asked.

"You bet, Gabe!"

Abby slowly unwrapped the crudely wrapped gift. It was a box. Inside the box was a hand-carved wooden cross. It was made of a dark wood. On the back of the cross Gabe had carved, "To Jack and Abby—For the best time of my life. —Gabe."

"When did you make this, Gabe?"

"In the hours that you and James were in Sudan—remember?"

"I do remember. Thank you, Gabe."

Both Abby and I gave him a big hug.

As we were eating, my bureau chief acquaintance from the Addis airport came over to where I was sitting.

"Jack, I'll need to talk with you later. My newspaper wants me to do a story on the plight of the Nuer tribe. They want to run a series of articles."

"Hey, that's an answer to prayer." I told him.

Each of the team stood up and gave a short summary of the medical mission just completed. Dr. Terry let Dr. Mike speak for both of them.

Oliver Thomas came up to me and gave me a big surprise. He stood close to me and whispered in my ear, "Jack, when you get back to the USA, someone will contact you and offer you a job. Please consider it. That is all I am going to say about it, and we never had this conversation."

"You got it! Thanks!" I shook his hand.

I decided to wait and tell Abby about it when it happened. It would be on my growing list of employment opportunities.

****

Abby and I were to take Ethiopian Airlines back to Addis where we would spend two nights at the Blue Nile Hotel. Fred and Mabel wanted to take our place in Selasie on the trip from Gambela to Addis Ababa. Gabe would certainly give them the ride of their lives.

From there it was back to Minneapolis where I would meet my sons and they would meet their mother's husband. I would become a dad once again—but this time an active one. I would also need to choose a career from several options and opportunities that lay before me.

All of this because I attended a basketball game one Saturday night.

I didn't know what God had in store for me. Neither did I when I met Abby in Frankfurt. But God knew.

Abby and I would just trust in the Lord and love each other.

****

The End

CPSIA information can be obtained at www.ICGtesting.com
Printed in the USA
LVOW12s1017111013

356398LV00003B/6/A